DEATH IN A CORNFIELD

and Other Stories from
Contemporary Taiwan

Death in a Cornfield

and Other Stories from
Contemporary Taiwan

Edited by
Ching-Hsi Perng and Chiu-kuei Wang

HONG KONG
OXFORD UNIVERSITY PRESS
OXFORD   NEW YORK
1994

Oxford University Press

Oxford   New York   Toronto
Kuala Lumpur   Singapore   Hong Kong   Tokyo
Delhi   Bombay   Calcutta   Madras   Karachi
Nairobi   Dar es Salaam   Cape Town
Melbourne   Auckland   Madrid

and associated companies in
Berlin   Ibadan

Oxford is a trade mark of Oxford University Press

First published 1994

Published in the United States
by Oxford University Press, New York

© Oxford University Press 1994

British Library Cataloguing in Publication Data
available

Library of Congress Cataloging-in-Publication Data
available

ISBN 0-19-586178-7

Printed in Hong Kong
Published by Oxford University Press (Hong Kong) Ltd
18/F Warwick House, Taikoo Place, 979 King's Road, Quarry Bay, Hong Kong

Preface

> . . . *the isle is full of noises,*
> *Sounds and sweet airs, that give delight, and hurt not.*
>
> *The Tempest* 3,2

AMIDST the dramatic—some would say unprecedented—transformations in the political, economic, and social scenes in the Taiwan of the 1980s, short story writers on the island found themselves avidly capturing these phenomena from artistic viewpoints and with bold innovations. The result is a harvest of short stories as varied in techniques as they are diverse in themes—two prominent features of the 13 included here.

When the idea for this volume of English translations was conceived in 1986, it won the immediate blessing of Mr Hsiung Hsien-chu, then Director of the National Institute of Translation and Compilation of the Republic of China. Over the years, the project continued to enjoy unreserved support from Dr Tseng Chi-ch'un and Dr Li-yun (Nancy) Chao, his successors, and the able staff of the Institute. Many other people have also given timely and generous help along the way, too numerous to be recorded individually here. We are grateful to all the translators and, of course, the writers represented in this anthology. Special thanks go to the following persons:

Mr Chan Hung-chih, a discerning critic and bibliophile, who came up with a lengthy tentative list after long and assiduous research; Professor David Der-wei Wang, then our colleague at National Taiwan University and now of Columbia University, who first went over each piece on that list with patience and critical acumen, and then wrote the succinct and insightful Introduction that greatly enriches this book; and Professor J. I. Crump, Jr., Professor Emeritus at The University of Michigan and a long-time friend, who most graciously served as chief advisor on matters of usage and style.

Ching-Hsi Perng
Chiu-kuei Wang

Acknowledgements

Permission for translation and publication of the stories in this volume have been kindly granted by the following:

'Mountain Path' (Shan-lu): from *Shan-lu*, by Chen Ying-chen (1984, Yuan-ching Publishing Co.); by permission of the author and the publisher;

'Azaleas Wept Blood' (Tu-chuan t'i-hsieh): from *Tu-chuan t'i-hsieh*, by Liu Ta-jen (1984, Yuan-ching Publishing Co.); by permission of the author and the publisher;

'Between Two Generations' (Liang-tai chih-chien): from *Hsing-chia ta-shao*, by Pao-chen (1983, Chiu-ko Publishing Co.); by permission of the author and the publisher;

'Life' (Jen-sheng): from *I-chou ta-shih*, ed. Chin Heng-wei (1985, Shih-pao Wen-hua Publishing Co.); by permission of the author and the publisher;

'The Rapeseed' (Yu-mai-ts'ai-tzu): from *Yu-ma-ts'ai-tzu*, by Liao Hui-ying (1983, Huang-kuan Publishing Co.); by permission of the author and the publisher;

'Old Love' (Chiu ai): from *Chiu ai*, by Su Wei-chen (1985, Hung-fan Books); by permission of the author and the publisher;

'Death in a Cornfield' (Yü-mi-t'ien chih ssu): by P'ing-lu, first published in *The United Daily* (1983); by permission of the author;

'Night-time Frolics' (Wan-chien te yü-lo): from *Tzu-yu tou-shih*, by Huang Fan (1983, Ch'ien-wei Publishing Co.); by permission of the author and the publisher;

'Everybody Needs Ch'in Te-fu' (Jen-jen hsu-yao Ch'in Te-fu): from *Lai So*, by Huang Fan (1980, Shih-pao Wen-hua Publishing Co.); by permission of the author and the publisher;

'Tung-p'u Street' (Tung-p'u chieh): by Huang Fan, first published in *The United Daily* Literary Supplement (1991); by permission of the author;

'The Policy Maker' (Chueh-ts'e che): from *Pu-hsiu che*, by Chang Hsi-kuo (1983, Hung-fan Books); by permission of the author and the publisher;

'The Scholar of Yang-hsien' (Yang-hsien shu-sheng): from *Yeh-ch'ü*, by Chang Hsi-kuo (1985, Chih-shih Hsi-t'ung Publishing Co.); by permission of the author and the publisher.

'Rustic Quandary' (Ts'un-jen yü-nan chi): from *Liu-shih-chiu nien tuan-p'ien hsiao-shuo hsuan*, ed. Chan Hung-chih (1980, Er-ya Publishing Co.); by permission of the author and the publisher.

'The Rapeseed' and 'Death in a Cornfield' first appeared in English in *The Chinese PEN* (Taipei Chinese Center, International P.E.N.). Permission for their inclusion here has been generously given by Mrs. Nancy Chang Ing, editor of the quarterly; both pieces, however, have been revised for this anthology.

Contents

Introduction

THE 1980s saw Taiwan undergo its most drastic transformation since 1949. The old hegemonic power was fading away, while a new order was yet to be established. Challenged by mainland China's new open-door policy and by burgeoning dissident powers from within, Taiwan struggled to remold its political structure. The economic boom may have brought Taiwan prosperity unknown in modern Chinese history, but it accelerated the disintegration of traditional value systems. Taiwan of the 1980s was a society full of changes and uncertainties; it took on a double image of a brave new world and a paradise lost.

The 13 stories in this anthology depict these cultural and political changes and uncertainties. They do not merely represent the changing Chinese manners and morals of the island society at a crucial historical moment; they call into question the norm of verisimilitude that has always claimed to make representation possible. Readers can resort to the conventional term 'realism' describing such stories' formal and thematic traits, but a reading will soon lead readers to rethink the conditions of the real, encouraging them to place the 'real' in quotes. In other words, the writers of these stories only 'appear' to be locked in the old form of realism; beneath the familiar narrative patterns they adopt, one discerns signals that anticipate a 're-forming' of the real.

To take Shu Kuo-chih's *Rustic Quandary* as an example. It begins with a typical day in the life of a small, provincial village. Idle farmers, routine work, monotonous scenery constitute a seemingly bland but serene picture. This pastoral serenity is disturbed when a stranger appears in the village. The villagers and the stranger never make contact, but by being there, the stranger has interrupted the villagers' rhythm of daily life, arousing in them an array of emotions ranging from curiosity, suspicion, fear, and indifference, to fantasy. Life goes back to normal, as the stranger finally disappears.

Rustic Quandary may at first appear to be a continuation of the nativist literature that prospered in Taiwan in the 1970s. The encounter between the villagers and the stranger might well recapitulate the confrontation between a declining rural culture and the intrusive forces from the outside world. But an informed reading will show that Shu Kuo-Chih has written a parody, an exposé, of this nativist narrative. The stranger's appearance does not so much bring about the subjugation and suppression of village life, as provoke and release agitations ever latent in the village unconscious. Vaguely aware of the restless undercurrents beneath the drudgery of their daily work, the villagers have always been looking for something to happen, unable to make it happen on their own. Shu Kuo-chih restates the conventional dichotomies of 'innocent country' versus 'depraved city' and of 'peaceful nature' versus 'agitated civilization'. Contrary to the tidy closures of the nativist writing of the 1970s, his story is significantly open-ended.

With the disappearance of the stranger at the end of *Rustic Quandary*, nothing seems to have changed in the village. Will the villagers go back to their work as usual? Maybe yes. After all, nobody knows who the stranger was, where he came from, or what he wanted. However, this story about 'nothing' captures the strange uneasiness beneath the village's attempt to re-establish surface tranquility. Something must have happened, though no one can name what it is. It is the villager's (and narrator's) inability to articulate what really happened or is happening—the absence of a 'proper meaning' that will contextualize the real—that brings home the historical and moral ambiguity underlying the story.

The quandary in which Shu Kuo-chih's villagers find themselves can serve as a thematic denominator for the stories in the anthology. It exemplifies both the condition to which Taiwan writers were confined in the early 1980s and the condition from which they derived their most polemical material. That Taiwan writers were confined in a cultural–historical 'quandary' peculiar to their place and time is itself a position which our age, over and over again, puts into question. So it is only natural that the writers of this anthology will be seen to adopt three modes of situating themselves within a painful interrogation of the real: a mode of re-presented history, a mode of gendered subjectivity, and a mode of simulated modernization.

Re-presented History

Four writers, Ch'en Ying-chen, Liu Ta-jen, Pao-chen, and Lu Fei-yi, touch on the changing political and historical consciousness of Chinese people on both sides of the Taiwan Straits. Both Ch'en Ying-chen's *Mountain Path* and Liu Ta-jen's *Azaleas Wept Blood* borrow the form of detective fiction, and with it they attempt to unravel the enigmas of history and authority that haunted generations of Chinese. In Ch'en's *Mountain Path*, an old woman mysteriously develops anorexia and is dying from starvation; neither her family nor her doctors can discover the cause of her disease. In Liu's *Azaleas Wept Blood*, the narrator is desperately looking for clues to the cause of his aunt's insanity. These stories end by revealing, retrospectively, the two women's youthful involvement in the communist movement, an involvement that they invested with fanaticism and passion, devotion and betrayal.

Ch'en Ying-chen and Liu Ta-jen were two of the most brilliant and controversial writers in the 1960s. For their supposed sympathy with the Chinese Communist cause, Ch'en spent years in jail while Liu was forced into self-exile. Both resumed their careers as writers and political activists in the 1980s and gained high public profiles, a fact that measured the changing political climate in Taiwan.

Mountain Path and *Azaleas Wept Blood* commemorate a period in which thousands of Chinese youths dedicated themselves to a forbidden ideal. Ch'en Ying-chen and Liu Ta-jen neither argue nor apologize for the ideological vision for which they sacrificed so much. As artists and ideologues, their concerns are: How could a once noble revolutionary ideal go rotten so fast in the fresh air of history? How could unconditional dedication entail falsehood, betrayal, and self-destruction? In the aftermath of the Great Cultural Revolution, where could a writer find a place to stand in the treacherous currents of art and politics, silence and senescence? In the words of the old woman in

Mountain Path: 'If the revolution fails on the Mainland, does that mean . . . your long-term imprisonment [has] turned into meaningless punishments more cruel than death or life in prison . . . ?'

For an ideology that has mythologized history, what actually happens in history may well serve as History's most ironic self-critique. Not unlike the old women trapped between their desire for History and their unhappy realization of history, both Ch'en and Liu are puzzled by an apparently endless play of paradoxes which stands at the end of their hermeneutic quests. If *Mountain Path* is a painful confession of an ex-revolutionary, or if *Azaleas Wept Blood* is a poignant indictment of socialist illusions, it is not due to either story's political topicality so much as to their authors' moral and ideological bravery, evident in their writings about illusions without necessarily knowing what was illusory and what was not.

For the old women in the stories, the only way to assure the meaning of life as it should be is either to cut short life (and time) or to lose one's mind, acts which would at least freeze their own histories into the crystallized narrative form of History, with a proper beginning, middle, and end. Ch'en Ying-chen and Liu Ta-jen see a residual desire for self-delusion in these actions. For them, the only way to maintain their integrity as writers and revolutionaries is to write, to sustain their ideological nostalgia, while at the same time questioning and even denying the validity of what they write.

On the other hand, both Pao-chen's *Between Two Generations* and Lu Fei-yi's *Life* can be read as a sharp contrast to *Mountain Path* and *Azaleas Wept Blood* in dealing with political issues. Pao-chen criticizes the refugee mentality of some of the Mainland émigrés in Taiwan; Lu Fei-yi deplores the family tragedies resulting from the confrontation between the two Chinas. Given their ideologically 'correct' standpoints, neither Pao-chen nor Lu Fei-yi is a naïve patriot, however. The most interesting parts of their stories ponder the dubious terms of patriotism in a volatile historical context, thereby upsetting the conservative discourse they seem to inhabit. Pao-chen sees an unlikely obsession with (the Republic of) China in those who are openly cynical or pessimistic about her fate. Lu Fei-yi insinuates the absurdity of the political status quo by means of a tearful melodrama about family reunion. Their benign narrative proves to be critical and self-critical. In this sense, they echo Ch'en Ying-chen's and Liu Ta-jen's rhetorical and conceptual strategies.

Gendered Subjectivity

Female writers have played a crucial role in modernizing Taiwan's fiction over the past 30 years. Their voices became even stronger and more diversified in the 1980s. Responding to the burgeoning global feminist movement, women writers are examining their own experiential and psychological problems in a highly polemical way. For some of the writers, feminism is not an end but a new starting point from which both male and female can explore the issue of subjectivity, public and private. These writers may raise more questions than they can answer, but the occasions on which these questions are raised have been some of the best moments of recent literature in Taiwan.

Liao Hui-ying's *Rapeseed* deals with the bitter-sweet relationship between a mother and a daughter. The mother is a victim of her own marriage. For 30 years she took care of her five children while her husband fooled around outside, squandering the family fortune. Against the stereotype of the docile, suffering mother in conventional literature, the mother in *Rapeseed* is a strong woman. She participates in choosing her husband back in the days when arranged marriage was the norm (therefore may be seen as partially responsible for the failure of the marriage), and is harsh in bringing up her children. With this imperfect mother, Liao Hui-ying makes an ironic case for the ideals of feminism. The mother may very well be a powerful model in a pre-feminist era, but she derives her strength not only from her fortitude and resourcefulness but also from her bigotry, selfishness, and bad temper. Her daughter, with all the newly acquired virtues of a modern, liberated woman, appears surprisingly conservative and old-fashioned. Can Liao Hui-ying, in construing feminism, have made an anachronistic mistake?

A similar ambiguity may be found in Su Wei-chen's *Old Love*. The story is about a woman's fruitless romances with three men at three different stages of her life. Instead of following a fashionable feminist formula, Su Wei-chen gains her inspiration from traditional gothic stories. Drifting from one man to another, Su's heroine is indeed more like a ghost than a human creature. Su's seemingly obsolete manner of storytelling, however, may point at an ingenious critique of Chinese women at the threshold of their feminist consciousness. In a man's world, women are symbolically ghosts, without substantial grounding. But women's ghostly status may also constitute an ubiquitous power, one that haunts and 'possesses' men. Su's heroine does die at the end of the story, leaving her suitors forever in a state of living death.

Another woman writer, P'ing-lu, expands the theme of gendered subjectivity, discussing it in the context of history and national fate. Her story *Death in a Cornfield* tells of a Taiwanese man's mysterious suicide in a cornfield in America, followed by an overseas news-correspondent's Sisyphean search for the reason for that suicide. The story at first reads like a re-run of the perils of an overseas Chinese, fitted out with such familiar motifs as exile, alienation, and rootless desire for the lost mother country. An overseas writer herself, P'ing-lu does not provide an easy solution to this type of identity crisis, dealt with by so many Chinese writers. What she does add to it is a feminist dimension, thus engendering a new possibility of seeing (and hopefully solving) the crisis. As will be noticed, her male protagonists' desire for personal and national identities are paralleled with China, and their obsession with their (male) subjectivity and virility form a reciprocal relation, reinforcing as well as exhausting each other. This entropic circulation of political and sexual power is where the crisis of modern China erupts into consciousness, in so far as it is a male consciousness. With the mysterious death in the cornfield, and the reporter's failure to explain it, P'ing-lu announces the demise of the traditional male-centred search for, and discourse upon, personal and national subjectivity.

In response to rising feminist voices, the male writer Huang Fan writes *Night-time Frolics*, a comic story about a young couple's bizarre love-hate relationship. Huang Fan is one of the most versatile writers of the 1980s. In *Night-time Frolics*, he laughs away religious and ethical teachings about love and marriage, professing to examine the war between the two sexes where it first began—in the bedroom. He writes a comedy that mixes both feminist desire and misogynist fantasy. Put side by side, Huang Fan's story and those of the three women writers' form a highly provocative dialogue about the changing male and female consciousness in a modern Chinese society.

Simulated Modernization

The other four stories in the anthology bear on the consequences of the modernization of Taiwan. With impressive statistical figures on economic productivity and steadily improving reports on political democratization, Taiwan in the 1980s was seen as being proudly initiated into the club of developed countries. Authors writing in this period had a rather modern set of questions to ask. For all of its modern look, has Taiwan truly been modernized? What are the moral and emotional consequences of modernizing Chinese morality and emotions? If modernization has happened in other realms of Taiwanese society, can the writer engage the reader in a fictional dialogue on the new reality? More importantly, how can the writer recreate rhetoric so as to seem modern, perhaps even be modern, in the very act of narrating the modern?

Huang Fan and Chang Hsi-kuo represent two of the voices most critical of Taiwan's modernization. Their criticism of this modernity is itself openly modern. In *The Policy Maker*, Chang sees in Taiwan's prosperous high-tech industry a new discursive paradigm that not only transforms social relations but also becomes a narrative format that manifests the relations as a transformation. The story deals with a group of scientists' research activities, and its formal device seems fittingly to reflect its subject. Its narrative format is modelled on a computerized questionnaire, with 23 questions grouped into seven thematic sections, such as marriage and career. Each section is labelled with a computer-command-like heading, demanding a quick, perhaps automatic response from Chang Hsi-kuo's hero. Chang thus graphically extends his vision of an automated society to the story's narrative level, showing how linguistic features have also been determined by modern technology.

Given this narrative design, it does not take long for the reader to find out that the story is actually not about the power of the computer but about a power struggle among computer scientists. It has less to do with technology than with technocracy. Tear aside its mask of stylized rhetoric, and the reader finds that the story is amazingly familiar. It is a 1980s version of late Ch'ing exposé fiction, caricaturing human ambitions and follies in a cultural *Vanity Fair*. All the computational rhetoric is nothing but a wallpaper of modernity, scarcely hiding the crack between what the story proposes to tell and what it actually tells. This crack or inconsistency between form and content, however, provides Chang Hsi-kuo a paradoxical perspective, from which he catches a glimpse of Taiwan's awkward experience in her modernization, as well as the limitation of the existent narrative model of realism in describing these experiences.

Chang Hsi-kuo goes further in another story: *The Scholar of Yanghsien.* He rewrites an ancient fantastic story, mixing it with references freely drawn from the classic novel *The Dream of the Red Chamber*, from the modern, woman writer Eileen Chang's romantic stories, and from contemporary science fiction. Aside from parading robots and computers, quacks and magical gourds, Chang intends to tell a moral tale. He shows how thin the line is between ancient alchemy and modern-day entrepreneurship, and how easily men and women can be drawn into the endless chain of desires and deceits. The story provides an ambivalent look at morality and modernity.

Huang Fan's *Everybody Needs Ch'in Te-fu* observes the rise of a new class in commercialized Taiwanese society. Ch'in Te-fu is a self-made entrepreneur, a business tycoon, a philanthropist, and a celebrity. He is also a mercurial opportunist, an unscrupulous bidder, an irresponsible family man, and a buffoon. Ch'in Te-fu seems to personify the ethics of Taiwan's commercial society in the 1980s: vigorous, sly and constantly changing. Everybody needs Ch'in Te-fu. With Ch'in around, people feel strangely 'at home'. But the writer/narrator, Huang Fan also knows Ch'in Te-fu's vulnerable spots, his inferiority complex, and most significantly, his inglorious past. This makes Ch'in Te-fu's popularity all the more interesting. Huang Fan suggests that Ch'in Te-fu is popular not only because he is a projection of people's fantasies of becoming rich and famous, but also because Ch'in tests, on their behalf, the dark boundaries of taboos and the unknown realm of the future. Ch'in Te-fu is not merely a vulgar *nouveau riche*; he is also the scapegoat of a society that is in desperate need of establishing a new system of belief. His death at the end of the story is predestined, and it is no surprise that his funeral should turn into a muted celebration.

Finally, modernity and modernization cannot be acutely felt without a reference to temporality. No matter how unlikely it may seem, nostalgia or a sense of the passage of time constitutes part of every inscription of the effect of modernization. Huang Fan's *Tung-P'u Street* does not touch on any new aspect of society. It describes a boy's growing experience in a shabby corner of Taipei, before it became a metropolis. Instead of the dark humour and sarcasm he is noted for, Huang Fan injects an unexpected lyricism into the story. Still, one notices that the mood of nostalgia, once evoked in the story, soon calls ironic attention to itself. The story is as much a melancholy remembrance of things past as it is a self-conscious testimony to history, including modernization; something they consume vigorously so as to continue to feel the old difference between the past and present. This must be felt in a more modern way, with a modern self-consciousness of knowing that such nostalgia has always been felt, an escape from the present that the present stages for itself.

In their efforts to register the changing experiences of Taiwan in the 1980s, the writers of this anthology redefine the boundary of history and historical writing, engender a new male/female division of subjectivity, and delineate the contours of modernization as only modern writers can. All these stories lead the writers to reconsider, wittingly or unwittingly, the conventional canons of realism and responsibility. The anthology must stand for the changes it is obligated to describe; it presents the same reality it represents. Writing their stories in the Taiwan of the restless 1980s, these writers convey an unease while never absolutely certain of its origins, like the unease felt by the villagers in *Rustic Quandary*. Yet by being so faithful to their own agitated uncertainty, these writers are all the more successful in precisely fictionalizing their historicity, their gender, their modernity.

DAVID DER-WEI WANG
Columbia University

STORIES FROM CONTEMPORARY TAIWAN

Mountain Path

Ch'en Ying-chen

translated by Nicholas Koss

'PROFESSOR YANG, about the lady in Room Three. . .' Li Kuo-mu tried to say as he walked over to the nurses' station from inside the private room, following the supervising doctor who had just seen the patient. Two young doctors, Chen and Wang, stood respectfully by the side of the man being addressed as 'Professor Yang', a tall, thin, elderly doctor with a full head of curly gray hair. They listened carefully as Professor Yang read from the patient's thick chart and interpreted it in a low voice.

For the time being, Li Kuo-mu could only stand quietly at one corner of the nurses' station. Looking at the nurses in their white blouses and white skirts, white stockings and white shoes, and realizing how superfluous he was here, he began to feel guilty and uncomfortable. It was as if he had forced himself into a place where he should not be. As he continued to look around, he happened to see the broad-rimmed, black tortoise-shell frames of Professor Yang's glasses and behind them a pair of exhausted eyes.

'Dr Yang! Professor Yang!' he called. The two young doctors and Professor Yang calmly looked his way. The telephone rang. A nurse answered saying, 'Endocrinology.'

'Professor Yang, if I may, what is the condition of the lady in Room Three?' Li Kuo-mu said, walking over to them. Dr Chen pulled out a brand new addition to the stack of patient files.

Professor Yang started to read the file and simultaneously asked Dr Chen something in a low voice. Then, the younger doctor looked up and inquired, 'Professor Yang would like to know who . . . who you are to this patient.'

'Her younger brother,' he answered, but then laughed and said, 'No, actually I am her brother-in-law. She is my sister-in-law.'

He then took a name card from the pocket of his suit jacket and courteously presented it to Professor Yang. It read: 'Li Kuo-mu: Honesty Accounting Firm.' Professor Yang looked at it and handed it to Dr Chen on his left for him to staple to the patient's file.

'I'm afraid we still have to take a few more tests,' said Professor Yang in a low voice. 'Please explain to us again the circumstances of this lady's illness.'

'The circumstances of the illness?' Li Kuo-mu repeated. 'She just became weak all of a sudden. Such a healthy person to become weak like that so suddenly.'

Professor Yang was momentarily silent. His arms were folded. His left hand was very large and, as fitted his profession, immaculately clean. On his wrist was a gold watch; obviously a very expensive one. Professor Yang sighed and looked at Dr Chen, who said, 'What Professor Yang wants to know is if there is any apparent reason . . . for instance, excessive worry, or anger, or . . .'

'Ah. . .'

Until Li Kuo-mu had come to this famous medical school hospital in Taipei, nobody either in the private clinics or the hospitals had ever asked this kind of question. But, for the moment, facing this many people, he instinctively lied, 'Er . . . no, not at all. Not at all.'

Walking out from behind the nurses' station, Professor Yang said, 'Let's do it this way. You go home and think over my question carefully. I'm afraid we still have to do a few more tests on her.'

Li Kuo-mu returned to Room Three and found his elderly sister-in-law asleep. How thin her face had become over the past half-month, he thought, looking at it resting on the soft, clean pillow. Her private room had a carpet, a telephone, a refrigerator, a small kitchen, a television, and a bath. His wife, waiting for him to relieve her, had cleaned the room until it shined. She had now gone home to cook special food for his sister-in-law. The heater was exuding warmth. He took off his coat and quietly walked over to the window. All around the pond were broad-leafed tropical plants. The angle from the fourth-storey window made the water spouting high above the pond look like a light, white fog. It was as if sheer, white gauze were gently floating in the wind, creating flickering forms out of the thick, luxuriant leaves, the randomly-placed rocks, and the large, red-and-white carp in the pond.

Trapped in a late spring cold front, the sky outside the window was a heavy grey. So many hospitals, but he had yet to discover the cause of his sister-in-law's illness. Recently he too had begun to wonder if, indeed, her illness was related to some news she might have read. The words of the doctor—'for instance, excessive worry, or anger . . .'—continued to go through his mind. But no, there simply had been no excessive worry, and no excessive anger, either. Plagued by his worries, he watched the carp in the pond below, unaffected by fear of a cold late spring, still swimming grandly.

One day about two months before, Li Kuo-mu's sister-in-law had risen as usual, a little after four in the morning. After preparing the morning rice for the family, she went to the river bank for a walk with other elderly people from the neighbourhood. Then, a little after six, she returned to get the children ready for school. Shortly afterwards, when she started reading the newspaper, it suddenly happened. That morning, Li Kuo-mu's only daughter, Ts'ui-yu, a first-year student in junior middle school, knocked loudly on her father's bedroom door.

'Dad, Dad,' she shouted in terror, 'Dad, get up quickly, there's something the matter with Auntie . . . .' Li Kuo-mu and his wife hurried to the living room and saw their sister-in-law, her face full of tears and the paper lying at the foot of the sofa.

'What is it?' his wife, Yueh-hsiang, shouted. She circled the tea table and rushed over to sit on the arm of the sofa where her sister-in-law was. She braced her sister-in-law's shoulder with one hand, and with the other lifted the edge of her own night gown to wipe away the tears from her cheeks.

'Sister, what happened? Where does it hurt?' she asked, starting to sob herself.

Li Kuo-mu stood quietly in front of the tea table. His sister-in-law had come to the Li household over 30 years ago. The hardest days of these 30 years were long past, and throughout them he had never seen his sister-in-law, whom he respected even more than his own mother, cry so painfully. Why? He frowned and thought.

His sister-in-law, trying to control the streams of tears flowing down her cheeks, buried her head in her hands.

'Sister, say something, what's the matter?' said Yueh-hsiang, crying. Li Kuo-mu placed his hands on his daughter, who was standing in the corner, frightened.

'Why don't you go to school?' he said. 'Auntie will be better when you get home.'

Li Kuo-mu and his wife sat quietly in the early morning sun in the living room as their sister-in-law's crying gradually came to an end. That morning, he let Yueh-hsiang go to work. He, however, stayed at home to be with his sister-in-law. When he entered her bedroom, she was there all alone lying on her back. Her eyes, swollen from crying, were looking at the freshly painted ceiling. Her hands were outside the blanket, tightly holding the rolled-up morning paper.

'Sister,' he said, sitting on a rattan chair by the bed.

'Go to work,' she responded.

Li Kuo-mu said nothing.

'There's nothing the matter,' she suddenly said in Japanese, 'so don't worry.'[1]

---

[1] Taiwan was a Japanese colony from 1895 until 1945. During these years Japanese was the official language of the island. Thus, Ts'ai Ch'ien-hui, who was educated under the Japanese, was fluent in both spoken and written Japanese.

'I didn't feel like going to work anyway,' he said comfortingly.

'Sister, if there's something you want to talk about, why not tell me?'

She was silent. Her somewhat long face, marked by more than 50 years, was much whiter than usual. Those years had obviously left their passage on her forehead, around her eyes, and in the corners of her mouth. What kind of years had they been, he wondered.

'For the past 30 years, you've been like a mother to me. . . .' he said, his voice shaking with emotion. She turned to look at him and saw his eyes were reddening and were moist with tears. Smiling, she held out her hand for him to hold.

'Look, you are already over 40,' she said, 'your work and family are all already well established. I'm at peace.'

He started to rub her hand gently. Then, he used both hands to place hers on the blanket. He took out a cigarette and lit it.

'It's best not to smoke so much,' she said.

'*Ni-san*,'[2] he answered with the Japanese term he had used since childhood. Seeing the determined expression on his face to have her explain what had happened that morning, she sighed softly. He had always been an obedient child, she was thinking. But, from childhood, whenever he insisted on something, he never tried to get it by making a fuss, but often used that same determined expression of his to accomplish his goal. At last she handed him the rolled-up newspaper.

'I saw in the newspaper that they are finally returning,' she said. Li Kuo-mu unfolded the paper. He saw one tiny item that had been circled in red: four 'traitors', having served 30 years in jail, were released because of 'proof of repentance'. The authorities had the previous day handed them over to local police to return them to their homes.

Li Kuo-mu had little response to the item.

'That Huang Chen-po was your big brother's best friend.' His sister-in-law started to sob. Li Kuo-mu reread the item. Huang Chen-po had been returned to his home in Taoyuan; he cried as he embraced his blind mother who was well into her eighties. 'They were tears of hatred and also tears of joy and a new life,' the paper said.

Li Kuo-mu suddenly felt relaxed. He thought his sister-in-law had read about someone named Huang Chen-po and his life sentence; this made her think of his elder brother and she started to cry. That was all there was to it. Or maybe it was simply the sudden return to life of prisoners everyone had

---

[2]   In Japanese, the same word is used for an elder sister and a sister-in-law.

expected to starve to death on that deserted, lonely island prison which moved her to tears.

'That's very good news,' he said smiling. 'At the right time, I should go pay my respects to this good friend of my brother.'

'Ah?'

'I can ask him to tell me something about my brother,' he added cheerfully.

'No,' his sister-in-law said.

'Oh? But why?'

She silently looked out the window. A light rain had started outside where a few pots of her beloved orchids hung from a rusting frame.

'No,' she said, 'that's not a good idea.'

From that day on, Li Kuo-mu and his family sensed the change taking place in his sister-in-law. She became silent, even morose. She began to eat less and less until, half a month later, she just stayed in bed. It seemed as though she had aged all of a sudden. During that period, Li Kuo-mu and Yueh-hsiang, each day after work, took their sister-in-law everywhere to see doctors. If urged, she would obediently force herself to take the prescribed medicine with water. If not, she would leave the container on the stand by the bed, unopened. As the days passed by, she seemed to shrink.

Li Kuo-mu again thought of the words Dr Chen had spoken while trying hard to conceal their implication: 'for instance, excessive worry, or anger . . . .' These words weighed heavily on his heart. Loosening his tie, he dropped it beside the sick-bed. He and his wife took turns spending the night in a chair in the hospital room.

'But, how can I talk about that morning in front of those doctors and nurses?' he thought painfully. 'How can I tell them about my brother and Huang Chen-po?' He was sitting in a coffee-coloured chair to the left of the sick-bed. At this point someone suddenly entered the room. A pregnant nurse came to take the patient's temperature and blood pressure. The patient opened her eyes, obediently accepted the thermometer and allowed the nurse to take her blood pressure. Li Kuo-mu stood up so the nurse would have more room to work.

'Thanks,' he said as she left.

He sat down again in the chair and reached over to grasp the bony, dry hand of his sister-in-law.

'Did you get a little sleep?' he asked with a smile.

'Go to work,' she responded weakly. 'Why are you spending your time . . . with a useless person like me . . . instead of going to work?'

'It's all right,' he said.

'I had a dream,' she said suddenly.

'Oh.'

'I dreamt of that railroad track,' she announced in Japanese.

'Aha,' he said, starting to laugh, and thought of that winding track in Yingko, his hometown. In the early days it went from the coal mines in the mountain hollows, over the curves and bumps of the mountains, passing below the famous Yingko Rock, and ended at the coal piles by the railroad station. His home was an old farmhouse in a mountain hollow just past the Yingko Rock.

'When I married into your family, I was all by myself. I found your home by walking along the railroad tracks,' she said.

Li Kuo-mu felt a sharp pain inside. He looked directly at the fiftyish woman in the bed before him. For over a month now, she had seemed to be shrinking. Now she was lying on her side facing him. He adjusted the intravenous bottle connected to her right arm. Thin drops of sweat were pouring from her wizened and heavily-lined face. With a tired smile, she said, 'When I got there, you were sitting all by yourself in the door, looking rather dumb . . . .'

Sister-in-law often said this; in fact, she never tired of talking about her past. It had all begun exactly 30 years before in 1953. One windy, dry morning in early summer, a young woman by the name of Ts'ai Ch'ien-hui, all alone and carrying a small bundle, had taken the train from Taoyuan to the next stop, Yingko.

'Now, did she dare ask the way to the Lis' when she left the station?' she would often quiz the intently listening Li Kuo-mu as she recalled the past.

'Who would dare tell her? The Li family had had a son taken away and shot. So what should she do?' Then sister-in-law would sigh. But still she always wanted to talk about those terrible days when everyone was scared to death.

'At that time, in Taoyuan, friends would simply go out and walk the streets making contact with no-one,' she would say.

'If you saw so-and-so from a distance you would know he was still okay. If you didn't see someone for several days in a row, you'd assume he had been taken away.'

It was precisely during those desolate days that little Li Kuo-mu, sitting in the doorway, had seen her coming his way, walking along the railroad tracks. On both sides of the tracks were lush acacia trees. Black butterflies with two light blue marks on their wings were fluttering through the groves like the shuttles of a loom. He still remembered how the young Ts'ai Ch'ien-hui, walking down the railroad ties, occasionally raised her head and looked over at his isolated farmhouse, at him sitting all along on the cold doorsill. Silently and without embarrassment, they simply stared at each other. A flock of starlings in the acacias were squawking intermittently. At times, the repeated clunking of the train coming down the side of the mountain could be heard, at first very distant and then closer and closer, only to become distant again. This was how a sickly little Li Kuo-mu first saw his sister-in-law, as she jumped from the tracks and walked over to him, taking a path amidst wild reeds and tall grass.

'Excuse me, does Li . . . Mr Li Ch'i-shin live here?' she asked.

He could never forget that moment. He remembered exactly how he had looked up at her, lacking curiosity and without any fear. She appeared to be a stranger and looked at him with slightly swollen eyes. For a moment, he said nothing. Then he nodded his head. He had never felt like doing much when suffering from hunger. The moment he nodded to her, an embracing, loving smile slowly came to her thin lips. Simultaneously, shining tears fell from her slightly swollen eyes that were observing him with so much feeling. Wild doves in the nearby acacia were cooing. His little mongrel had gone off into the mountains scavenging for something to eat; suddenly it ran from behind the house and barked fiercely while wagging its yellow tail.

'Stop barking!' he said angrily.

When he turned to look at her again, she was laughing and using an edge of her cloth-tied bundle to wipe away her tears. Then he heard the voice of his mother from inside the house.

'A-mu, who is it?'

He silently led her into the dark house. His mother was lying in bed. The bitter smell of herbal medicine being prepared wafted in from the kitchen, filling the room. With great effort, his mother lifted herself part way up and said, 'Who is she? A-mu, who is this person with you?'

Young Ts'ai Ch'ien-hui quietly sat down on the edge of the bed and said, 'I am the wife . . . the wife of Kuo-k'un.'

Even though little Li Kuo-mu heard what she said, he didn't fully understand the significance of it. Then, after a stiff silence, he heard his mother burst into loud crying. 'My son, my dear son . . . ,' she then started to moan in chant-like fashion as she quieted down. Looking out the window, Li Kuo-mu realized that the sky had darkened. The ponderous sound of thunder was heard in the distance. His little yellow mongrel nimbly chased a couple of shiny green grasshoppers.

More than a year before, his brother Li Kuo-k'un, who worked at a coke factory close to Taoyuan, was taken away, along with some of his fellow workers, in broad daylight. And it was only two months ago that his father, who worked on the mine railroad, had gone to Taipei with the letter of notification in hand, and returned with a bundle of worn clothes tied with grass cord, a pair of old tennis shoes, and a fountain pen with a corroded point. That night, his mother sobbed, 'My son, my dear son . . . !'

'Not so loud,' his father said against the competing night sounds of cicadas in the low-lying mountain.

'My son . . . my dear son, my . . . son . . . !' His mother covered her mouth with her hands as the tears, saliva and mucus oozed from the cracks between her fingers onto the old bed.

'Sister,' said Kuo-mu, clearing his throat—which had become choked as he recalled the past—'Sister'.

'Yes.'

Just then the door to the sick room was carefully opened. Yueh-hsiang entered carrying fruit and a box of food.

'Sister, I've brought you some perch soup. . . . ' she began.

'The time I was sitting in the doorway,' Li Kuo-mu said. 'Can you remember how I looked?'

'A little boy, sitting there,' his sister-in-law said, shutting her eyes. A smile lit up her face and she said, 'You were a little on the thin side.'

'Yeah.'

'But what I remember most is what happened that night,' she said, suddenly opening her eyes. She looked beyond Li Kuo-mu's right shoulder as if she were focusing on a distant point.

'Pa asked why he had never heard A-k'un mention me,' she said, adding, 'I said, I . . .'

'You said your family opposed it,' he said laughing. He didn't know how many times he had heard his sister-in-law tell the story over and over again from the time he was a boy until now when he was a grown man in his early forties.

'I said that my family did not approve,' she said. 'I said A-k'un and I had arranged everything, and now that he's not around, you must take me in, I said.'

Yueh-hsiang came in from the kitchen carrying a big bowl of the perch soup and said, 'Wait until it's cooled and then try some.'

'I'm really too much trouble,' sister-in-law replied.

'After Ma died, our family was so lucky to have you,' Li Kuo-mu remarked pensively. 'I'll have Yueh-hsiang put some noodles in the soup.'

'No need,' she said, slowly closing her eyes. 'And then your Pa said, "Poor as this family of ours is, you're going to have to put up with a lot of suffering. Look at you—you aren't the type who's used to hard work." That's just what your Pa said.'

Li Kuo-mu thought of his father during those times. His medium-built body had muscles as strong as steel from many years of hard labour. Each dawn, he tied a big lunch box to his belt, put on his sandals made out of tire rubber —rather like the sandals of today—and walked to the Hsing-nan Coal Mine in the mountain hollow to work. Then, several times each day, Pa would whiz by on the coal cart as it sped down the hillside tracks in front of the house. After sister-in-law arrived, Pa grew to love her deeply in his own silent way. Each evening, filthy with coal dust, Pa would come home, sometimes bringing a little dried beancurd or salted fish.

Each evening, our little yellow dog would bark its excited welcome for Pa. Sister-in-law would put down what she was doing and, drying her hands, go to the door and say, 'Pa, welcome back.'

'Hm,' Pa would say.

Getting the water ready for him to wash with, she would also take him a stack of neatly folded clothes. 'Pa, wash up.'

'Okay,' he would respond.

After supper, she'd brew a pot of fresh pomegranate tea and place it on the arm of Pa's big chair.

'Pa, have some tea,' she'd say.

'Hm.'

Li Kuo-mu recalled the pleasing picture created at that hour by the lightning insects flying among the shrubs beneath the acacia trees. The mountains would resound with the jumbled melodies made by insects of the night.

Now, Yueh-hsiang was standing by the bed and, with a long thin spoon, feeding her sister-in-law the perch in the soup spoonful by spoonful.

'Does it taste all right?' asked Yueh-hsiang softly.

Sister-in-law didn't say anything. She just obediently ate the perch Yueh-hsiang fed her, spoonful by spoonful, chewing it very attentively.

Suddenly, this made Li Kuo-mu think of his own mother.

After Elder Brother had had his trouble, and especially after Father had brought back his remaining possessions from Taipei, his mother, who was weak enough to begin with, had violently coughed up blood on a couple of occasions and afterward could not get out of bed. Early in the first summer that Sister-in-law was with the family, Mother unexpectedly improved a bit, but once autumn came, when the wild reeds on both sides of the railroad tracks began to show their yellowish-white, cotton-like flowers, Mother's sickness took a turn for the worse. Then Sister-in-law had done just what Yueh-hsiang was doing now—feeding Mother spoonful by spoonful. What's different, however, is that now Sister-in-law is in a private room in the hospital; Mother had to lie in a damp, dark room, full of the smell of urine from the toilet bucket. Also, when Mother's sickness became worse, her spirits changed. She lost her temper easily and was impatient. Once when Sister-in-law was spoon-feeding Mother rice porridge, she deliberately spat it out dirtying the quilt and the edge of the bed.

'My life is already too miserable, don't make me eat any more,' she sobbed without tears. 'I'll die and get it all over with. Let me die and get it all over with. . . .' Then Mother said, 'My son, my son, my dear, dear son.' She made Sister-in-law break into tears, too.

Mother did not live beyond that autumn day. She was buried in Yingko's public cemetery at Mount Niu-p'u.

'A-mu, we should visit Mount Niu-p'u,' Sister-in-law said suddenly.

'Oh?' said Li Kuo-mu looking up in surprise and staring at her. Yueh-hsiang was wiping off soup from around Sister-in-law's mouth. After thinking, he realized that Tomb-sweeping Day was near. Every year on that day, Sister-in-law, Yueh-hsiang, and he would take a train back to Yingko and go to Mt. Niu-p'u to clean up around Mother and Father's grave. It was only the year before last that they had finally put up a tombstone for Elder Brother. Sister-in-law planted a pair of cypress trees by Elder Brother's grave and surprisingly, they took root and sprouted.

Sister-in-law had explained, 'After the jailing because of the Kaohsiung Incident, people aren't so sensitive about political prisoners anymore.'[3] So she decided, when the time came to place Father's remains in an urn, she would put up a tombstone for Li Kuo-k'un, too.

'She finished the whole bowl of soup,' Yueh-hsiang announced with pleasure.

'This year I won't go with you two,' Sister-in-law said faintly.

She was lying on her back. Outside the window it was gradually darkening because of the heavy clouds.

'Sister-in-law, go ahead and sleep, if you feel like it,' said Yueh-hsiang.

Li Kuo-mu automatically felt for his cigarettes but immediately took his hand away from his pocket. Sister-in-law was not like Yueh-hsiang, who was always complaining resentfully about his smoking. In the hospital room, he had already had to stifle his desire to smoke a number of times. It was too much trouble to go out for a smoke. In silence, he thought about the old and new

---

[3] The Kaohsiung Incident, which occurred in 1979, was a violent confrontation between supporters of an independent Taiwan and the police in the southern city of Kaohsiung. A highly publicized trial followed the incident and the opposition leaders were sentenced to long-term imprisonment.

graves filling Mount Niu-p'u and about the weeds that seemed to grow stubbornly there in anger or out of meanness. Along the path by the shrine for the Earth God, on the side of the hill with a roll-like shape, was Elder Brother's new grave with its freshly turned soil. After the tombstone had been put in place, the elderly worker called over, 'You can come and pay your respects now.'

He and Yueh-hsiang had taken sticks of incense from Sister-in-law so that each of them had three sticks with which to pray before the newly erected tombstone. At that time, Li Kuo-mu kept thinking about Elder Brother's bundle of clothes and pair of shoes that had been buried there—items that Sister-in-law had carefully preserved for over 20 years. He gave his sticks of incense to Yueh-hsiang to place in the incense holder in front of the tombstone. Sister-in-law and Yueh-hsiang began to burn paper money next to the tombstone. Li Kuo-mu suddenly thought of the picture of his elder brother that his sister-in-law recently had enlarged. His Western style hair-do had the rough cut of the 1950s. Elder brother was looking with determination at some unknown place off in the distance, some place far off under the Taiwanese sky. His somewhat thin face seemed to be full of inexhaustible confidence about his future. Where now is this body that once had been alive with youth? While Li Kuo-mu was at the university, he had occasionally heard his friends say that the bullet-riddled bodies of those who had been shot were now silently floating in formaldahyde at medical schools. Then he had wondered, as he did now, where his brother's body might be.

With an expression that could only be one of satisfaction, Sister-in-law looked at the new tombstone:

Born March 17, 1928
Died September 1952
Li Kuo-k'un
Erected by his Children and Grandchildren

Sister-in-law said that although he had disappeared in 1950, it was September of 1952 before Pa had brought back his possessions—she didn't remember the exact day.

'Why didn't you use the lunar calendar for the dates?' Li Kuo-mu asked.

'Your brother was a very modern person,' she responded. Explaining who the children and grandchildren of Elder Brother were, she said, 'Your children are his children.'

He still remembered that at that moment, Yueh-hsiang had unconsciously lowered her head. Ever since Ts'ui-yu was born, they had been waiting for a boy, but he never came.

'How fast the time has gone by,' said the old worker standing by the grave, smoking the stub of a cigarette about to burn his fingers. 'Over twenty-some years, A-k'un . . .'

'Indeed,' Sister-in-law had said.

The old worker, Wang Fan, had been his father's friend. Coal mining at Yingko had declined as oil gradually became the main source of energy. Wang Fan and Kuo-mu's father had been among the first to lose their jobs. Li Kuo-mu's father had worked doing house repairs at first, and then gone to Taipei to work part-time on construction. Uncle Fan, who had always worked part-time in the cemetery, then took it on as his full-time job. The same winter Li Kuo-mu had entered the university, his Pa died, falling off the scaffolding of a building-site in Taipei. Uncle Fan had put up the tombstone. Li Kuo-mu still remembered watching Uncle Fan filling in the grave with shovelfuls of dirt and hearing the dirt strike the top of Pa's thin coffin. Uncle Fan wiped away the tears on his cheeks and said under his breath, 'You old motherfucker, I told you to work with me in the cemetery, but you wouldn't listen, you had to go your own way and work in Taipei. . . . Fuck!'

His sister-in-law opened her eyes—he thought she was asleep.

'Where's Ts'ui-yu?' she asked, smiling.

'She's not back from school yet,' answered Yueh-hsiang, looking at her wristwatch. 'I'll bring her to see you tonight.'

'Now I can be at peace with your family,' Sister-in-law said.

'Yes,' Li Kuo-mu responded.

'Even though I knew it wouldn't be easy, I wanted you to get an education and you did,' she said.

Li Kuo-mu smiled bitterly. The year that Li Kuo-mu had finished elementary school, his Pa and Uncle Fan wanted him to get a job at the mine processing coal. Sister-in-law, however, would not agree.

'Pa,' she said, 'A-mu can study, let him study.'

Nevertheless, Pa remained adamant and would not allow the boy to continue his schooling. As a result, all the day long, Sister-in-law, whether cleaning vegetables, preparing meals, or washing clothes—even when sharing a lunch-box with Pa at the mine—would be on the verge of tears. Finally, around the supper table, Pa said with a sigh, 'I'm not sure we can afford it.'

Sister-in-law said nothing.

'A worker has to accept his lot in life,' Pa said angrily. 'Young K'un, now, the big mistake was to let him go to normal school.'

Again Sister-in-law said nothing.

'And they said that if he went to normal school, we wouldn't have to spend any money,' said Pa, lost in thought and shaking his head.

'A-k'un once said to me we should let A-mu study more and get a better education,' Sister-in-law finally said.

Li Kuo-mu saw his Pa put down his bowl and chopsticks. The black strands of the beard filling his chin were revealed.

'When . . . when did he say that?' asked Pa.

'When he was at . . . at Taoyuan.'

For a very long time, Taoyuan had been a mysterious and sad name to Li Kuo-mu. His elder brother had been arrested near the river separating Taoyuan and Yingko; it was part of a mass arrest at Taoyuan. As a child Li Kuo-mu had gone to the river bank more than once but all he could see were white river stones blending into a distant road. A mass of blossoming wild reeds in the riverbed would be waving in the wind.

'After all these years, you still believe in him,' Pa said weakly, fumbling to light a cigarette.

'It was because I believed in him that I could find this house,' she said.

Sister-in-law gloomily cleared away the bowls and chopsticks. Li Kuo-mu remembered ever so clearly how, under the yellowish light of the forty-watt bulb, the tears quietly streamed down the then very full cheeks of his sister-in-law.

Pa never said anything more about the matter but agreed to let him go to high school. A-mu passed the entrance exam with no difficulty and was admitted to a provincial high school in Taipei.

'I came to your house to suffer,' she said. The heater cast faint rays of red on her thin face. She pulled the blanket tucked under her chin down to her breast, saying, 'I came to your house to . . .'

Yueh-hsiang straightened out the blanket.

'I came to your house to suffer,' Sister-in-law repeated and then added, 'Now that our life is so much better . . .'

Li Kuo-mu and Yueh-hsiang listened quietly but without comprehension.

'Like this, our life like this, is all right, isn't it?' the elderly patient worried. Tears gradually welled up in her dry eyes.

'Sister,' said Li Kuo-mu, extending his hand to touch her forehead. She had no fever. 'Sister,' he repeated.

The patient peacefully closed her eyes. Yueh-hsiang sat for a while and then unobtrusively went to the kitchen to get another small bowl of perch soup.

'There's a little bit left over. Why don't you have some?' she said gently to her husband.

He took the soup and ate it by the bed, careful not to make any noise. She's probably just starting to confuse everything, he thought, noting the incomprehensibility of what Sister-in-law had just said. The light rain outside the window made him, for no apparent reason, experience a tender sorrow.

'Professor Yang is here,' Yueh-hsiang called quietly from in the kitchen where she was washing dishes.

Professor Yang, who was tall and thin, and Dr Wang pushed open the door together and walked in.

'How's her food intake?' Professor Yang asked, as if talking to himself, as he picked up the chart hanging in front of the bed that recorded the patient's eating and bowel movements.

'It seems to be very good,' responded Dr Wang quite respectfully.

'Her sleep?' Professor Yang next asked, looking at the patient, who was fast asleep, and then said, 'She's asleep.'

'Yes,' said Yueh-hsiang, 'she just fell asleep.'

'Hmm,' responded Professor Yang.

'Professor Yang. . .' Li Kuo-mu began.

'By the way,' said Professor Yang looking straight at him through his dark tortoise-shell glasses, 'have you remembered anything about what happened just before her illness?'

Li Kuo-mu immediately thought of Sister-in-law's shock over the release of the man called Huang Chen-po, who had been sentenced to life imprisonment.

'No, nothing,' Li Kuo-mu responded, looking at the peaceful face of Sister-in-law who was sound asleep. Despondently, and as if all were lost, he continued, 'No, I can't think of anything special.'

'So . . . ' said Professor Yang.

Li Kuo-mu walked to the door with Professor Yang and questioned him earnestly about the cause of his sister-in-law's illness. Professor Yang opened the door to the patient's room. A cold draft from the corridor blew against Li Kuo-mu's face.

'I'm not sure,' answered Professor Yang, frowning. 'I only feel that the patient hasn't the slightest will to live.'

'Ahh!' gasped Li Kuo-mu.

'I can't explain it,' continued Professor Yang, perplexity showing on his face. 'In nearly 20 years of practising medicine, I have rarely seen a patient who has lost all desire to live the way she has.'

Li Kuo-mu watched Dr Yang as he entered the room next door. His full head of grey hair was blowing every which way because of the draft from the corridor. 'No,' he said dispiritedly to himself, 'it can't be.'

He went back beside his sister-in-law's bed. Yueh-hsiang was now sitting on the chair he had been using. She was smiling at the patient, her hand under the blanket, holding the dry, yet warm, hand of the patient.

'Were you asleep?' Yueh-hsiang asked lovingly.

'No,' Sister-in-law replied.

Yueh-hsiang laughed, remembering that her sister-in-law wasn't even aware of Professor Yang's visit and was still drowsy.

'Yes, you were, Sister,' she said. 'You didn't sleep long, but you fell asleep.'

'I didn't sleep. I was just dreaming.'

'Do you want something to drink?' Yueh-hsiang asked. 'I'll get a glass of juice for you.'

'That endless railroad track,' Sister-in-law said drowsily in Japanese.

Yueh-hsiang turned around and looked at Li Kuo-mu who stood by the bed and was staring intently at the patient.

'You sit,' Yueh-hsiang said, going to the kitchen to prepare a glass of fresh juice. The words of Professor Yang rang in Li Kuo-mu's ears: 'I have rarely seen a patient who has lost all desire to live the way she has.'

'Sister,' he called lightly.

'Yes.'

'Me, too. I often dream of that long railroad track,' he said in Japanese.

There was no response.

'I'll never forget it,' he said, his eyes fixed on the profile of her sallow face. 'That year, Sister, when you started to work with Pa pushing the coal cart.'

'Oh, yes,' she said starting to smile.

'I don't seem to dream of it at night so much as during the day when I get lost in thought remembering all of those times,' he said in Japanese. 'Sister, couldn't you fight to go on living just because of that railroad track?'

She slowly turned her head and looked at him. There was a single small tear locked in the corner of her faintly smiling eye. Then she again closed her eyes.

It was getting darker and darker outside. The rain was still falling without a pause. Now he was thinking about that long, twisting track that frequently derailed the carts. The track began at the mine and wound its way through Yinghsih Mountain until it reached the coal yard at the station. The third year after Sister-in-law had 'joined' his family, she got a job in the mine filling in as a cart pusher. 'Other women do it, why can't I?' she said to Pa when he opposed her taking the job. Li Kuo-mu was then in the fifth grade. He often saw his Sister-in-law with padding on her arms and legs and wearing a farmer's hat. She looked just like the other women. In the heat of the sun, she and another woman, straining hard, would be pushing a cart full of coal step by step up the slope to the railroad station. Their clothes were always drenched in sweat. When school was not in session, little Li Kuo-mu loved to tag along with his sister-in-law as she pushed the cart. When they were going uphill, he would help push. On level ground, his sister-in-law would first push it for a while and then jump on, allowing the cart to coast on its own. He would stand in the cart enjoying the pleasure of just rolling along. Going downhill, they both would ride in the cart. His sister-in-law would be talking with him while cautiously braking, lest the cart run off the tracks taking the curves.

In the summer, when the cart sailed along the long, winding downhill stretch, it would make a whizzing sound that either roused the cicadas in the dense acacia groves on both sides of the tracks to chirp, or caused their chirping to intensify. Amid the whizzing and the chirping, the cart would slide along the tracks under the huge Ying Rock halfway down the mountain. Li Kuo-mu would then remember the legend about Cheng Ch'eng-kung and his troops camping under Ying Rock.[4] Each day, according to the legend, a large number of his men disappeared. Later, it was learned, a gigantic monster called Ying-ko lived on top of the mountain. Each night, it would come out and devour several soldiers. Cheng Ch'eng-kung at last became so angry that he blasted off the monstrous head of Ying-ko with a cannon. Ying-ko turned to stone and, from that time on, never bothered the troops or people again. Each time the cart passed below Ying Rock, little Li Kuo-mu found himself imagining that at any moment a mist would spit out of the rock and engulf his sister-in-law and himself.

The end of the line for the carts hauling coal was the coal yards behind the railroad station at Yingko. A number of companies shared these yards. It was a large area. When arrangements were made for a shipment of coal to the southern or central part of the island, the carts of the company involved would haul coal to the company's own bins and pile up mounds of the black coal, to await loading on freight trains for transport to its destination.

Many a time Li Kuo-mu went with his sister-in-law and her co-worker to push the cart up the high mound of coal to dump it out. Looking down from the temporary tracks placed atop the mound, beyond the bins made of old wooden ties, Li Kuo-mu would watch many children from poor families sweeping up and collecting pieces of coal in dustpans that had fallen off the carts before they had reached the bins. Sister-in-law would regularly take any occasion when the supervisor was not paying attention to throw big handfuls of coal outside the bin for the children to sweep up and take home to burn.

---

[4] Cheng Ch'eng-kung (1624–62), a loyal supporter of the Ming dynasty, led an unsuccessful resistance movement to the Ch'ing dynasty from Taiwan. He is frequently referred to in Western histories of China as Koxinga, a Dutch derivative of a Chinese title by which he was popularly known.

'They're poor just like us,' she would say. 'We have to help each other out.'

On the way back to the mine in the empty cart, sister-in-law started to recite softly in a chant-like fashion, 'Country folks, workers all, living in poor hovels, doors and windows smashed, three meals a day, potatoes each time. Every single dish, dried beancurd . . .'

Li Kuo-mu turned around and looked at her with surprise. With the sun slowly setting above the orange groves, half the sky over Yingko was shrouded in a golden red. The wind, coming from the grove of acacia trees, blew against the cart speeding down the slope, causing Sister-in-law's hair to fly freely.

'Sister-in-law, what are you singing?' he asked with a laugh.

His sister-in-law suddenly stuck out her tongue in surprise. As he looked up at her, her could see that her cheeks were pink from the day's work and her eyes sparkled in a way he seldom saw.

'Oh, it's nothing,' she replied smiling ruefully. 'You can't sing it. Not allowed to sing it. Not now.'

'Why?'

Sister-in-law said nothing. As they approached a sharp curve, she applied the brakes while adjusting her body to the degree of curve to maintain the balance of the fast-moving cart. The brakes gave out a piercing screech, while from a distance came the sound of wild doves calling to each other.

'Your big brother taught me,' she unexpectedly replied quite calmly after they had slid past the sharp curve. A sprightly black object then appeared leaping beautifully through the limber branches of the acacia trees.

'Sister, look!' he shouted excitedly. 'Look! A squirrel! A squirrel!'

'Your big brother taught me,' she repeated, looking directly forward, with a gentle gleam in her eyes, at the tracks stretching ahead of the cart. 'It's a song more than 30 years old called "The Three-character Collection". That's what your big brother said. When the Japanese were here, leaders in the workers' movement in Taiwan used the songs to educate workers and farmers to resist the Japanese. That's what your big brother said.'

'Oh,' he responded, not quite understanding what she was talking about.

'Your big brother, that year, was busy rewriting the original "Three-character Collection". The situation was not quite the same as when the Japanese were here. That's what your big brother said,' she said, speaking as if to herself. 'Later, things got tight. Your brother gave me his manuscript to hide for safe-keeping. When things loosened up, I was to give it back. That's what your big brother said.'

Little Li Kuo-mu just listened.

The cart gradually slowed down. After Nan-tzu, the tracks were level for a stretch and then began to go uphill gently. Sister-in-law jumped off and started to push a little. Li Kuo-mu, however, remained in it, lost in a silence so unusual for a boy his age.

Next? What happened next? What about my big brother? So many times little Li Kuo-mu wanted to ask his sister-in-law these questions, but in the end he kept them to himself. Nevertheless, even now, sitting in front of the hospital bed, his sister-in-law sound asleep, he still wanted to ask about what had happened to his elder brother—to get to the bottom of things. The years passed. He had grown older and become more educated, gaining a general understanding of the significance of the execution of his elder brother. But this only made him want to clarify everything. For over 20 years now, his father, his sister-in-law, and he, had yearned for Elder Brother, feared him and avoided the topic. He had become the untouchable wound for his entire family; indeed, for all of society. And yet, this hidden wound, imperceptibly, through the selfless sacrifice of his sister-in-law for his poor broken family, had been turned into an overriding power that forced Li Kuo-mu to 'stay away from politics' and to 'forge ahead'. This power had transformed him from the child of a poverty-stricken family into a college-educated adult. After many years of hard work, he had finally become a certified public accountant just a little over three years ago. He had rented a small, elegant, well-equipped office on the east side of Taipei where he opened his own successful accounting business. That same year, he moved with his sister-in-law from their old home in Yingko to an exclusive residential area in Taipei.

Three months later, Li Kuo-mu's sister-in-law finally died after a gradual weakening that medical science was unable to explain.

The evening of the day his sister-in-law's body was sent to the mortuary, Li Kuo-mu was alone in her room, putting her possessions in order. To his surprise, he discovered a very thick letter in a lacquer box containing her simple jewellery. 'Mr Huang Chen-po' was written on the envelope in her neat handwriting. Without thinking, he opened the unsealed envelope and started to read the letter that his sister-in-law had written in an elegant Japanese quite different from anything he had learned in college.

Dear Chen-po,

I am Ts'ai Ch'ien-hui, the same Ch'ien-hui you once so lovingly and sincerely cared for.

Do you remember that evening, so very long ago, in the little village of K'anting near Taoyuan, when you held my hand for the first time? You told me that you had decided to temporarily break off the engagement arranged by our families, because you were risking your life daily to better the living conditions of the workers. 'I ask you to try to understand my feelings,' you said. Even now I am not able to forget your look under that star-filled sky as you said this to me.

Half a year after that evening, you finally allowed me to meet Mr Li Kuo-k'un, about whom you had spoken with so much respect and enthusiasm.

That was over 30 years ago. But when I saw in the paper the day before yesterday that you had been released to your old home, I knew I now had to tell you everything, whether from a sense of morality or love. Those days, you had me call Mr Li 'Elder Brother Kuo-k'un', and it gave me a feeling of anticipated happiness. I remember Kuo-k'un laughed heartily and said to you, 'She's a good girl, Chen-po.' Then, with those bright, shiny eyes of his under his thick eyebrows, he looked at me endearingly, who had already begun to blush, and said, 'What a shame you're going to marry a fellow like Chen-po, who is intent on dying for the happiness of others!' We left Kuo-k'un and returned to Yingko by a long and winding mountain path. Along the way, you talked about so many things, about what you and Kuo-k'un were doing together, about your dreams, about the bright and happy China of the future, and I remember you asked me, 'Why, Ch'ien-hui, why aren't you saying anything today?' I couldn't hold back my tears and I replied, 'Because I'm thinking about all those things you have just said that are so difficult to understand.'

Of course, you didn't notice, my dear Chen-po, on that mountain path, my heart was filled with images of Kuo-k'un—his tenderness and warmth, his clear vibrant laughter, those determined and courageous dark eyebrows, his honest and concerned look. Because it's a thing of the past, because it is now 30 years later, because you and Kuo-k'un were honourable and upright men, when my heart—my heart that is approaching old age and has already experienced over 50 years of life—when this heart thinks back about the young me on that mountain path, it understands all too clearly the sufferings of a girl in love.

But, dear Chen-po, if time could travel backwards and history could be written anew, I would still be exactly as I was then; I would just as wholeheartedly be willing to be your wife. Indeed, even though I just quietly listened to your noble ideas and walked with you to the end of that small and winding mountain path, I knew without a doubt that I could have been a wife you could trust, a wife who would endure any human suffering without regret for the sake of people like you and Kuo-k'un.

Then destiny struck without mercy. Because I had already returned to Tainan for classes, I only learned much later in October of your arrest and the investigation. My older brother Han-t'ing was also apprehended and my parents almost went crazy. Not long afterward, I finally discovered that my parents' fear and grief came from watching the all-too-visible unfolding of the mass arrests at Taoyuan. They associated it with the terror they had personally experienced on the Mainland, and had secretly arranged conditions with the authorities under which Han-t'ing would turn himself in. Several nights in a row, Han-t'ing, my useless brother, went out with my parents and they came back at dawn. He deceived you and Kuo-k'un, his best friends and his fellow workers; nonetheless he was still arrested.

My dear Chen-po, whatever you do, control the shock and anger that you must feel. Please continue to read to the end this letter, written by the sister of a despicable traitor.

Half a year later, Han-t'ing came back weak and aged. You know how much he always loved me. Drunk and unable to endure the censure of his conscience, he told me, the many repercussions of his arrest, one by one.

I felt unbearable, nearly hopeless, pain, shame and sorrow for Han-t'ing, who had caused so many brave and selfless young men, good and honest men like you and Kuo-k'un, to meet such a horrible fate.

I somehow had to redeem the sins of my family. Dear Chen-po, these were the thoughts I had after the appalling events of those times that nearly destroyed me.

A year later, I read in the newspaper that Kuo-k'un and many, many other young men I had never heard you mention, were shot. (Two of them were straightforward young men whom I remember meeting with you at K'anting.) It was then I also learned you had been sentenced to life imprisonment.

At last I decided to pretend to be the woman Kuo-k'un had married while he was away from home, and to go to his parents'. I did this not simply because of my admiration for Kuo-k'un—and that admiration is something I have never revealed to another person. When I decided to do what I did, I actually had clearly in mind what you had often told me about the poverty of Kuo-k'un's family. You told me that his mother was an invalid. There was a much younger brother, and a father who worked in the coal mines. You yourself came from a family of some means and had three older brothers, so you had no worries about the family's future. Further, it was the deep, honourable, and selfless friendship that you and Kuo-k'un shared that allowed me calmly and with full control to make this decision. Thinking that I would never see you alive again in this life, I convinced myself to go to Kuo-k'un's home and to give all I could of my life, my soul, and my physical strength. I would honour the man who courageously destroyed himself for the welfare of struggling workers by sacrificing myself.

Dear Chen-po, full of the trust that I imagined you had in me, I presented myself to Kuo-k'un's poor, stricken family. I worked furiously, as if I were harshly driving another, making a slave of my body and soul. I entered the coal mines and worked pushing carts and piling up coal. Whenever I was physically and emotionally exhausted, I thought of those men who had died with Kuo-k'un and of those like you, exiled, it was reported, to a deserted island where not even grass grew, to endure endless punishment. Whenever I bathed and saw my body, once as young and fresh as a flower, wither day by day from the heavy manual labour, I thought of Kuo-k'un fallen on the Mach'angting execution grounds and now nothing but a pile of rotting bones, and of those of you whose lonely, ageing bodies and souls were imprisoned and completely forgotten by the outside. With such thoughts was my resolve renewed.

For many years now, because of you and Kuo-k'un, I have hidden in the deepest recesses of my heart, the dream that both of you often dreamt. When I'm lost in daydreams, I imagine the flag of your dreams flying high in the sky over our town and I can't keep my eyes from welling up with tears. I'm never sure if they're tears of sorrow or happiness. I don't understand politics very well, but because of you, I never gave up reading the newspaper. In recent years, wearing bifocals, I have been reading about various changes on the Mainland, not infrequently with the worries and doubts of a woman. My only major concern is, if the revolution fails on the Mainland, does that mean Kuo-k'un's death and your long-term imprisonment have turned into meaningless punishments more cruel than death or life in prison?

Suddenly, two days ago, I learned you had been released unharmed. Dear Chen-po, how happy I was to hear that! Thirty years of imprisonment must have been a tremendous burden for you. In the 30 years you were not here, people married and banqueted and completely forgot about you and the other men spending their days on that distant and deserted island. Thinking about this, I realized that with Kuo-mu getting settled into work and starting a family, our own life had improved considerably. Seventeen years ago we moved from the old farm house by the railroad tracks. Seven years ago, we moved to Taipei. As for me, thanks to the devoted love of Kuo-mu and his family, I've been enjoying a leisurely and comfortable life.

Dear Chen-po, I realize now that these past seven or eight years I had completely forgotten about you and Kuo-k'un—I'm shocked to think how far I have fallen without being aware of it.

The last few days, I have felt a painful embarrassment about Kuo-mu's carefully built house with its rugs, air-conditioners, sofa, colour television, stereo, and car. Didn't all that come about precisely because I taught and forced Kuo-mu to 'avoid politics' and 'seek detachment'? In the past seven years I have, to my surprise, completely forgotten my original willingness to suffer, to be self-disciplined, and, unafraid of death, to be willing to redeem the shameful sins of my family.

I have a feeling of desperate waste. For such a long time I felt I had given up my own family and through self-sacrifice had lived for others. I believed that on the day I entered the underworld, I would deserve praise from you and Kuo-k'un. Sometimes I even fantasized myself dressed in white and wearing red flowers, standing between you and Kuo-k'un and, like a god, receiving great honour from the workers.

Now your release from prison has reawakened me. Compromised and living on the products of capitalism like a tamed animal, suddenly and with much trepidation, because of your release, I remember those dreadfully difficult woods we walked in, which none the less were so full of life. Thus coming to my senses, I also felt that whatever light had remained within me had gone out forever.

Separated for 30 long years and going back to your old home, you probably found the changes earth-shattering. I am afraid that you who had 'struggled for the life that is man's right', after your release, will have to begin another difficult journey. Facing a world so completely 'full of tamed animals', won't your struggle now be even more difficult than before? I worry so much about you.

Please go forth to fight with the strength of steel. As for me, my life of failure must come to an end. But if you are still willing, please, as long as you live, do not forget that girl who once stood with you on that winding mountain path.

With all my respect,

Ch'ien-hui

With tears running down his cheeks, Li Kuo-mu put the thick letter written with such fine, flowing brushstrokes back into its envelope.

'Kuo-mu, what is it?' cried Yueh-hsiang in surprise as she entered the room carrying a bowl of frozen lotus-seed soup.

'Nothing,' he replied, gravely taking out his handkerchief and wiping away his tears. 'Nothing at all. I'm . . . I'm just . . . I'm just thinking about Sister-in-law.'

Li Kuo-mu started to choke. Looking up, he saw the enlarged picture of his elder brother standing under a clear blue sky, somewhere in Taiwan, looking into the distance.

Azaleas Wept Blood

Liu Ta-jen

translated by Nicholas Koss

THE ROAD was tortuously winding. After we entered the mountains, though the car slowed down, the previous night's rain had washed the road clean of cinders and it was more bumpy than ever. The shock absorbers of the little car were not exceptionally good; the situation worsened, especially when going downhill, the driver put the car in neutral and allowed it to coast. It seemed as if the bottom of the car was going to fall off. Loud, unexpected clanks and clunks were emanating from all over the car, especially around the doors and windows. When Ch'en finally pointed out our destination, I let loose a giant sigh, but there was still a long, steep, uphill road ahead that seemed pasted on the dark, damp mountainside and ascended with twists and turns.

Seen from a distance, the architecture of the sanatorium seemed to be inserted into the mountainside. The overshadowing forests and the floating mountain mist vaguely suggested the dragon-hiding castles of fairy tales. As we drew near, its whole flavour changed again. Now it was more like a YMCA building from the 1930s and 1940s constructed mainly of brick with sandstone for the foundation, but it had lost none of its solemn and imposing appearance. Regrettably, the wooden portions had not been taken care of for years and were decaying and falling off. The weeds growing randomly from the cracks and crevices around the eaves further added to an impression of disrepair and ruin.

After Ch'en made the necessary introductions, we followed Dr Hsu into the visitors' room.

'The long distance didn't keep you away, Professor Hu,' Dr Hsu remarked to get the conversation started. The chill of the mountain was more evident in the room, and I felt I had not dressed sufficiently warmly.

Dr Hsu appeared to be a man of strong and dependable character and years of experience. He was in his fifties and so must have been an intellectual of my generation. He preserved the etiquette of a traditional host.

'Please, let me give you some tea. Here in the mountains we have nothing special for guests, but the mountain spring water is something hard to come by elsewhere. . . .'

I patiently waited for my host to get to the main topic. I was sure that they had a good grasp of the background for my visit. The only thing that made me uneasy was not knowing how much they would be willing to reveal. I kept warning myself that the best strategy was to feign ignorance and pursue the matter when he unintentionally allowed an opening.

'. . . Professor Hu, I understand fully your determination. But my superiors have their concerns too. You know . . .'

Of course I knew. Five or six years had passed since I stumbled on traces of my aunt who had been missing for forty-odd years and began using every imaginable method to piece together a vague picture of her life. If I had not worked my hands to the bone and gone all the way to the upper levels of the Overseas Chinese Department of the Chinese State Council, I would never have reached here to receive this gracious, though casual, reception from Dr Hsu.

'. . . I am not intentionally hindering a meeting between you and your aunt. You've been separated for 40 or 50 years. Added to that, you've been in very different places. And there have been great changes both within and outside of China. The party had to take many things into consideration. All this being said, one condition is most important. Everything comes down to whether or not it's beneficial to the health of Comrade Leng Feng! I'm sure you can appreciate this. . . .'

Item by item, Dr Hsu explained my aunt's present situation. He didn't say a word about the time before she entered the sanatorium. I knew I would not likely learn anything about this from him on our first meeting so I didn't even ask. The taste of the tea made from the mountain spring water was indeed different. Since the quality of the tea leaves was not exceptional, it must have been the high mineral content which made the water rather hard. Not only was there a clean, refreshing feeling as I drank it, but it also left a bitter-sweet sensation on my tongue. The tea really had an indescribable taste. Then, for no apparent reason, I was suddenly tired with Dr Hsu's report. I just couldn't suppress my apprehensions about finally meeting my aunt.

She had been placed in the section of the sanatorium for the long-term treatment of severe illnesses. It was a place newly opened outside the east wall of the sanatorium's rear courtyard.

'It's not like this big building which is moldy and damp the year round. Over there the sunlight, the air, indeed everything, is much better,' Dr Hsu said.

I left Ch'en, who had accompanied me up the mountain, waiting in the visitors' room. Dr Hsu led the way as we left the long hallway and walked along the tree-covered cement walk of the back garden.

It was about four or five in the afternoon. I expected, since it was the beginning of May and days were already longer, that the sun would be shining brightly, but the back garden was full of old trees reaching to the clouds so that it was coldly dark and gloomy. I heard the first early summer sounds of the cicada, and they seemed to have a ring of sorrowful desolation.

'This past year, Comrade Leng Feng's illness showed definite improvement . . . ' said Dr Hsu. He then continued to describe her condition. 'Her weight has increased half a kilo. Moreover, for the first time in all these years, she has made a request on her own!'

'Oh? What request?'

'You know, of course, that she was not very calm during her early days here. Later, the Party organization of the hospital, after a period of observation, determined the special characteristics of Comrade Leng Feng's illness and the salient features of the history of the illness. The group came to an overall conclusion and decided upon a course of treatment that would combine medication and a regulated routine. With this group help, her explosive tendencies took a turn for the better, and eventually she settled down completely. But for two years—two whole years—she wouldn't even open her mouth. She didn't say a single word. . . .'

As Dr Hsu continued to render his account, he stopped at the end of the walkway and pounded loudly on the door with his fist.

'What was the request?' I asked. I couldn't believe that the old-fashioned double doors were locked from the inside with a large lock. This was followed by the sound of a bolt being pulled.

'She wanted a watering can with a long spout! The first one we sent over to her she didn't want and sent it back. She said the holes were too large and it didn't do the job. We then had one of the hospital's workmen make one for her specially. You see, for her to make such a concrete request was totally unexpected. . . .'

The arrangement of the section for severe illness was not at all 'so much better' as Dr Hsu had claimed, but it was brighter than the damp visitors' room and the dark back garden. Near the tall south wall there were even some ten rows of vegetables including frames for melons and bean vines. So there were signs of life after all.

The patients' rooms were a row of single-storey frame houses stuck on the mountainside. A concrete wall had been built along the slope to prevent landslides. Certainly attention had been paid to safety, but visually it merely increased the feeling of oppression. The front edge of the patients' rooms had curved asbestos tiles for roof gutters, which made the buildings look a little like the covered arcades of old streets in the south, but these houses were built in a makeshift manner; compared with the overall classical architecture of the sanatorium itself, they particularly appeared shoddy. If I had not been influenced by my first impression—always the lasting one—seeing them from a distance, I would have taken them to be storehouses for equipment.

I could hear nothing except the intermittent sounds of the cicadas and the droning of Dr Hsu's report. In a place that should have scores of patients, I could see no signs of activity from the inmates. Could it be that they were all locked in their rooms? My mind being bent by this little question mark, I was inclined to be suspicious of Dr Hsu's description just now of how my aunt's condition had taken a turn for the better. We walked directly towards the patients' rooms, and when we were about 40 or 50 metres away, my first question was answered. Beneath the covered walkway near the foot of the wall a number of long benches were lined up. On these, all in a line, were 20 or 30 people uniformly dressed in grey shirts and grey pants. Some sat with their arms folded, or heads bent. Some sat with legs extended or leaned back. There was no sound or movement, except two or three cigarettes quietly burning. The last faint rays from the setting sun cut through the walkway. The two benches to the west were already in the shade and unoccupied. This long row of human shadows, could not have been always motionless; pushed along by the encroaching shade, it must have been gradually shifting to seats on the eastern side.

'. . . The patient only has to make a request, and if it's within the realm of possibility, we'll come up with a way to fulfil it. Professor Hu, to be honest, even though all of the patients here no longer hold positions, in the past, they worked hard and effectively on Party business, and made definite contributions . . . '

I paid little attention to Dr Hsu's faintly self-laudatory report. Actually, as soon as I saw that row of human forms, involuntarily I came to a sudden stop. Was I shocked by suddenly coming upon that collection of grey shapes, or had my long-held hopes aroused too many delusions? Now that the reality was before me, I lost all self-control. Before I left America, my mother had sent me a picture of my aunt. It was an old photo from 40 years ago, a group picture of four people. On the back, indistinctly seen, was my mother's youthful inscription: 'Autumn Moon and Spring Wind are priceless, leaving a beautiful image before Blossom Hill'. Forty years of changes appeared vividly before my eyes. Unconsciously I fidgeted with my shirt and then immediately dropped my hands, not knowing where to put them.

'. . . Basically, as you know, we do not follow Western idealistic psychological analysis. We advocate depending on group therapy . . . . I've heard, and I'm sure you would know, that in America now the use of group therapy is very common. Is that the case?'

Led by my mother, the four sisters in the picture—Autumn, Moon, Spring, and Wind—were all dressed in the sailor outfits popular at that time. The large turned-down collars set off four clear, full, smiling faces. The one that stood out was that of my youngest aunt. The others had fringes and permanents. Only she had her hair bobbed like the progressive women of the day. Furthermore, even in that old, fading photo, you could discern that she alone had inherited my grandmother's deep, round dimples. My mother often said when I was little, 'Your youngest aunt was the most pampered, but she also had the most nerve'.

Just as I was focusing on that row of greyish human shapes, looking for my aunt, a male nurse in a white uniform trotted over to us, signaled with his eyes, and nodded to the east. I took two big steps aside, to allow them to talk over business, but at the same time I looked in the direction he had indicated and finally discovered why this section for severe illnesses appeared to be brighter than the back garden we had just passed.

It was enclosed on two sides by a high wall and on one side by the mountain, but the east side of the section for the treatment of severe illnesses unexpectedly had a broad, open vista. Above was blue sky and below was the mountainside. It was bordered only by a wire fence strung along the trees. This let in air and light. Beyond the wire, down along the mountain, appeared undulating hills covered with shrubs. Winding through the fields in the flatland below and on the lower levels of the mountain, were little paths in the fields that caught a light, airy mist.

Inside the barbed wire stood a two-tiered flower stand constructed of mountain rocks and wooden planks. On the upper tier was an assortment of flower pots. In the last rays of sunset, I saw an elderly woman. In her hand was a shining, tin watering can. With great concentration, she was watering one of the flower pots. Against the sunset, droplets from the long spout produced a neon-like effect by creating in the little space above the pot a tiny, dazzling rainbow of light. Avoiding the row of greyish human shapes under the covered walkway and silently intent on getting some sun, we walked toward that rainbow.

'Comrade Leng Feng, your nephew has come to see you. He came from far, far away, from America. Do you know America? Comrade Teng Hsiao-p'ing just went there on a visit. . . .'

The elderly woman did not pick up his gambit. I did my best to see if there was anything whatsoever in my aunt's eyes. I saw nothing at all. They were spiritless. The pupils seemed slightly enlarged. I had the feeling that they were so enlarged that they were unable to focus. They were quite different from the eyes I had seen of people who had taken drugs and were hallucinating. Although such eyes were spiritless too, they none the less seemed to emit a soft glow that suggested to the observer a spiritual state of complete defencelessness and calm contentment. My aunt's eyes, if they emitted any glow to speak of, were those of somebody in a state of extreme agitation and worry who had suddenly suffered a vicious, unbearable attack—like a fish hooked and struggling for life beached by the fisher; or like a trembling, frightened dog tethered in a 'sweet meat' restaurant at the precise moment it lifts its head to meet the onslaught of a gigantic bludgeon. I struggled to control myself, hoping to make eye contact with her from some angle, but I was left feeling as though I looked into an endless tunnel devoid of light. Finally I had to turn away from that piercing coldness.

Avoiding those eyes, I walked towards her, thinking to take the can and help her water. The effect of this action was unexpected. Even Dr Hsu had no time to intervene. As though by reflex, she snatched back the can and held it tightly with both hands. The moment I turned toward her, two little indentations unexpectedly appeared on her face near the edges of her tightly compressed lips—traces of her dimples on the now fleshless cheeks. They seemed trapped in the lines on her face, rather like unnatural breaks in the wrinkles. Her hair was not all white, only 60 or 70 per cent so. It was obviously not combed often. It lacked luster, and was tangled like a heap of old twine. This must have been the unwanted effect of what black hair remained. Its dirty look immediately evoked a sense of disgust. Her voice was surprisingly high and sharp, with the odd intonation of the speech of a deaf person.

She said, 'Mine . . . don't take . . . my pail . . . don't take . . . my flowers . . . don't take, don't take . . . you go away, go away. . . .'

She suddenly leaped over to the potted plant and protected it with her emaciated body. Dr Hsu quickly pulled me back and wanted us to raise our hands as if in surrender. The situation relaxed, and the elderly lady returned to her interrupted work, intently watering the plant as if nothing had happened.

From the villi on the leaves and the shape of the flowers, I could tell that it was an azalea, and it was an extraordinarily beautiful one. It was beyond all expectations in a place like this to see such an exceptional and lovely potted plant. Dr Hsu explained that it was a gift from the provincial secretary when he had visited Comrade Leng last year. It had many stocks, and was the type whose roots were partially visible. Off-centre in the square, dark-red porcelain pot, a yellow rock rose like a crag, surrounded and covered by a rich, green moss. The curly roots of the azalea were creeping into the fissures of the yellow rock. The main stock was as thick as an arm. The markings on it resembled a snake's shedded skin and somehow gave the impression of untold age and classical restraint. A few inches up, the stock first twisted to the left, turned right at a sharp angle and then went straight up the centre. One root developed many stocks, and these fanned out in innumerable branches, terminating in a green umbrella three times the size of the pot. Over that dense crown were scattered hundreds of bright azalea blossoms. The entire effect was of snowflakes, not a single one off-colour. However, where the pistils were barely exposed there were spots of scarlet. From the angle at which I stood, it seemed as if these hundreds and hundreds of brilliantly shining azaleas each had a little mouth full of thick, smelly blood. From so many throats the blood oozed, flowing slowly and unimpeded.

When I returned to the guest house, it was already past supper time. Through the intercession of Ch'en, I was able to ask Comrade Cook to make simple small dishes. I ate these in my room, where I sat facing the window with waving bamboo shadows in the dark night. I poured myself a large glass of Luchou liquor. There was a settled silence throughout the guest house. Everyone had gone to the evening programme, leaving the place a deserted city. Opening the window, I heard a chorus of frogs from the depths of the gardens and, occasionally, the crisp sound of fish leaping in the pond.

If I were to tell the story of my aunt, I'm afraid no-one would believe it. After 40 years, the first trace of my aunt came from a tabloid of the Revolutionary Red Guards. That year saw the last gasp of the 'Great Proletarian Cultural Revolution'. The library of the school in America where I was teaching, through a stroke of unexpected good luck, came by a huge stack of tabloids and mimeographed material published by the Red Guards. My school was not large, it could be considered one of the better second-rank, small universities. Naturally the library did not have resources to hire a cataloguer for Chinese material, so I, who taught Oriental literature, constituted the school's only Asian authority and was called in to volunteer to help to take care of this material.

In the process of cataloguing, I discovered a publication entitled *Luchou Battle Report*. It was a half octavo, laid out and printed quite crudely as a propaganda brochure. The pages were cut unevenly; no special care was taken over the kind of paper used, so red, yellow, blue, and white were mixed together. It was a scrawny volume of only 30 or 40 pages but errors were everywhere and even whole pages were missing. As for the content, each article had a surfeit of slogans and other such nonsense common to publications of that sort. The printer's enthusiasm was evident from the frequent, almost hysterical, use of exclamation points—every third full stop. Leafing through the publication, I could hardly avoid the suspicion that these pen-wielding warriors were neurotics all.

This kind of crude publication—indeed it was nearly gibberish—should not have wasted my time and energy in reading and putting in order. I had only to put on a call number and say the work was completed. But things were to transpire much differently. Luchou as a place in modern Chinese history was fought for by both the left and the right. It also happened to be my parents' ancestral home. Needless to say, it was the place where I could find my roots.

Perhaps mainly out of curiosity, I carefully read that copy of the *Battle Report*. Near the end, I saw an article the very title of which sent shivers up my spine: 'Cut off the Dirty Hands of That Counter-revolutionary, Revisionist, Two-faced Leng Feng! Eradicate Completely the New Counter-attack of the Old Provincial Committee!'

The name Leng Feng of course did not have any special meaning for me. But, in the second half of the article, the writer cited 'revealing material', which had this passage:

> *According to recent revelations, this Leng Feng is from an ambiguous background, and her life is filled with the crimes of a political pickpocket. Before she fell in with the revolutionary camp, her name was Leng Yu-feng. Originally she was an overseas Chinese disguised as a patriot! When she was a student at Shanghai University, she . . .*

The appearance of the name Leng Yu-feng immediately made me shake from head to toe. It was impossible, impossible that there could be such a coincidence. First of all, there are really not too many people surnamed Leng. Further, the given name, Yu-feng, was exactly correct. My mother had three sisters in all. For their generation, the character 'Yu' [Jade] always formed the first part of their given names. For the second character, grandfather, according to the order of their births, chose the four characters 'Ch'iu' [Autumn], 'Yueh' [Moon], 'Ch'un' [Spring], and 'Feng' [Wind]. I heard this explanation a long time ago. Additionally, the text had, 'Originally . . . an overseas Chinese . . . .' This narrowed the possibilities considerably. But the appearance of 'Shanghai University' made my original 'impossible coincidence' a bit shaky. Energetically, I continued to check through the skimpy Chinese material stored in our library. In the back of my mind I had the impression that somebody—I can't remember for sure whether it was my mother, my second aunt, or my third aunt—had once mentioned in conversation that my fourth aunt, after the '18 September Incident', had returned to Shanghai for college, and for a year she studied with the very well-known Communist Ch'u Ch'iu-pai. Urged on by that impression, in a little volume on the life of Ch'u Ch'iu-pai, I finally found the following:

> *At that time, Shanghai University was the centre for leftist intellectuals in that city. . . .*
> *The nominal President of Shanghai University was Yu-jen, a member of the KMT, but*

the actual running of the University was in the hands of Teng Chung-hsia, Yun Tai-ying, Ch'u ch'iu-pai, and K'ang Sheng, famous young members from the early years of the Chinese Communist Party. . . . Ch'u Ch'iu-pai's official position at that time was chairman of the sociology department.

Putting these clues together, I deduced that the Revolutionary Red Guards' 'political pickpocket' of the Cultural Revolution was in fact Leng Yu-feng—my fourth aunt, out of touch for more than 40 years. There was an 80 or 90 per cent chance my deduction was correct, but I certainly didn't want to jump rashly to any conclusions. For further proof, I wrote to my mother in Singapore, my second aunt in Taipei, and my third aunt in Hong Kong, asking them to tell me in detail everything they remembered about their sister.

Mother's response was the most prompt and simple: 'After your aunt left home still a girl, I heard nothing from her, I do not know what became of her. When I returned to China with your grandfather the year before last to look up our relatives, I searched everywhere for news of her with no success. Alas for those of us separated in times of cataclysm.'

The letter from my aunt in Taipei, though also general and vague, did contain one bit of concrete information I had never heard before:

The year Yu-feng graduated from high school, she fell in love with her Chinese literature teacher. Then there was not the openness there is now, and their relationship became the town scandal. The man's name was Lo, and I had heard that he was strongly inclined to the left. He was dismissed by the school authorities because of the scandal. I'm not clear about the details because I had just married your uncle and moved to Singapore. Your aunt did visit us in Singapore for two days after she had left home and was on her own. I do remember that her head was filled with fervent dedication to the cause! Your uncle and I wasted our breath trying to convince her otherwise, but she was a wild horse, not to be bridled. For our urging, we were scolded!

The last paragraph of the 'Cut Off . . . Her Dirty Hands' article in the *Luchou Battle Report* mentioned a Comrade Lo Ch'eng. Could it be the Lo referred to by my aunt? On this point, my third aunt's letter mentioned a man named Lo but with a different given name. From other circumstances, however, it did seem likely it was the same person. Furthermore, if Leng Feng once was Leng Yu-feng, and this Leng Yu-feng was my aunt who had simply changed her name, it would not be surprising if Lo had changed his name to Lo Ch'eng. There were only two years' difference in age between my third and fourth aunts. When young, they were the closest of all four sisters. Moreover, like me, my third aunt was a teacher, so I naturally found what she had to say rather compelling. My third aunt's letter was the longest and the most detailed, and it was clearly organized. Two of her main points had a decisive effect on my investigation. In the first place she said:

> *In the spring of 1932 your aunt left home to study in Shanghai. The first year after her arrival, she wrote to me regularly. Unfortunately, because I moved from place to place over the years, the letters themselves are lost, but I still remember something of what she said. Your aunt entered the sociology department of Shanghai University, but appears not to have devoted herself wholeheartedly to her studies. My impression is that she was always talking about things like acting in new-style plays, going to lectures and meetings, and fighting the Japanese to save China.*

What was really interesting was to compare this passage with the revealing material in the 'Cut Off . . .' article:

> *How did this two-faced Leng Feng penetrate the Revolutionary camp? In March 1930, the Chinese Left-wing Writers' League was formally established in Shanghai under the initiative of Lu Hsun, the cultural leader and great fighter for the proletariat! Those days the movement to fight the Japanese and save China had vigorous support from literary and cultural circles, and Leng Feng seized the opportunity to sneak into the Revolutionary camp. But it is easier to move mountains than change a personality! From the very beginning, she followed the reactionary path, nosed the asses of Chou Yang and company, the 'Four Real Men' whom Lu Hsun once scathingly denounced. She waved their banner and shouted their battle cries.*

If Leng Feng was indeed my aunt, judging from my Hong Kong aunt's letter, I deduced that from the spring of 1932 until 1933, my aunt had not yet joined any organization, and still wrote regularly to her sister, revealing her living situation and the state of her thinking. Probably around 1934, when, according to the 'Cut Off' article, she 'nosed the asses . . . of the "Four Real Men"' and 'waved their banner and shouted their battle cries', my aunt broke off the last remaining ties with her family and formally became what her later name suggested: a person totally devoted to the organization. When she changed her name to Leng Feng ['cold mountain peak'], would she have meant to suggest that she had abandoned the last shred of emotion? This is hard to judge from my present position, of course, but I found it difficult to drive the thought from my mind.

Another passage in my aunt's letter also kept going around in my mind for a long, long time, like a ghost you know does not exist, but which keeps haunting you all the same. This passage was probably, only probably, the decisive force that compelled me in spite of myself to finally find out what had happened to my aunt:

> *Even though we are over 40 years from the event, through it all I still feel that your aunt's absolute renunciation was partly patriotic, and the greater part of patriotism is rational. Nevertheless, living to my advanced age, one tends to look at people and the world with detachment, and I still feel that 'emotion' is fundamental to all things and the most difficult to alter. This, I'm afraid your mother and your second aunt, even today, are not willing*

to accept, and do not want to face. Your aunt's running back to China, ultimately, had something to do with that Lo Te-ch'ang . . .

On this point, the 'revealing material' of the 'Cut Off' article was even more vague and abstract, but on a certain level it was consistent with what my third aunt said. Of course, everything is based on the assumption that the 'Lo Ch'eng' in the 'Cut Off' article is the 'Lo Te-ch'ang' mentioned by my aunt. The article says:

> *In July of 1934, the situation in the Central Committee's stronghold was desperate. The Party decided to let Comrade Fang Chih-min command the Seventh Red Army and the Tenth Red Army combined as the 'Advance Party of the Worker-Peasant Red Army to Fight the Japanese in the North'. Passing through Fukien and Chekiang, the Army moved on to strongholds in Hupeh, Anhui and Honan. To prepare for this massive strategic deployment of troops, the Party ordered Comrade Lo Ch'eng to the area of his old home to arrange for supplies. The political pickpocket Leng Feng took advantage of this opportunity to sneak into the underground Party organization of our Province. From then on, she has been a danger to our district for as long as 34 years!*

Since Leng Feng was denounced for having her 'nose to the asses . . . of the "Four Real Men"' and 'waving their banner and shouting their battle cries', why would she take advantage of Lo Ch'eng's transfer to his home territory to run there, too? If those two hadn't had a special relationship, it would be very difficult to explain logically. What possible reason did the 'Cut Off' article have to pass over this detail so vaguely? This was only one of the questions I was vainly turning over and over in my mind. There were, of course, a great number of unanswerable questions, but I instinctively felt that Lo was probably the most important person to have influenced, or even decided, the fate of my aunt. To check the details of this mysterious man, I really worked like a dog, spending a great deal of time on meticulous research and investigation. I don't know how many times I phoned or wrote to American acquaintances who specialized in the history of the Chinese Communist Party, but finally I gained the enthusiastic help of one of them. I took the occasion of his trip to Taiwan for research to ask him to get me a document entitled 'Records of Destroying Communists in South-Eastern China' from the top-secret Shih-sou Archives. Following regulations, my foreign friend had to copy out this material in his somewhat wobbly Chinese hand. A couple of lines from these 'Records' helped me to solve the riddle of Leng Feng and my fourth aunt, of Lo Ch'eng and Lo Te-ch'ang, and of the exact relationship between them:

> *Among the prisoners who escaped during the prison break, the most important was the Local Party Secretary Lo Ch'eng. His original name was Lo Te-ch'ang, and he was from Luchou.*

As a child, he went with his father, a merchant, to South-east Asia. In year 21 of the Republic, he returned secretly to Shanghai, joined the Communist Party, and worked in the labour movement. In August of year 23 of the Republic, he was with the forces of Fang Chih-min harassing the north-western region of the province. When he was captured in December, his remaining forces, led by his lover, Leng Feng, hid in the mountains. After Lo Ch'eng was captured, through the urging and entreaties of our workers, he came to regret his actions and decided to atone for his crimes by co-operating with us. Unfortunately, our safety precautions were insufficient, and the remaining Communist forces were able to take advantage.

Going over the circumstances this passage unintentionally revealed, I thought about my aunt and Lo Te-ch'ang. The two of them turned against their families and their society and together returned to China to follow their dream. In the 1930s the place where generations of my ancestors had lived and died was remote, inaccessible, poor and backward. For a vague but beautiful dream, they lived through death and battle, a life woven of blood, and tears of love and hatred. I read again my elderly third aunt's letter: '"Emotion" is fundamental to all things and the most difficult to alter.' Hadn't she unwittingly, in a single phrase, exposed all the perennially false and wishful lies of man's life? Hadn't she vividly revealed what seemed to be the childish and senseless truth of my fourth aunt's life?

Having solved in this roundabout way the important riddle of my aunt's life, mixed emotions of instinctual family feeling and a vague cultural nostalgia crept upon me. For a long time I was deeply sunk in such emotions. It was not until I received a second letter from my third aunt, which amounted to a reprimand, that I realized what was going on: from the time I stumbled upon that copy of *Luchou Battle Report*, until I verified the identity of Leng Feng and Lo Ch'eng—no short period—I didn't believe it possible these two people were alive today. My aunt's letter, however, showed clearly that after she had received my letter seeking information about my fourth aunt, her immediate response was: Is she still alive? At the thought of my own callousness, I broke into a cold sweat.

My subconscious belief was not unrelated to the exclamation points that so caught my attention, scattered throughout the 'Cut Off' article. It clearly described the dangerous position my aunt was in at the time of publication. Further, the *Luchou Battle Report* was published in the late spring of 1968— just the time the revolutionary faction was in a life and death struggle for power. The old guard were up against the wall and fighting back by joining the 'three-in-one' forces of the young, middle-aged, and elderly. Because of the 20 July mutiny of Ch'en Shou-t'ung in Wuhan the previous year, military control, which had been supporting the leftists, began to waver and seemed to adopt the policy of sitting back and letting the others fight it out. Moreover, judging by the various indictments of my aunt listed in the 'Cut Off' article, together with news of the Cultural Revolution heard abroad during those years, it was impossible to believe my aunt could undergo such calamities without incident. Furthermore, today she would be nearly 70. For this reason, when I first wrote to my mother and my aunts, I deliberately omitted what had moved me to collect material about my fourth aunt. Naturally I could not let these elderly women know about the *Battle Report* with its hints of blood and death.

I gained a rough understanding of my aunt's situation at that time by summarizing the indictments enumerated against her in the 'Cut Off' article. Before the Cultural Revolution, my aunt had been a secretary in the Provincial Party Committee's Secretariat; not at the top level of leadership, of course, because after the revolutionary storm of January 1967, the old Provincial Party Committee was completely paralyzed. The old cadres stood aside. Those who were number one, two, or three were brought down by vicious denunciations. They lost their power, their homes were ransacked, they were paraded through the streets wearing tall dunce's hats, and then tossed into prison. From the text of the 'Cut Off' article, it seemed that my aunt probably was a key figure in the second level of the conservative group in the old Provincial Party Committee. Under the pretext of organizing incriminating material to expose the number one agent of the 'Chinese Khrushchev' in their province, they were secretly readying a counter-attack using the newly popular slogan 'Step up the Revolution and Promote Production' as the banner under which to make their comeback. They were planning to break into the 'three-in-one' leadership. Unfortunately for them, their plans were betrayed by the elderly Lin T'ien-fu, a subordinate of hers whose sense of purpose was rather weak. This then, was the background of that bloody and bellicose 'Cut Off' article in the *Luchou Battle Report*. When I first read it, I went through related material immediately and discovered that the name Leng Feng, so utterly reviled there, did not appear again in lists of Provincial Revolutionary Committees or subsequent rolls of leadership. This was probably why I reasonably concluded there was not the faintest hope my aunt was alive. As I think back now, did I so bury myself in the search for this person called Leng Feng, that although, step by step, I came closer to the truth, I refused to face the tragedy my subconscious was telling me must have occurred?

As for Lin T'ien-fu, the truly two-faced, the 'Cut Off' article treated him as a revolutionary hero who had returned to the fold. The exposé at the end of the article had been contributed by him. The only problem was that the exposure was not complete, but this could not be blamed on him. The copy of that crudely printed *Luchou Battle Report* I had in hand was incomplete. The last paragraph of the expose read:

> *For many years I have had a secret in my heart. Now at last, with my own resurrection, I can openly reveal it to the great Revolutionary masses and for that I feel great happiness. Blood must be repaid with blood! Comrade Lo Ch'eng . . .*

After the three words 'Comrade Lo Ch'eng' appeared 'Turn to page 39', but when I leafed through my own precious overseas copy of *Luchou Battle Report* I could find no trace of a page 39. I couldn't find a complete copy even after I had applied to interlibrary loan departments of other American universities. From the 'Cut Off' article I could sense that something must have happened between my aunt and comrade Lo Ch'eng. Furthermore, Lin T'ien-fu's exposé must have touched on it. But influenced by my confused emotional state, and nearly convinced that the parties involved were dead, I thought, why should I search out the rights and wrongs committed during my aunt's lifetime? If my third aunt's family instinct had not reawakened me, I probably would long ago have put away this piece of family history. I could never have shown, as Dr Hsu described it, a really 'indomitable' spirit so many years after the fact.

I stayed in Luchou for seven days. Besides the visits to my aunt, the reception unit had arranged many tours for me to choose from, so I spent a good deal of time visiting farm communes, factories, schools, scenic places and historical sites. My hosts appeared deeply distressed by the ten years of destruction wrought by the Cultural Revolution, and were properly humble about the achievements of their country, though it was easy to see they felt a sense of pride and satisfaction. On me, however, their guest from afar, these tours did not have the effect my hosts expected. For example, though the famous lines of the great poet Tu Fu—'Leaves fall from deep woods—rustling and soughing; The Long River rolls on, forever, wave after wave'[1]—ran through my mind, yet when my two feet actually stood on the banks of the muddy, rapidly flowing Yangtse River, the T'ang dynasty feeling the poem used to conjure up in me was completely destroyed. The industrial and agricultural accomplishments in the land of my forebears, where I felt a vague sense of rootedness, did have their effect. But I was raised in a large city in South-east Asia. The speed of change in the life of my own family was far beyond anything my compatriots in my ancestral home could imagine. Also, over half of my life

---

[1] Wu-chi Liu's translation. Wu-chi Liu and Irving Yucheng Lo, eds., *Sunflower Splendor* (Bloomington: Indiana University Press, 1975), p. 140.

had been spent in America, which seemed even more like a land of extra-terrestrials. So, after a couple of tours and visits, I felt a curious sadness about the self-satisfied introductions and briefings. Accordingly, after a whirlwind circuit of the area, I decided to concentrate only on my aunt. If the friend I had asked to take my classes hadn't had a previous commitment, I might have stayed longer, but, after I had pressed on with my investigation and searched for clues everywhere, I became aware that even if I stayed longer, I couldn't feel it would have helped anything.

The travel agency really outdid itself; nothing was overlooked. Ch'en, assigned to accompany my errands, was always on call. He spent his entire day just waiting for orders.

Once, just before I went to bed, it suddenly occurred to me that my aunt's pillow was too old and hard, which probably affected her rest. I phoned Ch'en. That very night he considered every possibility and even mobilized Comrade Driver to take a new pillow up the mountain that evening. The attitude of the manager of the travel agency, Mr Ho, was the same. Every other day or so, he would not only ask me how I was, but each time he came he would solicit my suggestions, continually repeating in a manner devoid of artificiality: 'Just tell me what you need. We're all one big family here! And please don't be polite.' I had no complaint about the meticulous and conscientious travel agency.

This meticulousness and conscientiousness on the part of the travel agency caused appreciation and guilt in me. But some things I couldn't mention for fear of appearing fussy or because I felt I couldn't further burden the staff. It was an embarrassing situation because these were all trivialities, and yet, if not done, life became very inconvenient; but I could only get them accomplished if I became thick-skinned and 'made demands'. Elsewhere abroad, you can personally take care of both big and little needs, but to attempt this in China would be fruitless, leading only to dead ends. Although Mr Ho insisted I had only to ask for whatever I needed, it was clear from their exertions to satisfy my requests that there were limitations to what they could do.

For example, after I had seen my aunt for the first time, I tried hard to size up the situation and finally decided to give up my original determination to be clever and pretend ignorance of past events. I would be straightforward and ask them directly to look for a copy of *Luchou Battle Report* published in the spring of 1968. I remember very clearly that this occurred after a busy day of sightseeing when we had returned to the guest house. As usual, before leaving, Ch'en wanted to go over plans for the next day, and then he asked me if there was anything else I wanted him to do. I saw Ch'en very carefully write down in his little notebook my request for the *Battle Report*. Two days later, I again pursued the matter. Ch'en responded with what seemed to be a great deal of surprise: 'Oh my! I'm really sorry. I forgot about that!' Only the day before I was to leave did I finally receive a copy. However, not only did it have the same missing pages mine did, but there was no trace of the article 'Cut Off the Dirty Hands of That Counter-revolutionary, Revisionist, Two-faced Leng-feng'.

On the way to the airport, Ch'en was very apologetic and said, 'I'm very sorry about this. I should have taken care of it earlier. Nowadays it is really impossible to find this kind of mimeographed publication from the period of the Cultural Revolution. This copy, so our superior said, was an internal publication not to be taken out of the country. But since you are one of us, I had a special permit issued to prevent any trouble at customs. . . .'

I knew it would not be easy to solve the *Luchou Battle Report* problem. Sure enough, I encountered more or less the same difficulties as with other key problems. For instance, what were the exact circumstances under which my aunt first became ill? I could not find a single clue to the answer.

Dr Hsu's response was typical—he would never touch on anything outside the scope of his profession or specialization. I could only get from him the date my aunt entered the hospital, the symptoms she had during her early days there, and the treatment. As for circumstances before her entrance, Dr Hsu would only politely smile and say with much regret, 'This . . . we are not too clear about. As you know, Comrade Leng Feng, reportedly, was single all her life. All these years, I'm afraid you are the first relative to visit her.'

I asked Mr Ho, manager of the travel agency, the same question. I knew the travel agency was not simply a business organization, so it was very unlikely that its leadership was ignorant of my aunt who had been with the old Provincial Party Committee and had been one-time secretary for the Luchou City Party Committee. None the less, he breezed over the matter lightly: 'Oh my! She suffered at the hands of the Red Guards. Who didn't during that awful disaster? It was a kill-or-be-killed struggle!' Then he politely switched the topic to new policies of the Third Plenary Session of the Central Committee and assurances from the leadership that there would be no more mass political campaigns.

My last dinner at Luchou was hosted by the highest level of local leadership. For more than ten minutes before taking our seats, Comrade Mayor kindly spoke with me about my aunt's condition. The parlour where we sat was decorated with Tientsin rugs, bamboo carvings and jade vases, and the walls were covered with Soochow embroidery and character scrolls. The mayor was short and plump, but his movements were extraordinarily agile. He enjoyed laughing and it was contagious. He gave the immediate impression of being a pragmatic man who was not only straightforward but shrewd, capable and experienced.

'I heard there's been considerable improvement. Is that so? Wonderful! Wonderful! Our material condition is poor. Please be understanding. How could we not fall behind after more than a decade of disorder! In so many places we have to start all over again. Comrade Teng Hsiao-p'ing says we must do everything that has been neglected. How true it is! Professor Hu, you have come from abroad. You must not be polite. Please give us as much advice as you can! Please, please don't be polite. . . .'

I then tactfully made a suggestion. No, I should say a demand. I asked him for the details of my aunt's public trial by the Luchou Revolutionary Party in May or June of 1968.

My tactful wording must have failed to entirely conceal the directness of the question. Comrade Mayor suddenly stopped laughing, and lowered his head, appearing to be lost in thought. He took a fierce drag on his Panda-brand cigarette and slowly raised his moon-shaped head, the hair of which was white at the roots.

Earnestly looking directly at me, his relentless interrogator, he said, 'Comrade Leng Feng did indeed make a great sacrifice for us, for the people, and for the Party. I completely understand your agitation, Professor Hu. Believe me, our feelings are exactly the same as yours. We definitely will make the greatest effort to bring about Comrade Leng Feng's complete recovery.'

In a roundabout way I further explained: I must know exactly what actual circumstances contrived to bring on my aunt's illness. Without this information, I had no way of determining whether the treatment she was now receiving was the only effective one. Similarly, lacking this information, I had no way of fulfilling my obligations as her nephew. I even ventured to suggest that I could unofficially seek help in America by finding specialists for this kind of illness and soliciting professional opinion to furnish the sanatorium or any other responsible unit for consideration. I don't know if this last idea was the straw that broke the camel's back. It caused his hearty laughter. He quickly tossed his cigarette into the white porcelain spittoon by the tea table. The butt sizzled for a second when it hit the contents of the spittoon.

He said, 'Good! Very good! Your suggestion is excellent, Professor Hu! In so many ways America is ahead of us. We must be open to learning from America. Please come back often in the future and give us more suggestions, many more suggestions. . . .'

He then stood up and said to the young man standing by his side, 'Li, is everything ready? Can we sit down to supper now?' Next, he shook hands with me and said, 'Let us go, Professor Hu. After you!'

Walking through the hallway to the dining room, Comrade Mayor said to me in all seriousness, '. . . Comrade Leng Feng, in effect, offered her life by marrying the Chinese revolution. She sacrificed everything for the Chinese Communist Party. If the Party won't take care of her, who will? Isn't that so, Professor Hu?'

During the next hour or more of toasting, it was hard to find an opportunity to pursue my request. Comrade Mayor's hearty laughter often produced an unexpected buffering effect. Often when his laughter subsided, I could not remember clearly what had just been said. Besides, the other high-ranking cadres at the table were all experienced at urging a guest to eat and drink more. Half the time I was fending off offerings from their chopsticks, and the other half I was trying to deal with their repeated toasts. The result was that by the end of the banquet, I was warmly joining their conversation about the latest hit song of Teng Li-chun, a Taiwan songstress who had just become popular on the Mainland.

During the seven days I was in Luchou, I went up the mountain five times. Each time, I stayed for at least an hour or two, and sometimes for half a day. My intention was simple. Besides observing for myself the daily life of my aunt and her treatment, I tried to establish some kind of communication with her. In this regard, however, I had little hope after my first encounter. Still, I thought I should try. The reason I gave myself was, that even if I couldn't get to her on a level of consciousness, I might influence her subconsciously.

Lacking any professional training in psychological illness, I had to depend on common sense. Dr Hsu probably could have helped a little, but he was a man of extreme caution. Whenever I took the initiative in anything, he would not offer an opinion. If I asked for his guidance point-blank, most of the time his response was noncommittal. In sum, whenever any decision was called for, he was able to steer clear of assuming any responsibility, without going against my opinion. The second time I went up the mountain, I showed him a picture of my aunt and her three sisters, and asked if I could show it to her. His response was: 'There should be no problem I suppose. But . . . I am a little concerned that she might over-react . . . but if you think it might help. . . .'

I carefully considered the matter as he had suggested, and in the end decided to show it to her. Whether it would help or not, I thought, I should at least give it a try and see if there could be any shred of contact. If there was a reaction, wouldn't that mean the stronger the reaction, the more the hope? I even thought that if there was even the faintest indication of memory, I should perhaps get in touch with overseas relatives and take her abroad for treatment, even though the implications of such a decision were numerous, and I had no confidence that it was the right thing to do. After all, my aunt was almost 70 and the flame of life was burning low.

Afterwards, I did not have to reconsider this option. For though I tried quite a few times to establish contact, her reaction could be described in two words: total indifference. Feigning distraction and taking advantage of a time when she wasn't paying attention, I placed the photograph on the wooden stand by her metal bed. All the way up to the last time I went to see her, the picture remained just where I had placed it. It hadn't been moved in the least and had collected a light film of dust.

My aunt's daily schedule certainly didn't seem to have been carefully arranged by any professional psychologist. It was no different from any other group life. Apart from the lack of purposeful and systematic exercise, it was much the same as life in the military. Basically, it was passive, protective and nurturing; its only purpose was to lengthen life. However, since I was fortunate enough to have two lunches there, it seemed that at least the nutritional value of the food was above average. True, the portions of meat were a little small, but considering the preponderance of elderly patients, there was probably no need for a higher meat content. There was even fruit after one meal.

With regard to treatment, I had to confess total ignorance. Even so, I could see the crudity of a treatment that completely discarded Freudian theory in the crucial matter of analyzing psychosis. To be sure, the general management, equipment, and medicine, though sub-standard, was adequate. Furthermore, they rather boldly resorted to traditional Chinese medicine—not without some beneficial effect. Once I happened upon a patient who had fainted from internal bleeding. They used a combination of Western and Chinese medicine to save her: giving her blood transfusions and having her ingest Yunnan white powder concentrate. Afterward I heard that the procedure did stop the haemorrhage.

Dr Hsu said, 'The methods proved effective in large-scale clinical experiments, with a high rate of success. During the war the Vietnamese fought to save their country from the Americans, I heard that American soldiers actually went to Hong Kong to buy massive quantities of Yunnan white powder.'

Even though the sanatorium was not for mass treatment, it somewhat resembled a field hospital. When Dr Hsu, the chief physician, called a staff meeting for consultation, they had to use little wooden stools and sit in a circle on the bare floor. Apart from the worn-out sofas in the meeting and guest rooms, the rest of the sanatorium was furnished with wooden chairs and tables. Since the supply of electricity was inadequate, the lights were dim. I discovered that on a cloudy day the microscopes in the laboratory were moved to a window sill, so that work could be done by outside light.

On the whole, my aunt's life was just a step or two above someone who had become a vegetable and lost all power of movement. Her heart was fairly weak and she had seriously swollen lungs. She could only do simple things by herself—stand, sit or lie down. She needed help to go to the bathroom. But what struck me as being beyond all explanation was that, at all times, whether she was lying down, sitting, or even walking in the restricted courtyard, she seemed completely passive, just floating along struggling for breath. But in the morning and evening when she watered the azaleas she came out of her deep depression and suddenly collected herself to become what could be called a complete human being, showing signs of the ability to concentrate. Dr Hsu also noticed this unusual phenomenon. He, of course, did not look at it from the perspective of psychopathology. He said merely: 'It seems unusual! Each day at this time Comrade Leng Feng clearly manifests consciousness of an "I". This flower pot is "hers", that sprinkler is "hers", she allows no one else to touch it. No one can make any sense out of it. Theoretically, an old Communist. . .'

Getting this far, he suddenly became as if aware of the contradictions, for he hesitated, never finishing what he wanted to say. I never drew his attention to this. Yes, one could certainly imagine Dr Hsu's puzzlement. As a Communist she should have no notion of a self. Now the only bit left in her consciousness that was above materiality was precisely that she tightly held onto an 'I'. For Dr Hsu to bring this up before the outsider he was facing would, of course, have been hard.

The day I saw my aunt for the last time—it was toward evening—impulsively I disregarded Dr Hsu's warning and tightly held her little, withered hand. She reacted so suddenly I couldn't tell if it was intentional or not. By Dr Hsu's yardstick, the reaction was a fairly strong one. My aunt forcefully withdrew her hand. I don't think it was motivated by fear, because she quickly turned around and in her odd deaf intonation shouted, 'Eat, eat, eat while it's hot, eat it up, eat it up!' I don't remember how I reacted then, but I do remember clearly that Dr Hsu uncharacteristically took decisive action, instructing a male nurse to escort my aunt immediately back to her ward. I protested strongly, but Dr Hsu said, 'When Comrade Leng Feng first arrived, she spoke this nonsense all day long. Only with much difficulty did she make some progress. I trust you are unwilling to see her regress to that stage?'

Leaving the customs at Lo Wu, my mood lightened, but I also felt unsettled. Before, during and after my return to the family home and visits with relatives, I had, for a month or so, unwittingly become accustomed to having others manage everything for me. A month is not a long time, but for an entire month, even something like going to the bathroom occasionally required someone to make arrangements ahead of time. It was only too easy for inertia to settle in. I boarded the train from Lo Wu to Kowloon; there were no assigned seats, so the urge to rush for one raised its ugly head. Next, there were no public announcements. I thought my ears would have peace and quiet for a spell, but then there was the terrible noise of peddlers going up and down the train hawking cigarettes, candy, cola, and ice cream. Suddenly all the cells of my body tensed to face struggle for survival. Yes indeed, never had I realized so clearly that I must once again stand on my own two feet and manage for myself life's big or little events which I may or may not encounter. I had immediately to reinstate the habit of making all necessary decisions. As the density of signs, advertisements, and neon lights increased, my mixed emotions intensified. They came from the paradox of a relaxed resumption of independence, and restlessness—as if I had lost something. The result was a baffling melancholy drowned in the clanging of iron utensils which, since it could not escape the dense impossivity of one steel and concrete jungle after another, reverberated twice as loud. At Hung Hom Station I held the still plump hands of my third aunt who was over 70, and my eyes filled with a prickling warmth.

I passed two very quiet days at my aunt's shut-in apartment. We ate very simply and I refused all banquets and other invitations. I turned off the television and the radio, and was even too lazy to look at the newspapers. All I did was drink tea with my aunt and her family and talk about our family. I exercised extreme caution selecting what to say about my fourth aunt's condition. On the principle of reporting only the good and not the bad, I talked at length with third aunt about her sister. Obviously the 'good' was not talked about in its fullest sense. I said her sister had not disappeared, and was receiving a certain degree of care. For my aunt's generation, it was a great joy to hear such things after all those years of no hope for her sister. All the ins and outs, however, of my continuous investigation—from the accidental discovery of the *Luchou Battle Report*, to the events leading up to my present inability to explain the origin of my aunt's illness and her current vegetative existence—were left unsaid, of course. I imagined that in her heart, third aunt knew life on the Mainland was necessarily poor and strained. From her own experience, however, she must also have assumed that a person who had been dedicated to her country's revolution and who had held a high position as a ranking cadre, even if she could not escape life's cycle of birth, age, illness, and death, should, with the concern of an all-powerful Party and under the care of professional physicians, live in quite satisfactory conditions, both spiritually and physically. On the other hand, when she heard that her sister had never married or had a family, my aunt became silent for a long while. Then with a certain amount of sadness I explained that great men and women probably learned very early to put family matters out of their minds. Didn't Premier Chou En-lai consider the country's orphans his own children? My aunt then immediately laughed at her own narrow view, and with a sigh went back to remembering her sister's special personality in the early days.

'Yes indeed, yes indeed!' my aunt said. 'What a character. She always took her family very lightly. That was her temperament. She could certainly put things behind her.'

Leaving my aunt's, I took a 'teksi' to the airport. She and her family insisted on seeing me off. I resolutely declined their offer saying I still had to go to Kowloon to take care of personal matters, and if anyone accompanied me, it would cause me inconvenience. They didn't insist. We waved good-bye on the steps of their Sha Tin apartment overlooking the bay. My aunt asked her eldest grandson to carry my luggage and put it in the taxi waiting on the road. Waving good-bye she repeatedly urged, 'Write to her often! I'll write tonight. You do, too!'

I told the 'teksi' driver to take me across the harbour, where I took a room in Wanchai at a second-class hotel. I immediately phoned a friend I had contacted before leaving America. He lived in a large apartment building in the Wanchai section.

We met at a little restaurant near O'Brien Street. As soon as we got together, he started complaining, 'Why don't you trust your friends! I phoned you any number of times, and looked everywhere—libraries specializing in this kind of material, archives, and research institutes. I went to them all. If it's not to be found, it's not to be found. Why would I deceive you? You didn't believe me so you came in person. I'll take you around myself and let you die happy!'

We spent three days running around university libraries on Hong Kong island and in Kowloon. We even used our connections at the American consulate and news agencies to check. My friend had not deceived me. If there was nothing, there was nothing. But, there is an element of coincidence to life. Just when I had given up all hope, the only extant copy of the spring issue of *Luchou Battle Report* for 1968 suddenly appeared.

That day we had returned to the United Research Institute on College Road in Kowloon. Our original purpose was just to say thanks and apologize for the many times we had bothered them, and also to say good-bye. Unexpectedly, an elderly man sitting with us researching the history of the Cultural Revolution brought up the matter.

'I hear you are collecting material on the Cultural Revolution in south-eastern China. Is that so?'

I didn't think much would come from this, so I only politely groaned in agreement.

'For some years now I have been working on notes for a collection of material related to the Great Cultural Revolution. I have at hand some things that are not easily available outside.'

And this was how unexpectedly and without the least cost I got a photocopy of the precious document which held the answer to the riddle of my aunt's life. Furthermore, though a few pages were out of sequence, it was a complete copy.

What follows is the entire text of 'Cut Off the Dirty Hands of That Counter-revolutionary, Revisionist, Two-faced Leng Feng' beginning on page 39:

(Cont'd from p. 27) . . . Sacrifice. Up to now there has been no knowledge of any of this! I now am determined to stand up and have the verdict reversed, to expose completely the crimes of that two-faced counter-revolutionary Leng Feng who wormed her way into the Party. For over 30 years she concealed her crimes from the people!

{Many, many currents of Marxist doctrine, in the final analysis, can be summed up in a single phrase: revolution is the right thing to do!}

At the end of 1934, the revolution in our province reached its low point. Comrade Lo Ch'eng unfortunately had been captured. Because the underground organization of the Party was almost destroyed by the enemy, the Central Committee of the Party, in the spring of 1935, assigned Comrade Chang Tse-sheng to continue the work of Comrade Lo ch'eng. He was to reorganize the remnants of the revolutionary forces in the mountains, to continue guerrilla activity and rebuild a working base!

Who'd have suspected that impassioned capitalist politician Leng Feng thought Comrade Chang Tse-sheng had stolen her leadership role. Deep down there was hatred in her heart!

{Top-level directive: Be especially on your guard against personal careerists and schemers like Khrushchev. Prevent this kind of evil person from usurping any level of Party and national leadership!}

After the unmasking of Hu Feng's counter-revolutionary incident in 1955, Leng Feng seized the opportunity to do her wicked deeds everywhere. From a few articles Chang Tse-sheng had written before Liberation, she put together a list of his crimes and strained to frame him as a remnant of the Hu Feng faction. Chang confessed under torture and was convicted of counter-revolutionary activity! He endured great physical suffering in jail, his old illness recurred, and he died without vindication!

{Get rid of the vermin, then we will be without enemies!}

What will make your hair stand on end is that Leng Feng laid complete responsibility for the sacrifice of Comrade Lo Ch'eng on the shoulders of Comrade Chang Tse-sheng! She said, ". . . after the success of the prison rescue, Chang Tse-sheng disregarded my strong opposition and began a ruthless effort to find enemies within. Blood flowed under his suppression and he repeatedly condemned Lo Ch'eng as a traitor. Not only did he execute Lo without a second thought, he also forced me to take a public stand on the matter and to make a clean break with Lo Ch'eng. Even more diabolically, he compelled me before the crowd to take a bite out of the warm, bloody heart of Lo Ch'eng that had been ripped—still beating—from his chest!"

{These passages are from secret material taken from the classified files of the old Provincial Party Committee by the revolutionary masses. This is ironclad evidence unintentionally revealing that Leng Feng framed Chang Tse-sheng! Further, through the exposures of Lin T'ien-fu, let us be clear that this miserable little, wet dog wagging its tail, is in fact utterly vicious and deceitful! She not only neatly got away with putting her murderous crime on another, but also managed to put the deadly weapon in his hand. She thought this way she would be beyond the law. Lu Hsun said the only way to treat a wet dog is to hit it! Teach it not to bite again!}

What stupid nonsense! Leng Feng thought that if she could silence Chang Tse-sheng she could change black into white according to her fancy. She didn't realize that still there was me, the surviving, tough old nut. I was an insignificant soldier then, and for many years now I have been oppressed by the power struggle. I had to play deaf and dumb, always saying yes to what I was told; still, my conscience has not been destroyed. Today, under the wonderful situation brought on by Mao Tse-tung personally launching and leading the classless Great Cultural Revolution that touches the very soul of men, with the support of the revolutionary masses, I must come forward and speak openly and honestly!

{We oppose whoever our enemies support. We support whoever our enemies oppose. This is the truth of the class struggle.}

Who framed Chang Tse-sheng then? Who was determined to murder Lo Ch'eng? It was none other than Leng Feng!

Around April or May of 1934, Comrade Lo Ch'eng was ordered to go to my old village. To protect his identity, the Party decided to let him marry Hsiao-p'ing, the daughter of an old friend of mine. For the occasion the village organized three days of celebration! But, three months later Leng Feng arrived with Comrade Fang Chih-min's Advance Party of the Worker-Peasant Red Army to Fight the Japanese in the North. As soon as she got there she raised a ruckus about the wedding. If the Party had not arranged this, and if the people hadn't been involved, she would have turned the heavens upside down! In December of 1934, Comrade Lo Ch'eng was captured at a safe house in Luchou. So was Hsiao-p'ing. It is detestable that Hsiao-p'ing, a young girl, defected to the enemy, unable to resist their threats and temptations. She caused serious destruction in the underground organization. At that time the general situation was fairly chaotic. The enemy bore down with much force and rounded up everyone. Comrade Chang Tse-sheng was not all that familiar with the actual situation. The comrades themselves were overcome with grief and depression. Under these circumstances, when Leng Feng repeatedly condemned Comrade Lo Ch'eng as a traitor, I too half believed and did not dare question it.

I recall that scene as clearly as yesterday, it is right before my eyes! The place of execution that day was the ancestral hall of the village. The guns of the attacking reactionary party could still be faintly heard! Leng Feng looked crazy, a poisonous glare coming from her eyes. After Comrade Lo Ch'eng had fallen to the ground, she jumped to the front, ripped out his heart with a knife, and stuck it in her own mouth, biting it furiously. Rushing into the crowd, she forced everyone to take a bite. To this day I cannot forget her savage expression *or her mouth dripping blood! How clearly I remember her noisily chewing, yelling at the same time, "Eat, eat, eat while it's hot, eat it up, eat it up!"*

{This is how the enemy bullies us. We must treat it seriously!}

We cannot resist the historical current of the Cultural Revolution as it flows forward. Let the one billion-strong revolutionary masses lift up their spirits, and vigorously strengthen their determination to fight! Let us carefully remember the instructions of our great leader Mao Tse-tung: "We must use our unspent courage to pursue other enemies, rather than lord it over those already conquered!" We must again turn upside down the upside-down history of capitalist revisionists! We must strike down the crafty comeback of the new counter-revolutionism of the old Provincial Party committee! Let us resolutely, thoroughly, absolutely, and entirely sweep into the dustbin of history people like Leng Feng, beastly restorationists, deceivers, and executioners!

Oral testimony of Lin T'ien-fu, member of the old Provincial Party Committee's Revolutionary Cadre.

Transcribed by the editorial staff of the Luchou Battle Report *of the united headquarters for the Red Revolutionary Party of Luchou.*

I had two glasses of brandy with my friend at a little bar in Tsim Sha Tsui. Since he had things to do in Kowloon, we parted company at the wharf. I boarded the ferry with throngs of people on their way home from work. I managed to find a seat in the front of the cabin by a window. Dusk was turning into evening and the waterfront gradually filled with lights that became brighter as night began to fall. Listening to the rhythmic beat of the ferry's motor churning the water, I gradually felt the effects of the brandy as it rose to my head. How lovely the sea wind that gently massaged my face, which was becoming somewhat numb. I told myself not to believe all that nonsense of the Red Guards. Lin T'ien-fu was some idiot whose brains had been messed up by the Red Guards. But, looking at the mass of constantly flickering lights halfway up the mountains behind the waterfront, and seeing behind that gorgeous brilliance the distant darkness of the mountain shadows, I was deeply disturbed pondering these questions. If that exposure by Lin T'ien-fu was all wild exaggeration, why, when he testified both for and against her, did he mention eating Lo's bleeding heart, a detail very hard to fabricate? How can I explain why my aunt, with over 20 years of experience in tough infighting, would suddenly be unable to stand up to the physical torment of the Red Guards and break down completely?

Finally the brandy disarmed me for a time. In a daze, I seemed to see the shadow of the gradually approaching mountain extend two huge arms and slowly close them, consuming in its gigantic, lumbering embrace the glittering, sparkling dreamland, awash in fancy, broken diamonds.

Between Two Generations

Pao-chen

translated by Chu-yun Chen

> *I've often said, your father and I are both simple men. Even so, living in those chaotic times, we never once shirked our duty in battle, nor did we pocket a single penny other than our pay. We did our best to serve China faithfully.*
>
> *Uncle Lai*

THE OTHER day I returned home to find two letters on my desk: one was a pale blue air-mail letter, already opened; the other was a sealed white envelope.

I picked up the envelope and opened it. Inside was a xeroxed letter from the Chinese Student Association at the State University of Oregon. The content included a general description of living conditions in the area, of the life of foreign students on campus, and provided the name and address of the student in charge of the Association. The postscript noted that a member of the Association would be returning home to Taiwan for the summer and would be happy to answer any further questions.

I then picked up the air-mail letter and saw that it was addressed to my mother from a family friend living in the United States. What was it doing on my desk? Curious, I unfolded the air-mail letter and glanced rapidly over the first few lines. In shock I learned that my Uncle Lai had passed away.

Even as I refolded the letter after reading it, I still found it hard to believe what I had read. I sat immobile for a while, then pulled out a drawer and took from it a half-completed list of names and addresses. My eyes fell on the entry I had typed just the night before:

Mr T C Lai
43579 NW 9th St.
Corvallis, OR 97330

I was preparing to go to the States for graduate study, and had been making a list of friends and relatives living in that country. Some were school friends of mine, others were friends of my parents. I knew that Uncle Lai had gone to the States a year ago to visit his son, but had never noticed to what city or state. It was not until last night, when mother gave me her little green address book to copy from, that I found Uncle Lai was actually living in Corvallis—the location of the University of Oregon and my own destination. The discovery made me jump up and hurry, address book in hand, into the living room for confirmation.

'That's right. Old Lai is in Oregon.' Father had answered, and then turned to Mother to ask whether he should write Uncle Lai to meet me at the airport. Mother answered quickly: 'No need for that. His host family will be meeting him, so there's no need to bother your old classmate. . . . On second thoughts, why not write old Lai just the same, in case he could do something later. . . . I wonder how his health is.'

This happened the night before. Now I stood staring at the cold, typewritten address in my hands, still unable to accept the fact of Uncle Lai's death. I opened the air-mail letter from Mother's friend again, and the following lines of writing leaped up at me:

> Hsueh-chih called me long distance tonight to tell me that Uncle Lai died yesterday morning (the 24th) of a heart attack. He experienced no pain. His heart had stopped beating for ten minutes before he died, revived for a short time after emergency treatment, and finally stopped altogether yesterday. I had talked to Uncle Lai only last week on the phone, and I can't believe he is no longer with us. The remains will be cremated and sent back to Taiwan as soon as possible. Hsueh-chih said it will be a very simple ceremony. He hasn't notified any of Uncle Lai's friends or old schoolmates in Taiwan, so would you please inform Uncle Yin and Uncle Chung of the sad news? Please don't grieve too much over the loss of a dear old friend. What is life but birth, old age, sickness and death? Birth and death, reunion and separation have always brought us extremes of joy and sorrow.

The next day I went to the American Institute in Taiwan for my visa. I had started out early and arrived when it was still dark. There were others even earlier than I, judging by the long line already packed in front of the building.

Finally I was issued a numbered slip to begin waiting my turn for an interview. I sat in the corner by a turn in the stairway, near the end of the line. Holding an envelope stuffed with documents relating to my application, I thought of the time five years ago when Uncle Yin's eldest daughter was preparing to leave for the United States. Uncle Yin's business suffered a setback at the time; he had a run of bad luck and things were not going well for him. Uncle Lai and his wife were in Taiwan then, and one day Aunt Lai came over to our house to visit. Before long the conversation turned to Uncle Yin's daughter. Aunt Lai remarked that Aunt Yin was proudly telling all her friends of her daughter's good luck in getting a visa: of how many of Huei-hsin's friends had been rejected by the American Consulate, but that Huei-hsin had obtained her visa without so much as a single question being asked.

I shifted my position on the stairway and reflected on Aunt Yin's exaggeration of the situation. 'So many were rejected by the Consulate,' she had said. It couldn't have been that serious. Wasn't it true that we follow our preconceptions when judging people and events?

As I sat on the floor with such random thoughts running through my mind, I began to notice something peculiar. Now and then people would come around from the front of the building, step over those of us sitting or sprawling in line, and walk up the stairs. Disregarding the blond, blue-eyed Caucasians, quite a number were unmistakably Chinese. Most were couples holding giant manila envelopes, with children in tow.

My curiosity grew. I wondered who these people were. Finally when I could stand it no longer I stood up and walked over to the foot of the stairs. There a sign on the wall, in both Chinese and English, stated clearly: American Citizen Services. This reminded me once again of Aunt Lai, and of the time my younger brother almost created an embarrassing scene. The picture rose vividly in my mind . . . .

'Citizen, this citizenship thing is critical. If you don't have it you simply can't survive in America. Look at me. Old bag of bones that I am, I've still got to fly to America once every year or so; or they'll revoke my permanent residency. I keep telling him we shouldn't have to be doing this, we're getting too old. Look at him, looking smug while I natter!'

Uncle Lai was half reclining in the sofa, with the buttons on his flowery shirt undone, showing a floppy undershirt. One leg hung over the armrest, the toes flexing in dark brown socks. He was almost completely bald, but a few hairs were plastered against his skull, and his temples showed white. His face was fleshy and lined but the half-closed eyes were alert. His hands lay folded on his protruding stomach, and he was smiling but silent.

Aunt Lai herself must have been well past 50. Her hair was cut short and straight like somebody's little sister. She was always complaining about the heat and humidity of Taiwan summers. Beads of sweat ran down her neck.

'It's much more comfortable in California. The winters aren't so chilly, the summers not so hot. D. C. is bad, almost the same as Taiwan. The last time I was in Washington I was sweating the whole time. The two of us almost died from the heat.'

Aunt Lai sighed and went on: 'It's all his fault. He should've renewed PR earlier. When we get our citizenship in a couple of years everything will be OK. We'll come back to Taiwan to live for a while. Second sister and I can have some fun together while you two old boys stay at home and fend for yourselves.'

Aunt Lai's face expressed a variety of emotions; she closed her eyes and rocked her plump body back and forth. Uncle Lai's booming laugh rang out. Then he remarked in his north China country dialect: 'What's new about that? We won't starve. Before we got married, Chien-teng and I batched it together and we got along fine.'

'You think I don't know what that was like? A pile of ragged quilts on top of the bed, a pile of smelly socks underneath,' Aunt Lai retorted.

My father's face flushed red. Uncle Lai laughed until he was hoarse. His mouth was wide open, and he shook all over. Aunt Lai stared at him and shook her head.

'Second sister, he's really hopeless . . . . Oh, by the way, I almost forgot because of the interruption, I saw Lao Yin's daughter, Huei-hsin, in New York this time. We were just coming out of Macy's. She called out to me first, "Isn't it Aunt Lai?" I was startled. This daughter of Lao Yin's, God help her, she hasn't even gotten her PR yet. I asked her why she hadn't applied, she said her husband was still working on his Ph.D. at Stony Brook, and they wanted to wait until he got his degree. Well, the truth is, it is not so easy nowadays to get a PR, and lawyers cost a fortune. You know him—if it weren't for my nagging every day we wouldn't have our PR now. Everyone in America wants the three P's, especially Chinese students—you know the three P's: the first is a Ph.D.; the second is PR, the permanent residence permit; and the third is property, real estate. On this last trip we stopped over in San Francisco to visit an old friend. They had just bought a house in the Bay Area. Cost them 230,000 US dollars, with a bay view. It's a lovely view . . . .'

Just then I heard from the room which my two younger brothers shared the sound of furniture being knocked over. I got up quietly and pushed open the door. It was just as I thought. The older brother was red in the face, while the younger one was hanging on to him for dear life. The two were wrestling fiercely.

I shut the door at once and pulled them apart. All of a sudden the older one lost his taste for the fight. He righted an overturned chair and went back to his books without saying a single word.

'What happened?' I asked my youngest brother. I was experienced enough to know you always ask the younger one in this kind of situation.

'He wanted to go out and tick off Aunt Lai. I told him not to.'

'Hush, quiet,' I stopped him anxiously. Voices and laughter could be heard clearly from the other side of the door. Such talk would cause considerable embarrassment, to say the least.

'What's eating you, kid?' I patted him on the shoulder as I sat down on the bed.

'I hate it when they talk about that PR business. What's important now is not whether we can get permanent residence in the United States; it's whether a Chinese can get decent permanent residence rights on this planet.' My brother's voice shook with emotion.

Taken aback, I remained speechless for quite a while. I looked at the pimples and acne scars on my brother's face, told him to concentrate on his studies and not bother about such problems. When I returned to the living room Aunt Lai was still holding forth.

'On the plane from LA to Tokyo we met several Chinese couples. Everyone soon got to talking and we found that all of them had gone to the States to update their PRs. The husbands were all in the airline business, you see, and they could fly free, so they thought they might as well seize the opportunity. The woman sitting beside me was fun. She told me her husband's office had nicknamed their trips the "Back-to-the-Fatherland Movement".'

After getting my visa I made a trip to my Alma Mater. Having just spent ten months in military service, I felt a little disoriented as I walked the campus. It then came to me that this was summer vacation. No wonder it looked so empty. But I bet myself that good old Tuo-tze would be in the lab.

I walked the familiar path, turned and saw the gray walls of the department building. At the start of my senior year, Tuo-tze had just left for his military service. I wrote to him, describing how I felt entering and leaving the building every day. After spending three or four years in the same place, it's difficult not to feel some affection for it. Tuo-tze had answered from training camp, and told me that my letter made him feel homesick. Now that he was ensconced on the second floor of this building as a graduate student himself, I wanted to know how he looked.

I looked in on the department chairman first. He was happy to see me, asked whether I had received a scholarship, and how my plans for departure were going. Then he remarked that Li Hung-yao had been admitted to Cal Tech, the top honour for this year's graduate class in our department.

The chairman warmed to the topic and talked about several others who had completed military service and dropped by the department hoping for help finding jobs. Of course he would do all he could, but not everyone would get what he wanted. One graduate wanted to return here to work as an assistant, but there were no openings. Furthermore, even research assistants nowadays had to have a Master's degree. The graduate had left in disappointment, the chairman told me regretfully.

Upstairs I found my friend Tuo-tze. He had his feet up on the desk, reading.

'Hi, old man,' I knocked on the open door.

He looked up at me and jumped from his chair.

'Hey, I heard you're leaving? Which school? Any financial aid? You've gained weight, man.'

Tuo-tze seemed happy to see me, as though he had met 'a friend from home abroad'. I know this isn't the most appropriate way to describe it, but the feeling was much the same. He closed the book he was reading and began to talk. He told me repeatedly how different graduate school was from college. He even had to stay in the lab and sweat over his experiments during the summer vacation. I knew that he and his girlfriend had broken up while he was in the army, so I asked him whether there were any 'new ripples on the old pond' this past year. He shook his head and looked crestfallen for a moment. Then he perked up again.

'Hey, there were quite a few good looking ones among the freshmen last year,' he said.

'Oh? Then why aren't you in hot pursuit?' I joked.

'Forget it!' he made a face. 'They're at least five or six years younger, maybe even seven or eight years. As a younger sister, maybe; but if you're really looking for a wife, no way. There's too much difference in our thinking. The generation gap is wide, you know. I couldn't, shouldn't, wouldn't.'

I laughed, momentarily transported back to our undergraduate days. Time and the river never flow backwards but even the briefest of memories offers some comfort.

After the laughter there was a short period of silence. I walked over to the window. Only two or three students passed on the walk below, increasing the air of desolation. Didn't I use to do that on the same path? Tuo-tze's voice came from behind me.

'When I had just gotten back I used to mess around looking out of the window, but it got too depressing. Now I don't have the courage. Well, no, it's not that I don't have the courage. Anyway, I just avoid looking down.'

'Why depressing?' I turned to look at him.

'You know what the poet says, very simple. Each generation giving way to the next, like waves!' He raised his eyebrows.

It was lunch time. We walked over to the 'student-class restaurant' by the campus gate. We talked endlessly as we ate, as if we had an endless treasure of memories. We were a pair of white-haired palace maids reminiscing over old court glories.

On the way home I mused on Tuo-tze's behaviour—surprised somewhat at the change in him. I remembered when we were undergraduates we had been good friends, but since he was a class higher, there had still been a certain reserve in our friendship. Today, he not only spent the entire day dragging out both clean and dirty linen with me, but wouldn't even let me pay for lunch. Why the sudden closeness? Watching the scenery slip by outside the bus window, I thought it must be because he had spent too much time looking down from the study window.

That night Uncle Lai sang so beautifully. It has been three years, but the scene remains fresh in my mind. The way he looked with his hands crossed in front of his chest, his eyes staring into the distance, relaxed and confident.

The Yins and the Chungs arrived at our house in the evening. Uncle and Aunt Lai had come at about three o'clock in the afternoon.

My father's college friends usually held a reunion once a year, my parents didn't always attend. This time the Lais had travelled from their home in the Philippines to Hong Kong, where they spent a month on business. Then they came over to Taipei, according to Aunt Lai, 'to see old friends'. My mother invited a few intimate school alumni to our house for 'pot luck' in honour of the Lais.

Frankly, my mother's cooking is not all that special, so we seldom had guests to the house for dinner, only occasionally for an informal gathering, with everyone pitching in to wrap *chiao-tzu* and pot-stickers. Both my parents are from northern China and *chiao-tzu* are their speciality. Our home-made dumpling wrappings come out thicker in the middle and thinner at the edges, and the dumplings themselves are mouth-wateringly plump and attractive.

That day my mother took special care over the meal. She prepared three different fillings: minced pork and cabbage, minced beef and celery, and the fancy mixed specials. It took my father the entire afternoon to chop the meat by hand. Uncle Lai took one look at the bowl of minced beef and happily remarked he knew my mother would serve his favourite. My mother, her face aglow with heat and exertion, laughingly replied that the most tasty filling would be the fancy special.

'There's dried shrimp, egg yolk, mushrooms, glass noodles, dried tiger lily, black fungus, carrots, bean sprouts. The fragrance alone will bowl you over.'

While my parents were busy in the kitchen, the guests sat watching TV in the living room, cracking watermelon seeds. Uncle Chung kept popping fruit drops into his mouth. His wife nagged at him to stop, saying he'd spoil his appetite and wouldn't be able to eat the delicious dumplings.

In the early evening the TV station showed a variety programme with dancing and singing. I remember there was a trio of singers newly arrived from Hong Kong, each holding a guitar, writhing as they belted out their song. The host described them as 'the teen idols of South-east Asia', who had 'returned to the motherland to entertain their young compatriots'.

As the group finished one song, the camera suddenly caught a close-up of the lead singer. One eye was half shut, the other wide open. He slouched dejectedly, his mouth hanging open. His hair was plastered on his forehead, his face looked tired, bewildered and dazed. The shot lasted for a few seconds, then disappeared as a commercial came on.

Aunt Yin remarked that the group was very popular. She had seen crowds lining up to buy tickets for their concert a few days ago when she passed by the China Sports and Cultural Stadium. Uncle Lai snapped: 'You call that singing? Look at them. They look more like demons than human beings. Can't stand their dead-beat look, and their singing's atrocious. All they do is roar. What's so great about them?'

Aunt Yin said in some embarrassment: 'Aren't they also popular in Hong Kong? They attract the young. Young people don't like the same things we do.'

'Hey, Sister dear, you have no idea. We were in Hong Kong just last week. These singers are hot in Hong Kong precisely because they're typical of the aimless young in that colony. But why in the world should we import such types to Taiwan?'

Uncle Yin cracked a watermelon seed and smiled. His wife, who disliked losing at anything, retorted: 'Lao Lai, you call their singing atrocious. Can you sing?'

Aunt Lai laughed, trying to dispel the threat of a conflict: 'His singing sounds like a cracked gong.'

Uncle Lai stood up suddenly, his manner serious, and said: 'Of course I can sing.'

At this moment my parents appeared with two large platters of steaming boiled dumplings. Father called out to everyone: 'Come on, come on, grab a seat.'

Mother said as she arranged the table: 'Oh, did I hear something about Lao Lai singing? How about after we eat?'

'Now, Sister, haven't you heard the saying? "Puff on a full stomach, sing on an empty one"? You can't sing properly after eating.'

So saying, Uncle Lai walked over to the TV set. I turned it off, and everyone started clapping to encourage him.

It was very quiet in the room. Aunt Lai frowned and whispered to Aunt Chung: 'There he goes showing off again.'

There was an ink-brush painting of the Great Wall hanging above the TV. It showed a grayish structure winding over darker mountains like a huge dragon. Perhaps inspired by the painting, he chose to sing 'The Ballad of the Great Wall.'

Wan li ch'ang-ch'eng, wan li ch'ang, Ch'ang-ch'eng wai mien shih ku-hsiang, Kao-liang fei, ta-tou hsiang, Pien ti huang-chin shao tsai-yang.

Uncle Lai's voice rose loud and clear, evoking vividly the ten-thousand mile wall stretching endlessly over the terrain, the fertile land, golden with millet and soybean, where people lived in abundance and peace. His words summoned up a surge of warmth and nostalgia. I was stunned, never having known he could sing so well.

K'u nan tang, pen t'a-fang, Ku jou liu san fu mu sang.

If the first stanza described a calm and idyllic landscape, the second presented a torrential storm, portraying the wars and calamities which brought widespread suffering, causing the inhabitants to be displaced, families scattered and members to die. I was amazed at Uncle Lai's skill in expressing such a wide range of emotions. The old song was intensely moving.

Sze-wan-wan t'ung-pao hsin yi yang, Hsin te ch'ang-ch'eng wan—li—ch'ang—.

The song ended in a thunderous climax, declaring the one and only wish of the entire population of 400 million—that the new Great Wall stretch on and on to eternity. The enthusiastic applause that greeted the song must have surprised the neighbours.

Uncle Yin yelled, 'Encore, encore!' Aunt Chung begged for another song. My father urged everyone to the dinner table, saying the *chiao-tzu* would get cold and be no good.

Mother's dumplings were a great success that day. Everyone was full of praise. Uncle Lai said he had been all over the world, but never had he tasted such delicious dumplings. Mother thanked everyone happily.

After dinner there was a large platter of sweet and juicy 'bell fruit'—a local product. Uncle Lai remarked that in the back garden of their first home in Taipei on An-tung Street, there had been a 'bell fruit' tree, but since they were new to Taiwan no one recognized it and the fruit was left uneaten. It was not until neighbourhood children knocked on the door asking for some that they realized the fruit was edible. Uncle Lai's reminiscences started everyone off remembering the old days.

The conversation gradually turned to Chungking. Uncle Chung said he remembered people living upstream along the Chialing River cleaning out their chamber pots in the water while those living downstream used the same water to wash vegetables and meat. Before I could stop myself I blurted out: 'How filthy!' Father laughed and said that the younger generation had no idea how the older one lived.

Things were very lively in the living room. I went into the kitchen, where my younger brother was doing the dishes. There was quite a large pile that night, so I set about helping him.

I don't remember when Uncle Lai came in, walked over to the refrigerator and poured himself a glass of ice water. He drank it down and poured a second glass. I noticed the ridges of fat on the back of his neck and the thought came to me that Uncle Lai should probably watch his weight.

My brother put down the bowl he was washing and with his hands dripping stared at Uncle Lai. I said to myself the kid is up to something, and I was right.

'Uncle Lai, you made a mistake in the song,' he said.

'Oh? Where?' Uncle Lai asked as he patted his stomach lightly.

'It should be 800 million people, not four. Even our song book at school's been changed. There were 400 million people, but now it's 800.'

Uncle Lai nodded in agreement. Then he closed his eyes and said slowly: 'Change the song from 400 million to 800 million. One thing's still the same—China is still waiting for us to save her. Too bad your uncle is getting too old.'

He opened his eyes and stared at us, but I had the feeling he wasn't seeing us. 'Coming to Taiwan these last two years I see the place really prospering. When we first came we lived on An-tung Street. Hoping East Road was much narrower then, with fewer cars. But I've often said, the standard of living here in Taiwan is getting beyond needs and verging on waste. Take cooking oil, for example. Whether peanut oil or soybean oil, at least half is dumped into the sewer or thrown into the garbage or blown away through the range-hood. This is sheer waste. Back in the Philippines I'm always telling your Aunt Lai not to use so much oil for cooking. I remember we used to say: a drop of oil equals four ounces of good fortune. You young people know nothing of that. Look at this fat on my stomach. All from social dinners. We eat very simply at home. I was telling your Aunt Lai just the other day, even the *mao-erh-t'ou* the rickshaw drivers ate were quite nourishing.'

'What's *mao-erh-t'ou*?' I asked.

'In some of the smaller eateries in Szechuan, they used to put a large pot of boiling water on the stove and then cover it with a steamer made of bamboo slats. The steam from the boiling water kept the bamboo cover hot and wet. Well, the rice they put in that steamer-cover—that's *mao-erh-t'ou*. The rickshaw drivers would come in, help themselves to a bowl of *mao-erh-t'ou*, order a stir-fried dish, plus a side dish of pickled vegetables and a pot of soup, hot and delicious . . . . That was the life.'

Uncle Lai half closed his eyes and nodded, as if he could actually taste the *mao-erh-t'ou*. I almost shared his memory.

My brother cocked his head and asked, 'Uncle Lai, how come you sing so well?'

Uncle Lai laughed and beamed with pleasure.

'I loved to sing in high school. Now I'm getting old, it's not so good any more.'

Uncle Lai stopped as a wave of laughter came from the living room. We all emerged from the kitchen to see the women smiling, the men red in the face with laughter. Everyone looked like a mischievous little school kid. They must have been talking about the past again.

After my own graduation, whenever I came across old college friends we would laugh together over trifling matters, too. On those occasions I would think of my father and his friends. I realized human beings have the same emotions; our lives are all filled with loves and hates. We can listen to one another, understand our feelings and sympathize with them.

After that night at my house we lost touch with Uncle Lai for a while. The three Lai children were scattered over three continents. Hsueh-yung, the youngest, ran a business in Singapore and often travelled to Taiwan, but I don't remember his ever coming to our house. Actually, we of the second generation hardly knew each other. Sometimes I would receive a wedding announcement and not recognize the name of the bride or groom until I saw the names of the parents. Of course we were on more intimate terms with a few of the children of my father's friends, but in general, it was difficult to hand down the friendships of the older generation to the younger.

Of the three Lai children, Uncle Lai's favourite was the daughter in the middle—Hsueh-jen. Perhaps influenced by her father, Hsueh-jen went to Rome to study voice after graduating from the National Academy of Fine Arts. I don't know if she unconsciously wished to realize her father's unfulfilled dreams of becoming a singer.

After the children had all left home, Aunt Lai came from Taipei to visit us in Tainan, and told my mother she had decided to join Uncle Lai in the Philippines. When Mother asked about the children, she replied light-heartedly: 'They have their own lives.' Mother later told us how much she envied Aunt Lai her freedom.

Aunt Lai may have sounded carefree, but she still worried about the children. She wrote from the Philippines, complaining about the stubborn-ness of her daughter. The Lais had wanted to send her to the United States, where her older brother now lived and could take care of her. But Hsueh-jen insisted that schools in the States offered only training in instruments and that for voice one had to go to Italy. In the end she departed for Rome, leaving her mother frantic over her welfare. Mother said Aunt Lai missed her daughter so much she would often cry her eyes out. After the crying, Uncle Lai ended up taking his wife to Europe. I heard my mother remark wistfully once, 'How I envy your aunt Lai: she's been around the world.' Well, maybe not around the world exactly, but to many places just the same. We have a snapshot of the two of them standing in front of a flower clock in Switzerland. Uncle Lai looks annoyed, but Aunt Lai is smiling. On the back Aunt Lai had written: 'The old man looks tough as iron, the old lady beautiful as a flower.'

Soon after my graduation from college I was drafted for military service. I arrived at Feng-shan in early July to begin three months of basic training.

It was a hectic life. Near the end of our training came the Mid-Autumn Festival and a few days' break. We were all overjoyed. 'Rookies love holidays.' I managed to squeeze onto a crowded night express for Taipei.

My family was glad to see me. Father said I had become stronger; one brother said I had got a tan, the other said I had lost weight. Mother busied herself in the kitchen. Despite my protests, she poured me some milk and started to cook eggs. As I sat down to the dining room table, I saw an obituary notice lying on it. I opened it:

> *We are deeply saddened to announce the death, in the Veterans' General Hospital, of our beloved mother Mrs Shu-huei Lai on September 10, 1977, at 5:20 p.m. due to a heart attack. The funeral will be held on 20 September at 1:30 p.m. at the Taipei Municipal Funeral Parlor on Min-chuan East Road. . . .*

When Mother appeared with a bowl of noodles I expressed my surprise at the fact that Aunt Lai had died in a Taipei hospital. Wasn't she living in the Philippines? Mother put down the bowl and lowered her voice as she usually did when imparting important news.

'Their PR was up for renewal and they were just about to go to the States. Something came up at the last minute in Uncle Lai's company, so he had to take a later flight. Aunt Lai travelled alone, and on the way over here she suffered a heart attack. She was sent to the Veterans' Hospital as soon as the plane landed. It was lucky Hsueh-yung was in Taipei at the time. She regained consciousness for a short time in the hospital and kept saying she wanted to go back home to An-tung Street. What home on An-tung Street? She died in the middle of the night.' Mother blinked back tears.

'Did uncle Lai come?'

'Yes. He lay right there crying night before last.' Mother indicated the living room sofa. 'That afternoon at the funeral parlor he was smiling, saying to your father how happy his wife would have been to see so many people at the funeral. Then in the middle of the night he suddenly showed up here. I gave him pork liver noodles. He lay there and cried and kept saying he had treated his wife well. He had sent her to the best hospitals whenever she was ill.'

Mother spoke in a remarkable likeness of Uncle Lai's tone. I finished the milk and read the rest of the notice: 'She will be buried at North Sea Gardens in Tamsui.' I thought of Aunt Lai's incessant chatter about PR in our house that time, and my brother's reaction. I sighed. Too bad Aunt Lai had never known where her permanent residence was. Why did she say she wanted to return to An-tung Street while at the hospital? Was she confused? Or did she want to return to her roots? Where was Aunt Lai now?

I looked at the characters 'North Sea Gardens' and suddenly realized that with the change of only one character the name became 'North Sea Park'. Wasn't that the place where the Lais had their first date? Aunt Lai had told my mother the story of their romance so many times that even I knew it by heart.

They had met in the old city of Peking. Uncle Lai was then a student in Wen-hui High School. They had gone to North Sea Park on their first date. Aunt Lai had always kept with her a yellowed bookmark Uncle Lai had sent her after that date. On it was a love poem 'copied from God knows where'.

I've often mused to myself that people of Uncle Lai's generation were the first to enjoy the right to choose their own mates. To them, first love was was the sweetest flower of youth; not a single petal was to be wasted. Our family lived in Taiwan when I was a child, and whenever Aunt Lai quarrelled with her husband she would take the night train from Taipei to pour out her woes to my mother. But often these sessions would end in her tearful recollection of the time Uncle Lai and she were nearly separated.

It happened in late 1948. Conditions in northern China were rapidly deteriorating. Since Aunt Lai's family lived in Chi-nan, Uncle Lai travelled there with Aunt Lai in hopes of persuading her parents to come to Nanjing. At that time Uncle Lai's own parents were trapped in Ch'ang-ch'un, where conditions were so bad that they could not have left had they wanted to.

After Chi-nan fell to the Communists, Uncle Lai was still unable to persuade his parents-in-law to leave. He travelled south with Aunt Lai, but they were separated on the way. After Uncle Lai arrived in Hsu-chou, he tried every way he could think of to find Aunt Lai, but it was the eve of the battle for Hsu-chou, and in the general confusion, chances of locating any missing person were next to nothing. Uncle Lai stayed in Hsu-chou for a month or so, and completely discouraged, finally boarded the last train out of the city. As the train stopped en route in Fu-li-chi, Uncle Lai got off to buy roast chicken from vendors on the station platform. Completely by accident, he stumbled upon Aunt Lai, who happened to have been on the same train. As Aunt Lai told it, 'We held onto each other and cried our hearts out. He kept telling me to have some chicken. Who could eat chicken at a time like that? Besides, it wasn't chicken, it was crow.'

At this point aunt Lai would take out her handkerchief and sniff and weep into it.

When I was young I thought this made a good tale, full of interesting twists and turns. It was only later when I thought back to such stories heard in my childhood that I realized it was more than a 'tale of love and war'. Here was an average couple caught up in the suffering of the times, who provide a footnote to a chaotic period in the nation's history. Their story was repeated endlessly all over China. Because my own generation grew up in peaceful stability, we think of their story as a curious adventure. Everyone walks his own hard and weary path in this world. Who can fully understand another person's journey?

During the three months' basic training in Feng-shan, my days and nights were spent with college graduates from all over the island. I must admit that for a short time I felt confused. Most of the conversations of the trainees were reduced to banal comments on the looks of this girl or that one. Their fertile imaginations related everything to the subject of sex. In basic training our sergeant would recite the guidelines for standing at attention. No sooner had he said, 'The upper body must be kept upright,' than someone in the line would add: 'and the lower hanging down.' Some trainees chafed against the regulation crew cut. When on furlough in Taipei they would buy a wig to wear, then proudly tell everyone about it on their return. To my surprise, instead of making fun of them others would express envy and ask about the cost of a toupee.

In mid-August the then US Secretary of State, Cyrus Vance, made a visit to Peking. It rained incessantly in Feng-shan. Almost every night I tossed and turned and couldn't drop off. A rustling sound came to my ears from the next bunk. Peering through two layers of dark grey mosquito netting I saw my neighbour sit up, hold a hand to his mouth, inhale vigorously and then lie down again. Curiosity aroused, I inched closer and asked him what he was doing.

'Were you awake? I . . . it's only my asthma. I had to use my medication, an inhaler, you know.'

'You've got asthma?' I asked, unable to see his face through the nets.

'Yes, since I was a child. It's always like this whenever I'm tired or catch a cold.'

'Then you could've been exempt from military service.'

'I know. I was almost rejected at the basic training camp at Mount Success. So when I took my physical at the time of the exam for the reserve officers' training I didn't let on I had asthma.'

'Why not?'

'Because my father's in the military. He wants me to go through training. He said I would never regret doing my duty and serving my country. It's okay. After this defence training it'll get easier.'

That night was a great revelation to me. I thought of another friend. Being very thin, his weight was near the cut off point for exemption from military service. After college he tried his best to get the exemption, even taking pills to induce diarrhoea and fasting before the physical. Despite all his efforts his weight was still one kilo over the lowest limit, so he was drafted anyway. I came across him once at the train station as I waited for the southbound train. He looked weak and sickly, and was full of complaints.

After basic training we were sent to different branches of the services and I lost contact with my asthmatic bunk mate. It was not until Uncle Lai mentioned his older brother that I recalled the fellow trainee who had to get up in the middle of the night to stop an attack.

Uncle Lai returned to the Philippines after his wife's funeral. He came back to Taipei suddenly last year, and announced to us he had wound up his lumber business. He had decided to stay with his eldest son in the United States for the time being.

I was then serving as a second lieutenant in the north. When Uncle Lai arrived I happened to be at home on furlough. I remember he was wearing a white embroidered shirt that day and looked tired. I felt he had aged considerably. He told my father the lumber business in South-East Asia was going downhill, and it was too lonely in the Philippines without Aunt Lai. He wanted to take a break and then decide about the future. My mother came into the living room with a carton of cold milk, the sight of which set Uncle Lai off on his favourite topic.

He put on his glasses, looked at the carton and said: 'Look, even this carton is produced with the help of the Japanese. We Chinese are always losing out to them. They copy the Americans, but they are clever; they know exactly which Western products are needed, and what know-how it takes, and they set out to acquire it. Look at us, we're still asleep. We look up to the Japanese as innovators; actually the Americans are way ahead of them. The Japanese are thorough in everything they do. Once they set out to learn something, they learn it through and through. We Chinese really aren't up to much!'

I noticed my brother's expression darkening and was afraid he'd lose control again. Fortunately, just then, Uncle Lai headed for the bathroom. He emerged shortly with fists raised and grabbed my youngest brother, who was passing by.

'Young fellow, getting ready for your college exam?'

My brother replied shyly that he would not be taking the exam until the year after next. Uncle Lai asked him what department he wanted to enter. My brother said he had not yet decided. Uncle Lai let go of him and sat down again on the sofa.

'If I were you I'd put down different departments as options—music, astronomy—they're both good choices.' Uncle Lai went through the motions of looking through a telescope.

Then he looked at us. 'Young people should take advantage of their youth and study hard. When you get to my age the memory goes.'

'Uncle Lai, do you regret having gone to a military academy?' My brother asked off the top of his head.

'No, I don't. Every young man has the right to pursue his goal. We were no different. But we had to fight the Japanese to save China; we felt it was worth it to sacrifice our personal goals. We didn't complain. We could've blamed the country for not being stronger, but then, we had to ask ourselves: were we ourselves strong? If we were, what better way to prove it than by helping to save the country? We all thought this way in those days. Everyone rushed to enter military academies, but we all thought the only right way was to follow the central government in Nanking. We never thought of throwing in our lot with Chang Hsueh-liang or Yen Hsi-shan.[1] Take me, I'm a north easterner; but I chose to follow the Nanking government, didn't I? I wanted to do my bit to save China.'

Uncle Lai half closed his eyes in reminiscence.

'Before Ch'ang-ch'un fell to the Communists I wrote many times to my older brother. He was a minor official in county government. I urged him to leave the city and begged him to persuade our parents to leave with him. Finally, I wrote one last letter and had a friend deliver it by hand. I urged him not to follow Cheng Tung-kuo any longer—Cheng was vice-commander at the time. My brother was no soldier, he was shorter by a head than I. He was a scholar. He had no business staying in Ch'ang-ch'un. Then Shen-yang fell. I returned to Nanking from Hsu-chou, and found my brother's reply, also delivered by hand. He wrote dispassionately, saying no matter how bad conditions were, he would stay in Ch'ang-ch'un. He wasn't staying out of loyalty to anyone else, he stayed for himself, for the country. It's too bad I lost that letter. I can only remember the last sentence: "I carry out my official duties not for one person or one family, but for the people." The last news I had of him was that when Ch'ang-ch'un finally fell to the Communists he was caught and executed. My brother was as ignorant of military affairs, as he was uninterested in politics, but he died before he was 30.'

Uncle Lai turned around to look at me seriously.

---

[1] Chang and Yen were pre-war warlords in control of the North-east and North-west of China, respectively.

'You probably think your old uncle is always griping about this, beefing about that. I've always said, your father and I are both simple men. Even so, living in those chaotic times, we never once shirked our duty in battle, nor did we ever pocket a single penny other than our pay. We did our best to serve China faithfully. So when I see young people today wasting their lives, I've got to sound off.'

Uncle Lai stopped to drink the lemon tea my mother made, muttering to himself, 'Good tea.' The folds of wrinkled skin on his throat rose and fell as he drank.

'I used to say to my kids, go after your dreams while you're young. Learn whatever you want, I'd never stand in your way. You want to go to Rome? You've decided? No regrets? Okay! You go off to Rome! My wife was against it. She nagged me every day; faulted me for letting our daughter go off to such a far-away place all alone.'

There were tears in Uncle Lai's eyes. He took out a crumpled handkerchief and wiped them. Then he continued: 'I said, she wants to study singing in Rome today; if you won't let her go, ten years from now it'll be too late. She's young only once. If she doesn't go now she'll regret it for the rest of her life. At that time my business was flourishing in the Philippines and we were well-off. Why stand in her way? Think of how we spent the last 30 years, right? Later, I applied for a Philippines passport to facilitate business. Chien-teng, you've probably heard people criticize me for that. My frequent trips to the United States these days—probably some of you think I'm opting for the comfort and security of living in America. Actually this PR thing wasn't my idea, it was your aunt's. I'm not blaming her, of course; she'd been through so much hardship because of me. That time in Hsu-chou, especially, she was scared to death, and after I'd gone to the Philippines, for the first few years she stayed here in Taipei to look after the kids. I know she had a tough time.'

I glanced at my younger brother's bowed head. Maybe he, like me, was recalling a certain scene.

Uncle Lai had planned to stay in Taiwan for a week. But he called unexpectedly the next day from Uncle Chung's house to tell us he was leaving early next morning, and 'to say goodbye to second sister and the kids'. Then he said something about the calligraphy having been finished and left with the Chungs for us to pick up. My father said he was surprised at the sudden change in Uncle Lai's plans, but all we heard was Uncle Lai's booming laugh coming clearly over the wire.

After my father put down the phone, I asked him why we had never known Uncle Lai was good at calligraphy. Father replied: 'Ah, Uncle Lai's got the best hand of all of us.' He then went on to tell us that his family had been a prominent one in Ch'ang-ch'un and when Uncle Lai was a high school student in Peking he was already widely known for his many talents.

The next day I went over to the Chungs' house to pick up Uncle Lai's calligraphy. Father spread out the sheet of paper and we all crowded around for a look. It was a poem in the classical style, seven characters to a line, eight lines in all, written in the 'slim gold' Sung Dynasty style script. The poem, by the Southern Sung poet Lu Yu, went:

> *The glass shows graying temple locks from passing years,*
> *But cherished in my heart the elixir of loyalty.*
> *In lame old age I quit the fight—*
> *My campaign armour grown too tight.*
> *Sad indignation battled my longsword's steely chill.*
> *Ten years' campaign to Ti-po and beyond—*
> *My youthful ardour drove toward far Hao-lan.*
> *Our borders never lack for strife: can you believe*
> *This generation idly stands looking on?*

In the lower left hand corner was a line of smaller script dedicating the poem to my father in fulfillment of a pledge made 30 years ago.

Father explained that Uncle Lai had promised to do a hanging scroll for him when they were both living in Nanking. After so many years, what made him think of his long-forgotten promise all of a sudden? Father said he must have the poem mounted.

After he left for the States, Uncle Lai seldom communicated with us. Then in August or September last year he wrote to say that just before he was to return to Taiwan he had fallen ill and had had a gall bladder operation. More surgery was scheduled for later, and now he was recuperating in his son's home.

My mother was full of sympathy for Uncle Lai's plight. She urged my father to write and comfort him. Father had never been good at writing 'sentimental stuff', and kept putting it off. Maybe he never got around to writing the letter at all.

In early December Mother sent a Christmas card to Uncle Lai. On it was an ink painting of mountain scenery, with a small boat returning to shore. We soon received Uncle Lai's card. It was a plain one with the words 'Merry Christmas' on the cover. Inside on the left, Uncle Lai had written a few words sending his best wishes and telling us he was feeling much better. He also mentioned he wanted to come back to Taiwan to see what he could do for his country. At the end was a postscript: 'Hsueh-jen got married in October to a Chinese student in Europe. He too studies music.'

On the left side of the card Uncle Lai had written, with a brush pen in the familiar Sung Dynasty script, a classical couplet saying that life itself is an endless journey with no fixed harbour, there is no need to look for a boat home.

I did not know whether Uncle Lai had written the couplet himself or was quoting someone else. Neither could I fathom his feelings at that moment. This was the last time he wrote to us.

While I was busy getting ready to leave, I received good news from two of my friends. One classmate wrote to say he had been hired by the China Steel Corporation, another friend from military service told me he was starting at the Central News Agency after some tough competition. The latter told me excitedly over the phone that he was having a business card printed, and wanted to take me to dinner. I usually try to avoid welcome-home or going-away affairs but I was happy he'd been taken on by the Central News Agency, so I accepted.

Returning home from the dinner I came into the living room to find the new hanging scroll on the wall and my parents admiring it. Uncle Lai's calligraphy was now beautifully mounted. I read the poem to myself again. As I came to the final lines I turned to look at the picture of the Great Wall over the TV set and recalled Uncle Lai singing 'The Ballad of the Great Wall' that day in this very same room. Suddenly all the memories came crowding into my mind.

'Y'know, we still owe Lao Lai 30 silver dollars,' Mother said.

'How come?' Father asked.

'It was when we were boarding the boat at Huang-p'u in Shanghai. Old Lai came to the dock to see us off. You'd gone off somewhere, and he asked me whether we had enough money with us. I admitted we didn't have much and I was a little worried. Lao Lai said that wouldn't do, and straight off counted 30 silver dollars into my hand. I think he came prepared to give us the money. I told you about it. Have you forgotten?'

'Then how much interest should there be on that after 30 years?' Father asked.

I returned to my room, dazed with a multitude of thoughts and feeling slightly dizzy. After a while it occurred to me that I ought to write to the Chinese Student Association in Oregon. I picked up their xeroxed letter. It said:

> Corvallis is located near the ocean in western Oregon. With beautiful scenery, its longitude and latitude are similar to those of Harbin and Ch'ang-ch'un. Because of warm currents from the Pacific there is only light snow in winter, but the four seasons are distinct. The students here live and study in harmony.

I closed my eyes and thought of the couplet on Uncle Lai's card. Life itself is indeed an endless journey, but the journey from Ch'ang-ch'un to Corvallis was such a long one.

Life

Lu Fei-yi

translated by Ching-Hsi Perng

MORE than 30 years passed before he met her again. More than 30 years! How terrifying that the better half of one's life passes just like that and all aspirations and hopes eventually evaporate.

Not that the idea of meeting her again never occurred to him, but when the possibility becomes a reality, everything looks like a dream instead. While in the airplane, the passenger sitting next to him struck up a conversation, asking him where he was going. He answered, 'Hong Kong,' but added, 'is this flight going to Hong Kong?'—as if he could not truly believe he would make it, and things might go wrong at any moment.

And now, he and she are standing in the room, facing each other. He sees her, hears the sounds about them, and knows that all this is real. After more than 30 years, he meets her again.

He crosses the room to shut the door, and the lock clicks softly. Somehow, he seems to hear surprise in her voice.

'Leave it open,' she says.

He reopens the door, looks about outside, and says: 'They're all gone.' He shuts the door again.

She no longer insists. In the air, a strange atmosphere is congealing: it is so thick one can hardly utter a word in it.

He sizes her up and, before he knows it, says: 'You haven't changed much.' Actually that is not how he feels. He only realizes what he has said after he says it.

It takes her a second or two to understand him, as if those few words were abstruse and obscure. In the congealed air, one's senses seem to turn numb, except about oneself: all of a sudden she feels herself standing extraordinarily enormous.

'I'm old,' she says.

He has been gazing at her, not ready to comment, but now that she has mentioned it, he thinks she is quite right. He has thousands of times imagined the meeting with her, and has mulled over what to say and how to say it, but it has never occurred to him that the first moment of their reunion would steal away like that. And it is impossible to start over again.

He finds himself a chair and, pointing to the sofa, says: 'Sit down.'

She sits down, clearly feeling the springs being pushed downward. All the people who were in this room have left, each leaving a void in the air.

They had followed them from the station, all the neighbours, relatives, and colleagues. They jostled around her, chattering all the way from the station to the hostel. Now, they are all gone, leaving her alone to face him.

'That was a crowd,' says she.

'Yes, and I wonder how we recognized each other, it's been decades.'

'Yes,' she echoes.

The train had barely pulled to a stop when he was led up to her. He asked her, 'Are you Comrade Yao?' She heard the Neighbourhood Secretary forestalling her by eagerly replying, 'Yes, yes!'

Then, the crowd in loud voices asked: 'Is it him? Is that him?'

Only then did she take a good look at him, and he it was! He is sitting on the chair, dully staring at the floor, smiling: he looks like the man she knew, but slightly changed in appearance. She knows he is still the same man; it's just that, at this moment, she suddenly isn't sure how he used to look.

'Must have been a long ride?'

'Ah yes,' he laughs. By now he has calmed down, but mixed feelings begin to surge in him. 'This is really unexpected,' he says. Life is a bit too full of the unexpected.

'Yao-tsu and . . . they didn't come?' he asks.

'In a couple of days. Tickets are hard to come by. And you weren't sure you'd arrive today.'

'Oh,' he says apologetically, remembering the telephone call he made from Kowloon. All she could say on the phone was 'Come back, come back,' and he could hear those around her yelling: 'Ask him to come back, ask him to come back!'

'Is everything OK with you?'

'Just fine,' she says, her voice stiff, as if she is talking about some family affair to a stranger. 'Yao-tsu works in a factory, and he only gets home twice a year or even less. Where Yao-min works it's better, but still it's only every two or three months. . . . Says he's saving money—he has a girlfriend already.'

Vaguely he listens. Actually he knows something about that, having corresponded with them several times in the last two years. 'Yao-tsu must be thirty-something now?' he asks.

'Going on 40 already,' she says, a little irritated.

'No girlfriend?'

'In the early days, because he was a 'Rightist,' he couldn't think of marriage. The last few years, things have changed for the better, but he's no longer young. If it weren't for the shift to the right in recent years, Yao-min would be in the same predicament and have no girlfriend.'

'In fact, all this is my fault.'

'Let's not talk about that!' she snaps. Her tone shows impatience.

'How about you yourself, doing OK?'

She takes a look at him, says nothing, but lowering her head, she resumes toying with her cuff button.

He watches her unbutton it and then button it up, fiddling monotonously. Suddenly she raises her head and, with a smile, asks: 'And you? I heard you've got a second love.'

He is somewhat struck by this term, although he knows in this country husband and wife are alluded to that way. He smiles and wrings his hands, a little embarrassed. Looking at the two or three calluses on his hands, he replies: 'Ah, yes, we've been married for over 20 years. . . . Little did I think I could return today.'

'Mm, little did we expect,' she says.

He takes a look at her. He cannot detect any resentment, yet he feels she's a bit offended all the same. She keeps smiling indifferently.

'It's thanks to her, actually, that I could make this trip home,' he says, placating, trying not to sound defensive. 'You see, I am not settled down in the United States yet.'

'I know, . . .' she interrupts him, angry that he has made her feel she is currying favour with him.

But he goes on: 'We just opened the shop in Los Angeles. The beginning is always hard. After all, America is not our country.'

She looks at him with unconcern, not caring what he is saying, then edges in by asking: 'Isn't there a son?'

'Ah yes,' he says. 'We're lucky he was a good student. Otherwise, we couldn't have gone to the States.'

'Surely he's married?'

'H-hm,' he says, suddenly noticing the sadness and callousness in her eyes.

She does not say any more, but sits quietly, her fingers scratching the sofa, each scratch leaving a trace on the plastic sofa-cover.

Outside, a waiter knocks at the door. Before he can even stand up, the waiter opens it and walks in. She stands up at once, quite alarmed, and explains in a hurry: 'I, I am his love.'

Comrade Waiter pays no attention to her; he simply fills the thermos bottle and leaves. She remains standing for quite a while before sitting down in embarrassment.

'Some water?' he asks.

She shakes her head, somewhat annoyed.

Outside the window, cars pass by occasionally, and the *ding-ling* ringing of a bicycle bell accompanied by the chirping of some unknown insect reminds him of the South Airfield District in Taipei, where, in the streets on summer evenings, the same kind of noises used to flow by.

'Sure you don't want anything to drink?' he asks.

'Sure,' she says. 'When does the hostel close?'

'At eleven. It's still early.'

She glances at her watch, as though eleven were a long time away.

She is really changed, he thinks. Fatter now, and wearing glasses. In her glasses she looks conservative, ponderous, and the eyes in the frames look duller too. He had not imagined she would change into what she is now: in his mind, she was always either older or younger than this.

He must also look different to her. He recalls his life the last several decades, mostly spent, in no extraordinary way, in the Japanese-style housing unit: the '8-23' [August 23, 1958] Artillery Battle [in Quemoy] was fought and won; President Chiang Kai-shek passed away; the housing units were turned into apartments; children have grown up. . . . More than 30 years slipped away just like that: 'in no time', as they say. Thus, he and she, having led independent lives for more than 30 years, are like two people with nothing in common.

'How long are you staying?' she asks.

'Quite a few days, surely. Now that I'm here, I'd like to look around.'

'You should visit your elder brother . . . ,' she starts to talk about serious matters now, producing a piece of notebook paper from her pocket to see what else she wanted to say.

He listens, chiming in from time to time. Outside the room, people walk by, their slippers and shoes making different sounds on the floor. Outside the window, the unknown insect is chirping. Just like the days of the past 30-odd years. Human voices, insect chirping, and car noises loudly flow by all day long, all year long. And now, after more than 30 years have passed, he is listening to her mumbling about household matters.

'There, take this incense-stick,' says his elder brother. The relatives and neighbours around him also press him, muttering words.

He takes the incense-stick, and as he gently blows on it, a spark of red flares. On the table are offerings to some unknown Buddha, in dark gray. On the four walls are set commemorative wooden tablets, with Chinese characters large and small on them.

At least the tablets for his parents are next to each other, and around them are those relatives he knows. The incense smoke wavers, and those people, separated from him by the smoke, crouch between the lines of characters.

'The ashes are kept in the pagoda,' says his brother. 'Usually, we all come here to worship and make sacrifices.'

He faces the tablets of his parents, pays his respects, and bows. Someone takes over the incense stick, saying, 'That's fine, fine, fine.' People on all sides break the silence at once, and chattering is resumed.

High up in the hall hang a bell and drum. There is no wind, but it is dark and cool. Human voices linger round the tall columns and high beams; there are sighs and laughter. He looks at his elder brother, and then at the tablets of his parents. He kneels down to kowtow on the slate floor. All the voices die down, except his own. His tears drip.

Once out of the hall, it is hot again. A group of people pause at the steps, hesitating. The sunshine cuts through the eaves of the shrine, and a square of light is formed in the courtyard. Steam seems to rise from the green slate floor. A swallow darts overhead.

After some ceremonious yielding among the elders, his brother, holding him by the hand, leads him away. The sunshine stays on his neck, making him itch; one of them is trembling, and both feel a biting cold.

They have lunch at a restaurant, with many guests. Sitting next to him, she just keeps eating, as if resentful of those who have come. In the presence of others, she is especially cold toward him.

His elder brother keeps raising his chopsticks, entreating: 'Have some more, have some more.' It seems that as age comes on, you too easily become a mother hen.

Looking at those at the other two tables, where they are heartily enjoying their meal, he grins in embarrassment and says: 'I hardly recognize them now.' His elder brother makes no response to this but, his eyes half-closed, smiles his satisfaction: 'It's worth it, it's worth it—my first meal ever in a restaurant!'

During the meal, some of the guests come up to toast him with tea or wine, all saying: 'You're truly welcome,' and then they engage in a study of how they should address one another. The vicissitudes of the world seem to pass before his eyes, and they're transformed into so many cups of tea and wine that he takes in. She tries to stop him, saying, 'Not so much, not so much.' Not far away, the waiters watch them, coolly.

On the way back to the hostel, the same crowd follows, as if no one needed to go to work. He hears a woman say: 'Be quiet. This is going to be a new experience for you.' The one next to her chortles and shoots back, 'Don't talk like a hick,' in a voice that sounds no less excited.

The crowd follows him to the hostel. Comrade Janitor pulls a long face and requires everyone of them to sign the registry. Watching them do it, Comrade

Janitor also comments acidly: 'You sure have enough friends and relatives!' Then, as if afraid this remark has offended the guest, he adds: 'Oh well, this happens with everyone coming from abroad.'

The receiving room is filled with his group, all the others having left understandingly. Since every chair, big and small, is occupied, some have to stand, which they don't seem to mind, for then they can move about and look around. One of the children even goes so far as to peep into the rooms of other guests.

While he and his elder brother are chatting, several relatives their age join in the conversation. One of them, whom he addresses as cousin, says: 'It must be great to live in America! They say in America, anybody can make much more than we do here!'

He smiles at this, finding it hard to make any comment.

Another says: 'Studying abroad is permitted now, and if some relative or friend overseas is willing to help. . . .' As this draws no response, the speaker tries to save face by adding, with a laugh, 'Well, of course it isn't that easy either!' He joins in the laughter, recalling his own small shop, and the kids who rush in every morning, shouting, 'Hurry up, Mac!' Making sure that she is talking with somebody else, his elder brother asks: 'My nephew is doing well, I hope?'

He is speechless for a moment before he sees what his brother means, and he replies: 'He's alright. He's in real estate now.'

At this they all look confused. He smiles, explaining: 'He started out as a physics major, but transferred to computer science because of the job market. In the past two years he's been a realtor in the Los Angeles area, buying and selling houses—his clients are mostly Chinese.'

While they listen, these people keep nodding with approval, in a way becoming the elderly. One of them exclaims: 'That's nice—it's nice to study physics.'

His elder brother also smiles and says: '*Your* nephew is learning a foreign language on his own. In his work unit they're pushing foreign languages. When you get a chance, give him some advice.' He then called the young man standing by the window to come over for an audience.

'Oh, he's grown so tall, and sturdy!' the visitor remarks.

'Cares for nothing but basketball. Nothing but straw in his head!' says his elder brother. 'Come over here to greet your uncle.'

The young man, eighteen or nineteen, mumbles something awkwardly. Someone tries to egg him on: 'Come on, let's hear you say a couple of sentences in a foreign language. Remember your uncle's an expert!'

The young man is no speaker; he stumbles and halts, but finally finds an excuse to move away. Having done this, the boy turns his head around to look with great admiration.

All of a sudden, he recalls the time his own son had just arrived in the States. Every time he answered his son's letters, he would smooth the envelope onto the window, and trace the address against the sunlight.

'No problem in America, I suppose? Can you communicate?' asks his elder brother.

'It's OK,' says the visitor. 'I can understand everyday conversation. Where I live, there are lots of Chinese, so I don't have much to do with foreigners.'

'Yeah, it's always a problem dealing with foreigners,' they come to a unanimous conclusion.

His elder brother sighs and remarks: 'In the last few years, because our country has gotten strong, we aren't afraid of them. But in the early years— boy! how we suffered!'

Thereupon someone says: 'Yes, yes indeed. Still, we've got a lot to learn, a lot to learn. We're still way behind, way behind.' The others just nod at this, without making any comment. The afternoon sunshine stays in the courtyard. The twittering of birds comes continually from the huge trees, but aside from that, it is an extremely idle, sleepy afternoon, in which one can doze off at any minute.

'Your wife's quite something,' says his elder brother. 'I don't know how your family survived when all of them were branded "rightists". Yao-tsu even begged for food. Can you imagine, such a little kid. I was really at the end of my rope, and couldn't do much to help. When your wife went through forced labour in the countryside, Yao-tsu lived on my wife's milk, and he was already more than a year old. Not that he couldn't have been weaned, but, the fact is, there wasn't anything else to feed him.'

'I know, I know,' he says, in part because he is afraid to hear any more.

His brother takes a look at him and goes on: 'Luckily, we are all safe and sound; otherwise, I . . . honestly, I wouldn't know how to face you.'

He keeps patting his brother on the shoulder, feeling sad himself. Those around them, seeing his brother so depressed, can say nothing but all retreat into their own sorrows. Close to the door sit several women; they don't hear the conversation, but, judging from the sight itself, they can sense the sadness and their talking stops. The birds outside the window twitter more merrily.

When it's time to say goodbye, a crowd of people bid farewell at the entrance of the hostel. Comrade Janitor, who has dozed off, half awakes and glances up now and then. He bids farewell to all the relatives and friends,

young and old, once again each reviewing the other's title. Some of these
people will be with him for several days more: others, less close, he may never
see again, but all of them show great reluctance in parting.

All of a sudden Comrade Janitor flies into a rage: 'Damn it! Will you stop
making that racket on a hot day like this!'

Taken aback, they turn around to look, and then, realizing the rebuke was
aimed at the birds in the trees, resume their reluctant leave-taking.

His elder brother is the last to leave. Casting a significant look at him, he
says: 'Ask your love to come back for a visit, too.'

He is extremely shocked by the word 'love'. Although by now he's quite
used to the term, he is still surprised to hear it from his own brother. He
watches his elder brother walk slowly away, spotty shadows of the leaves of the
tree running up his back. He shuffles along, showing his age: indeed he is an
old man left behind by the times. Suddenly a hair-raising terror seizes him.

Yao-min's train arrives first, so he is the first to visit him at the hostel. He is
waiting in his room making tea, when he hears shuffling of footsteps outside.
It is she who opens the door, and immediately a crowd appears. Though he feels
a little dizzy, he can see Yao-min walk up.

'Call him "Daddy", say "Daddy"!' shouts one of them, more enthusiastic
than the others. But Yao-min fails to call him daddy after all; instead, he lowers
his head, as if in thought. He takes a look at her, standing by, nervous, tears
trickling down.

'Yao-min,' he calls out with a smile. His nose prickles, much to his surprise.
People around keep exhorting: 'Say "Daddy"!'

'Daddy!' Yao-min mutters, rather embarrassed. Somehow, on occasions of
joy or sorrow, parting or reunion, there are always lots of people on hand as
spectators.

When everyone is seated, he finds Yao-min has brought a girl along. 'This
is Chao Yun,' Yao-min makes the introduction.

She adds, 'Yao-min's girlfriend, the one I mentioned to you.'

They make some sort of greeting to each other. He is gazing at her when,
suddenly realizing that this might be his daughter-in-law, he turns away.

He turns instead toward Yao-min, who is looking at him. As soon as their
eyes meet, Yao-min lowers his head again. He gazes at his own son and feels
quite sure that the latter cannot recognize him. The boy was still in swaddling
clothes when he left home, and now he's so big, just unbelievable. It is a kind
of good luck, but it is also very sad. It is as if he had awakened from a dream
to find that he has everything, except for the decades that are lost.

Someone starts to talk again: 'Congratulations! A reunion between father and son. . . .' Thereupon everybody busies himself chatting idly. The advantage of having idlers around is that they help ease the embarrassment of having to face each other squarely.

They are talking about Yao-min's childhood. A neighbour who is a bit older than Yao-min banks on his seniority and sighs: 'Poor child, he used to go along with his elder brother begging for food, and when they chased him, he couldn't run; he'd stumble and cry, "Brother!" . . .' Everyone laughs, but can't think why.

She, too, laughs, and then wipes her tears away, remembering she was in the labour camp then, where every night she bit the quilt and sobbed, so heartbroken she only wished to die.

'Now it's alright,' someone tries to dilute the sad atmosphere. 'For a change. Finally. Things couldn't be better.'

All nod in agreement. There is silence for a while.

'Are things OK in America?'

'OK,' he replies, and not knowing what else to say, he repeats: 'OK.'

'It's great to have this kind of foreign connection these days,' someone joins in breezily.

Yao-min takes a look at Chao Yun, and they gaze at each other and smile.

'I've brought you something,' says he, getting up to fetch it.

Seeing that it's gift-giving time, relatives and friends all bid good-bye, as if by tacit agreement.

'Don't go yet; let's talk some more,' she entreats.

'No, no, no, you ought to have some small talk by yourselves,' someone replies, knowing there will be other occasions to see each other again.

He never thought it would come to this, all because he mentioned gifts, and so he also pleads: 'Don't go: I've brought *you* things, too.'

One of them suddenly pulls a long face, as if angry: 'No, no. We'd be insensitive fools if we stayed any longer.' Off he goes, as if washing himself clean of something.

Others, though still smiling, also insist on taking their leave: 'Indeed it's time we went. We'll come back some other time.'

The crowd gone, the room seems to turn into a teacup that has been shaken, and an uneasy air sways in it. He takes an electric shaver and other things from his suitcase and gives them to Yao-min; there are a couple of more valuable items, such as money, he means to give him when they are alone. He also presents Chao Yun with a coral necklace, made in Taiwan but sold in great quantity in US supermarkets. In fact it is not cheap, but it makes a good present because it looks much more expensive than it actually is. Yao-min helps Chao Yun put on the necklace, as if it were the gift for the wife upon first meeting. He smiles as he watches. This is no occasion for many words, he knows.

Yao-min begins to talk about how he and Chao Yun got acquainted; he tries to listen, but always gets lost, and so does she, all the while picking up this or that.

'Didn't think I'd come back, did you?' he jumps in with the question.

For a moment Yao-min is dumbfounded. The mother answers instead: 'Your return was always on his mind. He even asked for an extended leave this time.'

'That's right,' Yao-min says. 'And, more than I could hope for, here we are, together.' He looks at his father: although his mind tells him this man is his father, his heart still keeps its distance.

'I owe you apologies—didn't take good care of you,' he says.

Now Yao-min can't think of what to say.

After supper, Yao-min takes them to town for a movie, a love story. As he sits in the theater and watches the plainly dressed young men and women chatting romantically, his thoughts wander back to his own youthful experiences.

In the dark, he takes a look at Yao-min, who is holding hands with Chao Yun; lights and shadows leap on their faces. Yao-min is over 30 already; though he looks younger than his age, the boy is no longer a young man. He feels rather sad.

After Chao Yun has left, the three of them return to the hostel.

'When are you getting married?' he asks Yao-min.

'This year, I think. Depending on the financial situation.'

'The sooner the better then,' he is thinking of the money intended for Yao-min.

Yao-min makes no comment. He is deep in thought for quite a while before asking: 'Dad, you're doing fine in America?'

He takes a look at his son, pulls a chair over, and sits down seriously: 'I've been in America only a couple of years, so I'm not settled yet. But, don't you worry, it's easy to do well in America; in a few years, my business should amount to something.'

Yao-min is listening. After a while, he mumbles: 'I've taken up a foreign language recently.'

'Oh?' he says. 'Meaning to go to America?'

Yao-min says nothing but looks at his mother.

She doesn't say anything, her face turned toward the window.

'Take your time,' he pats his son on the shoulder. 'There will be a way.'

'Dad,' Yao-min again looks at his mother as he asks falteringly: 'There's a younger brother, right?'

He also looks at her, but she remains utterly motionless. He says: 'Your younger brother is in business—he's worked like hell to stay in America. As a matter of fact, his interest still lies rather in physics.' That last sentence was meant for himself, for Yao-min cannot understand. He looks at his son and says with a smile: 'Work hard on the English. I used to study it hours every day. You're young, you can learn fast. Once I'm back in America, I'll send you books.'

Yao-min laughs. He laughs too, remembering how, in the past, he would get up and recite lessons from *English 900* in the yard of the dormitory. He wonders what Yao-min would think if he knew that.

'Study hard!' he pats Yao-min on the shoulder, once again realizing his son is no longer young.

That night, he stays in the hostel alone. He tosses and turns, simply unable to go to sleep. He thinks of the last few days, of his wife and sons, extremely depressed. Night at the hostel is unusually quiet, with the occasional chirping of insects creeping in from the window. The moonlight gently embraces the earth, looking particularly bright when there is no other light. He walks to the balcony, and looks at the earth bathed in the moonlight, and the slightly undulating mountain ranges that encircle this city. He can hardly believe that all this is real. He seems to be in a dream, a dream that has for some decades past accompanied him wherever he went.

In the extremely quiet night, faintly he hears a rolling sound, like the breathing of the earth. Perhaps it's the river, he thinks, although the river is quite a distance from here. He grew up in this city, until adolescence, but that was a long time ago. Right now he stands at a certain point in life; there is no past, only the future.

He suddenly recalls another point in his life. That moment, he was standing among a group of people, staring at the speakers on the platform and listening to the waves of sound that came from the loudspeaker; then they raised their right hands and read the words of a pledge, pledging loyalty to America.

He has the same feeling now that he did then. At this moment, he feels like a solitary grain of millet in the great earth.

Yao-tsu is supposed to come straight to the restaurant for dinner with them, but for some reason he keeps them waiting.

'Is the train delayed?' he asks.

'I don't think so,' she says. 'The train is seldom late. Maybe it's the traffic on the way here.'

While Yao-min is waiting downstairs, he goes to the window and looks down toward the street. 'So many people!' he says.

'It's always like this when people get off work. That's probably why Yao-tsu's late.'

At first he tries to find Yao-tsu among the crowd, then he realizes it is impossible, for he does not know what Yao-tsu looks like. So he simply takes in the street scene.

There is still daylight, but tinted with the grayish yellow characteristic of dusk. The street is brim full of pedestrians and bicycles, like a flood tide. There are also a couple of military trucks, that keep honking '*ba-a, ba-a.*' At the edge of the road, a couple of carts pulled by men hesitate, unable to cross the street.

'But you haven't gone to work for quite a few days now,' he says.

'It's 'overseas guest first' now. Usually it's difficult to get leave.'

'The Chinese are gifted with a human touch, after all.'

She takes a look at him and says: 'Maybe so now. During the Anti-Rightist Movement, whoever dared to . . . . Great neighbours and relatives they were then!'

There is resentment in her voice—it must be grievances piled up in the last few days. He doesn't dare to pursue it, so simply switches to Yao-tsu: 'Yao-tsu still remembers me?'

'Perhaps not how you look, but he cannot forget you . . . having suffered so much because of you.'

'I should have taken you along then.'

'Why bring that up now?' she says impatiently, turning to go downstairs and tell the waiter to hold the meal for now.

When Yao-tsu arrives it is almost dark. He is followed by Comrade Waiter, who asks impatiently: 'Everybody here, eh?' Yao-tsu sits next to his mother, handing her a basketful of fruits and vegetables.

'Why are you so late?'

'Why? It's crowded!' Yao-tsu replies, all the while not giving his father a single glance.

He looks at Yao-tsu, not knowing what to say either. He calls to Yao-min: 'Get your big brother a pair of chopsticks.'

Yao-tsu takes the bowl and chopsticks, then finally takes a flustered look at his father.

'Would you have recognized him?' she asks.

'Looks like him,' Yao-tsu says, sizing his father up.

'He was only four—four, right?—how can he remember?' says the father.

She makes no reply. A moment passes and then, she suddenly says: 'After 40 years apart, you talk nothing but this nonsense when you see each other!' She bursts out crying.

The waiter comes with two dishes, still steaming, but the vegetables are yellowed already. No doubt they were reheated.

'Let's eat,' he says, and serves both Yao-tsu and Yao-min. As she watches the father and sons, her suppressed tears drop again. Yao-tsu puts his arm round her shoulder and says coaxingly: 'There, there, c'mon and eat.'

After dinner, Yao-min suggests they call a cab, so his elder brother might get a taste of a car ride. Yao-tsu says: 'No way. I sat a whole day and a night on the train.'

He says: 'Let's take a walk. I wonder how much this place has changed.'

People in the main street have dispersed; only a few bicycles rush by occasionally. Two rows of street lights extend all the way along the road, and behind them, thick foliage covers the sky.

'This is the better place after all,' he says.

'What's good about here? All worn out and torn down.'

He doesn't know how to explain it but, seeing the two rows of trees with dancing shadows, like river banks, he responds, 'These trees are wonderful.'

Yao-min looks up and stares at the trees, but fails to find anything remarkable about them. Instead, he exclaims: 'There are stars!'

He, too, looks up, searching. Yao-tsu takes a look at them, and does the same. But she says: 'Why such a fuss about stars?'

Yao-min is still watching the sky as he walks, saying, 'Fine day today.'

He smiles.

Yao-min smiles too, and, lowering his head, he kicks a piece of rock on the way and says: 'I wonder if stars are the same when you watch them in America?'

Looking at the strip of starry sky sandwiched between two rows of swaying leaves like a river of stars, he remarks: 'How can you see this many stars in America? Only lights, or high-rises. Not even trees like these, only lawns, and those are surrounded by wire fences too.'

Having heard this, Yao-min waits a long time before saying: 'There's not a single high-rise here.'

They go out of their way to where they once lived. The old house is still there, a little worn though, and surrounded by additions here and there.

'Incredible, to have survived all these years!' he says.

His hands on the wall-top, Yao-min hops along to glimpse the courtyard and residence inside. He says with a laugh: 'Brother used to straddle this and recite his Russian lessons.'

Yao-tsu looks blankly at the wall. Yao-min continues: 'That's because the girls from Twelfth High passed by everyday. It was for them that Brother recited.'

At this, she casts a sorrowful look at Yao-tsu. But Yao-tsu takes it rather calmly and says with a smile: 'How strange—I can hardly remember what happened before.'

The whole family stand in front of the wall. A gust of wind blows from the long street fluttering their clothes. On the eaves of the houses a few fallen leaves scurry about. The moonlight stays on the tiles, as if it had done so for millennia.

'Daddy used to play flute in the yard,' Yao-tsu suddenly remarks.

Yao-min looks at his brother in disbelief: 'Really?'

He, too, looks at Yao-tsu curiously: 'How do you know?'

'I seem to have a dim recollection, but then I'm not sure: maybe I heard it from uncle, as a boy.'

'Haven't played it for decades,' he sighs, vaguely conjuring up the dim past.

'During the Cultural Revolution, many houses were raided. He confiscated a flute from somebody and hid it, and secretly learned to play it,' she says. It happened more than ten years ago, and she mentions it with great calm.

'And I was given a good beating by Mom,' Yao-tsu laughs.

She also breaks into a laughter, while deep inside she is extremely sad.

After a long pause, she sighs: 'Ah well, that's all over.'

Yao-tsu does not go home with Mother, but stays in the hostel. He goes downstairs to register for Yao-tsu. When he returns, Yao-tsu hands him a package.

'Nothing much,' Yao-tsu says. 'Just a cheap thing made locally. Bought at the free market. Quite cheap. But took me a long time, too crowded.'

'No wonder we had to wait so long. I thought your train was delayed.'

He opens the package to find a tea-set—a pot and some cups made of bamboo, it appears, and wrapped in fine bamboo threads. 'But I'm not sure if you drink tea in America?'

'I do, I do,' says he, almost in tears.

As father and son are making beds, he notices Yao-tsu watching him. He laughs and says: 'I'm old now.'

Yao-tsu makes no comment, but goes on to finish making the bed.

'How have you been all these years?' he asks.

Yao-tsu pauses for a while and says: 'Well, nothing special. I've had my share of troubles. But I'm just sorry I didn't get much education.'

'Give yourself time, give yourself time,' he says. Yao-tsu smiles dryly, and is about to say 'There is no time left' when he checks himself.

'Your mom told me you're still not married. . . .'

'. . . I will; after all, I mustn't keep Mom worried over this.'

'Remember to write me about it.'

'Sure,' Yao-tsu says.

The beds are made. Both are silent for some time before he says: 'As you know, while I was in Taiwan I got married again.'

Yao-tsu interrupts him, saying: 'I want to take a bath.'

He finds it hard to go on, so he watches his son go into the bathroom.

Outside the window, the moon is still clear and bright. The leaves are fluttering and dancing in the wind. There is no insect chirping tonight. From the bathroom come splashing sounds.

When he too is done washing, he finds Yao-tsu smoking on the balcony, in contemplation.

'What's on your mind?' he asks.

Yao-tsu looks toward the great earth, dark and deep, outside the window, and replies: 'I wonder if Mom would be willing to go to America.'

He is struck dumb by this, not knowing what to say. After a long while, he asks: 'How about you?'

Yao-tsu turns around and laughs self-mockingly: 'I'm going on 40 already. . . . Regardless of what has happened, this is my home.'

Father and son make a pot of tea. He offers a cigarette to Yao-tsu, asking: 'Any plans?'

Yao-tsu replies: 'I'll wait and see. My unit is carrying out a new policy. I'll wait and see.'

He says: 'So I have heard many people say, and your uncle also says things are better now.'

Yao-tsu smiles dryly and repeats: 'I'll wait and see.'

Looking at the unperturbed face of Yao-tsu, he realizes that he really does not understand these people, or what they think. Yao-tsu sits straight, puffing out a big cloud of smoke, and says: 'Anyway, we've got to look ahead, we've wasted so many years.'

'Yeah,' he sighs. 'It's all up to your generation now.'

From his side of the smoke screen, Yao-tsu looks at his father and remembers the Anti-Rightist Movement, when he was so beaten he could hardly stand up, and also how, when he smeared the ground with vomited blood, someone shouted: 'A bloody liar! A bloody liar!'

But right now he is calm.

'When are you going back?' Yao-tsu asks.

'Not sure yet. We'll see,' he says. 'I don't know when I'll be back here again.'

Yao-tsu smiles. He gazes at him and knows that he is his father—that much he knows. After so many years, he suddenly appeared. Nothing will change. He will leave, and after that the days will be the same as always. There'll be only himself and Mom. Yao-tsu pours his father some more tea. Seeing his father's hands holding the cup, he suddenly thinks of the blood that circulates in his own body. He hurries to light a cigarette, so as to drive away such thoughts.

Outside of the window, the insects chirp again, and the big river—the big river rolls *gung-lung, gung-lung.*

On the eve of departure, a roomful of relatives and close friends gather again. Several women sit in a circle to lament. One of them sighs: '*Ai*, time flies, and it's time to say goodbye already. That day at the train station, when they had just met each other, he couldn't say a word, just stood there stupefied. Finally, because we nagged, he opened his mouth, and it was—"Comrade Yao"! Ha, ha, ha . . .' They burst into laughter all together, holding their sides and wiping away tears. With much restraint they manage to stop laughing: '*Ai*, that was just a few days ago, and now he's leaving.'

She laughs with them, so hard that she keeps wiping away her tears.

Yao-min and Chao Yun are chatting in a corner. He sees them and walks over to say: 'Take good care of Miss Chao, and remember to write me when you get married.'

Chao Yun lowers her head in embarrassment. Yao-min watches her, laughing. Yao-tsu sees this scene, gives his brother a pat on the head, and prods him good-naturedly: 'What's so funny, dummy? You and Miss Chao should be paying respects to Daddy together.'

Some clamour for a photograph, and make him sit next to his elder brother, who holds him by the hand in excitement, constantly shouting: 'No, no, not until I've wiped away my tears.' After many attempts, the picture is finally taken with tears of laughter running all over their faces.

Those present in the room pose in small groups. 'Take a picture of husband and wife,' someone suggests, and all applaud in agreement.

She resists determinedly, repeating, 'Don't, don't,' but in vain. She smoothes her hair and straightens her dress, still complaining: 'At my age. . . .'

One of them shouts: 'Sit closer, closer. . . . Cheese. . .' And then, 'click', it is done at last. She touches her hair again, wondering how she will look in the picture. He says: 'Let's take a group picture.' At this, several start jockeying for the job.

At last all those in the room are gathered in one place. Adjusting the focus, the photographer keeps moving backward.

'Can't get us all in, eh?' someone remarks.

'Too many people!'

'That's China, nothing but people.' Everyone in the room bursts into laughter.

Suddenly he realizes that life, the life of the Chinese people, always fluctuates, like this, between tears and laughter.

The Rapeseed

Liao Hui-ying

translated by I-djen Chen

WHEN Keke, my older brother, was born, Father was only 23, and Mother was not quite 21. She had attended a school for brides in Japan, her dowry was 12 gold bars, 12 big trunks full of silk and woollen material, and many pieces of top quality furniture, brought over in a black sedan and trucks.

Black Pussy Cat, the doctor's youngest daughter, was finally getting married. In those days, perfection such as hers was eyed with envy; her beauty and her family background brought out droves of matchmakers from nearby towns and villages, and many a young doctor had already broken his plumage and been turned down. Now she was finally getting married. What caused eyebrows to lift was that the groom was neither a doctor by profession, nor was he of the same social-economic background. He was only the son of a school teacher from a neighbouring town and graduate of a technical college. According to reports, the doctor liked him because he looked like a simple and sincere man; the young man's hair, prematurely white and casually groomed, made him look much more honest and reliable than the fashionable doctors wearing French hairdos and Western style clothing.

A year after the wedding they promptly had a boy, which pleased the maternal grandfather so much he could hardly keep his mouth closed from so much grinning. He himself had taken six concubines in succession, and still had not been able to produce a son. This birth was a disappointment and a great let-down to many who had been hoping Black Pussy Cat's marriage would come up short.

I do not know how long the happy days lasted. I only know that for as long as I could remember, Keke and I often had to hide in the corner watching our father throwing things around furiously. Mother would be screaming loudly, calling upon heaven and earth, her hair in great disarray. Quite a few times mother left home after a big battle, while Keke and I, who had long ago learned to be alert to expressions on the faces of adults and did not cry easily, were hastily packed off to stay with Aunt Fu. Three or four days later our old, white-haired grandfather would bring our resentful mother back. Never a man of words, Father was completely speechless before Grandfather, who was himself not a man of many words. The two of them would sit by the door in the setting sun, wordless. The old man, who had had great wealth, great influence, who could 'freeze water with a shout' and whose face was heavily lined, no longer looked awesome, but was a picture of senility in the setting sun. To the son-in-law, the old man's silence was not so much a reprimand as a request that he be good to Daddy's spoiled youngest daughter. However, the tight-mouthed young man was no longer the simpleton who had panicked and sat on a wash basin when he was being looked over before the marriage.

I held on to my mother's skirt as we dragged ourselves to the black sedan parked at the entrance to the village to see Grandfather off. Our aged grandfather turned around and, looking at his daughter, said with a sigh: 'Kitty, a woman's fate is like the seed of the rape plant. A father can only try to make a choice he hoped would be right for you, but, after all that picking, we still got one like him. Your papa's love for you turned out to be your undoing. It is your destiny. Your old father is over 70, and will look after you in his remaining years. Your husband is not like your father. There's no way he'll spoil you as your father did.'

When we got back home, Papa had already left. Mama held me in her arms and said to Keke, sobbing broken-heartedly, 'My silly boy, do you really think your mama has no place to go? Your mama has one foot inside the door and one foot outside. She cannot take the step because of you children.'

Situations like this, with mother and children crying in each other's arms, often happened in our younger days. In those days maybe we only wailed from panic and fear, when we saw her crying. Could we understand how a woman felt, sobbing away in a corridor, holding two young children in her arms during the twilight hours of the day?

The year after Titi, my kid brother, was born, our grandfather, who had been sickly for a long time, passed away. Mama practically crawled back to her father's house all the way from the bus station, wailing as she did so. On the day of the funeral, Father took the three of us and tottered around among the relatives in a state of stupor. Mother cried her heart out. I was used to her crying, but that time she did not cry in the same way as she did after a fight with Father. It was a soulful wail as if she had lost her only support in the whole wide world, and even Grandfather's several widows had to come over and comfort her.

Father wore the mourning of a son-in-law, but seemed absent-minded in contrast to Mother, who sprawled out mourning on the floor. He also had no patience with us. When Titi would not stop crying he cursed him with a few choice four-letter words. I followed him around timidly the whole day. Sometimes he walked too fast, and I did not dare tug at his trousers to slow him down. Later it often came to me that in those days Papa did not belong to us. He was all for himself. He tried to live the good life of a bachelor, which he missed, but he was the father of three. Maybe many times he forgot that he was.

But didn't he sometimes think of us? In those days when he was rushing about and seldom at home, he, to my surprise, brought me a big doll with fluttering eyes. When he beckoned with that golden-haired doll and bade me to go to him, I could only stand at a distance, watching a big man who was a stranger. I was full of fears and doubts. The expression on his face then must have been sympathetic, otherwise how could I remember, after so many years, how patiently he coaxed his startled young daughter to accept his generous gift in that old tile-roofed house in the country?

When I was six I attended the free kindergarten run by the factory for family of staff and workers, and I had to take Titi along. He attended the lower class, and I the upper class. At home I helped my mother to do chores like washing the rice before cooking, wiping all the *tatami* floor mats, or playing with the hateful Titi. On rare occasions my mother would look at me and say, 'Ah-hui is a good girl. Children from hard-up families are more mature. Who else can help your ill-fated mother but you? Your older brother is a boy. He plays all day long and is not the least aware of the suffering of his mother.'

Actually I was very envious of Keke. I thought he had a happier childhood. At least he was able to stay out of the house and play all kinds of games with his friends day in and day out. He had no patience with Titi, the cry baby. He hit him when he cried, so Mother never asked him to look after Titi. What's more, when Papa and Mama fought, he was either out frolicking or so soundly asleep he could not be disturbed. I was always the timid one: I could not let go; I could not leave mama and Titi behind; I could not be like other village kids frolicking around in the orchard or the planting field as if I had no worries and no cares.

Keke seemed to have no fear of Papa. Honestly, I think he came from the same kingdom as Papa. When Papa came home he usually brought him popular magazines like *Oriental Youth* and *School Chums*. He was king among the village kids; they all played up to him just because he lent those magazines out. One time Mother hit him. He cried and said, 'You hit me! I'm going to tell Papa to beat you up!' Mother hit him harder and cursed him between breaths, 'you short-lived, unfilial son. I carried you for ten months and gave birth to you, and you have the nerve to say you would tell your shameless father to beat me up. I'll kill you first.' As she hit him again and again she started to wail.

When I was seven I went barefoot to the only elementary school in the village. I was not the only barefoot child in my class, so I was not especially concerned, but in the second term I was elected class president, and was embarrassed to stand barefoot at the front of our class line-up. Besides, all the other barefoot children were from farming families. I went home and told

Mother, 'The teacher said Papa is a mechanical engineer. We are not poor, and I ought to be given a pair of shoes. She also said it's dangerous to cross the irrigation ditches unshod. There are water snakes and plants that could hurt a person.'

Mother said nothing. That night, after supper, after she put my one-year-old sister Meimei to sleep, she told me to put my feet on a cardboard where she traced their size and shape with a pencil. She then picked up a package wrapped in purple cloth and said, 'Ah-hui, Mama is going to Taichung. You go to bed. When Mama comes back she will have a pair of cotton shoes for you.'

I pointed at the wrap and asked her, 'What's that?'

'Something your grandpa gave Mama. Mama is going to sell it and buy you shoes.'

That evening I tried to stay up in anticipation, half of me wanting to believe her, half in doubt. I struggled hard to keep my eyes open, listening for passing buses on the only highway through the village. Finally I dozed off into a fitful sleep.

When I woke up the next morning there was a pair of maroon shoes beside my pillow. I put them on proudly and walked back and forth on the tatami mats. What was more exciting was that breakfast was not the usual gruel but a piece of red bean paste bread from the store Yi Fu Tang. I ate it slowly, peeling off small pieces of the outside layers until there was only the small center ball of red bean paste left. Then I ate it lingeringly.

After that day, Mama regularly took things out of her trunk and went to Taichung in the evening. The next day each of us would always have a piece of red bean bread, and tasty dishes would appear on the dinner table for a few days. Mama never failed to take opportunities such as these to lecture me.

'Ah-hui, you're a girl. You'll have to manage a household in the future. Mama will give you a few pointers. Go to the market place at noontime when the peddlers are about to call it a day. That's when you can get things cheap. If you're luckier than I, then good, otherwise you'll have to know how to get along.'

Gradually, Father came home more often; still he regularly went to Taichung after work. He'd come home and tidy up and leave. He still screamed at Mama at the top of his voice in our two-room apartment, loudly and rudely. They had no patience with each other. In those years it was a luxury to have them converse quietly and softly. They had been raising the roof for such a long time, it was often hard to tell whether they were quarreling or not, but the picture of Father's furious face, the sound of Mother's shrill voice, and a picture of him throwing her to the floor, punching and kicking her, appeared before our eyes again and again.

So days crept by slowly. Once, Mother took a look at Papa's pay envelope, threw it on the tatami floor right then and there, and cursed in a loud voice, 'You shameless four-legged beast! What else are you good for besides keeping that whore! If your four kids had to depend on you, they would have starved to death already. A salary of over a thousand dollars and only two hundred dollars is left! How can I feed the four of them with that? When you're messing with your cheap woman, did you ever think of your children who are about to die of starvation? What a disgrace! Supporting another's wife! Are those brats of hers yours? Don't tell me that these four are not.'

They cursed each other. My younger brother and sister and I made ourselves small in a corner. Suddenly Papa got hold of the meat cleaver and threw it at Mama. The cutting edge landed on Mama's ankle. For a split second nothing happened, then bright red blood started to gush out, looking like countless poisonous snakes crawling on Mama's white foot. I cried out in fear. My brother and sister started to too. Papa took one look at the three of us and left the room furious, slamming the door behind him. Mama did not cry. She looked around for cigarette butts, opened them up, threw away the wrapper, and put the tobacco to the wound to stop it bleeding.

That night I felt very cold. I kept dreaming of Mama all covered with blood. I cried and screamed, and promised to avenge her.

When I got to second grade, I still stood at the top of my class, and was named model student. My classmate Ah-chuan, who also lived in our village, told classmates, 'Li Jen-hui's father is a bad man. He's the lover of a woman in our village. So can she be a model student?'

I took off the button given to model students and hid it in my school bag. I did not wear it again that term, and I never spoke to Ah-chung again after that. I still wore my maroon-coloured cloth shoes, now gaping open at the toes, and I still went through the rice paddies on my way to school, swinging a rice stalk in my hand. But, oh, how I wished I could leave this place, here there were a bad woman and a schoolmate who bad-mouthed me behind my back. Surely, there must be some place where no one knew about Papa; and I would take Mama there with me.

One night I was awakened by strange sounds. I opened my eyes and heard the terrible noise of a raging storm blowing against the roof tiles, and, from beyond the bamboo fence, the rain rattling in the branches and trees. Beside me, Keke, Titi and Meimei were sleeping soundly. I heard Mama calling me in the dark in a little voice. I crawled over Keke, Titi and Meimei and knelt beside her. With great effort she said, 'Ah-hui, the baby in Mama's tummy is dead and I can't stop bleeding. Go get Aunt Chen and Aunt Fu to come and help. Can you do it? I tried to wake up your older brother, but he's so fast asleep I can't wake him.'

Mama's face was icy cold. She told me to get her another deck of toilet paper. I scrambled up, suddenly afraid that Mama was going to die. I said to her in a loud voice, 'Mama, you mustn't die. I'll go get them, but you've got to wait for me.'

I threw on a raincoat and went out barefoot. The eucalyptuses swaying back and forth sounded like witches laughing all over the village. When I came to the winnowing ground, I suppressed Ah-chuan's stories of ghosts and dashed across it. I stumbled and was sure the ghosts were after me. Picking myself up I ran on. The raindrops hitting my eyes hurt so much I couldn't keep them open. I stumbled on with all my might. Aunt Fu told me to go to the Chens and ask Aunt Chen to go back with me and help while Aunt Fu went for the doctor.

Then I ran through the other half of the village to the Chens' home. There I ran headlong into the bamboo fence and their big dog barked at me furiously from its cage. Aunt Chen waited until I finished my message, picked up a flashlight, put on her raincoat and followed me out.

'Poor, poor soul! Your dad is not home?'

I shook my head, and she looked at me and shook hers too. Walking beside her all of a sudden I felt drained. I almost didn't make it back home.

After the doctor left, Mama finally fell into a deep sleep, Aunt Chen said: 'Poor, ill-fated soul! What bad luck to be married to such a man! If it hadn't been for an eight-year-old girl, it would have been the end of her today.' Then she added, 'I wonder who that lousy husband is going after now?'

I knelt beside Mama and touched her face with my hand to make sure that she was only sleeping. Aunt Fu took my hand away and said, 'Ah-hui, your mother is all right. Go to sleep. I'll watch over her, don't worry.'

Mama's face was ashen. I refused to go to the inside room to sleep but stubbornly sprawled beside her and stared at her. Somehow, however, I fell asleep.

That year on New Year's Eve, the traditional steamed cake was already made. Mama, grumbling regretfully that the cake had not risen as much as it should (thus indicating there was no hope of prosperity in the coming year) muttered softly to herself as she sharpened a knife to kill the cock we had reared for more than a year just for this occasion. Just then four or five big guys came by. Father paled as he was summoned. They did not come into the house but sat by the door. They neither touched the tea Mama offered nor paid any attention to Mama's polite conversation. They just kept pressing Papa with questions.

'You're an educated person. How can you do such an awful thing?'

'How can you sleep with someone else's wife? What about ordinary decency?'

'Whoever does this should have the tendons of his feet cut.'

While those men cursed away angrily, Papa stayed to one side, head lowered. Mama too sat on the other side, her eyes red, muttering all the while to herself.

This went on the whole morning. I stayed in the backyard watching the big cock. He stood on his two strong legs and shook his long neck as he pecked at a shorter chicken. Well, he probably would not be killed today—Mama would have at least given me a fat chicken wing, but now. . . . Very regretfully I turned to look at a flock of turkeys that would not be ready for slaughtering until the Ghost Festival on the fifteenth of the seventh moon next year at the earliest. Also, it was New Year's Eve, but we would be eating neither chicken nor rice noodles, and the chance of our getting new clothes or new shoes was even more remote. When would those rude and crude people be leaving?

My unruly younger brother, Titi, began to sob. I was too hungry to bother with him. Besides, I felt like crying myself, so I stayed put. He started to holler. Keke covered his mouth with his hand, and Titi hollered even louder. Keke slapped him, which only resulted in Titi letting himself go and crying with all his might. This scared Meimei, who had been lying there quietly and she started crying too. Mama came and slapped Keke really hard and said to me angrily, 'Ah-hui, are you dead?' So I had to climb onto the tatami mats and pick up Meimei. I in turn cursed our unruly Titi, 'Are you dead, Ah-hsin?' What kind of New Year's celebration was this?

While we were making this ruckus the men stood up, and the leader among them said: 'Two thousand dollars would be a mere opener considering the magnitude of this shameful affair. We would not have let you off so easily today if it hadn't been for your four children, who also have a New Year's Eve to celebrate. This affair should be ended with a certain grace. Tonight at seven o'clock we'll be waiting for you at my house. Don't forget to set off a string of firecrackers. If you're not on time, I'm afraid it won't be pleasant for you.'

Papa and Mama knelt by the door watching them leave. Mama turned into the house and walked straight to the kitchen. She picked up the freshly steamed New Year's cake and started to slice it. Papa stayed by the door for a while, then he timidly followed her into the kitchen and said, 'The money for tonight—I have to have it somehow.'

Mama's words came out like rushing water as she screamed back, 'Have to have it? It was your doing; you end it! You slept with the woman; you try to find the money to cover up your shame. You and your shameless lust! Does it matter if our children are starving to death? Are you a man or mouse?'

There was no stopping Mama once she started. She cursed him and cried and cursed some more. She took a long time slicing the soft cake, but she was not putting the slices into a pan. The stove door was still covered by a rag. If she did not uncover it soon the fire would not be hot enough for cooking, but she was so mad that I didn't dare remind her of it.

At long last, the cake was fried. Mama then went through her trunk and searched for a long time. Red-eyed, she wrapped up a large bundle with a piece of cloth. Papa brought out his new-bought 20-inch Philips bicycle and was waiting for Mama at the door. Mama told Keke and me, 'Ah-chiang, Ah-hui, Mama is going to sell some stuff and pawn the bicycle to pay those people. You two older ones have to look after the younger ones. If you're hungry you can have some of the cake. When Mama comes back, Mama will cook for you. Be good. Do you hear?'

I gazed after them as they left. I wanted to ask, but dared not, if the cock would be killed. I could only ask Keke, 'What does "pawn" mean?'

'Stupid! It means to sell. To sell something for money. That's what it means. Don't you even understand that?'

Papa and Mama came back very late. The cock, of course, was spared. We had salted gruel that evening. We did not go through the usual worship ceremony, so, of course, there were no special things to eat. Sooner or later that cock would meet its fate. It would be killed. So thinking I fell asleep with a ray of hope in spite of disappointment at not getting any New Year's Eve money.

After school started, Mama went there to get a transfer for Keke and me. We were going to leave this place. I was so happy that I forgot my vow and ran up to Ah-chuan and said to him bluntly, 'We're moving to Taipei.'

The startled and stupid look on his face pleased me no end. I ran away thinking to myself: why, he's nothing but a small boy who likes to bad-mouth others.

We moved to Taipei and rented a house from my aunt Tsui-hung. Mama kept the big chickens and the native chickens near the water pump, and she also bought some American broilers. It was said that this kind of fowl grew fast, and would start to lay eggs in four months. Soon we would be eating exorbitantly expensive eggs without having to use any money at all.

Papa bought a second-hand bicycle and rode it back and forth to work. He got home early those days. An easel was set up in the living room. When he had time he often put on his shorts and started to paint, using many different colours. Our neighbours sometimes asked for his paintings. He got carried away and painted more and more. Although Mama did not tell him not to paint; she usually commented contemptuously, 'What good is it? It won't bring in money for food.' Sometimes when she was in a foul mood she'd say: 'Other husbands think of ways to make money to bring food to the table so that their wives and children can lead good lives. Your father only brings his monthly salary which isn't enough to make ends meet.'

Be that as it may, I was happy to see Papa home regularly. Furthermore, he fought less with Mama. He seldom talked to me. I thought he probably did not know how to. I had always, since infancy, watched him from a distance, but he often took Titi by the hand and, carrying Meimei using his other arm, he would buy the kind of steamed cake that cost ten cents a piece, and he never failed to bring back one each for Keke and me.

Keke and I both attended elementary school across the bridge; he in the fifth grade, I in the third. In those days intensive tutoring started in the third grade. Some five or six in my class had no intention of entering junior high, and they had to help the teacher with odd jobs. The rest, who had to take a city-wide examination, all took part in the intensive tutoring programme, because many important subjects were covered only in the tutorial sessions.

After our transfer I realized that the teachers in Taipei based their assignments on reference books. In the country we had never even heard the term 'reference books'. They cost over ten dollars each. Keke was in a higher grade and closer to taking the city-wide examination, so he needed several such books each term. We could not afford to buy all that were needed, so Mama made the decision that his were given priority. Therefore, for three or four weeks in a row, my teacher lashed the palm of my hand with a thick strip of rattan because I had not done my homework. Did the teacher think this kid from a rural district was beyond help?

At the end of every month our teacher would announce, 'Tutorial fees are due tomorrow.' The next day I would watch some 60 school mates lining up to pay. The going price then was 30 dollars a month. The rich students paid one or two hundred. I sat there shamefaced, watching the impressive line disperse, then I had to brace myself and sit through our teacher's loudly announcing the names of those who had not paid. For a week or two following this, fewer names would be called every day until finally mine was the only one. I couldn't take it any more, so I tried to discuss it with Mama: 'I don't want to be tutored any more.'

'Isn't it true that many subjects are covered only in these tutorial sessions?'

I nodded and said, 'I don't really have to take the examinations for junior high school.'

'You want to live the kind of life your Mama's leading?' Mama pulled a long face and lectured me sternly: 'A woman with no skills has to depend on her husband for a living. If she marries well, then it's her good fortune, so be it. If she marries an irresponsible man, what's she going to do for food? Eat sand? Your mama is not exactly unschooled. I even went to Japan for a few years of schooling. Didn't I have a good life when I was young? But I married and had children, and it finished me. I didn't go out to work, and the second half of my life is worse than others.'

'But,' said I haltingly, fingering the corner of my skirt, 'because I don't pay the tutorial fee, my name is called every day, and they all turn and look at me as if I were a freak.'

'In a couple of days I'll try to manage it. Mama will get twenty dollars.'

'All the others pay thirty; that's the minimum.'

'Be happy we can pay twenty. Ten dollars short can't be helped. So we are poor!'

Payment of monthly tutorial fees was met in this dragged-out manner. Often, no sooner had I paid one month's expense than the others would begin to pay for the next month. The shame I had to suffer having my name announced in class and for the sidelong looks of my fellow students was compensated by the honour of always getting the highest marks in the monthly examination.

The next year Keke was 1.5 points short and had to go to the school of his second choice. It was regrettable, but I think Mama was pleased nonetheless. He was her first-born. For a child from the country who had nothing to do with tutoring and reference books until the second term of his fifth grade to squeeze through the narrow portals of a provincial junior high school, was something that made even our ever lukewarm Papa, who never bothered with his children, happy. However, in order to raise money for Keke's tuition, which was over two hundred dollars, and to manage the additional expenses for uniforms, Mama was really squeezed. Papa buried his head like an ostrich as if all this had nothing to do with him. Mama could scream all she wanted pacing in and out of the house, calling him 'useless' at the top of her voice for the thousandth time, and he would still stay in his corner painting his pictures as if nothing had happened.

In those years Mama got up at the crack of dawn to start a fire outdoors. She first used a few sheets of paper from our old exercise books, on top of which she then piled a few pieces of thinly sliced kindling and finally some briquettes. When we got up there would be two bowls of freshly cooked rice waiting for us. In Keke's bowl there were two eggs; in mine, only one.

Mama's explanation for this discrepancy was that Keke was a boy; he was growing; he ate more rice, therefore he had an extra egg.

Once I ate only the part of the rice that was mixed with egg and refused to eat the little bit of plain rice left in the bowl. Mama scolded me, 'What a waste, Ah-hui! Do you know how much a catty of rice costs?'

'Why can't I have two eggs?' I muttered. 'I clean the chicken droppings every night. Keke never had to take care of them.'

Mama was taken aback. After a long pause she said, 'Why are you haggling? A woman's fate is like the seed of the rape plant: it grows where it falls. The good fortune of a woman before she is married doesn't count. Mama was fair. Poor as we are I let you go to school. In another family you would have been sent away to work as a housemaid long ago. Your older brother will have to carry on the Li family line. Why are you bargaining over him? Who knows what name you're going to take later on?'

Mama lowered her voice gradually, picked up the dishes and went back in.

After that I learned to eat my bowl of rice with its one egg wordlessly, and I no longer complained about too many chores after my tutorial session: Keke could swim all he wanted or play basketball, and he didn't even have to do dishes.

I had a lot of homework in the two years before the city-wide examination. In school I dutifully did all my work, but after school I did only my homework; I no longer dug into my other books. When I recalled how the household turned topsy-turvy over the registration fee, and how Mama had to struggle to meet household expenses and Keke's tuition, I decided deep down in my heart that if I did not pass, I would simply quit school.

In the sixth grade I entered a school-wide art competition and won first prize—a box of 24 water-colours and two brushes. I showed them at home, extremely pleased with myself. Mother, who was in the middle of doing dishes, rolled her eyes and said angrily, 'Do you think that's great? You'll be like your good-for-nothing Papa, paint, and paint and paint. Did all that painting make any money? Give up this art business right away.'

I never thought Mama would get so mad or that I would be the object of her scorn. The prize, though something I could never afford, turned sour. After that, I never talked about it when I entered composition competitions or poster competitions. In those days, when I came home with my report cards, Mama would look at them and put her seal on them. She never asked why I dropped to the second place in my class that month, nor did she utter any encouragement when I was back on top. I thought, so what if I do well or poorly! No one cared. That being the case, I no longer took extra tutorial sessions in the evening, but I still remained one of the top three in my class.

The day results of the city-wide examination for junior high were made known, Mama woke me up from my afternoon nap and snapped, 'Did you die in your sleep? The radio has been announcing the results all afternoon. Bet you didn't pass. Then see if you can still sleep like a pig.'

I rolled out of bed and stood by our neighbour's door to listen to the broadcast. I stood there so long I thought my legs were going to break. They were still announcing the names of boys. I didn't dare go home nor had I any idea how long I had to wait. While I was hesitating I saw Papa coming back on his bicycle. He yelled happily before he reached our door, 'You passed! You passed!'

Mama came out from the house and said anxiously but angrily, 'Of course she passed. The question is which school.'

'Her first choice! I knew it would be her first choice!' Papa parked his bicycle and gestured for me to go to him, eyebrows raised and face flushed. 'The list was already published in the paper. Do you want to keep listening anyway?'

Those were probably my best, most glorious days. Father, who seldom dwelt on things concerning me, was inexplicably happy. He told people repeatedly, 'She scored quite a few points above the admission score. Got 25 points for composition, a real high score.'

Was mama also pleased? She never told anybody and kept busy as always. I was not spared any chores as a result of the examinations.

It was at this time that Papa got some side jobs doing mechanical drawings. He did not negotiate with the people about payment. Mama blamed him for not knowing how to haggle, and he would reply, very sure of himself, 'It won't happen! It won't happen! They won't short change us.' As it turned out, after burning the midnight oil for a few nights, he was completely taken aback by the meager sum they paid him. After that he was no longer enthusiastic about that kind of job. Papa took a day off on registration day and took me to school on his bicycle. We had to spend the entire morning lining up in the auditorium, going to one desk after another. I did not know what had happened to Papa, but he seemed unable to stop talking to other parents on the line. The conversation was about how many points the other children scored, or which elementary school they were from. Whenever he found some one with grades lower than mine, he was pleased beyond description and would say, 'See! Quite a few points lower; almost had to take second choice.' When I was being measured for my uniform, he became even more excited and said repeatedly, 'In all Taipei only your school issues this kind of uniform.'

That day, Papa treated me to a bowl of beef noodles for lunch and gave me five dollars. He said, 'Don't tell your old mom about it. We'll charge this against registration fees.'

I felt guilty deceiving my extremely frugal mama, but when I thought of Papa, who had always been hard up, and who now at long last had an opportunity to show his daughter a sincere, childlike concern, I had to keep my peace.

After school started, Papa became more interested in my studies than I was. Whenever I picked my English textbook, he would say, in high spirits, 'Come! Papa will help you.' He would pick up the textbook and read on and on, in a Japanese accent, unmindful of anything else, until Mama gave it to him, 'Crazy! The girl is studying, and you're disturbing her. She has an exam tomorrow morning. Don't you know that?'

Father was most interested in helping me with my homework during junior high school years. His favorite statements those days were, 'Ah-hui is like me,' or 'Ah-hui's calligraphy is beautiful, like mine.' The gist of it was that anything good about me I got from him. Mama would always mercilessly pour cold water: 'Heaven forbid! Worst fate if she is like you!'

Papa probably was quite happy with himself during those years. He often gave me a couple of coins when no one was looking and indicated that I should not mention it to anybody. I saw him hide a few dollars clumsily in his shoe, and predicted they would be discovered by Mama. They were. From then on he began hiding money all over, in places he thought were safe. Perhaps he was in too much of a hurry when he hid them, or maybe he moved them around so often he would forget where they were, but later when he looked for them he couldn't find them. He would end up sweating profusely and, braving the danger of Mama's scorn, would have to ask her help. The end result was we all had to help him look, or it would cause another loud quarrel. At any rate his private savings would automatically go to the treasury. I was well aware that he always held back some money for himself to buy a pack of cigarettes or to hand out a few dimes secretly to us kids, but I never could bring myself to tell Mama. Was it because he was so disingenuous? Was it because I realized that no one should have designs on such a naïve person? I kept quiet.

He might have been able to manage a continuous flow of petty cash, but registration time was always an embarrassing time for father. When pressed, Mama told us to ask Papa for money. His usual answer was, 'Ask your old Mama.'

'Mama told us to ask you.'

'Where can I get money? I give her all my salary, and I don't know how to turn things into gold.'

If we pressed further, he would lose his temper and say, 'Quit school then, since there's no money.'

The frustration was repeated time and again. It made us feel that Father was a caged beast who could find no way out. He was a free soul, fit only to lead a carefree life by himself. To burden him with the responsibility of being the head of a household only made him look inadequate. He had married too young. It was the same with our mama whose dreams were shattered too early in life. Each of them cherished his or her own wild dreams; neither knew how to deal with the crude realities of married life.

The years went by, with members of the family at times submitting to fate, at times rebelling noisily against it. Mama was pregnant again at 37 with my youngest brother, Hsiao-ti. Every day she would waddle all around the house with her protruding silhouette and a heavy heart, either squatting under the faucet doing the laundry or taking care of something. Just before the baby was born, I brought out my piggy-bank (which contained two years' savings) from where it was hidden under my bed. I handed the bank to Mama silently. She gave me our rusty axe and said, 'The money is yours. You break it yourself.'

Even before she could finish speaking, she started crying. With one stroke I broke the bank, dimes flew all over the floor: there went my young dream of joining a hiking trip along the East-West Cross-Island Highway. Afterwards mother and daughter sat opposite one another in a dark corner in the kitchen silently stacking dimes: one, two. . . . Why was life like that?

After graduation from junior high, I passed entrance examinations to both the senior high school and the normal school for girls. Mother insisted I go to normal school.

'It's free,' she said. 'Besides, what's the point of a girl getting so much schooling? It's not as if you were planning to remain an old maid. A nice, reliable job ought to be good enough for you.'

I don't know whether it was because that was the first time I had ever opposed my mother and held firm to my own opinion, or because, starting that year, Father was hired for work in the Philippines and earned a salary much greater than before. In any event, Mother eventually agreed to allow me to continue on to senior high.

Those years were quite the opposite of the bad years past. The days seemed to slip by smoothly and quickly. Father was far away in a foreign land, and he kept part of his salary to enable him to once again live the satisfying life of a bachelor. Being separated by mountains and seas also seemed to have diminished the sharp conflicts between them. Every week he sent back loving words showing concern and longing. He even took pains to refer to every member of the family. Occasionally he sent us gifts by people returning from that distant land, specifying which was for whom. They were for the most part not very practical items. He also carefully wrapped up clothing he bought for us in sizes he imagined us to wear and sent them by air. All this was done by the same pair of hands that had beaten us and led us about.

Mama half the time grumbled about his unforgivable past; at other times she looked forward to his letters and gifts; always half-complaining and half-smiling in a helpless manner. But who wanted to find fault with this kind of life? We now even had money for non-essentials, and she no longer had to rack her brains to get the bare necessities of life.

When I passed the entrance exams and was admitted to college (for this Mama had prayed and burned a stick of incense twice a day, once in the morning and once in the evening), she looked at the report card and with the corners of her mouth drooping in a contemptuous manner, said, 'The pig does not grow fat, but the fat grows on a dog.'

This was truly a deflating statement to a girl's ego.

Then, she seemed to have forgotten her own words since she dashed about getting fresh flowers and fruit to spread on the sacrificial table. She told me to kneel down and kowtow 12 times. The clear outline of Mama's face looking solemn and kind, through the misty smoke of incense, watching me from above, looked very much like that of the Goddess of Mercy.

I remained my simpleton self. I drifted along neither fighting for, nor shying from anything. Like others, I also tutored children at their homes and started to write articles to earn my own keep. In the four more or less uneventful college years, I kind of took on the responsibilities of an older sister or mother, looking after a string of younger brothers and a sister: Mother started going to the temple religiously. She became a vegetarian and a semi-retired housewife. All worldly affairs concerning sons and daughters automatically became my inherited duty.

Father's glorious years were over. When he returned home he was long past employment age. He was able to devise jobs only because of his technical knowledge and experience, but he always found them unfulfilling. He was clearly inconsistent and changeable. Sometimes, on his way back from work when he had to change buses he would drop in at the Buddhist temple to buy an order of vegetarian noodles for Mama and show great concern urging her to eat it while it was still hot. At other times he might have a fit of temper just because she had gone to the temple to have a vegetarian meal. At such times he acted as if he would break each and every one of the idols on the sacrificial table. Sometimes he could be very patient and explain to Mother, sentence by sentence, foreign, or Mandarin, language movies on television. At other times he would ridicule her for not even knowing how to take a bus or to manage basic Mandarin. Mother still talked the way you chop kindling—splitting the wood with one sweep of the axe mercilessly and uncompromisingly. Time and again she numbered our father's misdeeds in great detail. Father, on the other hand, showed that he was most unhappy with the fact that Mother could not find a job and share his burden. One was now an old man whose back was bent, whose hair was whitening, and whose teeth were loose. The other was a housewife who had spent 30 years making ends meet; an old woman whose hair had turned gray and whose sight was failing. Yet the frequency and intensity of their rows were still as bad as they had been in their younger days. After 30 years of a hard life, after all the years of getting at one another, they still had not learned to live together without rancor. Hadn't they paid a price for all this? And all those hurts, were they injuries that could not be compensated for?

In those days Keke was unwilling to follow in Father's footsteps and look for a salaried job. He tried to set up his own business from scratch. It bled him dry, and he had no time for the family. That responsibility automatically fell on my shoulders. For a few years after my graduation, I was able to earn a fairly good salary, earned by blood and sweat. Maybe I was lucky; maybe I was driven by a stubborn desire to want to make something of the family. At any rate, I worked hard and moonlighted, holding other jobs. I made quite a bit of money through the years. Suddenly home began to look a lot different.

After making my way for a few years, I, who had always been placid, now displayed an excitable characteristic. In a business where the hens fought to crow the loudest, I was sometimes unable to fend for myself. The kind of life I lived before, drifting effortlessly as fate dictated, now seemed far, far away.

Mother had changed too. Maybe she was only reverting to her old self before her marriage, maybe she was trying to recover from 30 anemic years, but she became very demanding, very hard to please. The difference between now and then could even be been in the way she dressed. In the old days, in order that her children could have what they needed, she went unkempt, her face unwashed, and she never had a new dress from one year to another. She had even been mistaken for the kitchen maid. Now, whenever I went shopping with her she chose only Swiss or Japanese imported material. The kind I picked to have dresses made to wear for work every day was often too ordinary for her. After a few such shopping sprees, I became a favoured customer. When the stores got in new merchandise they never failed to call me at my office. I did what I could, and assumed I had boundless energy and that money spent, will somehow come back again. Besides, I felt Mama had gone through a lot in the past. Would it be possible for her to have another 30 years? If I could do something about it, why should I be stingy? So, season after season, I would carry large rolls of money and pay generously for her selections.

Mama could not go shopping by herself, so I shopped for her and for things like shirts, pants, sweaters and vests for Father. I had to guess the size. Mama now considered herself somewhat above worldly cares. She had long ago relinquished her control over miscellaneous practical matters, but she was never able to shake off such worldly sentiments as love and hate, or anger and scorn. Therefore, each time I bought a dress for myself I remembered to buy one for Meimei. I was quite a housewife in those days. Not only did I look after everyday matters like clothing, food, living and transportation expenses, but like an old biddy I coerced my younger brothers and sister to take all sorts of lessons after school. I feared they would grow up like me—good at nothing but school work; too cautious and dull. I even worried that they might not able to master a skill, and so urged them to learn more in other fields. Was it because in my day I was never able to get anything I wanted, and because I had missed too much? Now when I could afford what I wanted, I fastened my concerns on my sister and brothers like a fearful old mother hen. Come to think of it, deep down in me, didn't I have the same fears as Mama? Since that's the way I was those days, all I could think of was making money.

As for Mother, I don't know whether poverty had given her a permanent fear or whether she had reached such a mental state of greediness that she constantly complained to me about being poor. Sometimes she praised the children of our friends and spiced it up by pointing out how able and filial they were. Reading between the lines I was most deficient in every way.

A few years back I underwent unexpected major surgery and was bedridden for 40 days. My surgical expenses were paid by friends. Only then, when neither body nor soul was at my command, did I realize what a dreadful thing it was not to have any savings. At that point I joined a *hui*[1] at my company behind Mother's back. She shrewdly suspected it, however, and tried her best to find out more. She was most unhappy about my secret savings. At that time her own private savings amounted to hundreds of thousands. She didn't keep it in a savings bank but locked it up in her cabinet. She worshipped money. Should anyone in the family (with the exception of Keke) ask her for money, he or she would instantly get a sharp scolding. In the end, she would give, but less than asked for. Sometimes she would even throw the money into the far corner of the room for the petitioner to pick up.

Gradually her temper worsened as our family condition improved. Any one of us, young or old, could be the cause of her displeasure. She would curse us in a shrill voice, pursuing us from the room. Sometimes she was completely unreasonable.

[1] *Hui* is a form of insurance: a group collects money from its members at regular intervals; any member in need may enter a bid, and whoever pays the highest interest gets the sum.

The younger ones were likely to argue with her after she uttered two or three words. The quarrel once started, Mother would weep and bemoan her fate, tears rolling down her face and nose running. If anyone of us went against her, she would go back and enumerate each sin that each member of the family had ever committed. Not one of us was spared: this would go on for days. I really dreaded the way she would go on day and night, night and day, so in defense I would rail at whoever went against her. I had also learned to let her words all go in one ear and out the other, and never talked back. My brothers and sister accused me of spoiling her, and made fun of me, saying that I was 'stupidly filial' which made them look unfilial by comparison. However, considering all that had happened in the past, why not let her have her way now? We all owed her at least that much.

In those ten years she disapproved of all the people I associated with. Often she was rude to them over the phone, and sometimes kept visitors waiting outside in the rain. On the rare occasions when I came home late she would not let anyone open the door for me. She made me stand in the pitch dark alley listening to her obscene cursing drifting down from the fourth floor apartment—and I was already a twenty-year-old adult. But I'm sure she loved me in spite of her ways. When any of the others went against her she would suddenly remember that only this one daughter understood what she had gone through. Even though I seldom ate at home, when she went shopping for food she invariably remembered to buy kidneys for me. Many nights when I was exhausted and ready to drop off she would walk into my room to chat about this and that. At such times I seemed to see the face of that loving mother, bearing a resemblance to the very Goddess of Mercy, who looked down upon me as I lit incense and kowtowed after passing my college entrance examinations.

I wasn't actually following her anti-matrimony suggestions during those years. There was simply no-one to rouse my interest. I was just exhausted. All I wanted was to hide in a world where there were no quarrels, no hatred, and where I didn't have to break my neck getting ahead. Mother again and again cited examples of marriage failures among friends and relatives as warnings. She was most emphatic about incompatibility between Father and her who got along like fire and water. She said, 'Not to get married is not necessarily a misfortune. A girl's fate is like that of the seed of the rape plant: if the marriage does not work she will be stuck with it the rest of her life. This is the way with your mama. Look at you now. You dress nicely and go to work every day, and there's no need for you to wait on anybody. Now, what's wrong with that? Why should you want to get married?'

After 30 years of tears, Mother was anchored in a well of nameless fear. In her twilight years she became a devout Buddhist to curry favour with fate, but still things did not go as she would have liked. Everything irritated her: my brothers' careers, the friends they kept, their marriages. More than anything else, none of her three sons stayed with her; the sons whom she expected to continue the family line. They left home because they could not stand the atmosphere. As far as she was concerned, a daughter was only a daughter no matter how good. Only sons could keep the Li family incense burning. She had no praise and no respect for marriage.

Unfortunately it was just at this time I made my decision about marriage. To my surprise, however, she did not object strenuously. Maybe she was tired, or maybe it was because of my insistence. But when she finally nodded feebly as if she had no alternative, even I suffered a feeling of regret. When the final decision was made she iterated time and again, 'For better or for worse, it's your fate. You made the choice yourself.'

The wedding ceremony was hastily arranged. I didn't really care about the ritual formalities. However, when Mother showed the fortune-teller our *pa-tzu*, the eight characters denoting our time of birth, the year, the month, the day and hour, she found that the wedding date clashed with her horoscope. She could not personally see me off and she deeply regretted that.

'The Goddess of Brides rules supreme. I must stay away. I brought this girl up yet someone else will see her in her wedding gown. I raised a good daughter and can't even see her out of our door. I wonder if it was all worthwhile?'

The fact that my mother could not send me off in my white veil saddened me even more than Mother. She had sheltered me under her wing through difficult decades and made me what I was. She should be seeing me off personally no matter what. In my opinion, supreme though the Goddess of the Brides might be, she could not possibly outweigh a mother. Mother, however, persisted in her belief.

On the eve of my wedding, I put on my wedding dress for Mother alone. She stooped down on the floor of the apartment where we had lived for over ten years, feeling the white veil on the floor with her hand while looking up at this seed of a rape plant which was about to fall on an uncertain field.

I touched her graying hair with my long-gloved hand. She looked so helpless in the mirror; so old and feeble, as if she was unable to negotiate the distance to see where this rape seed was going to land. I fell down on my knees. For the first time in my life I held her in my arms, with her face pressed against my white-veiled breast. I wanted very much to tell her that I would be happy, that she could put her heart at ease, but when I looked at that face reflecting the countless sorrows of years past and saw how it had aged, I could only cry, 'Mama, Mama.'

Old Love

Su Wei-chen

translated by Susan So

HE did not fly home the day Tien-ch'ing was buried. Receiving the news, he set out wine and fruit on the terrace and, with only the sky as witness, lifted his glass to her memory.

That night, drinking alone, he got thoroughly drunk. In his dreams, he was not an alien in a foreign land. His drunken body seemed to be adrift in mid-air, and though he was not tied down, he was struggling to free himself; there was nothing for him to hold on to. He was not sure whether there had been tears or not.

The next day, he wasn't able to wake up from the night before. The pain he thought would go away after a time had become a heaviness he could not shake, pulling him ever deeper into uneasiness. At first he thought—it will pass and then things will be all right.

Closing in and backing off, not quite to the extent of an obsession, this that is weighing on him—is it enough to be called 'the past' or even 'that which will not pass?' He did return home while Tien-ch'ing was laid up in the hospital, but did he in fact obtain her consent? By then, Tien-ch'ing had unburdened herself of everything. She was resting quietly, watching and waiting for the conclusion to her destiny. She was in the habit of expressing herself; in everything one could see her independent nature. In actual fact, they had reached an understanding in their hearts. To them, appearances were at odds with reality.

There should be a certain process in one's life. Any period that is 'speeded up' or 'slowed down' could be called abnormal. A life drawn out or foreshortened is equally difficult for the imagination to cope with.

And then again, how long should one live? No matter what, it shouldn't be as brief as 34 years. Everything begun. All left unfulfilled.

Fortunately, the period Tien-ch'ing took to die he could say was peaceful, calm, and quick. Just as everyone was beginning to wonder how much longer was left to her, she, quite appropriately, left. What she herself was thinking, nobody knew. Not a hint—the way it had always been.

It had crossed his mind, the thought of their married life and how it would be. Would the days have been rational and calm, the way they had been before? At least that was the impression they had given to others.

Life is probably just that way. You can't say 'there's time' or 'there's no time', and even if you could, there'd be just as many regrets.

He said to himself: Feng Tzu-kang, it's about time you saw to your arthritis.

The western sun's shadow grew long, foretelling the long night, the long winter. Same old days, that's all. These were not difficult days, just a bit difficult to get through.

The Ch'eng family had one son and two daughters. The first born was left to stay with his grandmother on the mainland. Tien-lan was the youngest, six whole years younger than Tien-ch'ing. Tien-ch'ing was a mere toddler when her father left with the army for Taiwan; he was later joined by their mother. Tien-lan had never seen her brother, not even a photograph. This family had always been incomplete. When their mother arrived in Taiwan, her relationship with their father became, for some unknown reason, a matter of indifference to her. According to some, it began with her inability to adapt to the new environment. Whatever it was, she never recovered.

Their mother sat at home all day. She did no housework. Once in a while she'd tidy herself up and get dressed in one of her old-fashioned outfits (still made of good material) to go out—not anywhere in particular, just to go for a walk or to the movies. Tien-lan had in her memory the image of her mother walking alone down the long, long roadway of the military housing compound, turning to greet no one and being greeted by strange stares all along the way. At home, their mother was like a silent, slender lotus flower, withered after the sun came out, sitting under the green trees, afloat on the undying pond.

The first time Tien-ch'ing ran away from home, Tien-lan was still in elementary school. Coming home from school one day, she saw Tien-ch'ing trying on her dresses, one after another, not like someone about to run away from home, but rather like someone preparing to go on stage; the wrinkled clothes were spread out all over the bed. She discovered then that Tien-ch'ing's world was an adult's world, dazzlingly white and voluptuous, not at all like her own child's dream world.

'Where are you going?' she asked. Tien-ch'ing had once again put on her school uniform. Her face was a fierce white. All the mothers in the neighbourhood said that Tien-ch'ing was good-looking, that even the the merciless sun of South Taiwan had not left its mark on her. All Tien-lan knew was that when Tien-ch'ing came from night school, one of the male students would be with her. At first, they saw her to the village gates. Then, later on, they saw her all the way home to her doorstep. Their mother never saw a thing. On several occasions, their father had questioned her, but these episodes were inevitably interrupted by their mother's complaint, called out from within the house: 'Can't you people keep your voices down?' Their mother never got wind of the gossip circulating around the village.

That was how she used to watch Tien-ch'ing as she was growing up; and the watching was always from a distance. Later on, this became a habit. Theirs were two completely different worlds: their figures when they were still young and their fortunes after they grew up.

Tien-ch'ing ignored her 'where are you going?' She was lost in her own thoughts.

It was perhaps two months later that Tien-ch'ing came home. During this period, rumour had it that Tien-ch'ing had become a member of the delinquent youth gang called the 'Crape Myrtles'. Tien-lan wouldn't believe it. Tien-ch'ing was like their mother, keeping everything to herself; people can't stand that sort of person. When Tien-ch'ing disappeared again, the wagging tongues of the neighbourhood reported that she was pregnant. Tien-lan wouldn't believe that either. The family should be made up of the four— where could Tien-ch'ing have gone to? Why didn't she stay at home like the rest of them?

Father showed no signs of wanting to find her. He simply pretended it hadn't happened. At their house, night came early and dawn came later than at other homes. In fact, dawn seemed to make no difference.

The adult mind was beyond her comprehension. Not long afterwards, she saw in the papers the police calling for the gang members to voluntarily give themselves up to the authorities. The village was at once aflame with excitement. It was as if someone had struck a match and lit it up. You could see people whispering to each other in street corners, and people gathering here and there like cobwebs gathering dust. Even Mother was infected, uncharacteristically asking Father: 'Where is Tien-ch'ing?' 'Gone off to Taipei to study,' came the reply. Was it because he had ascertained that she had no sense of time?

Even the young Mr Yang, who was often seen chatting with Tien-ch'ing under that big tree by the alley, had no idea where she was. Several times, he stood in her way to ask Tien-lan if she had news of Tien-ch'ing. In the end, he went as far as to come to the house to ask after her, and was confronted by Father with the question: 'And who is she to you?' Tien-ch'ing came back on her own, dressed in a set of brand new clothes. Her tummy was not big at all. In fact, she looked like she had lost a few years, gotten skinnier and even paler than before.

By the time young Mr Yang showed up with Tien-ch'ing at the village gate, they had heard the news at home. He was pushing his bike with one hand and had Tien-ch'ing walking by his other side. He looked very tall and the two of them attracted quite a bit of attention. When they got to their doorstep, they stopped to exchange a few words. As they said goodbye, he said: 'I'll take care of everything for you.' Then, he stood there, watching after Tien-ch'ing as she went in the house. On thinking back, it occurred to her that the young men of that generation possessed a kind of uprightness. How old was he then? Barely 19?

When Tien-ch'ing entered the door, Father showed no emotion one way or the other. He acted as if he had seen her only yesterday; he simply told her to go wash up and go to bed. Mother, on the other hand, burst into a temper and shouted at them from behind her curtained window; perhaps she was angry that Tien-ch'ing had upset their routine. It would not have been the first time.

Soon afterwards, the young Mr Yang got himself in trouble. He was wounded somewhere in another village and had bled to death before anyone got to him. Tien-lan found it completely baffling; young Mr Yang was such a good student. His mother cried till she fainted on several occasions while she was at their house. Dusk seemed to have settled permanently into their house. Father made Tien-ch'ing kneel at Mrs Yang's feet. Stubborn as she was, Tien-ch'ing did exactly as she was told, and not only that, she cried. Since then, it seems, she never again saw tears flow from Tien-ch'ing' eyes.

For over a year and a half after that, Tien-ch'ing did not set foot outside the house. All day long, she sat at home reading or day-dreaming. Their home harboured two centres of silence; it grew quieter than ever. All those young men, delinquent or otherwise, who used to hang around their house, seemed to have disappeared. It was as if the quiet of their house had seeped out into the village; during that period, nothing happened in the village.

When Tien-ch'ing left home again, it was to go north to study at the University. In those four years, outsiders' impressions of Tien-ch'ing's appearance and understanding of her inner thoughts and emotions reached absolute zero. Tien-lan still remembered the day when entrance exam results were posted. In the village, families whose children had been admitted celebrated the occasion by setting off reams of firecrackers, filling the alleys with smoke and high spirits. Nobody thought it possible Tien-ch'ing would be admitted to college. That night, Tien-ch'ing went to bed early.

From then on, Tien-ch'ing's trips home mostly coincided with young Mr Yang's birthday or the anniversary of his death. The Yang family had moved away by then, and Tien-ch'ing's stay at home resembled that of a convict's time in jail. Village gossips did not forget her. Gradually, however, the talk turned to involuntary praise, as if they were comparing the hussies of the time with Tien-ch'ing and finding them lacking.

Their mother continued as she always had, regardless of births, deaths, illness, or age, regardless of how she might have felt. There were other paths in life to follow.

Everyone praised Tien-ch'ing for turning into a good girl. Tien-lan herself preferred the old Tien-ch'ing, the pretty, occasionally wild and irresponsible Tien-ch'ing.

The year their whole family moved north was when Tien-ch'ing stayed on for her second year as teaching assistant at the University. Everything remained the same at home. Tien-ch'ing studied aimlessly for the TOEFL. It was then that Tien-lan saw how lifeless and forced Tien-ch'ing's life had become; most people would find it hard to bear.

After she had grown up, Tien-lan found her sister less tall than she had appeared before, but the distance between them grew greater. Was it because Tien-ch'ing stopped growing?

One rainy night, she was still studying for her exams, when Tien-ch'ing came home at around midnight. After she took a bath, she sat at her desk in her usual manner, with her jet black, short hair half covering her face, sitting like that till all hours of the night. Tien-lan could then better appreciate various aspects of young womanhood, and discovered in her sister the kind of calm that few bystanders could have endured, the calm after great wind and waves, the calm that asks for nothing and gives nothing in return. All that others can ever see is the back view of her.

Tien-lan walked over to Tien-ch'ing's side. She had her book opened and was apparently memorizing the English vocabulary in front of her, repeating the words over and over, as if they had no meaning. She stood for a long time behind her.

When Tien-ch'ing finally noticed her sister's presence, she nearly jumped out of her skin. Immediately, however, she pretended that nothing had happened, and kept her head low. The pretence in fact made the moment even more awkward. Her heart was not in her books at all. Something else was circling her mind. Was it because of this sort of thing that she found it more difficult to study? Or was it because she was too far removed from the realities of daily living? She often grew shy in front of others, like a little girl, reminding one of those years long ago; perhaps Tien-ch'ing herself could not shake them from her memory. She never asked Tien-ch'ing whether the rumour about her pregnancy was true.

Since Tien-lan showed no signs of going away immediately, Tien-ch'ing had to make conversation, so she asked her what her plans were for the future.

'Marry someone,' she simply replied. Tien-ch'ing thought about this seriously for a while.

'What about you?' Tien-lan asked.

'No hurry, I'll wait and see,' came Tien-ch'ing's unhurried reply.

Wait and see? Could it be that Tien-ch'ing had no sense of time? Was Tien-ch'ing like their mother? A chill ran down her spine. Tien-ch'ing hesitated. Apparently she was considering whether or not to 'tell'. Hesitant towards her own sister?

'Why are you thinking of marriage?' Tien-ch'ing's words came from her lips though her eyes had not moved from the list of English words.

She had always remembered Tien-ch'ing's face as long and thin, but up close she realized that this impression was merely the creation of her imagination, born of the fact that Tien-ch'ing rarely smiled. Tien-ch'ing's face was in reality the sort that the Chinese call a 'full-moon face', small yet distinct, smooth and clear, giving a liquid impression.

'Isn't marriage enough?' She asked Tien-ch'ing in return.

Instantly, Tien-ch'ing grew sullen. She really couldn't stand that kind of attitude. Under the lamplight, Tien-ch'ing looked ageless, forever deathless as she was lifeless. That portrait of her told the whole story, of her present and her future. And her past?

She left Tien-ch'ing in her own circle of light; leaving her thus in her own world. Who ever entered into her world? Tien-lan couldn't help herself. She turned around to look back at her sister. Tien-ch'ing had not moved from her sitting posture; she was not looking forwards or backwards. All lines of communication between them were cut off. Was that posture the external manifestation of Tien-ch'ing's obstinacy?

Tien-lan returned to her bedroom and closed the door. She was not sleepy at all. She paced the room, all the while hoping to hear a little noise, some sign of life, a vibrant echo or the breath of time passing. Was it she who was the wild animal trapped?

Once in a while, they would receive invitations to go to a wedding or a funeral service in the village, like timers marking the different stages of life, going to these wedding banquets became their father's only form of entertainment. He would get irrepressibly excited before going, but afterwards he would deliberately keep silent about Tien-ch'ing's plans; he would not even mention them behind her back. In fact, in all those years they lived together as a family, she could well see that the person among them who knew most about the world was her father. He was also the most parsimonious; he let nothing go. Could it be because of this inability to let go that he didn't make any plans where Tien-ch'ing was concerned?

For the next few years, Tien-ch'ing continued to study for the TOEFL. It seemed like a long, long time. What stuck in Tien-lan's mind was the image of her with her head in her books and her back to the world on winter nights, and her closing the door completely.

In their generation, she had seen too many who had got by with flying colours without any effort. In contrast, it was unusual to see someone like Tien-ch'ing, who did nothing but concentrate on her studies and yet got nowhere. Even after she had passed the entrance exam for graduate school, she was still studying night after night. It was then that Tien-lan discovered the similarity between Tien-ch'ing and their mother: even their weaknesses held a portion of obstinacy. This was true even of the feelings Tien-ch'ing and Yi Hsing-wen had for each other.

She could not be sure exactly when their phone started to ring at all times of the night. Most likely, it was some time after Tien-ch'ing's entrance into graduate school. Quite a few times when she had come home late, she had seen Tien-ch'ing sitting by the telephone, the light turned dim, and speaking in a very low voice. It was obvious, however, that she was definitely not engaged in any kind of love talk, because it took her forever to squeeze out a few words. What sort of emotions could make one so silent? The person on the other end of the line, too, could not be one for the madding crowd, or he would not have called so late at night.

Another inexplicable picture of Tien-ch'ing, leaving one high and dry with no commentary, no satisfaction. Would this, too, become another representation of her life? Did not this state of Tien-ch'ing's mind reach it's dead end in emotional confusion? Their mother viewed life a total blank, their father was determined not to say a word about it. Who then could she ask? Could she have asked Tien-ch'ing?

The caller knew Tien-ch'ing's routine well. When she was out the telephone would never ring; five minutes after her return, something would happen. His call broke the long silence of the nights. He had no sense of time; nights were as days to him. In which spatial reality was he living? That was when T'ien-lan first started seeing T'ang Yuan and was therefore especially sensitive to the phone's ring. One day, it rang when Tien-ch'ing was out and she had picked it up in a hurry, asking, 'T'ang Yuan?' The reply came after a long pause. 'My name is Yi Hsing-wen. Is Tien-ch'ing home?'

She had heard of Yi Hsing-wen. Students are particularly aware of their teachers; particularly if that teacher is young and good, and particularly if he happened to be Yi Hsing-wen. The Yi family was a family of substance, with generations of wealth and scholarship behind them. Yi Hsing-wen had held important posts at various times in both political and academic circles and was somewhat of a public figure who attracted much attention. Young college students worshiped him as a god. She had not been sure that he was the one who had been calling, so instead of getting herself into a fix by saying too much, she simply and clearly said, 'She should be back soon!'

'Are you Tien-lan?' Yi Hsing-wen asked. She was stunned. 'Thank you very much! I'll call Tien-ch'ing again later on,' he continued.

When Yi Hsing-wen hung up she heard the line go dead, and in that instant realized that Tien-ch'ing would not live out her life in a calm and meaningless way; it was just a matter of time.

Never before had she paid so much attention to Tien-ch'ing's movements. When Tien-ch'ing came home, the telephone rang again. She knew it was Yi Hsing-wen. From the expression of her face she could sense that there was something going on between them. That phone call lasted over two hours. That night, Tien-ch'ing's desk lamp burnt till dawn. Outside the house, it was raining again.

Yi Hsing-wen did not stay in the country for long. For a time, one could always find news of him in the papers. It seemed as if a report of his being granted some important position would come any day. However, it never materialized. What appeared instead were innuendoes. The stories were skimpy at best, but reading between the lines, one could gather ample evidence concerning some sort of extramarital affair Yi Hsing-wen was supposed to be having. Moreover, the woman in question was apparently someone with such a muddly background that it was almost unmentionable; it had something to do with gangs and delinquents. Public opinion would simply not accept this liason. All these were words used by the papers.

So that was the end of that? Nobody knew. Tien-ch'ing appeared no different from her usual self. If only Tien-lan could rip that outer skin off her sister and get at the truth of the matter.

Yi Hsing-wen never appeared again. As soon as he came back from abroad, he left again. He appeared to spend most of his time in the air between destinations. It was as if he could not settle down in one place.

It was not until the day of Tien-ch'ing's funeral that Yi Hsing-wen reappeared. He went to pay his respects all by himself. His face was withered by grief. Tien-lan saw him from where she stood amid the others, and became convinced that there are some things that can never pass, even if human beings are unable to grasp what they are.

Yi Hsing-wen and Tien-ch'ing had not seen each other for how long? Three or four years? But how had his hair turned completely white at the temples and his person become so haggard? As he came forward to pay his respects, since

Tien-lan did not have to kneel down to his level, she had a good look at all of him. Yi Hsing-wen exuded a kind of calm just like that she had sensed from Tien-ch'ing. After he ceremoniously paid his respects, he backed up to the right side of the altar and stood there, looking at Tien-ch'ing's photograph hung above it. She congratulated herself for having chosen a photo of Tien-ch'ing in which she had uncharacteristically displayed a smile. When the dead are hung up above the crowd like that, a happy face could seem almost derisive; on the other hand, a solemn expression might suggest too much regret at having to leave this world. Only the faint smile on her face in this photo seemed appropriate. It said that there was no need to retrieve anything and no necessity to leave anything behind.

Perhaps Yi Hsing-wen did not feel the same way. He was standing in front of the altar as if no one else were around, Tien-lan could see that he had let himself slip into a difficult kind of time. She lifted her head to watch him several times, and recalled those nights, those rainy nights when he and Tien-ch'ing would talk on the phone. Perhaps they were more than talks, more like negotiations, after which he had left a certain kind of existence behind. Finally, it was Tien-ch'ing who in actual fact left this reality behind. Watching Yi Hsing-wen, Tien-lan, too, felt that nothing around them existed.

The couplets written for the occasion hung there like curtains on both sides of the altar; between them, the last act of a faded life was played out to the bitter end. Sad tears were the least libation one could offer. Their mother did not cry. Not a sound came from her. She looked horribly thin. Their father had on a suit he had not had the heart to throw out, looking like someone who came from another time. Tien-lan felt herself further and further removed from what was taking place. Perhaps it was unnecessary to be conscious of what was happening after all. The atmosphere remained oppressive to the end. Their mother collapsed; that finally gave the funeral some sense of tragedy.

Having seen as much, should Yi Hsing-wen be questioning the validity of the past? Or should he obstinately hold on to it? Even if he were to insist, it would bring him no joy for the future. But why shouldn't he insist?

Did Yi Hsing-wen know about Feng Tzu-kang? Feng Tzu-kang would not be showing his face today. He had promised Tien-ch'ing he wouldn't when he left her.

Yi Hsing-wen stood among the crowd as he watched the hearse and the funeral party take off. Tien-lan looked back through the cigarette smoke and the solemn faces to his face. She was just about to get into the back seat when she met his eyes. She gave him a meaningful smile. That smile, coming amid the confusion at the funeral parlor, captured the moment between them. She had meant it to express her deep regret toward the living who had been left behind. What had happened to Yi Hsing-wen's emotional life? Could he live with himself?

Dust shrouded the faces as they passed by, some leaving a clearer impression than others. Certainly, some people were meant to take seats at one's life-banquet, leaving their images engraved in the mind, whether they themselves know it or not. Tien-ch'ing's hearse did not arouse much attention as it passed through the city.

Half a year into Tien-ch'ing's hospitalization, Feng Tzu-kang came home. He packed his bags as soon as he heard the news of her illness. Fifteen years he had been away from the country with no accomplishments, domestic or professional, to show for it. Fifteen years? Difficult to imagine how they were passed. Were they like Tien-ch'ing's? When Tien-lan met him, however, she realized these questions were too normal to be asked of him. Some people do not acknowledge bitterness in life. There were indeed similarities between him and Tien-ch'ing. Was it the different stages in their destinies that made it impossible for their paths to merge? Since there was nothing to develop, it was natural that they fell into an impasse. If Feng Tzu-kang had borne it willingly, what about Yi Hsing-wen? Thinking about Yi Hsing-wen, it was impossible not to call up thoughts of Feng Tzu-kang.

For one whole month, Feng Tzu-kang had put everything else aside to spend all his time at Tien-ch'ing's bedside. He had come back in a hurry, and for fear Tien-ch'ing would not last, he had not even bought a present.

Feng Tzu-kang had come with his brother Feng Tzu-p'ing. The latter had been Tien-ch'ing's colleague and was therefore playing the go-between. When the brothers bumped into Tien-lan in the hallway, Feng Tzu-kang had asked, in all sincerity: 'Are they sure that Tien-ch'ing has cancer of the liver?' Immediately, she decided that Feng Tzu-kang and Yi Hsing-wen were the same type of person. Their speech revealed the passion they hid inside them. Feng Tzu-kang had also gone to see the doctor in charge of Tien-ch'ing's case to ask for a diagnosis; this, despite the fact that it was unclear what his relationship was to her.

Tien-ch'ing showed no sign of astonishment seeing Feng Tzu-kang. It was as if having had one thing delayed, nothing that followed would ever catch up. Feelings were the same way.

Tien-ch'ing had been very calm both before and after she went to the hospital. She expressed regret only at Feng Tzu-kang's having to rush home to see her. Often, after the tide of well-wishers had subsided, the two of them would be left alone in the hospital room: nobody knew what they talked about.

The hearse left the busy city behind and started to wind its way up the mountain path. For the purpose of leading the funeral party to the grave site, there were elaborate directions posted all along the way through the graveyard; this was to make it easier to guide the spirit West of the Great Beyond. The grave site lay just a little way outside the city, like the sojourn of a life that was neither too long nor too short.

After Tien-ch'ing was admitted to the hospital, the level of their parents' complaints grew, like a tidal wave, day by day: 30 years of keeping it in cannot easily be let out in a single day. Before they started on the ride up to the graveyard, Tien-lan had brought friends round and managed to persuade the two old people to stay at home. Having had to live in this world had been burden enough; let Tien-ch'ing leave it in peace.

Tien-ch'ing was faced with all sorts of injustice, but she was used to keeping it all to herself. Nevertheless, she owed Feng Tzu-kang an explanation, even though there was not much she could say.

'I'm very sorry, but I won't be able to study any more.' They had apparently made that promise to each other once upon a time.

When Feng Tzu-kang was there, the two old people had to stay away more often, and Tien-ch'ing was spared having to deal with their crying and complaints; she was temporarily granted peace in the time that was left. Then, whether there was understanding or forgiveness became unimportant.

How did Feng Tzu-kang feel, having witnessed all that was going on? Tien-ch'ing tried her best to make her period of illness a time of normality. She appeared as if she had removed herself from being the subject of her illness and become an observer. She smiled at her visitors and analyzed her condition with the doctors. Was she trying to tell the world to forget that this painful disease existed? Or had she never in fact been affected by pain?

By the last stage of the illness, even painkillers had lost their effect. All she did was hold the pillow down where it hurt and, from time to time, lift her head with an expression on her face close to indifference. An expression that was not in any way human.

Within the month, Feng Tzu-kang had helped them sell the old house in exchange for a smaller one in the country, with cash left over to put in the bank. The old house sold for an unbelievable sum. Feng Tzu-kang must have put in quite a bit of his own money.

On the day he took his plane, Tien-ch'ing walked with him all the way to the hospital entrance. She had on a lightweight green overcoat; outside, it was already spring. Under the green overcoat was the blue hospital gown. Their smiling faces were like those of actors at the conclusion of a play: nothing more will change the scene. Feng Tzu-kang was full of despair. His unhappiness certainly concerned more than himself. When Tien-ch'ing took his hand to say goodbye, she looked as if she had a great deal to say to him. But in the end, all she said was: 'There's no need to come back.' They all knew what she meant.

What if they had met earlier? Would he have walked out of her life just like that? Or would Tien-ch'ing have left him first? Wouldn't Tien-ch'ing and Feng Tzu-kang have made a great ending to the story? Or perhaps what went wrong was there from the very beginning? In any case, it was just as Tien-ch'ing's final comment put it: 'no need to come back again'.

It had not occurred to him that Tien-ch'ing and her sister would be so different. When he first met Tien-lan at the hospital, he was surprised to find her so young, surprised to find that she had made no arrangements for the future whatsoever. He had no regrets for having known Tien-ch'ing.

He had wanted to pretend to himself that he was not affected. During that month, he experienced such confusing emotions that he did not even want to analyze it. At the time, being with Tien-ch'ing day after day was hardly painful. On the contrary, there was a bittersweetness about the pressure of the day to day responsibility to be there. There was no way he could hope for a miracle, and he couldn't utter the platitudes of well wishers. All he could do was stay by her side. Even so, every day brought him a day closer to the day of departure and subtracted from the days he had left with her.

After everyone left, Tien-ch'ing would seem to relax a little. On occasion, she would even let go enough to joke a little. One time, when Tien-ch'ing had gone off to the ladies' room and did not come back for a long time, he went looking for her and stumbled into the nursery. He found her there, with her face glued to the window, looking at babies. He said to her: 'The doctors have come for your urine sample.'

'I know,' she said. 'They seem to be wishing even harder than I am for a miracle. Perhaps they will have fewer challenges when I'm absent.' He was feeling quite anxious, but was unwilling to show it, lest it should affect Tien-ch'ing.

In the wards for special cases were concealed many strange sensations, and stillness was one of them. He had no idea what Tien-ch'ing, fragile as she was, would be thinking when she was left alone in that stillness.

They used to take walks at the back of the hospital grounds. Along the long embankment, with the mountain ranges in the distance, they would admire the scene quietly. There was no need for thoughts of birth, aging, illness, or death. Their emotions were at their lowest ebb during these walks that were taken purely for their own sake. At those times, he would feel as if he were really Tien-ch'ing's boyfriend, even though they never talked about love.

Tien-ch'ing never mentioned America; never mentioned the fact that they corresponded nor what they wrote each other. She did not allow herself one shred of hope.

The emotional upheavals associated with cancer should have been even more difficult to deal with. Not so with Tien-ch'ing. She lay in bed, always, as if she were merely about to go off to dreamland, not as if she were sick—except on one occasion. On a particularly humid afternoon, when she had finally fallen asleep after dozing on and off for quite a while, she seemed to be having difficulty turning her body, as though she were held down by some kind of pressure. She looked as if she were in great pain. Since she had the intravenous needle stuck in her arm, he was afraid the struggle would cause her to hurt herself, so he held her hand to prevent her moving. She suddenly woke from her sleep, and for a while did not seem to realize where she was. When she finally came to, she let out a sigh and said, 'I saw him in my dream.' Which 'him' was this? He knew that she remembered. He had gotten over the years of jealousy a long time ago. Besides, he felt he was the most fortunate of them all. At least, he and Tien-ch'ing had the chance to reach a conclusion, even if it had no future.

He ought to be in the country, she continued, obviously having difficulty hiding the look of longing on her face. He wanted very much to go and look up Yi Hsing-wen, and not because he wanted to exchange ideas with him. What was there left to compete for, now that things had reached this stage?

Had Tien-ch'ing wanted to see Yi Hsing-wen? When a person has made up his mind and stilled his passions, whatever bubbles came to the surface after that remain just bubbles and soon disappear.

Was Yi Hsing-wen even alive and breathing in some corner of the earth? Did he still remember? Would he still welcome the anxieties that would accompany Tien-ch'ing's reappearance? For them both to account for the rights and wrongs of their relationship, such a meeting would probably fall outside of their allotment of time together in this life.

'Would you like me to look for him?'

Tien-ch'ing shook her head. Strange, he could read Tien-ch'ing's habits in love like a textbook of love.

In the end, Yi Hsing-wen never showed up. For Tien-ch'ing's part, once admitted she had not planned on leaving the hospital ever. Did this mean that they had been fated not to meet again?

One month is not a long time. They had met at the very last moments in life, he and Tien-ch'ing, which therefore also left them with too much unsaid.

It was as if they saw their lives turned upside down. That one month must have been the shortest month ever.

When they were not chatting, he would sit by her bed and read. When he first started going to the hospital, the medicinal smell stung his nose. Gradually, he got used to it. The experience was a little like facing the god of love and the god of death.

Tien-ch'ing loved to look out of the window. She would say whatever came into her mind. Time meant nothing to her. None of it had happened yet. The stop and go of the conversation was like the strand of their emotions, stopping now and then forming a knot before continuing on. He liked it very much.

All this, however, did not constitute love, and that fact made him doubly distressed. Why could Tien-ch'ing not commit herself to her closest companion? He saw how rapidly she wasted away. Although her weight loss had to come to a halt at a certain point, in the end all that was left that was round was her forehead. This roundness made her look particularly childlike, and it brought out in him the impulse to protect her as though she were a child.

He could not comprehend the depth of feeling a grown man can have for a little girl. Whenever she came into his thoughts, he would go to her; sometimes going to the hospital several times a day. Had he not returned home because of her? Could this be called a kind of relationship?

One time, he thought of her in the middle of the night. He believed she must have gone to sleep. But then, what if she weren't asleep? The thought made him want to go to her. Her condition was so prone to change that not only was it nearly impossible to tell how much time she had left, but the horrible pains that came with these changes were just as unpredictable. What if she were in pain? How many times had he been greeted by her solemn face as he entered her sick room? It was unbearable to see her locked in silence. He wondered what was in her thoughts after those bouts of torturing pain. Was she in pain the night before?

When he arrived late that night, she was indeed awake. She was propped up in bed, with her back facing the door, looking out the window, which must have been for her the source of life's tidings. He closed the door behind him and stood for a while before she turned her face to look at him. She looked at him for a long time.

In the room a dim light had been left on. He could see clearly the tears on her cheeks and in her eyes. What was she thinking? Because he was no longer a child, he could not allow himself to ask questions without reservation, nor could he appear too agitated. In actual fact, he nearly did both. He laughed at himself for being so inexperienced in life's emotions—he who had lived for so many years.

'Yang Chao?' She called out to him.

Not Yi Hsing-wen, but Yang Chao? Which world had she gone into? He did not turn on the lights, nor did he answer her. He went towards her and sat down. This time, he did not sit on the chair by the bed but went straight to her bedside. He wanted to ask her, 'Do you hurt?' Instead, he bent over and kissed her. If only he could lessen her pain he would be willing to let it pass from her body to his. Could illness be a kind of penetration? Like emotions, eating away at one? Tien-ch'ing did not resist him. He enjoyed the night sounds coming from outside the window and the dim light in the room. After his return to Taipei, he had suddenly acknowledged his feelings. He now knew what he liked and what he disliked. He was clearly conscious that he was not in a dream.

Tien-ch'ing's arms were full of needle marks. They looked like battle wounds, so many holes yet not one entrance for love. He held her hands tightly. He held her. He felt the warmth of her body and, at the same time, he was conscious of the fact that it was not for him that her temperature had risen. Because of their age, he found it impossible to express himself with a 'should we get married first?' Nor could he seek redemption. Perhaps, at their age, they had gone beyond the belief that love surpassed happiness.

He symbolically slipped a diamond ring onto Tien-ch'ing's finger. It wasn't purely for its beauty. He knew it would be used soon. It wasn't that he completely lacked imagination in his feelings for Tien-ch'ing. Only that those feelings were drowned out by other emotions all along. To have been able to bend down and kiss her, to hold her, to have had such a night as this, surpassed the emotions of receiving ten letters from Tien-ch'ing. Was that shameful? He didn't care.

The play had reached its climax, along with his emotions and all that he held dear. Was this 'The End'? The strange thing was, he was not a bit afraid even though he knew that death was a reality. He knew that Tien-ch'ing had never cared about what others thought. Then why should others have any regrets where she was concerned? Do the ticket holders in the audience have any right to refuse to leave the theater after the show just because they wish to stay and quarrel with characters in the story?

As their relationship gradually became more stable, it was time he went back to work. He had wanted to prolong his leave and stay with her, but Tien-ch'ing refused, giving the reason in six words—'in the end one must go'. Who did it refer to? Actually, prolonged illness tends to reduce illness to routine; too short a period deprives the emotions of the chance to adapt. He thought she would be left all alone from then on. Before he left, Tien-ch'ing handed him a package.

'My letters?' He knew what they were the minute she handed it over. Why did she have to be so ruthless? His heart sank.

'It had occurred to me that I would have the chance to give them to you face to face.' Indeed, she did, even though this 'giving' did not include her person.

'I thought it best that I left alone. . . . Don't let it bother you.' Tien-ch'ing lowered her head as she said this.

This was as far as he could accompany her anyway; so he did mind. He left her to an increasing daily sense of her individual self. But then, are we not all individuals?

The contents of their correspondence were unknown to any but themselves. Their romance was never carried on outside the hospital. Their relationship was, from beginning to end, like a life that existed in an air-tight world. How could it expect to breathe?

After his return to school, he continued to wait for news of her. He must ascertain what part of time and space she was in. The letters she returned to him were left in the bottom of his suitcase in the packet, the way they were given to him. He would probably never open them again. If he were one day to marry, he would burn them.

While he was waiting, he went nowhere. Occasionally, he would take a walk in the park. The parks overseas had no appeal for his eyes. He knew this was not the fault of the parks. It was as if he were the terminal patient chained down waiting for death.

Others continued to introduce him to new women. Even though he realized that youth was passing, he was not in a hurry. He couldn't say that his heart belonged to Tien-ch'ing, but he had, after all, taken part in her journey towards death, and death is not so easily shaken off.

His days were too routine. The more predictable his activities, the easier it became for the past to slip into his mind. The first time he received a letter from Tien-ch'ing, he did not open it in a great hurry. It felt very light in its airmail envelope. Just looking at the address on the outside alone, one could appreciate the delicate strength of the writer. He felt the weight of the writing. It had been a long time since he had expressed himself in written Chinese at all, not to mention expression that involved love. He could not remember ever seeing English words looking so much like Chinese characters.

It was not until he had reached the age of 30 that he learned how to appreciate a woman. By that time, there were no women around for him to appreciate. What sort of a person could have written such strokes as these?

He studied the letter over and over again. Her letter was really quite simple; the complications came from the way he felt about her. He couldn't remember why he had started writing to Tien-ch'ing. Perhaps because he had never been one for extended conversation and correspondence was just another form of give and take. In writing, a few words could convey much more depth of feeling. Now that she had responded to him, it occurred to him that the necessity for romance was not in question. At this juncture in life, it was more important to maintain normality. How he wished she would write more between the lines. Was this normal?

After he finished reading the letter, he went to a beer hall. He wanted very much to get drunk but the alcohol content of beer was too low. Like a shallow acquaintance, beer is merely filling and does not take one to the state of intoxication. He wanted to tell himself to hold onto consciousness, but he was too bloated to keep awake.

Because he hardly knew Tien-ch'ing at all he felt as if he knew her very well. Because there were so many blank areas, much was left to the imagination. Was that it? He did not try to analyze it. In any case, he did not experience any feelings of unfamiliarity. Indeed, in that state of consciousness, he had no 'feelings'. All he had was numbness.

When he got home from the bar he read the letter once again. Tien-ch'ing sounded formal and unimpassioned. The feel of years filled the lines. He was unsure of himself; he feared the irreversible, be it in things, time, emotions, or passages. He was afraid to hurt others. He had not anticipated that to start anything at this age to hurt was inevitable. At the beginning, in order not to allow this 'thing' to develop into 'hope', he did not aggressively pursue it. Not long afterwards, he noticed that whenever he had a long school break, he would grow restless. He'd be reading in the house, in the quiet of both the inside and out, knowing full well that there was no-one outside, and yet he would not be able to stop himself from lifting his head up from time to time, as if he were expecting someone. It was as if he was surrounded by too much life, like the atmosphere in a hospital nursery: simultaneously noisy and solemn. He was conscious of his own suppressed feelings and how those same feelings lay in ambush to catch him unawares. He was merely quarreling with himself. Therefore, he wrote Tien-ch'ing, telling her how he hoped she would come to America, and that she could continue her studies when she arrived. He knew she had prepared for just this purpose for many years.

This was the first time he had used the word 'hope'. She took a long time to reply. Did she feel insulted? He never asked, not even when they came face to face. He regretted it right after he had posted the letter. A little impulse of the moment should have been allowed to pass away. Instead, he had not only prolonged it but perhaps also invited more emotional complications than she could manage.

Tien-ch'ing's reply was in the tone she had always used in previous letters, not one bit more or less serious. He could almost enter her state of mind. He thought, 'She is opening up avenues of communication, even though her method is not obvious.'

At first, because of his guilty conscience towards her, he tried his best to keep their relationship going. As time went on, this developed into the testing of their two lives against each other. Through their differences, he discovered the readable Tien-ch'ing. He had no idea why it should be so difficult for two adults to communicate. More than once, the thought of making a clean break had reared its head in his mind. His life had already been half used up. What more was there to care about?

Fortunately, Tien-ch'ing was far away. Otherwise, they would have ended it all much sooner. It was only because they didn't have to face each other day in and day out that he did not decide to end it early on.

With the increase in the number of letters, he found himself going for more and more walks. It was not to cultivate a good habit that he did this, but there were certain moods he couldn't control. Tien-ch'ing never made it clear when she would be coming. He had gotten ready everything she might need, up to (and including) shampoo and clothes brushes. He didn't want to second guess his own motives for being so generous. He had never worried much about himself. In quiet moments, the feeling of shame and then of self-pity would come upon him. Such confusion was the result of having few romantic experiences, despite his years.

He felt compelled to ask her about her past. Tien-ch'ing told him everything. You might think it great that one should have a history; at least, it added interest. In dealing with historical events, one could enter in or leave out, believe or disbelieve, but writing one's own history was like fortune-telling for oneself. No matter what you will, it is your destiny. There is nothing you could have done to change it.

Yang Chao and Tien-ch'ing's destinies seemed to have been drawn up a long time ago.

That year Yang Chao was to graduate from a prestigious high school. His family had high hopes for him; the hopes were especially fervent for their only son. The good thing about Yang Chao was that he was not a bookworm, nor was he an idle Don Juan. It was difficult to tell from his clean-cut face what the future held for him. He was not like other boys of his age with whom one could tell the onset of manhood by their greasy appearance.

Because of his youth, Yang Chao tended to be earnest about everything. He was afraid to lose in anything, and this of course, included his hold over Tien-ch'ing. On her part, Tien-ch'ing didn't seem to object.

The two families, Yang and Ch'eng, did not have what you would call 'an established friendship going back generations'. Nevertheless, they had been neighbours since their arrival in Taiwan, and their fathers worked in the same company, so theirs could not be called a shallow acquaintance either. Since the affair was between the young people, the adults were reluctant to interfere. Besides, they had all left the homeland far behind and their hands were tied anyway; there was no point in fussing over it. Nonetheless, the Yangs were privately hoping that given time the younger generation would change its mind about the relationship. Yang Chao knew full well how his family felt. With merely a bamboo barrier separating the two families, there a deeper bond should have been established—or so Yang Chao thought.

Though Tien-ch'ing was born in the year of the dog, she had always disliked the company of others; she did not speak very well even at the age of ten. The young girl's personality, however, had little to do with how much she understood. In the environment of the housing compound, Tien-ch'ing was training herself to keep to herself. She was not like her mother: her mother kept to herself by denial. Tien-ch'ing was more straightforward. She made it clear to Yang Chao even when they were mere children that she would never marry.

Yang Chao never worried about that remark. If she didn't marry him, who would she marry? Because of their proximity, he was sure that their futures belonged to each other. Ever since he had known about girls he had known Tien-ch'ing. He could never get used to the idea of not having her face around when they became adults.

The first time he kissed her was in the fields behind the village. Tien-ch'ing did not even hesitate before slapping him. The slap chased away all his anxiety. He grabbed hold of her arms and questioned her.

'What right have you to slap me?' He could see every house and every face in the village.

'You? Who are you?' Tien-ch'ing was not a bit afraid of him.

He was sure Tien-ch'ing wouldn't run away, and as for their wedding date, that could be postponed indefinitely. So long as nobody else had her.

He went for her cheek once again, and she slapped him once again. He was satisfied. Their relationship was not without some effect on her.

When Yang Chao was preparing for the university entrance exam, Tien-ch'ing joined a gang. She didn't like to talk much but she liked to be among a lot of people. Home was too quiet. Her group had no money, but they had a great deal of spirit. They loved to be in places where excitement was cheap and direct. They had gang fights, went to the beach to swim and to the graveyard at night, or they would steal things. Except for theft, she was included in everything. Naturally, Yang Chao did not know about any of this. She was not afraid of Yang Chao. She was not even afraid of death. She didn't tell him of her actions simply out of habit. Yang Chao had to study and her mother was absorbed in the past. The group were nobodies; among them, she could relax a little.

Yang Chao would remind her once in a while of the results of study and how it would allow them to go abroad together someday. She lied and nodded. All along she had used passive methods cheating Yang Chao. You could call it a kind of perverse seduction. When she grew to the realization that she was a woman, whenever she was with Yang Chao she would feel dirty. On the other hand, she felt that Yang Chao was pure to the point of obscenity.

It was not that she despised Yang Chao. She just could not believe in their future together. Did they really have that much time to grow up and have to grow up in such a timed manner? She was afraid Yang Chao would simply tell her to be patient. When she slapped him she did so out of frustration. What was she to do with him now that he had gotten so close to her?

Then, one day, the school had scheduled an outing. Nobody cared at home. She had forgotten how indifferent her mother was to everything. It was not that she needed a reaction to her every action but at the very least she expected her mother to react a little. To continue to live like this was to let herself die of boredom.

'Since I'll die anyway this might as well be it,' she thought to herself. Not only that but she would die far away.

It was especially quiet in the housing compound in the afternoon. She suddenly felt that she was an orphan, existing outside of time. She slowly packed her bag. What was she waiting for? Yang Chao? Or was she waiting for time to catch up with her? The room was terrifyingly silent. Her mother was in the next room. Ridiculous really, that they should be under the same roof. She could hear her own breathing. Its rhythmic motion was like a spring in her heart bouncing up and down, up and down, meaninglessly, out of habit unable to stop. Or there was another possibility—that of increasing activity with the number of years she had lived. This scared her not a little. She was afraid that, in this depressed atmosphere, if she jumped about too much, she might fall hard to her death.

It was really rather strange, but she had this fear of pain all along. Imaginary pain was even more painful than real pain. She had never been beaten before, but she sensed that the pain of being beaten would be impossible to bear. This, because she had already experienced every other kind of pain. She knew that if they were to recapture her after she had run away from home, she would not escape a sound beating.

She felt something in her heart but not her hands. She finally finished tidying up the few things she was going to take with her. She could hardly believe it, but she could not find a single clean piece of clothing. In their house, it was not unusual, however, (since their father was busy and she, lazy) to have dirty clothes left piled up in the wash until they began to smell. She found it rather amusing that though there was no noise nor voice in their house, there were all sorts of smells around.

In actual fact, she had never had much in the way of clothing. The most presentable clothes in the house belonged to their mother. Her clothes, though old, were not worn. They breathed out a strange kind of breath. They had life, but not their original one. They were like mummies.

She had no choice but to wear her school uniform. White shirt on top of black skirt, she looked as plain and severe as a martyr.

Summer twilights are excessively long. That day was a difficult one to get through, as difficult as that passage through the village to its gate. It was torturously hot. She knew what those people were thinking. Pregnant? She was not as foolhardy as all that. The adult world was too full of matter-of-courses. She stuck her tummy out, pretending that there was no one around to look at her. Meanwhile, she was making up her mind where she could go. It was March, and the park was already full of greenery. Most of its scenic features were left over from the days of the Japanese occupation. Trees had grown tall but there were not many flowers. This was a black and white movie, not one to encourage the blossoming of the heart or youthful attitudes. She rambled on in the park, roaming all over, resting whenever she felt tired at the foot of some big tree. All she could see through the dense, dark shades of the trees were more trees. Not many people visited the park.

The sky was finally completely blackened. Her emotions too had receded to the level of the horizon, glowing with the colours of the twilight. The thought of home never even crossed her mind.

That night, the gang brought with them, from somewhere, rice wine, dried bean curd, jelly fish, and peanuts. She did not much like the taste of wine. Perhaps it was also because of her bad mood, but she was tipsy after just a few sips.

The boys soon started to curse each other, as if harsh language made the wine taste better. The alarming effect of alcohol to ignite whatever lay in its path was demonstrated for her. She discovered that the latent capacity of boys to quarrel was far greater than that of girls. Of course, perhaps the way she sat quietly by manifested another form of objection. She wanted to exist on the edge of these two states. Maybe it was because of excitement aroused by the wine, but the Big Guy started to put his arm around her shoulder and almost crushed her to pieces. She scowled but didn't say a word. The Big Guy said she was the most silently poisonous character in the Crepe-Myrtle Gang. She felt the pain around her shoulder concentrated in one spot. She thought it rather thrilling. It was a kind of meticulous pain, as opposed to the epic pain caused by whipping. Whether physical or psychological, pain had the same effect: the ability to tear apart your body and soul.

She could not identify the reason she was fond of such an evening, the starlight, the terrace, a pair of hands. Was it because they free the body from restraints? Why should summer nights be so short?

When the party started to dissipate, she finally became a little worried. Where could she go? The stars were not so attractive that she could gaze at them all night long. She was not willful to the extent of being such a romantic. She dawdled behind as she watched the other girls go off in different directions. She did not want to leave with them. Her self-respect would not let her.

'Ch'eng Tien-ch'ing is the most valuable property we have in the gang!' She thought the remark ludicrous.

In the end, one by one, everyone had left except for the Big Guy and herself. It was not until then that he asked, 'Leave home?' She thought of the strength in his arm and did not respond. The darker it got the more serious it became for her to make up her mind where she could go. So long as no one knew about it, she'd be fine.

As the night dew thickened, they wound their way through the alleys and finally ended up in front of a small hotel. Perhaps it was the lighting, but she found herself looking up several times at the two words: 'Elegance Hotel.' What was that supposed to mean? Besides, she knew that the Big Guy did not have a cent in his pocket.

'Don't worry, they won't want the rent till the morning. We'll settle it tomorrow.'

The Big Guy picked the room key up from the front desk and sauntered off to the room by himself. She followed behind him. In her hand she held all her earthly belongings. On the door, she read: 405. The number was etched in her mind.

She did not understand the Big Guy. Whenever the gang got together, they'd have a wild time, but nobody ever got serious, let alone discussed his aspirations. All she knew was that the Big Guy was studying at the university, though for some reason or other, he liked to keep their company.

The Big Guy didn't ask any questions. It was more than likely that they came from similar backgrounds and therefore understood without talking about it. Besides, it was unnecessary for them to ask each other how they felt; they simply knew.

After they had turned off the light, the Big Guy made himself comfortable on the floor, while she, with all her clothes on, as if she were in full gear about to go into battle, slept on the bed. Small as the room was, the air stuck together as if it were one piece of material. The electric fan let out a rhythmic rumble that was not at all conducive to slumber. 'What was the Big Guy thinking?' The thought kept turning itself over in her mind.

They slept the night away. She woke up more tired than before. She continued to stay at the hotel while the Big Guy went out looking for money. He returned at around noon and asked if she wanted to stay on. She guessed they would have found out at home by now that she had run away, and said: 'Yes.'

The Big Guy stayed with her another night. In the darkness, she asked him: 'Where did the money come from?'

'A few drops of blood is still worth something,' he replied with nonchalance.

She made him sleep on the bed. Gratitude had brought on the need for her to coax him a little, the way she coaxed Yang Chao. The Big Guy asked her: 'What do you want to do tomorrow?' Before they had finished discussing it, he had fallen asleep.

Just before dawn, she woke up suddenly with a strange sensation. In the early morning light, all things were roused and ready to come to life. She turned her head and saw the Big Guy staring at her.

How did it happen? Because she was too busy hiding her own embarrassment she could not remember clearly at all. The only thing she could say for sure was that she was willing.

To what degree were they in love? The Big Guy did not say and Tien-ch'ing did not ask. If that moment were a life condensed, she would rather spend it with the Big Guy. Being with Yang Chao made her feel so very, very tired. Precisely because it was too tiring to turn back, she prayed fervently that in this simple, enclosed way of life, she could separate out the joy of peacefulness. She thought of her mother, and discovered that she could now sympathize with her a little.

Afterwards, they changed lodgings a few more times. The weather got hotter and hotter. The pores of their skin breathed in unison in the confined space in which they found themselves. She felt sticky, greasy, disgusted. She had not become used to having someone by her side, a living person who was always there. Was that why the Big Guy never mentioned the word 'love'? She discovered that, compared to Yang Chao, he kept far too much to himself.

By and by, she got used to seeing that face every day. Then, Yang Chao appeared. The Big Guy was taken away to the Detention Centre and Yang Chao was asked to come for her. The first night when the Big Guy didn't show up, Tien-ch'ing didn't close her eyes all night long. Every pore on her body was opened wide like mouths trying to breath. She was so chilly she almost caught a cold.

Yang Chao's face was as pale as a ghost's. She thought his pain would sooner or later pass away. She had forgotten that Yang Chao was a grown-up child with no capacity to adapt.

Another ten days of rent was still outstanding. The Big Guy's student ID was kept by the hotel as pledge and Tien-ch'ing would not leave without it. Yang Chao asked how the Big Guy went about getting cash. She told him and he went out to do it.

Selling blood was obviously not the same as the martyr's spilling of blood, but what was unforgettable was her picture of him. Yang Chao grew up with a nature clear as glass. Now it was tinted with the colour of blood, seeping through to the outside, awash through the painting of his life.

Yang Chao paid the bill and asked her whether she wanted to go home. She really didn't want to. She asked him what his plans were and he said: 'To be with you.'

July was around the corner. Yang Chao should have no problem with the university entrance exams. If, because of her, his prospects were to change, how could she bear the responsibility? Let her account for herself alone. 'Let's go home!' she said to Yang Chao. At least let him pass his entrance exam first. It took time to forget someone.

In her satchel were clothes the Big Guy had bought her. Having been washed once, they have already lost one third of their colour. She took off all her clothes in front of Yang Chao to change into her new clothes. She wanted him to know everything, though she did not want to use speech to tell him. The room grew even more silent. She turned around to look at him and found him with his hands covering his face, with tears flooding out from between his fingers. Since he did not have a free hand to wipe them away, he had to let the tears fall. She thought how good it would be if only she could cry too.

'I really do want to go back.' For the moment, she had better continue to coax him.

'How I wish I were already 30 years old.'

If he were that age, then he could work, support a family, get married. The trouble was, she didn't even dare think about her own 20 years of age. Besides the old days were threatening to return, what's the point of talking about the years to come?

She helped Yang Chao wipe the tears off his face and went home with him. Her father pretended nothing had happened. She also pretended nothing had taken place.

The arrest and disciplinary action taken against the Big Guy was planned and executed by his own father. In addition, his father announced in the papers that whatever his son did outside of the home had nothing to do with him. Tien-ch'ing had seen the Big Guy's father. He was supposed to be a scholar, but his temper and spirit was more like those of a warrior. He was a university president.

Once the papers reported the incident, it immediately caused a scandal. The president of a university and yet unable to discipline his own son? It was too tempting a subject for writers not to expound on. The formers of public opinion were falling over each other to enter the debate. Journalists took a hold of the tail of the incident and refused to let go of it; they did not let go of Ch'eng Tien-ch'ing either.

After the incident became news, the university president couldn't extricate himself without some show of discipline. He staunchly refused to bail his son out unless the latter promised never to see Ch'eng Tien-ch'ing again. The most serious event has a way of fading into the past. Tien-ch'ing believed that the problem did not lie between herself and The Big Guy and their intimacy. It lay in the opposition between the Big Guy and his father. Theirs was a typical generation gap. She learned not to inquire. She did not want to know.

The affair finally involved Yang Chao. The most difficult aspect to handle was the birth of rumour at a moment's notice. In addition, people even came to school just to point their fingers at her. She could ignore them, Yang Chao could not. Yang Chao's grades fell through the floor. Despite all, he never said a word that hinted at his abandoning her. Neither did he ever blame her for her relationship with the Big Guy.

She knew Yang Chao really cared. So far as she could manage it, she went home straight from school. No matter what, she wanted never to see Yang Chao's tears again.

Just when she thought she had become used to her way of life, the body's memory began to react. Lying on her bed in the middle of the night without a trace of sweat, she would nevertheless feel moisture on her body. Something was flowing through her, something that made her lightheaded and weak, almost making her want to fly. She sorely missed the Big Guy.

She described the sensation to Yang Chao. He didn't say a word; he simply held her tight. This time, she did not hit him, nor did he kiss her. She recalled the first hotel she stayed in, and the room. In Yang Chao's arms, the feeling was completely different from that of being with the Big Guy. The latter had passion and was free of qualms. It was as if he would do the same thing whoever he was with. Though Yang Chao was holding her tight, he made no demands on her. The difference was in the degree of their emotions. Yang Chao behaved this way towards her alone. Did Yang Chao really have nothing more that he wanted from her? Tien-ch'ing felt the dark tidal wave that was flowing in her body freeze instantaneously.

The memory of the outside world was also in reaction. The gang that had followed the Big Guy came to look for her. They said since she was the Big Guy's woman, they would take care of her. In actual fact they merely wanted her to rejoin the gang. Now that her name was known, her reputation would be an asset in staking out their territory.

'What if I refuse?' She wanted to be by herself now. She had no need to be among a lot of people any more.

'Could you take back sucked blood?'

It was not the first time that they had stood in her way and refused to let her pass, or had messages taken to her. She turned away, wanting to leave, but they twisted her arm and forced her to stay, threatening her: 'Refuse us and that pretty face of yours will be sorry.'

This was not a gang rule established by the Big Guy. They thought they were standing up for the Big Guy, but in fact they were merely bullies. Tien-ch'ing was not about to surrender without putting up a fight. She struggled to free herself, but the one who was holding her down convinced her it was no use with a hard slap across the face.

They took her to an empty room. She was not trying to struggle free any more. If only they had known about this empty room before, things would not have developed the way they did. One could only blame the Big Guy's stars for not leading them here in the first place.

The only thing that worried her was that Yang Chao would probably think she had left home again when he came to pick her up at school and couldn't find her.

The whole crowd left together, leaving her alone in the empty room as punishment. She was surrounded by darkness, but she was not a bit afraid. She had survived more than ten years at home; was there a deadlier silence any place on earth than that? Sitting or moving around at home, she felt she was like the minute hand of the clock, ticking away blindly, passing the time.

When morning came she surveyed her surroundings. It was just like life itself. Just like life in its total emptiness. She shrank into a corner and sat down. That one day and night was very long. In the end they didn't have the gall to

keep her locked up for long. She was still a living person after all, and besides
it was no fun that way, so they let her go. When Yang Chao saw her, he didn't
even bother to ask.

'I'm all right,' she volunteered.

Now she was the one who was afraid he would be hurt, that he would let
his mind wander to the worst possible scenario.

'I hope you can live decently in the next few years until I graduate from the
university,' Yang Chao said distantly.

'Decently? I wouldn't dare hope for that much. But I'll make it all right.'

'Is it possible to make it?' There was poison in his words.

'You wait and see!'

For a whole half month she did not have anything to do with Yang Chao.
During that month, she discovered there was something wrong with her. Yes,
she was indeed pregnant. She wanted to laugh. Even if the Big Guy were
around, she might not necessarily marry him. In any case, he was not around.

Yang Chao accompanied her to the women's clinic. The doctor didn't ask
a single question before he told her to lie down on the operation table. She
forgot to take off her shoes.

When they emerged from the clinic, it was already dark. Yang Chao took
her for a meal of duck cooked with envigorating herbal medicine. He ordered
two bowls and placed them both in front of her. He sat there in the middle of
the crowded restaurant, thinking about something; there were people everywhere.

'Did it hurt?' Yang Chao asked her.

She wanted to cry but shook her head instead. If only she had learned to
shake her head sooner. If she had she might not have to learn to bear pain now.

Events came to a close. The Big Guy's father finally bailed him out. The day
the Big Guy was released, Yang Chao went looking for him right after school;
he still had his school-bag with him. He never got to see the Big Guy; he was
stabbed by several 'brothers', and on the way to the hospital he died from loss
of blood.

When she heard the news, the first image that flashed across her mind was
those bowls of duck meat.

The university president, with comet-like speed, sent his son away. She had
no way of going abroad so she stayed behind to complete the studies that Yang
Chao could not now complete for himself.

Later when she met the Big Guy again, he had already finished his studies
abroad and returned home. In addition, his reputation was on the rise. He was
Yi Hsing-wen.

Having been out of touch for several months, Yi Hsing-wen was completely ignorant of the news of Yang Chao's death. That he was sent off abroad in such a hurry, however, convinced him something untoward had happened. It was not until he had left the country that the facts about Yang Chao's death reached him by circuitous channels.

In the first half year, he had called long distance and written to argue with his father to let him come home. To no avail. Since he couldn't sit still indoors, he spent his days wandering the streets. Every face he saw was a stranger's. He was drunk numerous times. Drinking from the time he woke up to the time he could drink no more, he lost ten kilos in all. He then discovered that the only way home was to finish his studies abroad. He pretended to have forgotten all about the past and began to make applications for schools. He also sent Tien-ch'ing a letter. Reply to his applications soon came back with positive results. The letter to Tien-ch'ing, on the other hand, was like a stone sunk to the bottom of the sea.

During that period he concentrated on one thing alone—his studies. Why his studies? He could not afford to think of anything else. Because of his father's good connections, he very easily entered a prestigious university, had prestigious friends, made prestigious grades. Life seemed easy, but what about the heart? All about him he saw the alien faces of an alien people. He was clearly conscious of his own position. He would never ever like that environment, those people.

On countless occasions he would wake up in the middle of the night and think he was still at that little hotel. The darkness and the stillness were the same, but his cold, stiff body told him otherwise. In this way, he got into the habit of sleeping with his lights on. Since he did not want to see his surroundings he was left with the only option of closing his eyes while still awake.

With the approach of each vacation, his aunt would hide his passport. In the end, he simply gave up the notion that he could return home without his diploma. The days became a little less difficult to pass after that.

In his spare time after school, he worked at restaurants. It was not that his family needed him to make an effort at anything other than school work. He simply wanted to see if, in a place where Chinese people frequented, he could bump into someone he knew. Also, it gave him a chance to speak more Chinese and so bring up particular memories of the past. Unreasonably, he felt that nights were especially long abroad and the lights too many. He often forgot what day of the week it was.

During this period, his mother passed away and his father became president of one of the best universities. He did not receive the news till after the event.

His father did not want him home for the funeral, thinking time would dilute public memory. He, for his part, never touched on the subject. He knew the deadliest link in his father's fears was that of whether or not he remembered what happened before. He did not harbour much hate. When one has been abroad for long enough, one tends to wish away certain responses to life.

When he finally saw Tien-ch'ing again, it was after his numerous trips home to give lectures. He firmly believed that Tien-ch'ing must have known from the newspapers about his visits early on. Why then was she so perverse as to not look him up? He did not want to pursue that subject.

After all those years, Tien-ch'ing appeared much smaller than the image he had of her. He brought her to the hotel where he was staying. His suite was spacious and up-scale. He wanted them to come face to face with each other without reservations. This time, their surroundings were much cooler. That which had not changed was the stillness in the air.

'You knew about my coming back a long time ago?' he asked.

Tien-ch'ing nodded. This was the same nod that he had seen before when, all those years ago, he had asked her if it was her wish not to go home. He winced. He couldn't ask further. Should he have told her how much trouble he had gone to to find her? What did her not wanting to see him mean?

To his surprise, they sat till the morning. Trying to communicate with each other, they had made matters even more confusing. The room rent was taken care of by somebody else this time; they needn't worry. Besides, they had grown up quite some time ago.

Tien-ch'ing's silence made him realize that she hated him, and they had once been intimate. He held Tien-ch'ing's hand. Both her hands were cold, not the way it was when she was young.

'How can I pay my debt to you?'

'I owed you and your family.'

This was the first time he had taken a good look at Tien-ch'ing. The memory and pain of his youth could not be mended now. Again, he gave in to another impulsive action. He came straight to the point, 'I will take you abroad with me.'

The same old problems remained: marriage, contracts, public opinion. Only, now that they were adults, they could no longer solve problems by running away.

'Can we escape?'

How did Tien-ch'ing become so passive? By his estimate, even if they had to exchange time for space, they had a great future ahead of them. Events were outside of their control before, but problems created by time can eventually be solved.

Tien-ch'ing's quiet nature did not make their reunion an earth-shattering event. He swore this time he was not going to let it end with a whimper. He accepted the school's offer to stay on. His decision to stay led to a good deal of speculation by the media; they finally proved that they had guessed right.

Even though he thought there was a lot of time ahead of them, he still tried to grasp every opportunity to see Tien-ch'ing. He would even go straight to her classroom to look for her. Tien-ch'ing kidded him with 'once a gangster always a gangster.'

Poor Tien-ch'ing had already been looked at askance before she entered graduate school. When she finally did, criticism and rumour blew about. They were no more than speculations, on the possibility of her coming from a great family and on the likelihood of her ambition. Such speculations made him laugh.

The people he found most detestable were those around Tien-ch'ing, lying in wait for something to happen to them. Yi Hsing-wen expressed his displeasure; he did not want Tien-ch'ing to have other alternatives. At school, he had a reputation as a gracious scholar, but for some reason, whenever he came face to face with Tien-ch'ing, his old self would resurface and it was impossible for him to rise to grace.

He reckoned that in this lifetime, it was his destiny to have Tien-ch'ing at whatever cost; he would exchange his life for hers. He was willing to give anything just to make it up to her.

It was unavoidable. His violent mood swings were entirely unpredictable. They were brought on by his fear of once again searching for her. This unpredictability affected his work as well as his social life. When the news in the papers and at the university reached its most unambiguous, he volunteered to resign. It was at that point his father reappeared on the scene.

It was incomprehensible to him. Why was it that all his life in his role as son, he was unable to disentangle himself from his father? They were not enemies. Father and son sat down more than once in a series of negotiations over a topic that had no conclusions. He was never of the opinion that divorce was a shameful matter. Besides, even if it were, it was not a matter that called for the taking of a life. On the other hand, the loss of Tien-ch'ing and the suffering that that would bring would last a whole lifetime. His father could no longer withhold his passport. He had not wanted to go abroad before; it was the same now.

In the period of negotiations, he and Tien-ch'ing had arranged temporarily not to see each other. When he called, she was mostly quiet.

After his father left, his wife arrived from abroad. His father had arranged this marriage at a time when Yi Hsing-wen was the most indifferent to life.

Marriage of convenience, it was merely a case of making perfection more perfect. Ironically, it attracted all sorts of envy.

Since he and his wife were not truly intimate, he had never really opened his heart and mind up to her. Theirs was a civil relationship. This time, his wife lifted the facade of civility and quite plainly said: 'If you go ahead with the divorce, then be prepared to come and identify my body.'

In fact, they had never said anything in front of others about his relationship with Tien-ch'ing, past or present. Yet, almost everyone thought that he or she knew exactly what was going on between them. All those detached bystanders observed the two of them and came to their own conclusions from mere appearances. What if, once again, they were forced apart by circumstance? What if he lost touch with Tien-ch'ing? What would he do? Who would he fight to the death for her?

He finally decided that the status quo was the best situation for them. At least that way he could continue to see her. Caught in the current, what were they waiting for? Time? Why was it that once they came together news was bound to arise? Was it the abnormal reaction squeezed out by their going against the tide? Thinking about it, he realized there was something wrong. This was not the end.

Sure enough, his wife's family took rapid measures going through certain channels to protest against Tien-ch'ing to her school. He pleaded with Tien-ch'ing to quit school as a response, but Tien-ch'ing refused, saying: 'Where else can I hide myself?' She was indeed right. He, however, was afraid that, given the situation, Tien-ch'ing would finally sacrifice him. So he insisted that she quit school to give him a free hand dealing with them.

His wife kept pressing him to give up his relationship with Tien-ch'ing; he was unwilling to discuss their past with anyone else. That was their business and no one else's. Moreover, it was clear to him that, after such a long time, Tien-ch'ing was extremely unwilling to enter into conflict with anyone; any form of struggle would bring on too many memories. Yang Chao lost his life in just such a conflict. Yi Hsing-wen discovered that he was still unable to share the same front line with Tien-ch'ing.

He pressed forward with his plans for them, presenting her various strategies. He thought their best bet would be Tien-ch'ing's pregnancy; if they could only produce a child that was theirs. If they had a child, who could then say that they were not bound to each other?

It was then that Tien-ch'ing, looking out the window of the restaurant, told him about what happened at the women's clinic.

'We have already lost a child,' she said.

He was stunned into silence. And they said his relationship with Tien-ch'ing did not amount to much.

'It's all too predictable. The final outcome of this mess. What's the point? No one has long to live; I can't take much more of this.' She said this deliberately, taking her time. She even called him 'Big Guy'.

How many people would have to die before they were allowed to go on? He was willing to fight with his life. Tien-ch'ing did not comment. After she had left for home, it started to rain. He wanted to make sure she was all right, so he rang her up afterwards. Tien-lan answered the phone. He called her again later. Tien-ch'ing came to the phone that time and said she had been for a walk. He told her to have a good rest, that everything was going to be all right. Tien-ch'ing replied that there was no reason why she shouldn't learn from her mother and quietly hide behind the passing of time. He understood that she was saying goodbye. He heard her despair beneath the calm. She did not repeat herself. Goodbye need not be repeated.

He quickly resigned his position and left the country. He believed they would one day come together again.

The news of Tien-ch'ing's illness arrived at the same time as that of her relationship with Feng Tzu-kang. He felt that there was no such thing as justice in this world.

He did not go to visit her at the hospital. This way, maybe, she could live a little longer without suffering. The day Feng Tzu-kang arrived at the hospital, Yi Hsing-wen was also there, standing at a distance, secretly grateful to Feng Tzu-kang. He must remember Feng Tzu-kang's face. Tien-ch'ing deserved better luck in life. He had hoped that Feng Tzu-kang would bring her new life. For Feng's companionship in his stead, Yi Hsing-wen had only gratitude.

The day they buried Tien-ch'ing, he felt surprisingly light-hearted. If death were another life, then Tien-ch'ing had finally crossed over to the beyond; they had shaken hands.

None of them could detain her.

Death in a Cornfield

P'ing-lu

translated by Chang Jun-mei Chou

LATELY it has been raining all the time in Taipei. I've been sitting in front of my bedroom window going through the things that accumulated under the bed. Among the odds and ends there is a mouse-eaten old notebook I kept as a journal a couple of years ago. As I pick it up and flip through it, a few mouse droppings fall out and a gust of mildewy odour fans out from the pages. The odour stops my reading and pushes me to press my nose against the cold window, continuously rinsed clean by several days of pouring rain. Outside, against a background of rain and fog which have lingered for days now, the flat roofs of overlapping apartment buildings stretch into a grey blur. The only objects distinguishable are the cross-shaped television antennas sticking up from the cement roof tops, creating a scene like a deserted graveyard. Shying from such unpleasant associations, I shift my eyes to the inside of the room, but the inside does not reveal a much pleasanter view. The room is in the mess typical of a single man's lodging. All of a sudden, I cannot help recalling a 'once-upon-a-time' scene of a sunny house with green lawns, and also the mistress of the house. How simple and orderly it was there! With the recollection, a feeling of guilt overwhelms me like a nightmare, which results from my having abandoned, a year ago, both a marriage and a career.

As I begin to read the notebook, the scene of a beautiful cornfield flashes across my mind; so also my sense of righteousness and determination last year to do what I did. The events of that summer all come back, so alive to me that my life in the present begins to recede.

The summer in Washington, DC, that year was probably hotter than it had ever been. For about two weeks, the temperature was around 100 degrees every day. I was then a foreign correspondent for a Taiwanese newspaper. My name appeared often on the second page of that paper. 'Dispatch from Washington, DC, by correspondent so-and-so.' With such a nice ring to my title I should have had a splendid life.

Unfortunately, this was not so. As a matter of fact, I was at that time rather tired of my job. It was partly because the international situation then was so unfavorable to us that even reporters were affected and could not enjoy the privileges we were entitled to. We had to cope with politically snobbish circles; sometimes it was humiliating. In addition, I had to deal with the numerous visitors from Taiwan. I could never understand how there could be so many people from Taiwan, all sorts of people, coming to Washington, DC, on official visits, and it seemed that all of them, besides sight-seeing, wanted to have their names appear in their hometown newspapers after their visits. Somehow, the responsibility fell to me to arrange some kind of social function that would increase the news-worthiness of their visits.

After a while, I disliked the role of host for the visitors. In the first two years of my assignment, I asked several times, unsuccessfully, to be transferred back to Taiwan. Later I gave up the idea, mainly because my wife, Mei-yun, did not want to leave. A few years after that, I grew accustomed to the environment and I too became reluctant to leave. I then found ways to prove myself a valuable asset to my employer, showing off my talent in languages and my experience in the profession so as to make my headquarters think I was indispensable. However, the more conscientious part of me as a professional journalist felt I was rotting away in a unique manner.

It was during those years that I gradually formed the habit of reading obituaries. It became my daily routine to glance over the headlines of the just-off-press, still-warm papers and pick a few items to telex back to Taiwan. After that I settled myself down in a certain corner of the building, the news centre, and went through the obituaries one by one.

The reasons for forming such a strange habit were probably more complicated than I could explain. Firstly, a couple of years earlier my brother-in-law died so unexpectedly that I never quite got over thoughts about the uncertainty of life. Secondly, having seen some of the ups and downs of human society, I realized where true equality was possible, and thus had a somewhat strange feeling of satisfaction when I saw that all kinds of people, no matter how powerful during their lifetimes, inevitably ended up on the same path.

One day, the name 'Chen Hsi-shan' appeared in the obituary column, squeezed in a space as small as a classified advertisement. The few short lines gave the dates of his birth and death (a fairly young man, not yet 40), where he worked (Department of Housing Development), and his survivors (his widow, Georgia, and their daughter). I read it out absent-mindedly, while sipping a cup of coffee.

Why did I go back to the death of this Chinese man on the obituary page after I had finished reading the sports pages? A possible explanation is that I was extremely bored at the time, in that seemingly endless scorching summer. My colleague, Hsiao Ch'in[1], who covered local news, was on a trip to New

---

[1] *Hsiao*, which means 'little', often prefixes the name of a child or a young person.

York, so I didn't even have anyone to argue with. Before taking off, he had asked me to cover his job for him. 'Come up with a scoop. Let me see exactly what you can do,' he said, a cigarette hanging from the corner of his mouth; in his voice there was no hint of his taking me seriously. Thinking of the successful young reporter's arrogance, I took out the Cross pen from my pocket and outlined repeatedly that small rectangular announcement.

That day I made a few phone calls to the numbers recorded in my pocket address book, in an attempt to obtain background information about the deceased without bothering his immediate family. I hoped to find out that Chen was some sort of successful young man who might have been invited back to Taiwan to attend important conferences. If this was so, I could at least write an article in his memory, showing respect for scholars abroad. Unfortunately, it turned out that Chen was not particularly successful in any field and had no connections with any recruiting channels back in Taiwan. He seemed to have been something of a loner. Just as I was going to give up, one of my sources provided me with a piece of unexpected information: this man Chen had disappeared for about a month before he was declared dead. After his body was found, the case was hastily closed on the ground that there was no suspicion of homicide. This information aroused my professional curiosity. The dormant instincts of a former feature writer urged me to dig further. At least I should try to interview his widow.

At the same time, I argued with myself that this kind of news was Hsiao Ch'in's domain; if my meddling led to any trouble, I would be blamed for trespassing on his territory, and if I did dig out something at all newsworthy, my aggressive colleague would never let me follow it up. Thus reasoning, I lost interest in the case. Nonetheless, I did not tell Hsiao Ch'in about it when he came back from New York. Maybe the weather was too hot; anyhow I was too lazy to open my mouth. That week the temperature went even higher; some of the already thickly growing plants in the suburbs suddenly turned into tropical jungles.

It remained very hot the following weekend. Worse still, there was not yet even the trace of a breeze. That Sunday afternoon, sitting in our kitchen listening to the loud hum of the refrigerator, I stared at the overgrown lawn in the backyard. Mei-yun was at her choir practice. Before she left she told me to do the mowing; she said, all the neighbours' lawns had already been mowed. 'So what?' I thought. 'Keeping up with the Joneses?' It was too bad that her husband could not keep up with many Joneses. First of all, I had studied the humanities; so Mei-yun was not the wife of an engineer, architect, accountant, or lawyer. Fortunately I had earned a modest name in journalism and it helped her somewhat in the women's circles. Really stupid! How stupid could a man be if the goal he strove to reach was simply 'do not disgrace thy spouse'. If he was not stupid, he would not have a stupid woman who demanded that he keep up with the Joneses. The stupid woman said the neighbours' lawns were mowed, but so what? The problem was, I did not think it necessary to mow the lawn at all. 'There is a different kind of beauty in overgrown grass.' I waved my arms and groaned, but she had already left. The choir gathering was one of her favourite social activities, where she mingled with women of high society. Their performances for charities had earned them quite a name, and Mei-yun seemed to be their star soprano. Meanwhile I was supposed to sweat under the sun mowing the lawn. I pushed the kitchen chair back heavily and suddenly I had a desire to interview the woman named Georgia.

It was a week later when I finally met Mrs Chen. During that time, after the appointment was made, my curiosity increased somewhat and I even vaguely looked forward to the meeting. This was special in my uneventful daily routine; I kept it a secret from my colleague Hsiao Ch'in.

On the day of the meeting, sitting at a table near the aisle in the Four Seasons Restaurant, I began to worry whether Mrs Chen would change her mind at the last minute. Yes, over the phone she did promise to meet me, but all women were capable of changing their minds at the last minute. I felt restless and kept looking towards the entrance of the restaurant. Layers of wide-leafed plants were arranged around the door; the very density of the greenness looked threatening and suffocating. Whenever I felt depressed, I had the feeling I was trapped in a jungle where octopus-like plants were suspended all around me. The imaginary depth of the green was overwhelming and suffocating—or maybe it was just the overgrown lawn in my backyard. Mei-yun had once proclaimed with a very severe face that the lawn would eventually turn into a jungle if we let it grow freely. What's wrong with growing freely? I wanted to pursue freedom, too, and thought I would have to mow the lawn if I were not sitting here waiting for a woman named Georgia . . . .

Finally, thank heavens, Mrs Georgia Chen appeared. Along the aisle lined with palm trees came a tall, thin woman of about 30 with very thick, black hair and strong features. When she reached my table I could see several brownish freckles on her cheekbones. The pouting lips were calmly closed but the eyes shifted like little flickering flames, revealing her unusual energy. Before saying anything she opened her handbag and took out a calling card with the name of a trading company on it. Then she assaulted me, in rapid English with a Cantonese accent: 'Don't think I am unaware of what you reporters are after. I am a naturalized American citizen and know all my rights. I presume you understand that too. Please respect my rights. I don't want my name to appear in the newspapers. Don't try any tricks on me, or my lawyer will contact you.'

The lenses of her tea-coloured spectacles flashed against the background of tropical plants while she was talking. The combination of sunglasses and tropical plants reminded me of the seaside and the flat-figured women on the beach. I felt a little dizzy and disgusted. Georgia Chen's bluffing did not scare me but it disappointed me, unbearably. She was shrewd, but in a very juvenile way—just like one of those resolute-looking women you see in office buildings who only talk about disputes over rights and interests. I was disappointed, but I don't know what I expected. What had I anticipated? A weeping little woman twisting her handkerchief? Or a chic widow with a white flower behind her ear, like those described in old-fashioned Chinese stories? (Or, even more exciting, a bold 'merry widow' who did not hide her desire even in mourning?) How could I entertain such trashy ideas? I must be in a terribly trashy state of mind myself.

After Georgia Chen's solemn pronouncements, I told her in all sincerity that I had no vicious intentions and would not put her name in the newspapers; I only wanted to know more facts about her husband's death and hoped to be of some help if possible.

When she had relaxed somewhat she began to speak in Chinese. She lit up a cigarette and recounted the events surrounding her husband's death. It was more intricate than I had dreamt, and I was rather unprepared for that. My interest in the case came from a wish for a break in my dull routine of the hot summer. It came of course also from my curiosity about a young widow (Young? Definitely! Any woman ten years my junior is young!)—an idle curiosity which I should not have had. Therefore, psychologically I was not prepared for what I was hearing from Mrs Chen. But, being a more or less seasoned reporter, I made myself appear calm. She relaxed even further and seemed comfortable enough to answer all my questions. Her answers were brief and to the point. Her courage facing the questions impressed me favourably in a professional way. Finally I began to appreciate her frankness, which reminded me of my wife's carefree manner and how I had liked it when we first met. The daring self-assurance of this kind of woman automatically wins respect; but only idiots like me would have married one. And true enough, soon after we were married I was totally defeated by Mei-yun's haughty, pugnacious spirit. No wonder marriage was sometimes described as a combination of battlefield and graveyard. The battlefield was to test one's will. Anyone who could not pass the test would be buried there for eternal rest—not exactly for rest, but as a martyr. While I was looking at this spirited widow in front of me, a terrible thought suddenly came to me: 'Isn't it true that one gets what one wants?' Again I tried not to associate this woman with my wife. Yet the two must have something in common. Maybe it was the voice, crisp and piercing, accurate as bullets. What, then, was the story here? An exhausted man encountered an energetic woman? . . . *ta ta ta* . . . it was the machine-gun firing . . . the man was doomed to a life of hard work, and could easily lose his life on the way! . . . *ta ta ta ta* . . . I had to pull myself out of the imagined volleys of machine-gun fire to continue the interview with Georgia Chen. The following is what I jotted down in my notebook from what she said.

The Widow's Version

Hsi-shan disappeared about two months ago. He never came back after he went out one night. The next morning I felt something must be wrong and reported it to the police. Two officers came to our house and said they would enter the information into the computer. They told me that thousands of people went missing every year and only a very small number of them were found. . . . A little over a month later the police found Hsi-shan's body in the cornfield near our house. In this hot weather the body was already rotting, but the police said it was his.

The house we moved into last October was a new one. It was rural enough that there was still a cornfield in our neighbourhood. The body was found there. Why did he go out that night? Maybe he heard some noise, maybe he was walking in his sleep. Who knows? Those days when I got home from work, I was exhausted. Usually I fell asleep as soon as I could lie down after Hsiao-wei, our daughter, went to bed. It seems so improbable that someone would go out at midnight.

The police said it was most likely suicide. I don't believe them. One stupid officer even asked me whether Hsi-shan and I had quarrelled. I immediately asked him whether he and his wife ever quarrelled. Are there any husbands and wives who have never quarrelled? If you want to ask me the same questions, I can tell you Hsi-shan and I had been through much hardship together. There was the kind of attachment between us that came from sharing hard times and good times. . . . This is the strongest kind of bond between a husband and wife.

I was from Hong Kong. We got to know each other in a small college town in the States where there weren't many Chinese. I worked part-time. He dropped out of the university but could not get a decent job, so he had to work in a restaurant for some time. After I graduated and he got a job, we were married in a court by a justice of the peace.

Before he met me, he had some questionable friends. During the territorial disputes over the Tiao-yu-t'ai Archipelagos he joined his friends in protest demonstrations. He had even planned to go back to the Mainland to serve the 'socialist motherland'. After he met me he stopped seeing those friends and gradually settled down. Later he got a job in a government office. Recently, however, he talked a lot about returning to Taiwan, though he knew it was only talk. He had a record in Taiwan and, even worse, his name was probably on the blacklist. Anyway, I definitely would not go with him.

Now I have a trading company here, importing pure wool rugs. The business is not bad. I began it out of necessity. Before he got the government job, he never had any steady work. So the importing business was very helpful financially. We had to plan for our daughter's future; it takes a lot of money to raise a child here, especially a girl. Besides, there was the mortgage. Actually, I didn't want to have a child in the first place. Well, now she is fatherless, but her life is pretty much the same, except that I, instead of her father, pick her up from the baby-sitter. She still takes piano lessons on weekends. Now with her father gone, she is free of the pressure to learn Chinese characters. He even foolishly tried to teach the child to speak Taiwanese. Don't you agree that wasn't very sensible?

As a matter of fact, Hsi-shan didn't have much of a head on his shoulders; he was absolutely ignorant of politics. During the Tiao-yu-t'ai protests, he joined many other Chinese in the movement to 'identify with the motherland'. He didn't take into account he was Taiwanese; who could he identify with on the Mainland? In the last few years he changed his mind and wanted to go back to Taiwan. He said he didn't mind living in a poverty-stricken village as long as he could go back to the place he had grown up. I couldn't stand it any more so I told him very directly, 'Years ago your impulsive ideas might have been excusable because you were young. But now, you have a family and should be responsible for it. Unless you want to give up everything, you better stay here and settle down with me.'

He was rather dumb and, at times, unbearable, but he had no enemies. I simply can't understand how something like this could happen. Kidnappers would not pick on people like us. . . .

I really didn't hear anything that night. . . .

Watching Mrs Chen walk out of the glass doors of the Four Seasons, I put the notebook back into the pocket of my coat and leaned back in the deep soft seat. The more I thought over her words, the more confused I felt about the incident. Her Cantonese accent reminded me of the Hong Kong section in the Chinese newspapers published in New York. Those pages were mostly filled with either the romances of actors and actresses or sensational crimes like smuggling, kidnapping and drugs. But this was not Hong Kong, and Mrs Chen was not that kind of person. Then what could it be? Before I could come up with a satisfactory explanation, they began to serve dinner, and since I could not charge such a meal as a business expense, I picked up my jacket and left the restaurant. Outside, the pavement was still releasing heat accumulated during the day; the fog within my head dissolved into perspiration, dampening my whole body.

After I returned to my suburban home from the steaming temperature of the city, the cool air blown out by our heavy-duty air-conditioner sobered me up. I heard my wife's resounding soprano voice ringing out through the hallway. It was the afternoon for voice practice again.

I took a shower first. When I came to the kitchen to make myself a cup of jasmine tea I heard her singing a Chinese lyric: 'The dew captured the fragrance of a red flower in bloom; the momentary passion left only longing and gloom.' I was somewhat touched by the singing, or maybe by the sadness of the lyric. I could visualize my wife sitting on the edge of her bed combing her hair; I had an impulse to go in to tell her what had happened that day. Just then her voice stopped on a whole note rest. The pause gave me time to think of our tangled problems, to remember her stern face and her desire for the material things. I was, by contrast, a very lethargic, languid kind of person. Our differences had become irreconcilable, maybe because of our ages, or maybe simply because of the sad reality of human nature. Though I understood all this, often I still could not resist, and in this way further boosted her arrogance and degraded myself before her. The moment all this flashed through my mind, my hand fell from the doorknob.

The next moment, strangely, my mind drifted to a cornfield. Even more strangely, this time the swaying green leaves, layers and layers of them, no longer suffocated me. I visualized the body of Chen Hsi-shan lying there surrounded by cornstalks waving like warm ocean currents. His body was floating on the currents under the sunshine. I suddenly realized at that moment it might not be such a sad thing for someone to die that way if he could not do anything about his own life any more.

I made several more phone calls, trying to find out more about Chen Hsi-shan. A few days later I was put in touch with a colleague of Chen's, a man named Kao Li-pen, who took the English name of Jack. Originally from Anhui Province, he was older and had begun working in DC much earlier than Chen. I called to make the appointment and met Kao at the arch-shaped gate of his office building. I was wearing a Hawaiian shirt and had a notebook under my arm, very casual so as not to arouse any unnecessary suspicions. Unexpectedly, Kao was rather worldly-wise. Seeing me standing there, he walked towards me with a friendly smile and shook my hand warmly. From his looks, I guessed he had stood on a few docks in his time.

When our talk turned to Chen Hsi-shan, Kao's smiling face turned serious. A thin film of water could be seen in his heavily-wrinkled eyes.

A Colleague's Version

Chen Hsi-shan? When people said he had disappeared I couldn't believe it—until I went to his funeral. What a pity! He was really a nice man. How could a guy like him end up like that in the prime of his life!

He was so innocent that people liked to make fun of him. Even I did sometimes. Now I really regret that. He was also a perfectionist in certain ways. For instance, you could never find a single wrinkle in his shirt. He must have washed and ironed them every day. His family meant a lot to him —he had a large family photo in his office and he liked to talk about his daughter. Every afternoon he left the office at four o'clock sharp so he could pick her up at the baby-sitter's house. He never kept the child waiting.

Probably his only hobby was growing vegetables. He said he had lots of different kinds in his backyard and used to bring me Chinese varieties. They were good! Particularly the green turnips; they tasted just like the ones from my hometown.

Oh, the cornfield. I heard that he died in a cornfield. Chen had told me once that his house was in a newly developed area, completed just last October. He always went to look at it while it was going up. He was particularly excited about the cornfield nearby, because it reminded him of the sugarcane field in his hometown. He liked to talk about pranks in his childhood: the way he used to sneak into the fields to steal sugarcane. When caught, he said, the owner used to spank him but would also give him a bunch of sugarcane to take home. When he came to this part of his story, Chen would laugh and laugh. I believe he told me this story again the day before he disappeared. I remember that day I said jokingly to him: 'You better not steal the corn here. The farmers here have guns.' In hindsight, my words sounded like a bad omen. I really feel sorry I kidded him that way.

Beg pardon? . . . what kind of work do we do in our office? Oh, government offices are probably the same the world round . . . just busy work. It is true our English limits our job opportunities. . . . No, no, absolutely not. You reporters are over-imaginative. Brother, this is twentieth-century America, not eighteenth-century Africa. Just being a public official no way invites violence; or I would quit my job right now. . . . Don't let your imagination run wild . . . . By the way, if you uncover anything, please let me know. I miss him very much. It's not easy to find someone you can get along with in the office. Ai!—Ai!

He ended his account with a long sigh. His goodbye handshake was tight and heavy as though he was trusting me with the puzzle. Yet, actually, what could I do? I'm just a reporter, and this is America, where nobody really knows what's on anyone's mind. When I walked away from him, his sigh lingered in my ears.

According to Kao, Chen Hsi-shan was a rather passive person. That's probably why he worked for the government at a young age in the first place? The rows of fluorescent lights in the arched hallway of that ultramodern building went on glowing in my mind as if they were eternal lamps.

The cornfield might be an important clue, I thought. Its resemblance to sugarcane fields reminded Chen of his childhood, so it had a special meaning for him. Could it be this reminder of his childhood that led, directly or indirectly, to the tragedy? The tangled threads made me even more confused . . . .

Oddly enough, except for a momentary confusion, whenever I thought of Chen lying quietly in the cornfield, a cool feeling would begin and grow deep inside me. I became more and more aware that the cornfield scene brought a kind of inner coolness. It made me invulnerable to the summer heat that continued its unrelenting pressure. I became obsessed with the image of the scene. There must be some link between Chen and me. Yes, both of us were married to very capable women, except that he had a five-year-old daughter and I did not. It is good to have a child. If it had not been for my wife's extremely sound and logical mind, my child would also be five years old now.

I decided I had to have a talk with Chen's child, Hsiao-wei.

I went to see Chen's daughter at her baby-sitter's home. The child spoke very clearly and sensibly for a five-year-old. Her eyes were huge and pitiful, probably because of her father's disappearance. Her mouth, pouting, reminded me of her mother but the child did not have her mother's shrewdness and self-confidence. She was weaker and more submissive.

The Daughter's Version

Papa left. He hasn't come back since he went out the door that night. I still wait for him to pick me up as before at Grandma Liu's steps at a quarter past four.

Papa is very nice to me. He is more patient than Mama. He always goes to work and comes home on time. Mama sometimes comes home very late, after dark.

That night I heard Papa going out. I heard the doorknob turning softly. I was getting up to wee wee. Then I dreamed I heard a loud 'bang'. I don't know if it was a gun or not. . . . If only I had stayed awake, it would have been all right.

Mama always came home late then. Papa would stand at the front door and stare at the cornfield across the road. Sometimes the moon was round and bright. There were dogs, lots of them, barking far away. . . . Sometimes Papa had tears coming down his face. When I saw that I wanted to cry, too.

As soon as Mama got home, they quarrelled. Usually Papa mumbled a few words and then Mama yelled at him. They fought in English, so I didn't understand much, but I knew Mama blamed Papa for not helping her earn more. Once she said angrily, 'If you go back, I'll never let you see Hsiao-wei again.'

Mr Reporter, tell me, is it true that Papa will never see me again? He used to hold me in his arms and tell me he wouldn't go anywhere because he didn't want to leave me. When he was very unhappy, he often took me to the vegetable garden and showed me how to plant the seeds and how to water them. He let me feel the soil in my hand. It was soft and sticky. Papa said, 'This is the thing dearest to us in the world. It will never desert us.'

Mr Reporter, isn't Papa coming back? I want to tell him I wait for him every day. I've been waiting a long time.

Even after the little girl's waving arm had disappeared from my sight in the car's rear window, her large vague eyes remained in my mind. She had seen her father staring at the cornfield. She had heard a noise like a gunshot. Was she dreaming? Was the whole thing a dream? . . . When I looked into her eyes, I could believe her father really would come back and stand at the steps of her baby-sitter's house at quarter past four to pick her up. Why did I feel that way?

With this question in my mind, I still envied Chen Hsi-shan. No matter what he had lacked in his lifetime, he had had this child, a daughter who loved him. What did I have? Many years ago, when the exhausted obstetrician took off his gloves and laid his big hand on my arm to tell me they had to make an instant decision to save the mother instead of the baby, I was not sure how I felt deep in my heart. Did I wish they had made a different choice? How badly I had wanted a child! A child could be another self, a more hopeful self. Life could be renewed while the life I used to have remained only a timid and spiritless physical shell.

This was how I lost my first chance to have a child. When my wife became pregnant again, she had an abortion, saying that she did not want to take another risk. That was five years ago. Since then I deeply resented my wife's body. (Of course there were times I couldn't restrain desire.) It seemed to me what had been between us withered little by little ever since . . . . Or, perhaps, only I was dying gradually . . . .

After seeing Hsiao-wei, half the summer passed and I suddenly became very busy with visitors from Taiwan, for many newly-elected legislative representatives came to visit the American capital. Group after group I accompanied on tours of the north-eastern states. In the past I was always glad to do so because I liked travelling; it brought back many of the dreams of youth. There were opportunities to fool around with girls in bars, forgetting you already had someone at home. Of course these chances didn't occur very often, for the legislators had very tight schedules. But this year's trips gave me no time for enjoyment at all, particularly those with the 'nonpartisans' who wanted to meet as many Chinese from their districts as possible. The 'hometown folks' held various political views; many of them supported or sympathized with the Taiwan Independence Movement. The newly-elected representatives tried, on the one hand to maintain their nonpartisan stance, so as not to be labelled as leaning toward the Kuomintang. On the other hand, they avoided being used or trapped by any opposition faction. Theirs was not an easy job, but it was the price they had to pay for holding public office. What about myself? I paid an even sadder price, for I spent much of my time increasing the news-worthiness of their visits. I felt disappointed with myself and recalled more honourable days when I actually covered local news in Taiwan and considered myself the true voice of the people and the conscience of society. Once, before an election, I made some honest and shattering criticisms of certain undesirable candidates for public offices, and these were accepted and acted on. In those days even though I could only afford to eat at roadside stands, I ate my food with self-respect and professional satisfaction. Probably those were my happiest days, when I was fulfilling a newspaperman's real duties.

However, in a certain way, the time I spent on the road with the representatives was not all lost. By sheer luck I ran into a man who was a classmate of Chen Hsi-shan in high school. What's more, he remembered him. The following was what he told me, revealing yet another side of Chen Hsi-shan.

The High School Classmate's Version

He was the 'Little Plumpy' of our class, who was seated in the front row—seldom talked, not attractive, but always ranking among the top five. He was in charge of classroom maintenance for a few years and did very well in assigning jobs. However, it was not until our senior-year trip that he stood out in any way. Most of the harder-working students withdrew from the trip at the last minute because they needed more time to study for final examinations. Those who went for the trip were the more carefree ones. Chen Hsi-shan went with us and he was a top-ranking student. On our round-the-island trip, he entertained the whole group by telling jokes through the microphone. No one ever suspected he had such a rich sense of humour.

The last stop on the trip was at Chen's home. To get there we had to ride a little way on a railroad built for a sugar mill. The land around the Chen's house was all sugarcane fields. His parents gave us a really nice meal. I remember there was a plate of steamed chicken with thick soy sauce gravy. They were unsophisticated country folk, not speaking much nor eating much but plying us with food. When we were leaving, they kept bowing, saying we were admirable scholars; they also asked us to be good to their son.

After high school we saw little of each other. Chen Hsi-shan was able to study finance and taxation as he had hoped. I entered a different university and studied accounting and statistics. A year later I switched to engineering, which, I believed, would better equip me to win a girlfriend.

I ran into Chen Hsi-shan on the street a few times, but we didn't seem to have much to talk about, even though I liked him. Because I had seen another side of him during our senior-year trip, I was not surprised when in later years I heard he was taking part in the Tiao-yu-t'ai demonstrations . . . .

He took the protest very seriously and tried to organize a symposium to discuss certain national problems of China. When the movement fizzled and the symposium did not materialize, Chen became so depressed he couldn't continue his studies. That was a pity.

The next time I heard about him, he had married a very capable woman in the import-export business. I thought he had managed his life more successfully than the rest of our classmates. If I hadn't heard the shocking news from you today, I would still think he was enjoying an easy life in some obscure and quiet place.

That was my interview with the hardware engineer from Bell Laboratory. The representatives from Taiwan ended their intensive tour and I returned to

Washington, DC. It was late summer, still hot but no longer suffocating. My first act on my return was to clear my desk, throwing away the piles of newspapers and magazines which had accumulated while I was away. I threw them out not even glancing at them—the way I often handled news bulletins and releases. Even if I were to burn them all, I reasoned, what would it matter? The earth would keep on spinning as usual, tomorrow's papers would not suffer any setbacks, nor would anyone notice the lack of anything.

However, such irresponsible reasoning did not put me fully at ease. Was the map on the wall staring at me angrily and blaming me for insensitivity to some faraway parts of the world where serious calamities had just happened? Maybe I had become cold-blooded, or was indifference just a sign of professional fatigue? But to me, universal brotherhood could never be realized. I never was able to identify with unknown people in faraway places even though I had been dealing with foreign news for years. In that part of my job, I was merely a translation machine and nothing more, typing cold messages into a cold keyboard.

It was while tidying up my desk that I chanced to see a short article on Chen Hsi-shan. It was in a bulletin published by a leftist faction of the Taiwan Independence Movement. It read:

> Mr Chen—shan, of Pingtung, Taiwan, was devoted to the welfare of his hometown and was also very loyal to his motherland. His body was found in a field. The cause of death remains unknown. The organization is deeply concerned about his sudden death.
>
> Also, ten years ago during the Tiao-yu-t'ai Movement Mr Chen was an outstanding member of the group, noted for his courage in speaking out and for the contributions he made.

Another month passed without further progress in the case. As an amateur, I probably had reached a dead-end. During this period, I went to the police to pick up information, but was given the same official answer: 'There is no suspicion of homicide.' I also tried to contact Chen's neighbours but got no helpful information. In that new residential area there were very few houses nearby, and the Chens must have been rather isolated, for the neighbours hardly knew they existed. Each time I felt frustrated, something seemed to urge me to go to the cornfield—the only place I hadn't been to. Perhaps the answer was there.

Then came a day in early October. My wife and I again exchanged unpleasant words before I left home. The spat, as I remember, started over the unmowed lawn and wound up with the question of 'love', or the lack of it, between us. Mei-yun interpreted mowing the lawn as evidence of love for her, and she spoke the word 'love' with a holy radiance on her face. I could not help laughing. This was the first time, in spite of being irritated, I was able to remain calm enough to analyze the fictitious premises of her words.

That day, I arrived at my office building about noon. As I waited for the elevator in the lobby, the sun coming in through the large window drew my attention to the scene outside—picturesque Capitol Hill and the shimmering Potomac River. Just as I shifted my gaze from the dense green foliage on the banks to the flowing water, I was suddenly suffocated by a feeling of being trapped in a jungle. I felt dizzy. As a drowning man tries to grab at a piece of driftwood, I forced myself to think of Chen Hsi-shan, to think of him lying on the soil in the field with arms and legs stretched out, lightly brushed by the breeze and cradled by waving stalks, as a child held in his mother's arms— where one could find true peace and rest. I took a deep breath and a cool feeling gradually grew inside me.

My long postponed resolve to go to the cornfield grew stronger. In the past, on long afternoons like this, I often went to the bar on the top floor of the news building, bought a drink, and listened to the harpist play old songs from a couple of decades ago, songs which always brought back my faded dreams from the past. As I have mentioned earlier, I had certain weaknesses and easily became sentimental. However, this afternoon I kept thinking of the cornfield even after I had downed the first drink. I was worried that it would soon be harvest time, after which the field would be only cracked earth and dry stalks rustling in the autumn wind. Then snow would cover the field and finally it would become a vast blank stretch of grey. Ah! by then, it would be too late. That was too bleak a scene.

Slightly affected by the alcohol, I steered my car directly to Chen's house. After getting on and off the expressway a few times, I finally reached the end of the road where the Chens lived. The house came into view. The corn in the field nearby indeed looked like sugarcane, except for the barely noticeable brownish hairs at the tips of the ears.

I pulled the car to the side of the road and stopped. Leaning on the steering wheel, I wondered if I should turn back to the highway. In the darkening evening, the early autumn wind was a little chilly. Moreover, common sense told me I had gotten past thrill-seeking years after all. Yet there seemed to be a kind of force in the evening wind drawing me to the field. The edge of the corn leaves prickled my shoulders so that I had to walk sideways and pry my way through the field. Brief gusts of chilly wind gave me gooseflesh all over, but the soft rustling of the leaves sounded like faint panting, calling to me. Was it Chen trying to tell me something? Some secret hidden amid the green leaves and stalks? What was hidden there? His dreams? Secret dreams he had never realized?

The effects of the alcohol left me as I walked slowly into the depths of the rustling field, but, oddly enough, my heart pumped even faster. Treading the soil Chen had walked on, I almost felt I was stepping in the foot-prints he left that particular night. Right! He must have been looking for something that night, perhaps for an answer the way I was looking for one now. He had refrained from doing it until, inch by inch, the corn grew tall enough. Then, one evening, one scorching, airless evening, seeing the stretch of motionless cornstalks more like sugarcane than ever, he could not wait any longer. Then a highly-excited Chen walked into the field—and immediately found his dream broken. Tightly wrapped in the leaves was not sweet and juicy sugarcane, only a mocking illusion. The field could never resurrect the past he was looking for, just as he could never relive his childhood when right by his house there was a sugarcane field. His new house, a spacious one on the slopes, was perhaps also a dream. America, a dream of affluence and prosperity; marriage, a dream of absurdity; and Tiao-yu-t'ai? A dream of dislocated time and space.

I sat down on the bank. The moon came out and shone on the corn ears: ripe and full, wrapped in leaves along their stalks. Swaying in the breeze, the whole field appeared dreamily calm and peaceful. At that moment old dreams of my hometown came to mind. They were remote, vague, coloured with childish concepts and all built upon and expanded from limited and fragmentary memories. (When I was barely able to recognize the sound of guns, I became a refugee schoolchild.) In good years, the fields at home would normally be covered with vast stretches of green, but I could not remember whether they looked like the cornfield, or like the frightening jungles of greenness I often saw in my imagination. (Too bad I couldn't remember. I only remembered moving continuously with the troops from base to base, leaving behind us waves of hungry people.) . . . (Going south by ship, I went ashore every time the ship docked for food, driven by the constant hunger that pervaded the boats. I saw sugarcane for the first time at a peddler's stand. 'Bamboo?' I asked. The peddler gave me a scornful look in answer. That was my first impression of sugarcane.) Afterwards? After those days I seldom thought of my hometown and seldom shed tears, not even when I heard people singing folk songs about the fragrance of the ripening soybeans and sorghum. I concentrated on my studies in an evening school, and pursued my ambition to be a newspaper reporter who would speak for needy people.

Perhaps it was all a dream, I thought bewilderedly in the moonlight. Maybe simple wishes became complicated by rationalizing. Maybe what we see on the surface is a screenplay we substitute for the truth. Was it possible that Chen Hsi-shan was simply an unhappy man (like me!) who often had wanted to run away? ('Heaven help me! How can I harden my heart and just leave?') Probably he was planning his escape when he stood at his door, staring toward the cornfield under the moon. Perhaps that body was not his at all, and he was still alive, living comfortably soaking up sunshine on a Mediterranean island with a rich woman. I felt almost comforted as I continued dreaming in this vein. But just then the moon went behind a dark cloud, and I suddenly realized how stupid I was, sitting there in the dirt fantasizing about somebody I did not even know. I had to admit that, having had only limited information from fragmentary accounts, I knew very little about this man. My guesses were nothing but reflections of my own mental state. However, there was one thing certain about Chen: he had lived his life arduously and had tried his best to seek happiness even though he had not got much of it. I thought the vegetable garden in his backyard and his daughter who was still waiting for him to come back were all traces of his strenuous efforts. He had also worked hard to build a new home on the slopes near the cornfield, where he could watch the corn grow taller and taller, day after day, and grow more and more like sugarcane. . . . Compared to him, what had my life been the past few years? What did I have left now? What entitled me to pry into his life? Even this cornfield was his realm, because he had feelings about it and had watched it grow. In my life, the earth was much further from me. In my work, I had become so mechanical that even the little bit of romantic fantasy I once had was worn out with time. All that was left was an insubstantial living and an insatiable wife.

Sitting motionless on the bank and watching the moon obscured by the dark clouds, I felt the ground turning damp with dew and the wind growing stronger. When I raised my wrist to look at the time, the luminous dial reminded me of the inscription on its back: 'Uncrowned King'. The watch was a gift from the director of our newspaper, this gift to each new recruit to encourage him to live up to that motto. (I was then a greenhorn, but what high self-esteem I had when I got that watch! Now I had a better job but somehow I had lost the spirit.)

'I should try again, anyway,' I said to myself, somewhat moved by the vast stretches of fully-grown corn under the moon. I got up, dusted off my pants, and wiped clean the back of my watch on my hip pocket. Then I walked slowly through the rustling leaves and out of the field.

After that visit, I stopped digging for the cause of Chen's death. Instead, I asked for immediate transfer back to Taiwan and received permission a month later. I made arrangements for Mei-yun to remain in America and returned to

Taipei alone. Once back, I started from the beginning again, working a beat as a real news reporter.

Half a year later Mei-yun asked for a divorce on the grounds of our separation. I agreed at once. She came back to Taipei to complete the necessary legal steps. At the airport before she left, she looked at me gravely and said if I was to be sent abroad again we might be reconciled.

I thought I must tell her the truth. Holding her hand with its red-coated fingernails, I said, 'Now I'm middle aged I cannot make the same mistake again. I would rather stay here and do some solid work. The job of a foreign correspondent is one for younger people who can fight it alone. Maybe I'll marry a country woman and raise a bunch of lively kids. That's what I want from life.'

After that meeting with Mei-yen I hardly ever think about the cornfield any more. Occasionally when it does come back to my mind, I simply catch a southbound express train and as the train passes the Chianan Plain, the vast green fields of sugarcane outside the window become a sweet spring flooding my uneventful life.

Night-time Frolics

Huang Fan

translated by Chen-lai Lu

SU HENG stood obediently before the altar, mouth slightly open, eyes fixed upon the silver cross on the priest's chest. The cross glittered when the priest moved. Su Heng squinted, felt the bread slip onto his tongue, and heard a low voice saying, 'Holy Eucharist.' The man next to him in line pushed him lightly. Holy Eucharist. The bread soon dissolved into a pasty mush. Su Heng lowered his head and staring at his toes, he walked back to his pew.

Inside the church, the mingled rays from the lights and candles pierced, along with the sharp, vibrant voice from the choir, through the stained-glass window in rich mosaic, and penetrated into the endless darkness beyond. The priest slowly made an elaborate cross, turned and went back to the altar. When he moved, the loose, white vestment, revealed the linen alb he was wearing inside. It was stuffy and hot, the windows were shut tight. From among the bas reliefs of St Antony, St Francis, and St Joseph, fans turned. Su Heng rested his hand on the fluttering pages. Mass was almost over. He glanced at the words in the book, 'Kingdom of nations, power of the world, all glories belong to you', while watching the priest, with his head lowered, allowing the altar boy on his tiptoes to wipe the sweat off his forehead. The choir finally came to a stop, the priest raised his voice and said, 'May God bless all souls'—he was sweating again—'and bless us all.'

At last, everyone knelt down to pray. Su Heng closed his eyes, and placed his clasped hands against his chin. He felt a little uncomfortable with the posture. He twisted a little, and sighed with relief a few seconds later when he found his balance under his knees.

'Our Father in Heaven', he said to himself, 'our Father in Heaven, I've been good and devout today, really I have, I'm not so sure about yesterday, heaven didn't cross my mind the whole day yesterday, neither did holy grace. I was busy yesterday, it isn't important what I was busy with, Virgin Mary, what I did wasn't important, I can't even remember, but I have a favour to ask of you. This really embarrasses me. My luck hasn't been good, and it's unlikely to get better. Dear Christ, I couldn't ask you this, I'm ashamed to have done so. I didn't ask you yesterday; I don't remember what I did yesterday, It couldn't have been anything important anyway. I haven't done anything yet today, I haven't prayed. No! I don't mean that. I've been praying all the time, but haven't been begging for anything. For Lily to become more devout, for instance. Oh, no, it's not likely. I've prayed for that so many times. Maybe I didn't wish her to become devout; it would be horrible if she should become devout, for you are mine alone, dear Christ. No, you are Saviour to all. I beg of you to make my wife religious, make everyone more religious. I feel ashamed that I always ask for the same things, I'll ask for something else today. My dearest, dearest Jesus Christ, it is so very hot today. If only the church had air-conditioning, I beg of you to make the church air-conditioned. No, no, I shouldn't ask you for this, I shouldn't have asked for anything today. I'm really ashamed. I can only pray that you might make it a bit cooler, or have someone donate an air-conditioner. If you are willing, you would grant me this wish even without my asking. Dearest, dearest Virgin Mary, you certainly never say yes to people's idle prayers, nor to mine, like giving my enemies boils on their asses or making them fall into ditches, these are things I would never ask for. You may already have noticed my gentleness and kindness. No, you don't have to notice, you simply know. You always know whoever mistreats me, and they deserve their due without your bothering. Dear Christ, dear Jesus Christ, I'm not asking for anything, I'm simply praying, you know that. I'm devoted, and happy, and content, and joyous. Jesus Christ, Virgin Mary, in the name of the Father, and the Son, and the Holy Ghost, and all the saints, thank you all for listening to my prayers, thank you, thank you so very much, Amen.'

Su Heng rose from his devotions and looked around. Everyone had left except for the Italian nun, still kneeling. She always stayed behind. She was about 50, but it was difficult to tell the age of a nun. Perhaps in some sense they were ageless. Nor could anyone guess when the nun would leave her seat. He had been talking with some parishioners about the miracles of St Bernard and St Francis one evening in the Father's office when the lights in the chapel went off. They saw the priest appear in the doorway, but not the nun. She was probably still praying in the dark. Su Heng didn't know what it was like to pray in the chapel in utter darkness—there might be better results. No, 'results' was not the proper word. The priest was kind, he was Italian, too, and spoke Chinese. Perhaps he wasn't very kind toward the nun, for they seldom spoke to each other. The priest was very fond of children; the nun, perhaps more so. She used to bring candies for them. Once she offered a piece of chocolate to Su Heng. He shook his head and turned it down. The nun lifted up her face and said, 'It's all right.' Her accent was so odd, he almost laughed. Watching him suppressing his laughter, she too broke into a laugh and kept repeating, 'It's all right. It's all right.'

At the door of the chapel stood the Father and some members of the congregation, talking with animation in the cool evening breeze. The solemn-faced alter boy, back in plain clothes, went up to the middle-aged man who was talking to the Father, and caught his arm. The priest patted the boy's head. The boy made an impish face.

'Good night, Father,' Su Heng said as he passed by them.

'Good night.'

A long, distorted shadow appeared on the wall. Coming up to the place where the shadow gradually vanished in the light from the street lamps, Su Heng knew he was at the end of the lane. A pick-up drove by. The dust and the swirling air currents indicated that he had come to the ten-metre-wide main road. He crossed with caution.

Su Heng slowed down to get his breath; his slightly heaving chest slowly calmed down. From another alley five or six girls, who probably worked at a near-by textile mill, walked out briskly. They parted to pass him, and then joined ranks again. Su Heng looked at their uneven silhouettes, and overheard one of them saying, 'What a bore! What a drag!'

'What's the matter with you?' another said. 'It was your idea to come out.'

'I didn't know it would turn out so lousy. What a drag!'

'I wasn't bored—not a bit.'

They pulled away and finally disappeared into the shadow of a wall.

Su Heng kept on walking and passed a row of houses with scaffolding outside. A small bare bulb hanging down from a wooden ladder shone on small heaps of sand, bricks and stones, and steel bars and tools the workmen had left behind. He carefully stepped over a pit. When he saw street lights shining ahead of him again, he knew he would soon be home.

It was a row of about ten two-storeyed terrace houses. Down the end of the road the lane disappeared in the pitch black of paddy fields. In no time there would be houses shooting up in those fields. City folk were moving to the suburbs. A few cars sometimes stopped by the fields in the day. Su Heng would watch the people getting out from his window. The face of the obese one was familiar. Once, this fat guy even walked up to his door. With his head tilted, he hesitated for a few seconds. Su Heng pulled the blinds. He knew what the man was going to do, and waited for him to ring.

This night his wife answered the door. There were five or six women sitting in the small yard. Seeing Su Heng at the door, the one who was waving her fan stood up and said, 'It's time we went, Mrs Su.'

'You don't have to leave because he's back from church,' Lily said. 'Please stay a little longer.'

'That old fool of mine should be back by now. He took the kids to the movies.' Another woman cocked her ears pretending that she heard something. 'That must be his motorbike.'

Lily gave her husband a furious glare and insisted no further. The way she rose from the rattan chair was deliberately slow and exaggerated. The loose dress she had on couldn't hide her young body. Her hair was tied up in a bun at the back of her head with a rubber band, but her face showed an exasperated childishness. She shook her head and said something in a low voice to the woman beside her. At the same time, she shot a sideways glance at Su Heng, watching him, with hands drooping, nod goodbye to the guests. He soon closed the door. There were tables and chairs scattered in the yard. He let out a deep breath, walked to the chairs, took one under each arm, opened the screen door with the tip of one foot. His wife shouted behind him, 'Careful!'

'Don't worry,' he turned round to say. 'You should've gone to church. Don't you talk enough during the day?'

Su Heng went into the living-room, seated himself, crossed his legs, and lit a cigarette. His wife also lit a cigarette. They smoked in silence, each waiting for the other to break it.

'You change into another person every time you come back from church,' his wife said at last. 'You were fine during the day.'

No response. She gazed at him, at the face behind the haze of smoke. Lines were showing by the corners of his eyes when he frowned. He was completely different from the man she married: the way he talked, the gestures he used when he didn't want to talk—every move he made was different. She had just recently begun to notice some of his strange, petty motions. (Why only just recently?) Take for instance his daily shave, the excessive use of hair cream, worry over stains on his shirt, and the constant use of words such as 'sacred', 'immaculate', and 'peaceful'. Besides, he spent a lot of his time with the Bible. He even had a special pair of glasses for it. She was looking at him and thinking of the scene in the church. No, she shouldn't be thinking about it. She hadn't been to church for a long time. She had many excuses. She had a lot of chores to do; men didn't have such chores, nor did Fathers or Sisters. She used to be a faithful believer, enjoyed going to mass, and was awed by the service. The low, reassuring voice of the priest, the gospels, the beautiful paintings on the walls, and even the confessional—they were all so lovely. She remembered the first time she went to confession: she was blushing, telling the father hidden in the dark, about. . . what she said was. . . but she couldn't bring herself to recall that occasion. She was different now, she could not concentrate on any one ritual, life itself just might be the only ritual.

She kept her eyes on him, until he finished smoking.

'Time to go to bed,' he waved the smoke away. 'I have to get to school early tomorrow.'

He raised his voice a little when he said the word 'school'. She thought of the way he was at his school. Twice she went to his classroom. She stood outside the window watching him: he appeared to be languid and helpless in front of the blackboard, and the pupils looked absent-minded. A boy seated by the window stared at her intently out of the corner of his eyes; this made her move away. She forgot why she had gone there, but remembered clearly the classroom and his back in front of the blackboard.

'What is it, Lily?'

'Nothing,' she looked away and said in a low voice. 'You turn in first. I'll pick up the living-room.'

The Madonna on the wall was looking down at Lily on the sofa. She frowned at the bout of coughing coming from the other room. Spreading the newspaper before her, she started to read again what she had already read. Turning from the social columns to the ads, her glance stopped at the classified section. She was surprised to see the word 'Bible'. It was a moment before she went on, 'Bible Publishing, applications invited for the positions of . . .'

Bible Publishing, applications invited . . . She stood up, the words flashed again and again in her mind. With force, she tossed the paper away. This sudden outburst made her conscious of herself again. Irritated, she walked into the other room.

Su Heng was lying in bed, staring at the fluorescent light on the ceiling. There was a strange oval-shaped shadow behind the lampshade. He imagined it was a slowly expanding prairie growing into a jungle, and then he closed his eyes, listening for sounds from the other side of the wall. No, no sound at all. Lily just might be standing at the window, looking out in silence. A dog barked across the road. It was a grizzly, tawny dog, with an evil look in its eyes. Most of the time it just lay on the porch in front of the grocery store. It wouldn't move when people passed by, but you could feel its eyes searching you. The dog had stopped barking. A moment later he heard the soft sound of a chair moving. She must have stood up. She was standing up, yes, she was walking this way, walking this way. He opened his eyes then and watched the door. She walked in, face expressionless. She passed the bed and went to the window. Softly she pulled down the blinds. She felt her mouth open and shut several times, but there was no sound. She knew she was saying, 'You never learned to pull down the blinds before going to sleep, you. . . .' She said the words to herself several times before she managed to restrain her anger.

'Turn it off,' Su Heng said from the bed.

'What?'

'Turn the lights off.'

'Just a minute. I've got to try on a new dress.'

'Will you please turn off the lights?'

'What's the hurry?' she asked. 'Do you think I've been putting on weight?' She turned suddenly, stark naked.

'I'm a little tired,' Su Heng said. 'And I have to get to school early tomorrow.'

With arms akimbo and buttocks thrust out, she assumed the posture of a fashion model and walked round the bed a couple of times. The fluorescent light hanging from the ceiling added an almost translucent sheen to her fine fair skin.

'What do you say? Haven't I been putting on weight?'

'No, you should eat more,' he sighed. 'You're not gaining weight.'

'Mrs Wang next door has been trying to lose weight for three weeks, but I can't see that it's done any good.' She bent from the waist, her fingertips touching the floor, relaxed and breathed deeply. Lying in the bed, Su Heng looked at her helplessly.

'I don't need to diet. I'll be in the same condition at 30.'

'You won't get fat,' he said. 'How could you get fat when you go folk dancing every day?'

At last she switched off the lights and snuggled up against him all naked. He felt the weight that lifted up his body for a second, then the mattress resumed its original shape.

'You don't like my joining the folk dance group, do you?'

'I haven't said that, have I? You can join whatever pleases you.'

Su Heng shut his eyes. The coming of darkness made him comfortable, but at the same time vexed.

'You should have come with me to the club. It's a great place to have fun. So many people have been asking why they haven't seen my husband.'

'What did you say?'

'I said he'd been busy going to church.'

He felt her leg on his thigh. There was also a distinct giggle from her.

'Not everyday, only twice a week.'

'Twice, twice,' she clung close to his neck and, with lips next to his ear, cooed, 'twice, twice. . . .'

'Father said fewer people are coming to church. He said the day won't be far away when people will become used to the idea of attending mass in front of the tube.'

'That'll be nice. Has it ever occurred to you that you simply don't know where to put your hands when you are not in church?' she said. 'You weren't like that before. At least not before we got married. Don't you remember that you used to take me to the pictures on Sundays? You even whistled for taxis.'

She whistled.

'What's come over you, whistling so late at night?'

She whistled again, louder this time, while at the same time climbed over and sat astride him.

'What are you trying to do?'

She didn't answer. Instead, she fixed her wide eyes on his face.

'What on earth are you trying to do?'

Su Heng opened his eyes.

'Knock it off!' he said. 'What's the matter with you today, Lily?'

'I want to—' she said quietly.

'What?'

'You never—screw me—on this day?'

The word 'screw' took both of them by surprise. Su Heng thought he must have heard wrong.

'Where did you learn to talk like that?'

'Never mind where I learned it,' she said loudly. 'You never do it on this day.'

It was in church that they first met. She had on a white dress embroidered with lace, reading the Bible to the congregation in front of the altar. Her tone rose and fell in beautiful cadences, full of the joy of life. The expression on her face was solemn but at the same time enchanting. Silence filled the chapel, as if all were immersed in her voice. Su Heng couldn't take his eyes away from her. He noticed her every single movement. He watched her raising her hand, sweeping gently over her forehead. The hand drew a graceful arch in the air— what an adorable movement. He fixed his eyes upon her, totally unaware of what was being said. He couldn't concentrate his thought on anything. When she had finished the last verse, crossed herself, and returned to her seat, Su Heng was still staring at the empty altar, tantalized and lost.

'Why don't you come with me to church?' he asked. 'You might be able to find some... some significance. Don't you remember that you used to read the Bible before the congregation? Father said that if you're willing to try to be observant, you will become devoted. Besides, you can always go to confession if you should feel troubled.'

The word 'confession' led him to thinking. The peace, complete contentment, and the deeply religious mood after the evening mass would always sustain him through to the moment he went to sleep. He never had nightmares

on these nights. Lily told him that once he even laughed openly in his sleep.
What a miraculous change, by God! When he was in college, he had always
thought Christianity was merely an imported religion. There was no sense for
Chinese to believe in an alien god with blue eyes and blond hair.

Lily wasn't listening. She was lost for a moment, then resumed working on
him, and started to strip him of his pajamas.

'Lily, you are not listening.'

She ignored his words.

Her passion shocked him. She had never been like this all the years they had
been married. It might be the folk dancing. It might be all those neighbours'
wives.

His thoughts wandered away for a while, and when they returned to the
moment, he found himself having an erection.

'Oh, my God! Lily!'

'How do you like it, the way I'm doing?'

'Where did you learn this?'

'Mrs Wang has a VCR at home.' She bit his ear softly. 'At her place, during
the day, we . . .'

'After dancing . . .?'

The day wouldn't be far away when people could switch to sex programmes
after they are done with watching a Mass. Press a button and one could listen
to great sermons on the soul; press another and one could learn a whole series
of postures for copulation. Sex, a word to which the Church cautiously gave a
wide berth, but soul . . . Father repeats it dozens of times everyday. After God
created Adam, He went on to create Eve. But Eve was made from a rib of Adam.
Ah, yes, a rib! He felt a little uneasy, psychologically. He had just come back
from church, infused with thoughts on matters of the mind and of the soul,
feeling uplifted and purified and glorified. But physically . . . 'Aah, aahhh,'
Lily moaned. 'Don't talk.'

Her movements became more violent and wilder. She licked his sensitive
parts like a dog. He couldn't suppress his laughter.

'Beat me, will you?'

'Why should I beat you?' He stopped laughing. 'Why do you want me to
beat you?'

He tried to push her away. But it was no use.

'Ohh, ahh,' she held on tightly to his neck, tighter and harder. 'Beat me,
beat me . . . .'

'No,' he cried out. 'Let go, Lily. You're hurting me.'

'Never in your life! You never do it on this day!'

Partly because of the pain in his neck, and partly because she reminded him of what happened during the day, his desire died away rapidly. He finally pushed her away. He was sweating all over. Coming back from the bathroom, he saw Lily perched on the corner of the bed, clutching a pillow in her arms, watching him with a strange stare.

'That's quite enough for tonight,' he said tenderly. 'Be a good girl, Lily. Let's go to sleep, OK?'

There was no answer. It didn't really matter, he thought, if she answered or not. A moment later, he turned his back to her and closed his eyes.

I have to get up early tomorrow, he continued to think, and before I fall asleep, I have to say the Rosary. Nothing is more important than that. But a wave of sobbing made him open his eyes.

'What is it?' he turned and asked.

Lily cried louder.

'Oh God,' he said. 'Oh, my God!'

The cries stopped after a while. Again, there was an empty, strange look in her eyes.

'You really want me to beat you, don't you? With what?'

'Your belt,' she said, almost inaudibly.

'All right. Just this once. And then you be a good girl and go to sleep.'

There was a clear swish at the first flick of the belt. Her white, smooth, round buttocks trembled to the sound.

The shock sent tremors from the buckle to his fingertips, and then on to the back of his hand, his neck, and his brain. Oh, the whole house was shaking, the whole world quivering!

This must be the sound of primitive lust, he thought. Jesus Christ, Virgin Mary, the sound of the primitive lust. It was making a soul just purged ready to pounce. It was making a non-church-going woman into a whore. It was making the testicle-like earth rock in frenzy.

'What's stopping you? Go on beat me!'

'I told you it's just for this once.'

'Just once more,' Lily turned over, spread her legs far apart, feet kicking in the air.

'What the devil do you want me to do?'

'I want you to go on whipping me with the belt. If you don't want to,' she pointed below her belly, 'use your tongue.'

'What?' With mouth agape, one hand clutching that absurd belt, he stood helpless at the bedside.

'It's not such a big deal,' Lily said. 'Mrs Chang's husband does it, and so does Mrs Ch'en's.'

'No, no, I'd never. . .' he stuttered.

'Then beat me.' Lily changed her posture. Half-kneeling on the bed, her head on the pillows, she looked between her legs at her husband.

'Come on, come on,' she swayed her hips. 'Give your sweet wife a good lash.'

Faced with that spherical object, he flung the belt on the bed.

'This is crazy, Lily,' he said stiffly, 'crazy!'

'You bastard!'

'What?'

'You yellow bastard,' keeping her posture, Lily went on.

'You're timid—always scared of this or frightened of that. Y' know what students call you behind your back?'

'What?'

'Mouse,' Lily said. 'Don't pretend you didn't know.'

'How can you call me such names just because I won't do the disgusting things they do in porns?'

'Mouse,' Lily said, 'and it's got nothing to do with porns. Didn't you see how the neighbours' wives looked at you when you came in? I can't stand it any more.'

'I go to church. I come back home. What's wrong with that?'

'Everything is wrong. If you want to glorify God and sing His praises, do it in your heart. That's quite enough.'

'What kind of talk is this? You're only saying this to make me mad and beat you, Lily. Well, I'm not going to give you that satisfaction.'

'Clown! I'm not in the mood any more. I want some sleep.' She stretched herself. 'You go and say your prayers. Don't bother me now.'

A feeling of shame and anger flooded through Su Heng. He realized in his wife's eyes that he was not a man but a cringing coward. To be more precise, he was just a mouse. When the ladies in the neighbourhood greeted him with sneering looks, he was all apologies. An object of ridicule. He stood there, hands drooping, like a little boy who had been caught doing wrong. A little boy who had been treated unfairly standing at the door and bidding goodbye to the ladies. What was the matter with him? He should have told those boring and sacrilegious wenches to piss off! Yes, piss off!

'I'm no coward nor any kind of a mouse!' He glared furiously at Lily, still lying in bed.

'Go and say your prayers, don't bother me.'

'I'm telling you I'm not.'

'Hail Mary, full of grace . . .'

'Stop it!'

'Don't make me laugh! What's wrong with my saying a prayer to help me go to sleep? You are. . . this is religious persecution.'

'Stop it, Lily. Don't you push me.'

'Didn't I tell you just now, I'm not interested?'

'You have no right to mention the name of the Virgin Mary.'

'Why? Did I offend her?'

'Yes. You certainly did!'

'That's funny. You think Jesus is yours alone. I won't swallow that. You think I've even forgotten all the prayers? All right, I'll say the Lord's Prayer for you. Our Father, who art in Heaven, hallowed be Thy name. Thy Kingdom come . . .'

'Stop it, Lily.'

'Who's going to stop me?'

He had an obligation to stop her. When he picked up the belt from the floor, Lily shut her mouth and looked at him dumbfounded.

'What are you doing?'

'You asked for this,' he said coldly. 'Didn't you want me to whip you? This'll give you satisfaction, give you heavenly bliss, and give you meaning.'

So he started to slash with his belt, like a shepherd wielding his staff. He went to work in real earnest and abandon, oblivious of her painful pleadings.

Everybody Needs Ch'in Te-fu

Huang Fan

translated by Yuan-lin Huang

EVEN when I was young, I had a drastically different view of this society. I believed it wasn't what we were used to thinking it was. Thirty years later, at an annual tourism conference, I ran into a childhood playmate Ch'in Te-fu, and suddenly became sad—for no reason I could think of. I recalled that time in our lives still fresh in our memories (his face was lined with the markings of time, and I wasn't much better off); the swept asphalt streets, pedicabs, young girls wearing clogs, beggars, and the sluggishness, lethargy and gloominess that characterized the vicinity of Hua-hsi Street.

That same evening we sat in a restaurant called 'The Maples'. Through the alkaline glass that filters colours, we watched the throngs in the street and reflected on the forties: its scenes, old friends, and vanished childhood.

'Now this I remember,' Ch'in Te-fu said, 'this is the brand—Dragon Spring soda—you popped open the cap, and "luh!" out gushed a pile of bubbles. I always crushed the broken bottles and took out the marbles inside. Do you remember the big square in front of the Dragon Mountain Temple?'

'It's now been made into a huge shopping mall,' I said, 'not like what it was before.'

'That was where I played marbles with a gang of street kids, and I always won, won, won!—a wide pocketful of glass marbles, five for ten cents. Then, I could make pocket money with my own two hands. Didn't think—'

'That we would grow old.'

I interrupted him, getting impatient with this conversation. Those days I had lost interest in everything; nothing could motivate me. When Li-mei walked out on me, she left behind a savage, sarcastic comment: 'You're a freak who's already gone through change-of-life!'

A few days ago, I got a note from Ting-chia Entertainment, asking me to go to this year's tourism conference on their behalf. Since this was my only commission in some time, I made myself presentable, and dyed my hair. In fact, I had reached the most dreadful low of my life. It mattered little that I had had a rather brilliant past: my name was once closely associated with success; I controlled a legal firm and had a beautiful woman. But with the latter I made a deadly mistake and did not bring home the masculinity I showed in court. To borrow a phrase, 'Home was only someplace to stay'. When I realized the situation was so bad that I had to reorganize my life or else, it was already too late. Li-mei flung the car key on the table. 'Damn you!' she howled. 'I'm still young, do you understand? You freak, you've already gone through change-of-life!'

I couldn't afford to let this incident keep intruding on my thoughts. Two months later, I was sitting at the tourism conference table, looking as though I was thinking; suddenly I was surprised to find the person sitting opposite me was in fact my playmate from childhood.

Across the conference table, I idly watched Ch'in Te-fu. His wide forehead, his hooked nose, his coarse, somewhat savage face—they were not very different from the photo I saw in the newspaper two years ago. Then, I had heard nothing of him for five or six years. I had once heard he was involved with Wu Yung-han, Ts'ai Huo-shih and that lot—celebrities who used every means to evade the camera. Later, he told me proudly that in the past he had to rack his brain to think of ways to deal with the judiciary, and now it was the National Tax Bureau. Therefore, in view of his ever-increasing wealth and property, he had to add to his staff a Doctor of Law and two Economics Ph.D.s. These highly-educated intellectuals helped him construct an air of 'culture'. He himself elected two evening courses—'Management Studies' and 'English'. The black Mercedes Benz that was parked in front of the school gate, the chauffeur sitting up straight as a brush-pen in the driver's seat, Ch'in Te-fu trying hard to suppress his urge to smoke, staring intently at the blackboard with a bunch of young kids—these vignettes must have been most touching. Later he donated a million dollars to our Alma Mater, a cool one million! In fact, this amount was not very much to him. He was one of the few truly rich and powerful figures in upper-class circles in Taipei. They really despised him, mocked his background, his wife who dressed like a cabaret girl, and his lavish, extravagant, but utterly purposeless and tasteless parties. Nevertheless Ch'in Te-fu remained popular and was welcomed everywhere. He was the perfect representative of this rapidly-changing society which is getting more and more difficult to understand. These people stood in awe of his presence, hands thrust into pants pockets playing with coins that went 'click, click, click'. At the same time, they stared wide-eyed east and west.

The meeting was lengthy and boring, like all meetings not directed at reaching a conclusion. The Korean representative gave a paper on 'The potential of tourism in Asia', the Japanese a talk on 'A few basic concepts for smokeless industries'. The Koreans and the Japanese hadn't come with noble intentions. But, this is a world where everyone scrambles. I lit a cigarette. At this point Ch'in Te-fu nodded at me and smiled. He had finally discovered my name on the list of participants. I smiled back.

When the meeting was over, I got into his Benz. The car turned from Chung-shan North Road into Jen-ai Road. The neon light from the tall buildings and the fluorescent light from the two sides of the road intermingled and flashed on his face. That evening he was in high spirits. He unbuttoned the second button of his shirt. This was a pleasant evening in April—slightly chilly. Ch'in Te-fu rolled down the car window and spat forcefully into the street. For some reason, this action brought me great relief. To be honest, subconsciously, I had all along regarded him as quite a different person. At this point, he was talking about the sudden escalation of land prices, hotels, highways, supermarkets, and modernized public cemeteries, as if all these things had something more or less to do with him. As for me, I just looked out of the window from time to time. I had enough troubles of my own.

In the next few days, I forgot the whole business of the annual tourism conference and Ch'in Te-fu. During the day, I was busy with all sorts of fruitless 'waiting' and 'recollecting' games. In the evening, I kept switching from one TV station to another, from one soap opera to another soap opera. I began to enjoy those lengthy, uninteresting programs; there was no way of knowing when they would end the story. Maybe I too was hoping for an inevitable ending.

The district in which I lived was situated at the consolidated public bus terminal (after Li-mei left, I often hoped to catch sight of her in crowded places). Our bus-driver loved to brake suddenly and violently and then turn around and yell to the passengers who had been thrown topsy-turvy, 'Last stop! Last stop!' He imbued the words 'last stop' with a nameless kind of anger. True, everyone has a last stop, and there are bus stop signs along the way. What was strange was that very often people forgot to pay their fare or got off at the wrong stop. That fellow who stole Li-mei had long dirty hair. *Synthesis* once carried a poem of his—'A day without ending'—it was sentimental and maudlin! Really, truly ridiculous! Poets, littérateurs, artists, Ch'in Te-fu didn't think highly of them. As for me, I tended to be more cautious in my attitude. From a utilitarian point of view, Ch'in Te-fu could also call himself a philosopher or an artist. One of my clients, for example, was quite happy to call himself an 'artist of deceit'. This guy, in his fifties, also wore long hair.

If emotional deceptions can be regarded as a kind of 'fraud', then that no-good who wrote poetry should be locked up, because he was guilty of kidnapping by enticement. In truth, Li-mei took none of my possessions (I wish she had taken something, at least a photo of me). She left nothing behind either, not a silk scarf, a pair of pajamas, nothing. Only a note. After I had read it, I tore it up in a rage. Written with an eyebrow pencil, it said, 'I've gone. Don't look for me. I don't hate you. Li-mei.' If she had been more merciful, she could have written, 'Li-mei, who still loves you.' In the days that followed, I refused to believe it had happened. We were not bound by any legal marital agreement (there's nothing wrong with that; a lot of people do without it), but we were deeply in love, and very dependent on each other. (She even said she couldn't go on living without me. I tape-recorded that, but she erased it some time later. Now the blank tape simply went *sha sha sha*—like the way she laughed.) Day and night I waited for her to call—a sad little miracle that would be! One morning, I discovered a heavy beard had appeared on my chin, so I shaved in the bathroom mirror. At the same time, I drew the curtains and outside, the blue expanse of sky was cloudless; clear sky stretched thousands of miles, vast and fathomless. It was then mid-spring; the garden bloomed with azaleas, and creeping rattans twined their way up the white wooden racks. That's when I told myself, 'Listen, when you've finished shaving, change your clothes, shine your shoes, comb your hair. Everyone is waiting for you, lover boy!' I did it all and then I looked at myself in the mirror. I stared and stared until suddenly I couldn't stand it any longer and burst out crying. What appeared in the mirror was no lover boy! It was just a face lined with wrinkles, marred by sunken cheeks and bloodshot eyes—a face afflicted by eight generations of bad luck.

The telephone rang, once, twice, three times. . . . I let it go on ringing a while longer.

'Hello!' It was a man's voice. 'Is that Mr Ho?'

'Hello?!' he repeated. 'This is Ch'in Te-fu. May I ask . . .?'

'Ch'in Te-fu?'

'What's wrong, old boy? We saw each other just the other day. Are you OK?'

'Te-fu, it's you. I'm OK.' For a few seconds, my ears were filled with the buzz of quiet electricity; something must have flown into my head.

'I thought I had dialed the wrong number,' he said. 'You sounded a bit odd.'

'Lately very few people call me,' I said. 'I'm resting at home.'

'Resting? What for? The other day you looked great, remember? You even cracked a joke.'

'There's something wrong with me,' I said, 'something wrong with my head.'

The cigarette between my fingers was burning down. I tossed it into the corner, but it didn't hit the waste bin. The butt went out at once.

During the last hour, I'd hit the bin three times. The last time the bin caught fire. I'd run into the bathroom and got a pail of water. Now part of the floor was wet, and a burning smell lingered in the air.

'Ha!' he laughed. 'There is something wrong with me too. The doctor said it was really not that bad, something about its being benign. This guy is an authority on brain diseases at the Veterans' Hospital. If he says it's not serious, it's unlikely you'll die. Want me to introduce him to you?'

'Thank you. I only have a slight headache. A few aspirins will do the job.'

'Don't put too much trust in pills,' he said. 'Are you free Saturday?'

'Saturday? What day is it today?'

'What day? You really like kidding, don't you?'

I held the receiver away from my ear. His guffaw was unbearable. 'What day is it today? You are really convalescing! What day?' He laughed again. 'By the way, there's something I want your opinion on. How about coming over to my place for a talk?'

'Yeah, OK.'

It had been a long time since I had done anything that touched on my profession. After Li-mei had left, I handed the office over to another lawyer. You can't afford to smile sarcastically at your clients or keep asking them to repeat the question one more time. Furthermore, I still had some savings in the bank: the car had sold for 200,000. There was no need to lock myself up alone in my iron cage. The other day, a traffic policeman pounded on my car window. 'You mother—!' he snarled. 'You mean to tell me you didn't hear anything!? A dozen cars behind you, honking at you? You know you made everybody wait for the red light twice!?'

The driver started the meter. Outside the weather was fine. The street was packed with well-dressed pedestrians. A nice day, good for any kind of clothes; besides, this was a weekend. Oh! The weekend! I remembered how surprised Ch'in Te-fu sounded on the phone. 'What day is it today?' He sounded as though he were quizzing me. To survive in this highly refined, organized, standardization-first society, you had to carry a timetable around. Drivers install a big digital clock next to the meter. The Arabic numerals kept jumping: 3:20, 3:21, 3:22. There are a few other standards used for measuring your life: your payday, your wife's birthday, your kids' registration notices, traffic tickets, water and electricity bills, even court summons. 'What day is it today? You really know how to kid.' Who's joking? God knows! I used to have a gilt-edged pocket diary too. I recorded each month all my appointments and their gist, business that needed attention, important items, reminders (including Li-mei's monthly allowance check), medical appointments, and so on. One morning, suddenly I wasn't able to locate my appointment book and immediately my face turned pale. Time seemed to stop. I hurried home and when Li-mei opened the door, she was at first astonished and then furious. She thought I was playing private detective and spying on her. I hastened to explain, but how could I clear things up all at once? Finally, still angry, she said, 'You're getting senile!'

Getting senile! Thinking about it, I began to feel a slight jerking pain in my chest. My heart had never been in good shape. That arrogant young doctor at Ch'ang-keng Hospital once pointed to my cardiograph and said, 'We have to be more careful.' His ambiguous 'we' sounded like Li-mei's primary school teacher who announced to the whole class, 'Li-mei, come forward. Let us see how many times we should take a ruler to your palm?' She had had an unhappy childhood. Whenever she was depressed, she would complain that everybody picked on her. (After she had told me her childhood story, she concluded, 'Ever since then, I've held a grudge against anyone who picked on me.' That evening she had on her a blue and white striped dress. The neckline was very low, exposing the pinkish, silky top of her bosom. In the soft light, she looked very agitated. Her face was full of expression: the whites of her eyes showed and even the tip of her nose was trembling, as if in protest. At that very moment, the lovable little girl who had been picked on by others and who still harboured hatred for it was being resurrected before my eyes. I should have been warned of potential danger, but I was so captivated by her—completely, unreservedly.)

A guard opened the iron gate, a servant in a starched-collar shirt was already waiting.

'Sir, this way, please.'

We passed through a neatly trimmed garden. It was vast and spacious; out of luxuriant clusters of lilacs and daisies emerged the funny-looking head of an automatic sprinkler.

'Master is in the tennis court.'

'Tennis?' I was incredulous. 'He plays that game too?'

The servant remained silent.

After we had made a few turns, a tennis court surrounded by a wire fence came into view. The servant bowed and left. Ch'in Te-fu turned around and waved to me. I hung my hands on the fence and looked into the court through the wires. Ch'in Te-fu was in his all white tennis outfit. His forehead was covered with sweat and his face flushed. Below his bulging stomach were a pair of slender legs moving with tremendous agility over the orange-coloured surface. He deliberately showed off a beautiful backhand. He motioned and his opponent immediately stopped hitting the ball. She clasped the racket under her arm, walked to Ch'in Te-fu, took out a towel and wiped the sweat off his forehead. Together they came towards me.

'How are you, Lao Ho? What took you so long?' Te-fu said. 'Do you want to have a go?'

'I don't play,' I said, and took a quick look at his female companion. She was a lovely young girl: long hair, cheeks reddened by the sun, a pair of charming eyes.

'Mei-hsia, this is Big Brother Ho.'

'Big Brother Ho,' she said in a clear crisp voice.

'He doesn't play tennis, but,' Te-fu pointed to his head, 'he plays this.'

The girl burst into laughter, almost a shriek. Te-fu embraced her shoulders and a smile of contentment turned the corner of his mouth.

A short while later, I was standing in the sitting room which was floored with a green carpet. From the french window, I could see at the foot of the mountains lay glittering, gay, festive Taipei shrouded in evening mist. A peculiar city, I thought. Hordes of people, tons of garbage, and one damn fool.

'So what do you think? Nice view, eh?'

Te-fu's voice came from behind. I stopped gazing out.

'Whiskey or brandy?'

'Brandy.'

'Come!' He gave me a glass. 'To us, cheers!'

'To us, cheers!'

I allowed myself to sink into an enormous white leather sofa. Te-fu adjusted his position and lit a cigarette. In the mist of smoke, his expression kept on changing: one moment he looked very serious, in another, he was deeply agitated; then all of a sudden, he became sentimental and melancholic. He was talking about his childhood. (That sad place, filled with putrid, malodourous air; near Hua-hsi Street, beneath the low, dust-laden eaves, Te-fu's mother carries a basin of laundry; a bunch of kids, barefooted, are running around her: chasing each other, making a lot of noise, having fun. With one quick motion, she pushes them away. And then, in an injured voice she calls down the street. 'Ah-fu, come to dinner!')

'Nobody cares about my past,' he says angrily, feeling sorely wronged. 'I've had three wives and eleven sons. A bunch of rotten eggs. They're leading comfortable lives because of me, dammit! But nobody's interested—interested in knowing what Ch'in Te-fu is really made of.'

What are you made of, then, and what does that have to do with my ass? But I begin to understand: 30 years later, all ambitions fulfilled, he grew arrogant and supercilious. Now he lives in a luxurious villa that overlooks the city, that overlooks the whole human race. He's using me as a representative of humanity and telling me in detail about his family, his accomplishments, and his inner feelings, which I find crazy.

'I didn't have a penny, then; only these two fists.' He was getting more and more excited, and finally he rose from his chair. 'My old pa didn't have a penny to his name either. When the cock crew, he would drive me out of the house.'

'I remember your father,' I said. 'He was a good man.'

'The best father in the world,' he raised his wine glass, 'the best, best father, the very best.'

(Te-fu's dad was a notorious alcoholic. When he was sober, he was a pretty good mason. His greatest joys were drinking and beating up his son. One night, Te-fu's dad came home drunk and dropped dead in the big ditch beside the school. There was a hole in his head, and the water in the ditch was dyed red. The next morning, the corpse was surrounded by primary school kids on their way to school. Teachers holding sticks in one hand and their noses in the other, drove the kids into the classrooms.

Te-fu's mother cried for several days and her crying became an intermittent lament at night. His father's coffin took up all the space in the sitting room. Te-fu crouched at the door, looking blank. With a small stick, he kept writing in the sand, 'dead, dead, dead . . .')

'To all those who died. Cheers!' I said.

'To all those who died,' he said.

(When Te-fu's ma died, nobody knew where to find him. On the day of the funeral, Te-fu and a couple of young guys appeared before the coffin. He knelt down and burst out crying. They were all chewing betel nuts and spitting the juice all over the place.)

We went on drinking. Te-fu was a good drinker—his capacity was astonishing. His eyes became bigger and bigger, but he became more wide awake, more and more crafty and calculating. I, on the other hand, became hopelessly drunk. In a semi-conscious state, I told him about Li-mei. At this moment, Mei-hsia pulled over a cushion, leaned on his thigh, and cuddled up to him like a little rabbit. Te-fu gently stroked her hair and looked at me sympathetically.

'I'll help you find her,' he said.

I thought he was kidding.

One afternoon in May (April went by all of a sudden), I was wakened abruptly by the telephone while sitting in the rattan armchair. The way I got up scared away a few sparrows which were hopping to and fro on the terrace. I apologized to them and went to the sitting room. The telephone rang furiously, louder and louder, and more and more agitatedly. I took up the receiver, and allowed myself to lie comfortably on the sofa with the tips of my feet propped up. Having positioned myself that way, I suddenly remembered my pack of cigarettes left on the rattan chair.

'Speaking,' I said. 'Te-fu, how are you?'

'As well as your ass!' I was taken aback and my sleepiness vanished. He went on cursing for a while, as if Arabia, Iran, the US, and China Petroleum had deliberately formed an alliance to addle his eggs for him. By then, I was thinking desperately about that pack of cigarettes. Since I got back from his hillside villa, half a month had already gone by. We had communicated by phone a few times. Talking to him on the phone was both physical and mental torture. He could talk continuously for ten minutes without allowing you to interrupt.

'Oh well, forget it. It's no use talking to you about these things,' he said. His tone suddenly changed. 'Listen, Lao Ho, go get a pen and paper.'

He then gave me Li-mei's address, word by word, slowly and carefully. There was obviously suppressed excitement in his voice, as if he could see the expression on my face. Two hours later, I found myself standing rather stupidly in front of the gigantic mirror in Hao Lai Menswear Shop. In the mirror were a fashionable fellow wearing a blue Thai silk shirt, a white necktie, a pair of light-yellow, diagonally-striped trousers, and a shop assistant trying very hard to keep from laughing. He kept circling me, saying in a voice that you would use to cajole a child, 'You look much younger, much younger!'

Afterwards, I walked along Heng-yang Road towards the train station. On the face of every passer-by, I detected the same peculiar expression I saw on the face of the shop assistant. When I asked him to wrap up the clothes I had taken off and send them to my apartment, he was astounded, and stammered, 'Sir, are you going out like that?'

I gave him a furious look. 'And why not?'

Outside the window of the Chu-kuang first-class train, the darkness of night provided the best mirror background. I took out my comb and tidied up my unkempt hair (Oh, no! I'd forgotten to dye my hair). Li-mei was always

concerned about my hair, so I had tried every brand of shampoo at least once—
'566', '333', 'Herbal Fragrance', 'VO-5', but no shampoo could rejuvenate a
heap of ageing hair. Li-mei should have understood this. For someone who has
been tortured by love, someone who is getting on in years (I avoided using 'old
man'), every single one of his wrinkles, every one of his white hairs, should be
loved and cherished. She should have understood this.

The Chu-kuang train was like a shuttling fish in the depths of the ocean,
foraging through the vast fields now enveloped in complete darkness. The
clothes-dryers that appeared here and there on both sides of the railway tracks
during daytime, the electricity poles from which the paint had fallen, the small
vegetable gardens, heaps of rubbish, ponds covered with layers of oily green
duckweed—all now became obscure hallucinations disappearing, one replacing another.

If we could start all over again (maybe they had broken up after a quarrel)
. . . Li-mei was probably asleep at this hour, alone in a queen-size bed—her legs
curled, her little face covered with marks of tears. Even in her dreams, she
grieves and mourns for her betrayal of love. And see! Her benefactor is on the
Chu-kuang train, speeding ahead, moving like the wind. He's so anxious, so
desperate to forgive, to pardon her, to redeem her soul.

I must have fallen asleep. The ticket-checker came by a quarter of an hour
before. He woke me up very gently, and spoke to me in a voice that seemed
to come from another world, 'Excuse me, sir. Excuse me. . . .' After that I
couldn't go back to sleep. Slit-eyed, I surveyed the carriage. The slight
agitation caused by the ticket-checker had gradually subsided. The young
fellow sitting beside me yawned, his mouth twitching unconsciously. Then
his head drooped again. An old woman, half-awake, stood up and went
towards the toilet. After a while, she returned, still half-awake. A young
couple, hand in hand, head to head, entered the world of dreams, smiles
lingering on the corners of their mouths. What a tranquil, peaceful world. I
thought to myself: everyone was at some point along a line marked at each end
by 'Start' and 'Return'. Only I, confused for a moment, or perhaps just because
I was tired, was too tired to start, yet too tired to return.

Early in the morning, the train entered Tainan city, which was only half-
awake. When the first ray of sunlight penetrated the window, I greeted it with
a cold eye. The excitement and the anticipation I had had at the beginning of
the trip had evaporated without a trace.

I found a motel in the vicinity of the train station which faced a parking lot.
Taxis, tour buses, public buses came and went under the fly-over. Along the

street, newspaper hawkers and beady-eyed housewives. From the underpass emerged students and traffic police wearing white safety helmets which glittered under the sun. What kind of city was this? I stood at my window and gazed at the place for a while. Then I went into the bathroom and turned on the tap. In no time the bathroom was filled with warm steam. Until that moment I did not realize I had brought no luggage. I called the service counter and asked them to send up breakfast and a set of underwear. The maid pushed open the door and entered. She showed no sign of surprise and I felt much relieved.

Breakfast was plentiful: ham, eggs, toast done to a golden-yellow, but I only drank a little milk. Sometimes it was enough simply to look at food. After Li-mei left, I stopped my daily half-hour jogging, but hadn't put on any weight as a result of my eating habits. This regulated my weight in a natural way (no need for Peggy's Diet Plan). Occasionally I would bring back from the market ready-to-eat food—biscuits, canned or dehydrated food. Some time in April, I spent a whole morning moving the refrigerator to the sitting room and put it right beside the TV set (a great advance in industrial art and civilization). I would take a bite of biscuit, and drink a little milk. There, bathed in the multi-coloured rays, I knew, somehow, that I was consuming so many units of protein, vitamins, and male hormones.

After I had taken a bath, I relaxed in bed. I hoped I'd fall asleep right away, so that when I woke up, I'd feel alert and energetic, ready to bring a happy ending to the comedy, 'A thousand miles to win the hand of a beautiful lady'. But what should I say first? What would Li-mei think seeing me in such good spirits? Maybe I should look sad and pitiable. I could embrace her legs and weep hysterically. But for a guy whose hair was already half-white, who looked haggard, wearing these fashionable clothes, to embrace a woman's legs and cry and sob hysterically—that might not look too good.

Or, what then? I lay in bed, tossing and turning, not a hope of falling asleep. I got up, lit a cigarette, and paced back and forth. After half an hour, I looked at my watch, adjusted my tie, and went downstairs. In the street, I hailed a taxi. I gave the driver the address, he nodded, and the car dodged in and out of the narrow streets. On the way, a thousand thoughts flooded my head—past memories, future hopes, fantasies, aspirations—all these bounded around in my mind. My face in the rear-view mirror was like the scenery outside—moving, changing, randomly and unpredictably. It was May then, and the weather was getting hotter. When I took out the fare, my hand was shaking slightly. The driver noticed it but said nothing.

With a great deal of effort I managed to press the door-bell. Not until the sound of the bell came seeping through the crack of the door did I realize that I was actually rather pathetic, and stupid, too.

The door opened, a middle-aged woman poked her head out.

'Excuse me,' I said faintly. 'Does a Miss Li Li-mei live here?'

'Li Li-mei?' She took a good look at me, from head to toe. 'You mean Mrs Hsu?'

'What?'

'Sir, you are . . . ?'

'I am. . . ,' I must have blushed, 'I am her uncle.'

'Please come in.' I could see an expression of relief on her face. 'But you came at an inappropriate time. Both husband and wife are at work. What a dear couple, so in love with each other.'

I followed her into a sitting room very simply furnished. She talked to me as she walked, but her voice seemed to get more and more remote, and more and more indistinct. After that, I don't remember how I actually sat down on the sofa, how I finished a cup of tea, or how I returned to the train station and got the north-bound train.

As night fell, we came into Taipei. Because it was still early, I loafed around in the Hsi-men district crowded with people. I even went to see a movie, but I don't know what it was about. I wandered around until one or two a.m. When I got home, my head was completely empty but I was still wide awake. I took a bottle of liquor, sat in the terrace, and finished it, drink after drink, drink after drink.

For quite a long time, I allowed myself to sink into a whirlpool of thoughts, regrets, self-mockery, and cynicism (at certain moments I thought about my wife who had passed away years ago, and my son who is in America). Living was no longer a fresh, interesting affair. Moreover, I had already passed the age at which renewal was possible (the times test old age, and old age mocks the times). In other words, I was content with the status quo (what choice did I have?)

This lasted until one day, probably in November or December. It was raining outside. I had dinner in town, opened my umbrella, and passed through a number of streets; the streets were glistening with rain. At the door of my apartment I shook the raindrops off the umbrella and stomped on the doormat. At this moment, a soft, small voice came from the corner of the wall. I turned around and couldn't believe what I saw.

'Big Brother Ho?' this time I heard the voice clearly. 'It's Mei-hsia.'

'Oh!' Mei-hsia was completely wrapped in a big, brown overcoat. Her face was slightly pale, and raindrops clung to her hair. When she saw how surprised I was, her mouth twitched for an instant.

After a short while, we got into a taxi. The driver had the heater turned on, and a trace of colour gradually appeared on her face.

'All you had to do was call,' I said. 'You didn't have to come all this way.'

'Te-fu said the same thing too. But I thought,' she said, 'it'd be better to come in person.'

'What did the doctor say?'

She shook her head, then she fixed her eyes on the windscreen wipers swinging from side to side. The water marks kept vanishing and emerging. The rain got heavier and heavier and lashed the roof of the car with a rattling sound. I lit a cigarette, looked at her beautiful silhouette, thought about Te-fu, then about Li-mei, then about this twisted and complex world. A long sigh escaped me.

The car stopped in front of the main entrance of the Veterans' Hospital. I glanced at my watch and it was already eight o'clock. Hurriedly we passed through the main hall which was resplendently lit, and entered the private wards. The rooms were on both sides of a corridor carpeted in red. Mei-hsia opened a door and inside was Ch'in Te-fu in his silk pajamas propped up on a pillow. In his hand was a TV remote control.

'Sit, sit, sit!' He turned off the TV with one motion, flung the remote control to one side, and yelled, 'Mei-hsia, make some coffee.'

'Are you OK, Te-fu?' I found a sofa and sat down.

'Extremely well, extremely well.'

He sat on a pillow, legs crossed and arms folded, looking like a sort of dignified sultan.

'The doctor said operating on this is like having an appendix out. Nothing serious. You had your appendix removed? No? You should go and do it, find out what it's like.'

Mei-hsia brought the coffee. I said, 'Thank you.' I was looking at Ch'in Te-fu who was busy talking, gesticulating with his hands. His face was much thinner. Because of excitement, his cheeks were red, but that couldn't hide the dark circles around his eye sockets. At this moment, he was talking about his many sufferings, his courage, and his misfortunes. How was the doctor? Not bad, but he seems a bit gawky and clumsy. The nurses? The nurses shouldn't wear white uniforms, the funeral colour is so depressing. It would be nice if they wore street clothes. Who made these rules anyway? Did anyone from the family come to see him? They all came, but he threw them all out. He couldn't stand the thoughts hovering in their heads. He was not dead yet, and he was not going to die.

'Damn it!' he snarled. 'If they make me real mad, I'll give all the money to orphanages. Mei-hsia, come closer. Wouldn't you say that's the right thing to do?'

Mei-hsia cuddled up to him like a small bird.

'You're joking,' I said.

'Who's joking? But this time, ha-a-a . . .,' he stretched out the sound, 'everyone is going to be disappointed. Lao Ho, do you know how long a person needs to stay in bed after an appendectomy?'

'Maybe five or six days.'

'That's wonderful!' He grinned contentedly.

'Lao Ho, let's make a date? Let's have a tennis match.'

'Tennis?'

'Oh, well, forget it. You don't play that stuff. Something else then, anything will do. What can you play?'

I didn't answer. I thought he just liked to play jokes on others and himself. He understood that himself, but he didn't know how to stop.

Then he rambled on, getting more and more agitated, more and more incoherent. All this time Mei-hsia did nothing but gawk at him. As for me, I tried to toss in a remark or two, here and there—Oh, good! That's true! That sort of nonsense. To be frank, why should I spoil the scene when I could see he was feeling so exuberant, so interested in what he was talking about. But finally, when he said he wanted Mei-hsia to have a chubby little baby for him, we were all stunned. After a few seconds, he coughed a couple of times, felt rather embarrassed, and put an end to the topic.

I took the opportunity to stand up and stretch my arms and legs. Mei-hsia had come in a downpour to fetch me, just to let me hear him babble! I walked round the room, and put my hands on this and that. All this time Te-fu's eyes seemed to follow me very closely. I turned around and went back to the sofa I used before. I raised my head, and was about to utter something polite in order to take leave, but was taken aback by his facial expression.

'Lao Ho,' he said, 'I didn't ask you here to listen to all this nonsense. I want a favour of you. Mei-hsia, take that briefcase out of the wardrobe and bring it over here.'

Around midnight, carrying his briefcase, I returned home. Inside it were several contracts, stock certificates, financial charts, and one whole volume devoted to tax evasion (just in case). All these belonged to their 'Underground Highway Bureau'. When Ch'in Te-fu spoke of 'them', he could not suppress a malicious smile. The 'Underground Highway Bureau' was a legal company with an enormous organizational system (I was well acquainted with these sorts of tricks). There were more than 100 coaches-drivers, conductresses, solicitors, bodyguards, and a whole bunch of guys who were free-loaders. When they first went to Ch'in Te-fu for partnership, they didn't ask for a single cent. This was very puzzling, but useless to speculate about. Because the division of labour in this outfit is very finely drawn, there are all types of investments, among them, the mere provision of capital was the lowest kind. I believed that Ch'in Te-fu's 'antennae' reached to every level. Quite obviously, his contributions were in the arena of technology. The recent rapid development of the company was really quite amazing. Buses leaving for major cities in the north departed every 20 minutes. In the main lot were bulletin boards showing travel schedules, travellers who never stopped coming and going, and voices that came booming through speakers all day long. Behind every worn-out public bus on the highway followed one of Ch'in Te-fu's limousines. These were air-conditioned, furnished with deep foam seats and tinted windows. When Ch'in Te-fu handed these documents over to me, he looked me right in the eye. The expression on his face was complicated. I had to tell him that I no longer did this sort thing, that I was getting old, both psychologically and physically, I was getting old. He burst out laughing, the wrinkles at the corners of his eyes falling into creases, but his eyes were bright and clear. He laughed for a while and said I could use this money; a 30 per cent commission would see me through my old age without worry. Having said that, he cocked his head and looked tenderly at the young girl beside him, 'And there's Mei-hsia.' At that moment, I could see a trace of sadness stealing through his eyes. Maybe I was wrong, because then he began to complain about the hospital, the operation, his wives and kids who did nothing but jabber and yap all day long, and about those muddle-headed managers of his. Just at that point, the doctor and a nurse opened the door and entered quietly. Ch'in Te-fu saw them, uttered a sigh, and made a helpless gesture. The nurse held a thermometer. She looked serious and cautious. The doctor nodded. On his face was a plastic smile. I stood up; it was time to go. We shook hands, squeezing each other's hands very tightly. I was almost out of the room when he suddenly blurted out, 'Thank you.' I was taken by surprise.

The next day, I didn't get up until noon. The weather was very cold, so I put on a woolen hat, wrapped a scarf around my collar, and got on the bus that went to the centre of the city. Inside the bus the air was misty; passengers were trying hard to avoid eye contact with each other, but it was hard to see the scenery outside the windows. When we reached downtown, I got off, and after I had lunch at Mei-hsin, I strolled towards the New Park. There were very few people there. Fallen leaves covered the ground. I found a bench and sat down, thrust my hands into my pockets, and gazed languidly at the dry fountain, and the red-and-white pavilion.

In the evening I went back home, switched on the lights, and caught sight of the briefcase. I shook my head—all right! This would be the last time. For the next few days, I got very busy without really being aware of it. I went to a number of places, met with a number of people, and did a great deal of talking. Again, without being fully conscious of it, that supercilious, confident lawyer Ho complete with his masculine air had been resurrected.

In mid-November, a few days after the birthday of the Founding Father, I got an unexpected phone-call from Mei-hsia. She whimpered, 'Te-fu died.' What she said after that I could not hear through her crying. I hurried to the hospital at once. The room was cold and empty; there was only a nurse cleaning up. She said the patient had already been sent to the funeral home. I was stunned; I hadn't even been able to see him for last time. After a short while, I regained my poise.

'What happened?'

'The operation wasn't successful,' the nurse said. 'He never knew.'

Te-fu passed away very quickly, he didn't feel anything. This was probably the best way to go, just like going to sleep. Sometimes I thought about my own death: would I be sad, frightened, or angry at the fact that I had not been treated fairly? When Father passed away, I was still in college. That morning, he bent down to tie his shoelace. When the tip of his finger reached the ankle, the blood vessels at the back of his neck suddenly burst. He gave out a loud cry, collapsed on the ground, and all at once blood gushed up to his head. His plump face became red all over. We carried him to bed. At that moment, he burst into a fit of hysterical crying. Did he know that he was going to die? Was he frightened? Was he sad? I don't know. A few hours later, he breathed his last, still wearing the suit he wore to work.

On the day of Te-fu's funeral, I put on a black suit, so that I would look more appropriate. The taxi circled around the main entrance but couldn't find a place at the curb. So I got out in the middle of the road. The policeman on duty frowned but didn't say anything. Inside the funeral parlour was another spectacle to behold. I think every celebrity in Taipei was there. Cameras held aloft by news reporters kept on flashing. Propped against the walls were countless flower wreaths and long strips of cloth with elegiac couplets. In the centre of the hall stood the enormous, three-foot-square coloured photo of Ch'in Te-fu. He looked down puzzled, at the busy and noisy crowd as well as his wives and kids. They looked blank and expressionless. They were bowing to the sympathizers in the fashion dictated by the rites.

I stood on the balcony outside the hall for a while and observed the whole scene from there—the solemn, festive, grandiose funeral ceremony proceeded according to schedule. In the middle of this, the arrival of a cabinet minister caused some disturbance. The reporters came at him in a wave. Continuous flashes of light lit up his smooth and glittering forehead. Mr Minister leaned towards the microphone. He could hardly open his eyes. I believe he said something like this: everybody needs philanthropists and entrepreneurs like Ch'in Te-fu. His passing was indeed a great loss to all of us here as well as to society in general.

His voice was then overwhelmed by others and after a while he stopped talking. Mr Minister, accompanied by others, went to the Spirit Tablet and paid their respects to the deceased. When he came out, the reporters moved aside so he could pass, and one clown stepped on my foot. I uttered a few silent curses and retreated to the side door which was less crowded. There stood Mei-hsia and an old woman with lavish jewellery twined all around her. When she saw me, she looked delighted.

'Big Brother Ho, this is my ma.'

I nodded.

'Mr Ho,' the old woman said.

'Why don't you go over to the hall?'

'*Ta tai-tai*[1] would not allow me to go in there.' Mei-hsia lowered her head, as if she were going to cry. The old woman quickly grabbed her hand.

'Oh,' I changed the subject. 'Looks like everyone is here.'

A few seconds of silence lapsed. The old woman asked, 'What kind of numbers are we . . .?'

'You mean how many people are there? Let me see . . .'

'Big Brother Ho, my ma is not talking about that.'

I turned around and met the peculiar expression of both mother and daughter.

'She meant,' Mei-hsia seemed to be making a great effort, and blushed for a second, 'she meant what did Te-fu leave me. How much is there?'

Even when I was young, I had a drastically different view of this society. I believed it wasn't what we were used to thinking it was. Thirty years later, at Ch'in Te-fu's funeral, I recalled that time in our lives still fresh in our memories: the streets of swept asphalt.

'About ten million,' I said coldly. 'Ten million.'

'Oh!'

---

[1] Literally 'First Madam' or 'Oldest Madam': that is, Ch'in Te-fu's first and legal wife.

Returning from the funeral I was surprised to find a letter in the mailbox. It was sent by my son from the US. I opened it as I walked towards the terrace. It was evening, and a light breeze had come up. The scenery near and far juxtaposed and overlapped. I unfolded the letter. It said he wanted to tell me a wonderful piece of news (Pa, I'm sure you are now as excited as I am). He had finally been granted permanent residence in the States; and he was getting married to a local overseas-Chinese girl. He hoped that I would be able to attend the wedding. At the end of the letter, he even signed a stylish English name. I looked at it for a long time and was finally able to figure out what the characters stood for—'George Ho'.

After I read the letter, I put it back into its envelope, and tore them both to pieces. I watched them fall slowly onto the street: some fell on the roofs of cars, some fell into the gutters, and one fragment was blown into the flower pot on my neighbour's balcony. It was getting dark; the yellow chrysanthemums in the flower pot, which were as big as the palm of a hand, were swaying listlessly in the wind.

Tung-p'u Street

Huang Fan

translated by Yuan-lin Huang

TUNG-P'U STREET was situated alongside the railway tracks. On each side of the street there was a row of bungalows with black-tile roofs. There was hardly room for a walk-way. When the trains passed by, first came the steam whistle, followed immediately by a vibration that caused the dust on tree trunks and on window frames on both sides of the street to shake down. When winter came, the air being nippy and raw, the steam whistle sounded fathomless and far, as if it came from some mysterious dreamland. The tree trunks were grayish-white, as if smeared with a layer of powder; leaves blown by the wind fluttered to the ground. They fell noiselessly among the egg-sized stones poled between the wooden sleepers, dropped on the grass near the fences, and into the little glistening puddles beside the highway.

The highway ran down the main street, and as trucks drove through, they sometimes ran parallel with the trains. The driver would poke his head out, seemingly gesturing at the trains that refused to slow down. By the time he withdrew his arms, the truck would have reached the end of main street. From there it headed north, and went round a heap of rubble. What came into sight then was a vast expanse of brownish-red—it rose slightly, and eventually arched into a small hill. When you climbed to the top of it, streets, houses, and the railway tracks below looked like stains left carelessly on a piece of red cloth.

In the afternoon or evening, we often sat on that slope and surveyed the deserted and empty thoroughfare, the dust covered tree-trunks, and the squat little houses that looked a bit comical. Sometimes we looked off in that direction, flung out stone after stone with all the strength we could muster, but our stones could only reach the small pond covered with duckweed. Sometimes we would roar and yell as we raced downhill, until we came to that heap of rubble. We stood among rotten wood, distorted iron bars, and fragmented pieces of mud. This had been the Ts'ai's house that had burned down. It was some distance from the street. We got into the habit of looking through it for something, or hiding there as the sky gradually darkened. When it was totally dark, we would say goodbye to each other at the entrance to the street. I put my hands into my trouser pockets, at the same time repeating to myself a few completely meaningless words, and casting blank looks at the houses near me as they were gradually swallowed up by shadows. When these shadows disappeared in the yellow light of a dim street lamp, I realized I was standing at the entrance of that long lichen-covered alley. I stood there in thought for a few seconds, turned around and watched my companion slip into his back door. I stood there until I was sure there was no one behind me, then I plucked up enough courage to deliberately focus my eyes on this mysterious, dark, and horrible alley, allowing myself to be overwhelmed by fear, and then with quick steps I hurried home.

When spring came again, we put our schoolbags on our shoulders, leaped on our bicycles, and passed by the heap of rubble, the red-soil knoll, and the still and arid waste that lay behind the hill. I always followed Chih-ch'ing. He was taller than I. His bicycle was heavy and clumsy, the kind with straight handlebars; the seat was an old-fashioned leather cushion that made your buttocks ache. Chih-ch'ing pedalled it as though he were engaged in some obscure kind of religious dance. Riding along a narrow path, he talked to me without turning his head. His voice was mixed with his breathing, the sound of the wind, and a strange kind of echo from the wasteland. Having passed through the narrow part, we rode abreast of each other. Chih-ch'ing deliberately turned his handlebars towards me, in a threatening fashion. In response, I stretched out my leg, and kicked his front tire.

When we both fell down, Chih-ch'ing yelled, 'Oh! Oh!'

'If only we didn't have to go to school, it would be so wonderful!' I said as I sat on the ground.

'Didn't have to go to school, didn't have to go to school!' Chih-ch'ing mumbled.

But we went to school after all. Our school was situated beside the big bridge which was then newly-built. We leaned on the window sills and gazed at the cement bridge glittering brightly under the sun. During dry seasons, the level of the stream dropped; stones and boulders with strange shapes appeared in the bed of the stream, and the lower buttresses of the bridge laden with moss could be seen. I often dreamed of this bridge. In my dreams it appeared in different shapes: sometimes its form was distorted, to an extent that became horrifying; sometimes it was transformed into a circular track in a stadium, and people and vehicles went round and round endlessly.

After school we deliberately made a detour which took us to a close-up view of the bridge and the multi-coloured vehicles that crawled along it. There was a small heap of soil, one side of which faced the bridge and was covered with low shrubs and little wild flowers. We pretended it was a fortress. The thickest branch was a canon and canon balls were shot from there, aimed specifically at vehicles on the bridge.

'Ping! Ping! Ping!' Chih-ch'ing cupped his hands into two tubes and pretended that they were binoculars. 'No hits!' I would say when I got tired of playing the game. However, more often we could bombard it very accurately, and knock it flat. I saw the cars fall into the stream, one after another, until it was so full the river could hold no more. The rest of the cars on the bridge could do nothing but turn around and leave, through the old street that passed by our house. Afterwards, we would slide down the mound, laughing and yelling, and run towards the tree where our bicycles were parked. One afternoon, while we were sliding down the mound, Chih-ch'ing suddenly informed me that his family was planning to leave Tung-p'u Street. 'It is a dead street,' he raised his voice, as if to announce it to the world: 'A dead street!'

Between shock and astonishment, I stopped what I was doing. The strange-sounding words were like dull, frozen echoes coming from a cement pipe. It became a force propelling me to scramble up the mound. My ears were filled with all sorts of sounds: whistle of the wind, thumping of the heart, Chin-ch'ing's yelling, and the sound of something shattering. Finally I stood atop the fortress that once belonged to us. Now it had been completely destroyed by enemies from the other side of the river. I felt I was standing on a lonely grave. The bushes hung their heads, the little flowers lost their colours, and many ghostly shadows arose among them. I stood there until it was almost completely dark. Then I slid down the mound, and ran towards the wasteland, alone.

One morning after that day, I sat under the sign of an abandoned bus-stop, and stared at Chih-ch'ing's house where people were busy packing. A small truck was parked in front and the truck was packed with beds, old furniture, and some cartons. Chih-ch'ing ran over to me from time to time, and we exchanged a few rapid words. His face was flushed with excitement. This damnable excited expression made me immediately abandon the thought of talking to him about 'our small hill', 'the rubble heap', 'the bridge', and stuff like that. Chih-ch'ing's father had his sleeves rolled up, which exposed his thin, pale arms. His forehead was continually sweating, so that his wrinkles, caught in the sunlight, became small, winding rivers. I heard him saying in a loud voice to the neighbours, 'Oh! That place isn't bad!' He took a deep breath and continued, 'Business! Right, there will be business.'

Oh, oh, oh. I was puzzled: why was my father the only one who hadn't shown up? 'Where's your father?' I was worried that people might ask me that. Where was my father? I saw that all the men who lived in the street were surrounding the truck, but my father? I stole several glances toward home. I strained my eyes, but could only make out one shadow that was darker than the darkness inside the house. Then the shadow stirred; I knew my father was there. I could even sense the direction of his gaze—he was looking intensely at me too.

I ran after the small truck. Chih-ch'ing waved goodbye to me from the midst of the furniture. I ran as hard as I could, until I heard a strange ringing in my ears and thought my chest would burst. In front of the heap of rubble, my feet stopped but my eyes followed as the truck disappeared behind the red earth hill.

When I climbed into bed, it was already very late. The whole afternoon, I had roamed, alone, in the vicinity of the rubble heap, pretending that Chih-ch'ing was right there beside me. Once a northbound train emitted a sharp and frightening sound that pulled me back to reality. I ran to the railway tracks, and when the engine sped by, I leaned as far as I could toward the speeding train. I seemed to hear people talking on the train. What they said was . . . .

Once, we made a bet on who could hear what the people on the train were talking about. We would get so close to the passing train that our cheeks would almost touch the side of it. This feeling was frightening but thrilling. For a long time after the train had passed, we still stood by the tracks, as if dumbfounded.

'What is this spooky place called?' somebody on the train had asked.

'It's called . . . called . . . '

I stepped into the middle of the road and stared off at him in anger. Now both the train and Chih-ch'ing's face had disappeared. I looked for a suitable target. In the grass near the wooden sleepers, something moved. A sparrow! A sparrow! I stooped down and grabbed some stones to kill it with. I must kill it. There was no alternative!

I pulled the blanket over my head, and tried hard to think about something pleasant. I thought of our English teacher who asked Fatty to pronounce a word that required the tongue to curl. Fatty blushed all over, his throat emitting a strange sound. He tried a few more times, but the sounds were all wrong. The whole class burst into hysterical laughter and the one who laughed the loudest was Chih-ch'ing. His guffaw vibrated in the small space under my blanket. I couldn't put up with the noise anymore so I pulled down the blanket and let my eyeballs roam about in the dark room. After a while, my eyes were fixed on the wall that was used for hanging my clothes in the daytime. I tried to picture the shape of the clothing, my school uniform, but it gradually turned into a human being. I looked away quickly. Then I heard, through the plank wall, faint sounds, audible but fragmented. I guessed it was Father's footsteps pacing to and fro, followed by Mother's coughing. Then they whispered to one another. I concentrated on the wooden partition, and heard a few garbled words.

'Had moved . . . '

'This time . . . it wouldn't work . . . '

'The more . . . the more . . . '

These words formed a strange and indistinct mosaic in my mind, like an anagram or a puzzle board. I tried to piece them together. I turned over and the whispering was gone.

Darkness, silence, and sleepiness all descended at the same time. I closed my eyes. From somewhere on the rooftop came the yowl of a cat. It sounded like a mourner's cry but also like a summons. I joined her on the roof (which was covered with tiles). She pranced there in a most peculiar and fascinating manner—her paws not quite touching the tiles, she raced under the star-lit sky. Delightfully, joyfully she skittered carefree as if there were nothing whatsoever to worry about. Silently she leaped across Chih-ch'ing's home. She tiptoed lightly up the red-soil hill, glided down like a bird, and scudded over the darkened wasteland. She headed north, sweeping like the wind across the stream which glistened in the light of the stars. She sped under the dimly-lit cement bridge, and entered at last a serene, peaceful, noiseless world . . . and I fell into a deep sleep.

The next day after breakfast, I stayed at the table practicing pronouncing English words aloud.

'Ee-er . . . ah-m . . . ah . . . m . . . m . . . '

'Ah . . . m . . . '

I heard a tiny voice from behind, 'What's that?'

'Ah-m, is "a-r-m", that means hand.' I turned around, and looked at Father, who was sitting in the corner smoking. His back was to the light so his whole body seemed to have sunk into the wall.

'Hand . . . oh . . . hand,' he muttered. He paused for a while, 'How's school?'

I didn't know why he asked that question. Maybe it was just something to say; he didn't really want an answer. At this moment, my mother came from the kitchen and stopped between the window and the dining table. A shadow swept across my eyes for she was standing right in the middle of a shaft of light coming through the window. The black skirt she had on turned immediately grayish-white. When she moved, it was like waves in the sea. When the gray waves became still, I heard her saying, 'Do you mean, "How's school"?'

'Nothing much.'

I closed my book, and sighed a sigh of relief. Now I couldn't concentrate on my English vocabulary. I hated having to memorize something early in the morning. Maybe today our English teacher would give us a short vocabulary test. I simply can't remember English words; I am bound to do badly. When my parents see the grade they would ask . . . and then I would say . . . I would say . . .

'Nothing much?'

'There are a couple of transfer students,' I said. 'Several families have just moved into the school district.'

'Oh,' he grunted again, as if he regretted having asked such a question.

After a long silence, I left the table. My mother immediately took my seat. My father went on to smoke his second cigarette. The match illuminated his bony, dark-skinned face. After I said goodbye, I put the schoolbag on my shoulder, and went towards the front room. The front room was where Father carried on his business. I passed through heaps of plastic tubes, metal bars, toothed wheels, and all kinds of metal pieces. When business was good, my father even took in a young apprentice who slept in the corner where I put my bike. He used to crouch, motionless, between two racks (he was like a rack himself) sorting out the bent nails. Sometimes from the back would come Father's shouting and the apprentice would reply after quite a pause. Because of that, my father always said he was stupid. One thing he often did for my father was to go into the street to call my ma back home. My ma loafed around with her neighbours all day long. In those days, she used to wear a Western-style dress with alternating red and green stripes. Occasionally, truck drivers driving by would make vulgar gestures at her. The young apprentice had gone away and my mother had put that Western-style dress away in the wardrobe. Truck drivers no longer appeared on our street, and the drivers of those few cars that passed by kept their heads inside. Except for dust, there was nothing to be seen.

'Ah-m . . . ah-m . . . , ' I jumped on my bicycle, while trying to fit this English word into a tune in my head and chant it.

My bicycle passed by door after door, all tightly shut. Before I arrived at that fearful alley, I slowed down. I cast my eyes casually towards that alley. In daylight, I realized again that I was in fact, a big fool: the fear that came at night was, of course, totally baseless.

It was a shallow, blind alley. A big lump of stucco had fallen from the wall on the right-hand side, and exposed the red tiles beneath. Uncut grass extended from the corner of that wall to the entrance of the alley. Recently somebody had chalked Arabic numerals and letters along the wall. When the rain stopped, traces of the words would shortly reappear. I passed by here many times a day, but never ran into the one who wrote on the wall.

'1, 2, 1, 3, . . . ah-m . . .' my voice echoed in the quiet thoroughfare. Then I accelerated, and headed towards the wasteland full speed.

A downpour came at noon. I stared aimlessly out of the classroom window. A short guy came up beside me; he also poked his head out of the window. I saw that he was one of the new transfer students.

'That's my home,' he said to me, after a while.

I looked in the direction his finger pointed. Out of a screen of rain and mist, a gigantic monster slowly emerged—that was the bridge, that was the bridge, that was the bridge—it was like a hideous, sunken rock poking its head out at low tide, and staring at you with a malevolent expression.

The downpour went on until evening. When the rain stopped, an evening fog rose and the sky was filled with black clouds floating slowly by. Foreground and background mingled in a confusing mass, as if it had been swept up in a mammoth maelstrom. The wasteland that lay below the current was shrouded in a thin layer of mist. Rocks, bushes, earth mounds seemed foreshortened, and pressing towards you. The edge of the wasteland had, on the other hand, taken on a strange aspect, as if it were smeared with a layer of oil, faintly reflecting a brownish light.

I rode my bicycle and slowly approached the street that seemed to be the centre of the circulating airstream. Looking down from the knoll, it appeared that the grayish houses and branches might at any moment be thrown into the sky. The railway tracks were like a rope end that had been wrenched out of shape; in the distance it became a black line. I longed for some moving object to appear right then; a small red dot moved slowly along the black line, and when it became distinguishable to the naked eye, it was separated from the railway tracks. It was a red taxi cab. When it reached the entrance of the street, it stopped and a brownish figure stepped down from it. I raced down the slope at my best speed, but when I arrived at the entrance to the street, both car and human had disappeared. I gazed in the direction the the cab had disappeared. I searched for an answer as I pushed my bicycle listlessly, and passed once again down the street that had become deserted again. When I passed by the entrance of the alley, I cast a quick glance at the writing on the wall. It had become totally blank; the rain had washed everything away.

At dinner, I kept my head down, pretending to concentrate on my food.

'Uncle A-Szu came back,' said my father. 'Did you see him?'

'I heard the car,' my mother said. 'He didn't say hello to anyone.'

'I saw it,' I interrupted impulsively. 'A cab, a red cab.'

They both turned and looked at me.

'What did he come back for? Back to this place . . . ' my father continued.

'Maybe he couldn't get used to living in town.'

I lowered my head again, and concentrated half of my attention on the food; the other half thinking aimlessly about the man: what he looked like. He was an old man, his body odour was not pleasant. I wondered if I would have that kind of smell when I grew old. His sons (there were several of them) built a booth for him outside their house. I remember it was made of bamboos and planks—looked like the movable props used during fun-fairs at school, and there he would sit from morning till evening. His eyes, filled with matter, stayed fixed on the centre of the street. Occasionally a truck stopped in front of him and the driver would shout to him from the cab, but the old man remained motionless. Unless you stepped down from the car yourself, he wouldn't hand you a packet of cigarettes or a bag of betel nuts.

'How did you know?'

'I heard about it.'

'Who told you about it?' My father asked. 'How come I know nothing about these things?'

'You spend the whole day sitting over there,' my mother cast a quick glance at the corner of the wall. 'His son came back once.'

'Back? What for?'

'Probably to persuade people to leave this place. His son told everyone he ran into, that his father is drinking all the time.'

'Oh?'

'Just like you. Smoking—drinking all day long; he does nothing else.'

'Not the same,' my father said, coldly.

'Not the same?'

They almost got into a row. I looked from one face to the other, and they looked at me at the same time. There was no trace of anger. Secretly I was disappointed. Suddenly, I had a funny notion: I hoped Father would stand up in fury, bang his hand on the table, vent his wrath on the furniture, and beat me up. Then he would rush into the street and snarl at every tightly shut door. I hoped to hear this; I longed to hear anything frightening and unpleasant.

'He's old, he can't . . . '

'. . . start all over again,' my mother finished his sentence.

'Can't . . . start over . . . ' he stretched the last two words. 'He can only— wait for death to come.'

'Wait for death . . . ' my mother muttered, seemingly agreeing with him.

Lying in bed, I thought about the conversation at the dining table, but in a little while, a TV programme we saw that evening came to mind. It was very funny, and I laughed out loud; but I couldn't remember anything about the story—a woman broke something in the kitchen, or something like that, but what was so funny about that? Father, who was sitting beside me, must have been puzzled. I should have taken a good look at his facial expression. It had been a long time since I saw him smile. What did he look like when he smiled? The wrinkles on his forehead would crumble together? Or his nostrils would enlarge all of a sudden? Just like the janitor in our school—it seemed that the janitor was not as tall as I, because he was always bent, looking for something on the floor. Once he scared me when I saw his shadow squatting in the toilet. That's when Wu Shih-lin came towards me, Wu was that transfer student. He pretended to be very scared and said, 'Who is that man?' 'That's your father, your father, your father. . . . ' My thoughts turned again to the transfer students. I couldn't understand why I disliked them so much. During gym I would deliberately kick the ball wrong, so they had to run to and fro to pick it up. When we played baseball, I would throw the ball at them, the harder the better. Then teacher would run to them—everybody would run towards them. But I wouldn't say a word; I wouldn't say sorry. Neither would I apologize. If anyone asked me I'd say, 'They deserve it, deserve it, deserve it.'

I think I lay there for a long time before I fell asleep, and then I started to have a nightmare. It was a really scary dream. I opened my eyes, but the frightening sound still echoed in my ears. A train had just stopped in front of me. It was dead silent all around. I entered the carriage; the seats were floating in the mid-air. I walked from the last compartment forward. All the way I didn't find any passengers. I continued to walk. The seats parted before me, without a sound. I came to the locomotive and saw a man lying in the driver's seat. His skin was so white it seemed he had been coated with a layer of lime. I turned over his body; it was Chih-ch'ing. He stared at me coldly; his eyeballs were completely white. I was so frightened I screamed, but the scream was drowned out by the steam whistle suddenly shrieking.

Now, fright quickly drove away all thought of sleep. I sat up in bed. Dream! Terrible dream! The room was completely dark. I didn't know what time it was. If it was four or five o'clock, then I would stay up and not go back to sleep until daybreak. I stretched out my hand, and fumbled for my watch on the night-table. Then, a shrill, horrible groan sounded. It leaked through all four walls. I gave a loud cry, and pulled the blanket all the way over my head. Dream! Terrible dream! This frightening sound was a tangible object pushing, pressing, and crushing the blanket. At this critical moment, the lights were turned on. I heard Mother calling my name.

'Ma, what noise was that?' My voice was trembling.

'Your papa went out to take a look,' she sat on the edge of the bed and adjusted my blanket. 'Probably a wild dog.'

My eyes passed by her stern silhouette, and stopped at the open door. The light in the room was just enough to illuminate a corner of the corridor outside the door. There was a wall-lamp there, but it hadn't worked for some days. At night if you wanted to go to the sitting room, you had to feel the walls along the way. The walls were icy cold and humid, like inside a tomb. I didn't know why Father wouldn't fix the wall-lamp. Now he was courageously chasing after a wild dog, but why didn't he have the courage to repair the wall-lamp? I looked at my ma again, and found that she seemed to share the same thought. The corner of her mouth moved slightly, but the smile only lasted a few seconds. When she turned her face towards me, the smile was crowded out by the wrinkles on her forehead. She frowned tightly and said to me, 'That dog—.'

More moaning and groaning interrupted her words again. Together, we turned towards the door. Helped by the bright light, and driven by false bravery, these words suddenly slipped out of my mouth: 'Ma, don't be afraid—,' I must have blushed momentarily.

I realized I was 'playing adult'; at the same time, I felt rather stupid. Fortunately my mother didn't notice her son feeling uneasy. Her eyes concentrated on a single spot, as though she could see through the wall and into the thoroughfare which was enveloped in complete darkness. There my father was chasing a wild dog. In his hand he held a lead pipe (that kind of pipe could be found everywhere in the front room) frantically hitting the dog, which woke people up from their dreams. When my father lost his temper it could be frightening. Once, he almost beat me to death. With one kick I was kneeling on the ground. Now I could still feel the intense pain that was caused by the heel of his shoe hitting my calf. I tried to imagine how the dog would feel and at the same time I felt uneasy because of the stillness that once again engulfed us.

'No more groaning,' my mother leaned forward and listened for a while.

'It was beaten to death,' I said.

'What was beaten to death?'

'That dog.'

'Oh.'

We continued to listen for other sounds. After a while, we heard a mix of footsteps and conversation in hushed voices passing by our house, and disappearing down the other end of the street. After a while, a slight sound, like a mop being dragged along the floor, slowly drew near the door.

'It's your father.' My mother stood up. The sound paused at the door for about half a minute.

'Not your father.' My mother sat down in disappointment.

I hadn't really paid attention to my father's footsteps. In the dark thoroughfare, the footsteps told us he was there, still within our reach; he hadn't disappeared with the dog. Suddenly the sound of the door opening: my mother stood up immediately. This time she said in a louder and happier voice: 'I was right. It is your father.'

We waited with gratitude, looking expectantly to welcome father's appearance at the door. He was wearing a gray jacket and on his feet were a pair of slippers. The strong light made him lift his hands to cover his eyes.

'You're not asleep yet?' He asked as he lowered his hands.

When they left, they switched off the lights for me, and so, together with the room, I sank once again into darkness. I had thought about a dog beaten by father until it was half dead, but father said, 'That was no dog, it was old man A-Szu. Drunk as a mud-puddle, he was . . . woke up everyone in the street so they could see he was drunk as a mud-puddle.'

I had imagined not only that it was a dog, but that it was beaten half to death by my father.

All the men in the street had got out of bed (perhaps they all wanted to be courageous, heroic dog-beaters, too) and then the would-be heroes simply carried the old man home. One or two of them stayed behind to take care of him. My father said he looked really awful. I thought he couldn't possibly be more awful than the school janitor who had deliberately crouched to scare me. My father said the old man looked like a ghost. The man who stayed behind to look after him was probably A-Hsing. He had no wife or children. It must have been very frightening to sit up with a ghost all night long! My father didn't say this, that was what I said. I also said that the old man's yelling was really horrible. My father said: 'Just think of it as a dog barking and it won't be so bad.' I didn't know which noise I preferred. However, before I fell asleep (I didn't know when or how), I seemed to hear several kinds of sounds. The one I liked most would be Father's footsteps. They sounded like the rustling of wind in the treetops, or the sound of my ruler scraping on the desk— something I used to do when I was bored . . . .

Sha . . . la . . . sha . . . sha . . . la . . . sha . . .

For the next several evenings the sound of old man A-Szu could be heard, from time to time, at both ends of the street; sometimes at midnight, sometimes in the wee hours. They filled my dreams with all kinds of hallucinations. I don't know if he did the same thing during the daytime, too, but according to some people, I think my mother said this, the old man either passed out or staggered up and down the street with a bottle in his hand. The empty liquor bottles that I discovered along the walls confirmed this. Every day before I went to school, I would count the empty bottles along the street. After school, I would count them again. If there was an additional one or two, then the old man had been there during the day. Doing this was as meaningless as making chalk marks in the alley. After a while, I stopped counting. The only grocery store that was left in the street was doing a brisk business. One night I heard rapid knocks on a door. I guessed it was the old man pounding on the store door. I was frightened, and was awakened by a storm of knocks. A while later, that familiar moaning and groaning once again floated down the street.

A couple of weeks later, Sunday afternoon, I finally ran into the old man. He stopped mumbling to himself, and slowly turned his face towards me.

Slowly—he said—'ah', 'ah'—

He stuck out his tongue at me—'ah'—he said again—'ah'—

He opened his wet mouth—'ah'—'ah'—when he opened it he bit it once or twice—'ah'—his eyes were also wet—'ah'—he looked at me as if peering through a transparent piece of glass,—'ah'—'ah'—the hand holding the liquor bottle was also drawing the word in the air—'ah', 'ah'. He was finally convinced I was a piece of glass—'ah'—he turned his face slowly—'ah'—he stopped pronouncing the word. Oh—oh—he started mumbling to himself—oh—.

Old man A-Szu finally died. I was neither surprised nor sad. It was something like the monthly exam at school—it happened anyway, willy-nilly. Day and night my parents talked about when he would die . . . so did everybody on the street. 'Oh, he won't live long. . . . Won't get through this month . . . not possible . . . I dare say . . . just wait and see, wait . . . ', counting how many steps it would take the old man to reach death. It seemed to be the only thing here that was definite and certain. Several times, I passed the door of his house and noticed a white paper with the words 'IN MOURNING' pasted there. A breeze blew one corner of the paper. I seemed to see right through the wooden board behind the paper and into the sitting room where the corpse was placed; there was a little light bulb hanging from the ceiling. Its faint yellow glow dissolved into the air and fell like a drizzle; beating on the corpse which resembled the body of a child.

The corpse, wearing a big black gown, was lying on a wooden bed that had been moved out from the bedroom. A lot of people went in and out, and all made an effort to speak in a low voice. The shadows of these people were reflected on the walls. Then many more shadows appeared—his family had returned. The hubbub then became greater and greater, as if people were quarreling with each other, but one voice louder than all the rest brought the quarrel to an end. When the family of the deceased carried the corpse out of the sitting room, Mother and I (I was hanging onto her sleeves) also left, following the others. The street was dim and quiet. It was already very late.

The panting of the pall-bearers could be clearly heard. After a short while, someone ran across the street and turned on a lamp under the eaves (that was the grocery store that sold liquor). The person turned, his face was against the light, and so I couldn't see clearly. He came closer and closer, mumbling, 'I had no alternatives . . . . I . . . really . . . didn't expect . . . ' Finally he got hold of someone. They stood beside a truck and they gesticulated to each other. My mother tugged my arm forcefully: I knew what she meant, and we walked away as quietly as possible. Some distance from the scene, I looked back and saw that the corpse had been put onto the truck. Beside the grocery store owner there were a few others I didn't know, but I couldn't understand why none of us felt the slightest sense of sorrow.

By the time the white paper that said 'IN MOURNING' was blown off by the wind, it was already June. The weather grew hotter and hotter. I took off my short-sleeved uniform, tied it around my waist, and passed through the wasteland that was scorched by the sun, it continued to emit steam. The parched earth seemed to have been burnt by fire. A tiny whirlwind several steps away blew up a small circle of dust, red and hot. My palms holding the handlebars seemed glued to them. A patch of sweat grew on my back. I looked around hoping to find a cooler spot, but none could be found. The setting sun had stretched the shadow of a small clump of bushes to the foot of the cliff. The stand that sold sweet ice came to mind. That was the season when many people along the street would bring out their rattan chairs. They sat in the shade of the trees and gazed at vehicles passing down the thoroughfare. Sometimes they shouted to each other across the street. Occasionally my father would sit with the neighbours in the shade in front of the the door using his fan. When someone came into the shop to buy something, the delicate, high-pitched voice of his apprentice would be transmitted through the back door. Chih-ch'ing and I passed in front of them, walked across the railway tracks, and arrived at the little bog. We took off our shirts and sat among the bushes. Nearby several other kids had taken cover. They belonged to another gang, and looked at us with hostility, but we were not afraid of them. We talked to each other but watched our enemies out of the corner of our eyes. One time Chih-ch'ing jumped up and fought with one of them—a big burly fellow. I still remember how fierce he looked. Oh, that summer, the sweat and the little bog. The summer when sunshine and fighting were all tangled up.

I sped down the slope to the thoroughfare with the wind behind me. The squeal of my brakes drew no attention. I wanted to ring the bell, but it had broken long ago. The doors on both sides of the street appeared closed. If they

were not they would show as a small dark hole, but it was difficult for anyone
to look inside. The rattan chairs under the eaves had disappeared; few families
were left on the street. I counted the several holes which were pitch-dark. In
my heart I wished secretly that a few people like uncle A-Szu would come back
and stagger around again.

I parked my bike in front of my door, and peered in. There was no
movement. I supposed Father was squatting under the storage racks. I crossed
the threshold. After I had closed my eyes for a second and adjusted to the
darkness, I still didn't see Father. Lately he often bent down in different places,
counting different things—water-taps, thick wires, plastic tubes of different
lengths. I was puzzled by this: what was the use of counting these things? The
number was always the same. It was not like working algebra problems. When
I came across formulas, when I came across the same kind of situation, I would
calculate secretly: $X^2 + 2X + 1 = 0$. There, you can put any number into the
formula—multiply it by 5, multiply it by 78, the solution is the same: no one
can fool me with that kind of trick. My father counted his 'scrap copper and
rusty iron' over and over again, as if once he stopped counting, some of them
would go missing. 'Scrap copper and rusty iron' was not a term I invented. My
mother did. My mother wanted him to sell off all the stuff and leave this place,
but my father wouldn't agree to that. He said it wasn't possible to get good
prices now; and that wasn't all he said. Probably because of what he said our
family never moved. I wondered what Chih-ch'ing was doing now? When
there were a lot of kids on our street, we could play a lot of games—kick-the-
can, cops-and-robbers, whatever. I hated to think of staying in this place and
spending the whole summer all by myself. Neither did I want to spend it
squatting and counting plastic tubes. I hoped that we could move to the
seaside. There you could strip to the waist, and wear only a pair of shorts. When
you weren't swimming, you could walk on the soft, wet sand, and make funny,
deep footprints.

I kicked a tin can so hard that it let out a 'DONG!' I wanted it to hit the
wall, bounce back, and let me kick it again like a ball, but the can let me down:
it tumbled to the corner of the wall and stood there upright and rigid. Without
a second look, I walked away in the other direction. I passed through the dark,
airless hall and on the way dropped my schoolbag and stuff. The idea of taking
a cold shower was exciting, so I walked towards the kitchen. It was empty:
since my mother wasn't there I couldn't get permission to do anything. I
opened the back door and found Mother standing in the backyard, gazing into
the wasteland. The way she stood was like the two clothes-horses beside her.
Their shadows, twisted and distorted, and entwined around each other, were
creeping up the wall. A few pieces of clothing and a white bedcloth hung on

them. There wasn't any breeze, so that everything in the backyard resembled Mother—docilely and silently they gazed at the wasteland.

My footsteps caused her to turn her head. She said: 'I'm waiting for your father—went out early in the morning—went into town to take care of some business—very likely he'll sell the copper scraps and rusty iron—the old motorbike probably doesn't have enough gas—you're sweating all over—go wash up this minute—go now—your father should have sold those things a long time ago—I saw you coming down from the slope—didn't expect you to be home so soon—in future don't ride your bike so fast—put on a clean shirt—did you run into anybody on the way—at this time of the day you probably wouldn't run into anyone—your father will be back soon—he's an adult so he should know that the motorbike needs gas—when the things are sold, we'll move into town—I'll get you some clean clothes—clothes are hard to wash—hard to wash—hard to wash—.' She said so many things that I could only remember 'very likely he would sell the copper scraps and rusty iron'.

So, that was why Father went to town, to take care of this business. While showering and eating, I thought about the matter. When I sat down at the dining table to do my homework, I sketched a mental picture of my new home. Then I sketched it with a pen. It looked awfully artificial, like publicity posters produced by building companies. I drew three or four coconut trees, a straight-line highway, and buildings clean and tidy. And cars! Oh, yes, lots and lots of cars! I drew them until the highway was crammed with cars—all kinds of cars: cabs, buses, private cars, ambulances, fire engines, police cars . . . even a couple of cars I couldn't name. My mother sat beside me, head bent, mending my school uniform. It was the long-sleeved winter uniform. I opened my mouth to tell her summer was approaching, but I don't know why, I didn't do it. I put down my pen, cocked my ear and listened intently for sounds in the street. I couldn't hear anything. A train going north passed by, and left behind a vacuum-like silence that still stayed. My mother mending my uniform seemed to have slowed down. Maybe she was straining her ears, too, hoping some kind of sound might break the silence.

By some curious impulse, I reached out and turned on the television. The garbled sounds made my mother jerk her head in surprise.

The second time she raised her head, my father was standing by the dining table, looking at us. His face was red all over, and he motioned me to turn down the volume. When I passed by him, I could smell liquor on him. I thought Mother also noticed it. She frowned, and asked him what I wanted to ask: 'So, what happened?'

I turned down the volume of the television so far that only the screen was left—actors fighting each other silently.

'What do you think?'

My father seemed to be making a great effort to suppress his excitement, and was rapping the table with his knuckles, 'Ko, ko, ko . . . '

'Guess!' Ko, ko, ko . . .

Guess! Guess! Guess! I looked at him and then turned around to look at Mother. The guys on the TV were still fighting back and forth. My father fixed his eyes on the TV for a moment. The images jumping up and down seemed to have punched him in the eye, and caused him to start back suddenly, surprised and frightened.

'Of course you can't guess—ko, ko, ko—of course you can't —ko—we're not moving after all—ko, ko, ko—wait till I go out and park the motorbike and I'll tell you about it.'

Mother and I looked at each other. My father wove out. Our eyes followed his back until he disappeared at the entrance. Then the noise of someone moving things came from the door. It was hollow and monotonous, as if dozens of people were knocking on doors along the street at the same time. Then an even greater noise reduced everything else to silence.

My father howled at the top of his voice: 'Fuck!'

The summer holidays finally came. Part of the homework assigned for the summer was to write a diary. I hoped I could faithfully record everything that happened each day in my diary, but somehow I was never able to express myself clearly. I remember the entry that appeared most frequently was: 'a truck went by.' I thought Teacher would be puzzled: why did I spend my day doing nothing but counting trucks? A truck came! A truck came again! So what? Trucks came and went, like what I did every day, like brushing my teeth and washing my face. Our teacher would say this: you wash your face and brush your teeth every day, would you write that down every day? When the first truck came into Tung-p'u Street, everyone rushed out to look at it. Mother and I stood under the eaves watching how it churned up great clouds of dust, and seeing Father's face gradually emerge after the dust had dissipated. He and a few others stood under an enormous sign that read 'Highway Hotel'. They were all grinning.

July 2

The truck was here again! I put down my book and rushed into the street. . . .

July 3

Way off at the foot of the slope, several trucks side by side, heading towards the thoroughfare. . . .

July 4

A truck stopped in front of me and the driver opened the door. He was wearing a bright red baseball cap. . . .

July 5

At midnight, I was awakened by the sudden braking of a truck. . . .

(I really couldn't explain these events clearly. That was a summer filled with sunshine, dust, the noise of trucks, drivers' shouts, and women's laughter. Everything that happened seemed to have come from a strange continuous dream that kept circling round and round the same centre-point. Illusions of all kinds scuttled and chased themselves in the hot, hazy streets filled with litter. All tangible objects—drifting dust, plastic bags, bits of paper, dried grass roots—had transformed and gave forth an essence of corruption which itself became a tangible object. It crept into your stomach and intestines, wrenched your liver and entrails apart, distorted your five senses, and then it gnawed into your soul bite by bite.)

July 12

Drunk drivers were jumping up and down and shouting in the street. A couple of them were teasing the hotel waitresses and making them run around like crazy, shrieking and yelling.

July 13

A truck crashed into a tree. . . .

July 14

This evening, mother and I walked to the place across from the hotel. We stood under the eaves and peered inside between the gaps left by a whole line of parked trucks. The place was full of smoke. The racket reached all the way down to the end of the street. Several women in red appeared and then disappeared. I thought I saw Father's back, but Mother said it wasn't him, because he was working in the kitchen.

July 15

Two workmen were fighting in the street. Their noses were bloody. . . .

(And there was this thing which I was too embarrassed to write in my diary. But I . . . it happened a couple of days after July 15—it was getting dark and a man chewing betel nuts called to me at the corner of the alley. He unzipped his pants and exposed his private parts. It was an enormous ugly thing. He stuck out his tongue, and kept shaking it.)

July 20

Today was 'back-to-school day'. I rode my bicycle past the wasteland. On the way I came across a lot of trucks and one mini-truck.

July 21

A few families moved back to the street. I and the Lai kids drank soda at the grocery store.

(In the days that followed, circumstances changed somewhat. It appears I had lost interest in counting trucks. Wasteland, the boy, and rubble heaps once again entered my life. Those days the main features of my diary were vivid and detailed reports of how I dissected frogs: with a penknife, I cut the frog from its neck all the way to its dead white belly. Blood, organs, intestines, all popped out one after another. . . .)

At the end of the month, Father seemed to have been transformed. He was in high spirits all the time. His guffaw was loud and clear, and his home appearances were erratic. I was often awakened at midnight by his pounding on the door, demanding to be let in, but the next day, early in the morning, when I got out of bed, I couldn't find him. My mother put on that attractive Western-style dress with alternate red and green stripes. Occasionally, when people came in to buy things, she would giggle nervously. Most of the time, she sat in the doorway and gazed off at the hotel. Although my father had a small share in the hotel, he never allowed her to go there. We all wanted to take a look at the place. Some time later, a woman who worked there described it to my mother (I wasn't allowed to listen). The woman tittered as she described the place. As she talked, she shook her knees in a most inelegant manner. All the women lived in old man A-Szu's house. When night came, the house seemed to have caught fire. The big neon light at the door was so bright you could hardly look at it. The old man's body had once lain in that hall. Now lights were turned on even during daytime. A lot of people went in and out. Actually, I knew what people were doing in there—that kid from the Lai family once told me, using a very dirty word.

The word was. . . .

August

I began to feel fed up writing journal entries every day. I started to write only once every two or three days, then once every week. Because of this, some events recorded in the diary could never really have happened. Like helping my mother mend the dining table—in actual fact, I only handed her the hammer and the nails. And the one about my father saying he planned to open a hotel himself: perhaps it was something I dreamed up. On another 'back-to-school' day, the story of telling my schoolmates the street would be restored as it had once been. I even talked about air-conditioned limousines (tour buses). This kind of vehicle could be seen on the cement bridge only once in a while. There was one thing I could be absolutely sure about: among these fragments and made-up stories (on which day it happened I had forgotten, but the date's not important), I wrote a sentence in a matter-of-fact way—Today, a woman in our street died and a number of policeman arrived in a car.

The journal entries stopped at the end of August: the holidays ended then.

One Sunday after school started, I took out a small stool, sat under the eaves, and waited for the appraisers from town to come. Behind my back sounded quarrels between my parents. Over the value of every item, they argued endlessly. From the end of the street came a strong breeze that drove these noises away, and made me shut my eyes for a moment. When I opened them again . . .

Time seemed to have come to a standstill. The entire street seemed to have been frozen. Dust no longer flew around. Sunlight, indifferent to what was going on around it, covered the empty street. The huge signboard that used to attract a great deal of attention now stood desolate, lonely and abandoned, looking down the street. The signboard that said 'Highway Hotel' opened its expressionless, pathetic eyes, as if it were trying to tell a distant, tragic story.

I blinked as hard as I could, to drive away the picture that tried to fill my mind. (Many pairs of legs surrounding a hotel waitress lying in a pool of blood. Her eyes turned white, the muscles on her face still twitched slightly. She was wearing a bright red dress; her naked calf had turned red because of the blood. A black high-heeled shoe inlaid with pearl flowers was resting peacefully at the mouth of the alley; the other shoe, for reasons unknown to us, was firmly gripped in her hand.) Again, I blinked as hard as I could, and the noise of my parents quarreling once again floated into the street.

'Look at this carefully again . . . . No matter what you say it's certainly worth 200 dollars.'

'This price . . . you'd think . . . people would . . . '

'It's just rusted a little . . . '

'If only it had been sold two months ago . . . '

A black spot in the distance caught my attention. It was like a rock rolling down the slope, coupled with an increasingly loud roar: bo, bo, bo, bo . . . . Now

I could see clearly: it was a motorbike. Then I turned, faced the door, and cried at the top of my voice:

'Pa, the man is here . . . he's here!'

Like a miracle, that man made us move out of Tung-p'u Street. I'll never forget that day. Our emotions were a mix of agitation, sorrow, excitement, longing, and reluctance to depart. My father threw the last chair onto the truck, turned around and looked at the quiet street. He then announced proudly, 'We are the last ones to leave.' When he spoke, he sounded like a general who had dealt the enemies a heavy blow but who was forced to sound retreat.

After we left Tung-p'u Street, we settled down in a street in town. The house was directly opposite a filthy little park. The neighbourhood dumped its garbage in a place originally designed to be a fountain. Beside the park, there were a few buildings in the process of construction. By day, a deafening tumult of noise came through the window, but once night arrived, the entire street became deadly quiet. The dried twigs, the stone benches, the fences and railings in the park were like ghostly shadows moving to and fro. Sometimes a car sped by; the headlights shot through the windows, and brought these shadows into your dreams, like it or not.

At midnight one wintry day, I was suddenly awakened by a strange-sounding kind of scream. I listened intently; I had heard that noise somewhere before. I thought about it for a while, then I put on my clothes and walked into the sitting room. In the dim light, I saw Father standing beside the window.

I moved forward, and looked through the window, but there was only complete darkness, there was nothing at all.

'What was that noise?' I asked.

My voice was trembling.

The Policy Maker

Chang Hsi-kuo

translated by Ching-Hsi Perng

A. Go To . . .

Problem 1.   Enter through the left-hand door, turn left, walk 20 steps, then turn right, cross the long corridor, and open the last door. What do you see?
Answer: A black lacquered screen, on whose top right corner the peeling paint bares the colour of the wood.

Problem 2.   Enter through the right-hand door, turn right, walk 20 steps, then turn left, cross the long corridor, and open the last door. What do you see?
Answer: A desk, on which are placed a platter-glass desk-top with a green-felt base, two telephones, a small calculator, a fountain-pen stand, and an inkpot.

Problem 3.   Enter through the back door, walk through the guardroom and the toilet, and then open the side door on the right. What do you see?
Answer: The backs of bookshelves made of Chinese cypress and covered with spider webs. Underneath the bookshelves are a pair of sneakers.

Problem 4.   All told, how many policy makers are there?
Answer: I don't know.

Problem 5.   All told, how many roads are there that lead to the policy maker(s)?
Answer: I don't know.
   Key to the Problems
   1. The policy maker.
   2. The policy maker.
   3. The policy maker.
   4. One.
   5. Infinite roads.

B. If . . .

Problem 6.   The ministries concerned have decided to set up a Commission for the Promotion of Photochemistry in the form of a trust, a corporate body, with government and the private sectors each raising 50 million dollars to fund it. What is your judgment on this?

Answer: A successful policy maker must first collect information, then analyze the data, and finally form a judgment.

(1)   Collecting Information: I am already 56 I am very tired although I jog in the morning and do hand exercises I participated in the P'u Chung-ch'iang Run for Self-strengthening and also morning-jogged with Wang Yung-ch'ing but my belly is still protruding my hair thinning day by day[1]

I am already 56 I am very tired thirteen years ago at Oakland University I almost made the department chairman at the last moment I was betrayed by Fan Shu-t'ung who joined forces with the Indian colleagues and the Old Jew the venerable Ching-wen happened to come at that time trying to talk me into returning to the motherland so my mind was made up now Ching-wen has passed away and now I have no friend in the court neither here nor there I am already 56 I am very tired still tomorrow I'll jog never leave until tomorrow what should be finished today work hard on signing the reports have someone pour tea

(2)   Analyzing Data: for the routine meeting tomorrow it will do to just send Associate Director Wu I should go to the annual conference of the Association of Photochemistry later to give a lecture no need to draft the lecture just drop the bomb on the bureaucracy for concocting pretexts to pile one bed over another to give vent to my oppressed feeling *I was just about to ride [to heaven] on the wind but feared that heaven's crystalline palaces and towers so high would be for me too cold instead I dance and cavort here with my shadow*[2] Pao Shih-chien came again to touch me for money this man is sly and shrewd someday he'll be somebody so I have to pretend to be serious about this we agree to co-sponsor the International Conference on Photochemistry and will contribute 200,000 dollars

(3)   Forming Judgments: planning for the Commission for the Promotion of Photochemistry is afoot and full steam and its establishment is a cinch it worries me who will head the Commission it is customary to invite a Chinese scholar from overseas to accept the job condescendingly for a short stint for as long as the dragonfly can stay on the surface of the water and like a spring dream leaving not a trace Fan Shu-t'ung seems the most likely candidate Hu Chien is also possible Sung Fu-sheng would be perfect he's temperate and has no students to work for him whoever I recommend for the job of executive secretary he will certainly accept Hu Chien has been away for years and has

---

[1] P'u Chung-ch'iang was a phenomenal long-distance runner who stayed in the United States but who made frequent visits to Taiwan in the early '80s; Wang Yung-ch'ing is a business tycoon in Taiwan.

[2] The italic lines here are from a *tz'u* poem by the Sung poet Su Shih; the English version is that of Eugene Eoyang in *Sunflower Splendor: Three Thousand Years of Chinese Poetry*, eds. Wu-chi Liu and Irving Yucheng Lo (Garden City, NY: Anchor Press / Doubleday, 1975), p. 350.

seldom come back he has no firm relationship with anybody Fan Shu-t'ung is the most hateful one fortunately the venerable Ts'ai happens to be his arch-enemy I should join hands with Ts'ai to oppose Fan in the unlikely event of failing I will retreat and try to save my own skin if I cannot take control of the Commission for the Promotion of Photochemistry I must at least hold fast to my own position and boycott the Commission so that it will never amount to anything I'll then see how long Fan Shu-t'ung can go on with his one-man show those young men in the Association of Photochemistry should be useful Pao Shih-chien is also capable but this man is too ambitious and I simply cannot afford not to guard against his defection

Problem 7.   (Yes or No) Should you go to Man-ch'ien's place for lunch?
Answer: Yes.

Key to the Problems
6.   The battle is as good as lost.
7.   No.

C.   Then. . .

Problem 8.   (Multiple Choice)
Man-ch'ien is acting up again. How are you going to deal with it?
(1)   Appease her by coaxing.
(2)   Play deaf and dumb.
(3)   Make a clean break with her.
(4)   Risk hypertension and have a brawl with her.
(5)   Other (write down your answer in the blank provided).
Answer: Play deaf and dumb.
It's the same old problem.

'Why don't you get a divorce?'
'. . . .'

'You lied to me when you said that because you were married abroad, you had to go back to that country to get a divorce. I know nothing about foreign laws and have been duped by you all these years. I didn't know the truth until Shi-chia, by a slip of the tongue, let it out. Humph! You weren't married overseas at all, but in Nanking! Chang Pi-ching, be fair and answer this: Why did you deceive me? For fear I might make a scene, was it?'
'. . . .'

'If that's what you fear, then that's just the thing I'd do. Now that I've thoroughly investigated the case, you can no longer fool me. If she won't come back, you can place a notice in the newspaper demanding that she return in three months. If she doesn't come back by then, you are perfectly justified to file for a divorce. What's so hard about that?'

'. . . .'

'You don't want to publicize it, right? Chang Pi-ching, you are afraid of losing face? And why should I not be afraid of losing face? Do you know what Li'l Ch'uan's playmates in the kindergarten say about him? He's your son, and yet you have the heart to see him humiliated like this?'

'. . . .'

'Li'l Ch'uan and I have become the butt of jokes wherever we go. Now you're satisfied, eh? You're satisfied, eh?'

'. . . .'

'Your house overseas you gave to her, and all your money to boot! What have I got? She is smart, and knows how to protect herself. I'm the only fool, and because of me Li'l Ch'uan has to suffer.'

'. . . .'

'If you won't place the notice, I'll do it for you. Instead of some of us losing face, let's all be shamed!'

'. . . .'

Truly there is nothing I can say. The child is innocent, and one way or another the problem has to be solved. It's been some time since Man-ch'ien threatened to place an ad in the paper, but she's become more ferocious recently, probably because the child is going to school. All this is the fault of Shih-chia and his big mouth. Some people are lucky, some aren't. The venerable Chou keeps two other 'small residences', and he is doing just fine. Why should I, of all people, have the ill luck to meddle with a woman given to crying and brawls?

Problem 9.   (Fill in the blank.)
Because you didn't take a nap, you feel languid in the afternoon. After the visitors from the Ministry of Economic Affairs have left, you recline on your chair and doze off, again dreaming of _____.
Answer: Chungking.
One group after another, people jammed the air-raid shelter. In the dark, only the faint light of one or two flashlights could be seen. Layers of shadows, like ghosts and goblins, besieged me. A child cried, wanting to get out, but was soon stopped by the mother—as if terribly afraid that enemy aircraft might hear the underground cry. The air became foul; I almost suffocated. I don't know how long I stood it. Maybe a few hours, maybe a few centuries. All of a sudden the crowd surged like waves. 'The iron-gate is shut and won't open! Help!' People screamed like beasts, and struggled like worms. I pushed away the layers of ghostly shadows and moved forward in the dark. I'm only seventeen, I can't die in this place, I've got to push my way out of it! Push my way out, push my way out, push my way out. . . .

From the endless darkness of deep under the earth, I gradually emerged. I could still hear the crying of people. I was crawling on their bodies, crawling over countless heads and arms. Too many people and not enough oxygen: I've got to push my way out! Push my way out, push my way out. . . . Barely opening my eyes, I find crouching in the chair, in the spacious office, only myself. Outside, maybe it is still a crowded world, but I don't have to push myself out. I've already pushed myself in, where there's only me, and I'm quite safe. I don't have to push out. I'm quite safe. I'm quite safe.

Key to the Problems

8. Make a clean break with her.

9. The dream fairy.

D. Else . . .

Problem 10. If, 13 years ago, you had made department chairman at Oakland, what would you be now?

Answer: Four-forty. Ring for the maid to call Wang the chauffeur. Pack up the briefcase, open the door, cross the long corridor, turn left, walk 20 steps, and then turn right. The car is waiting at the main entrance. Associate Director Wu stands by, radiant with smiles. Get into the car, and Associate Director Wu closes the door. Good-bye, Mr Director. Good-bye.

Key to the Problem

10. Four-forty. In the supermarket, pushing a cart, tamely following Mei-fan and walking past row after row of canned foods. Want vegetable oil? No, we've got some at home. Want some peanut-butter? Yes, take one. Instant macaroni is on sale, 15 cents off a box. Get three. American cheese and Swiss cheese—get one of each. Want some bread? Take two loaves. One box of granola. One bag of doughnuts. Go back to the first row and get a jar of fresh orange juice—Li'l Sis caught cold yesterday. The price of TV Weekly is up again, by five cents—forget it. Did you bring the credit card? We can't use the credit card any more this month. Well, then, check or cash? Go to the bank tomorrow morning, be sure not to forget. Thank you for shopping with us. Here are the coupons. Good-bye.

E. Begin. . .

Problem 11. (Translation) Translate into everyday speech the opinions expressed in the second meeting of the Preparatory Committee for the Commission for the Promotion of Photochemistry.

(1) Ts'ai (Commission Member): 'In recent years our industry has made rapid progress, a fact well-known to the world. In order to develop it further, we must upgrade our labour-intensive industry and make it capital- and technology-intensive. Besides efforts made by industry itself and assistance

and incentives provided by the government, all leadership units in charge of technology must also co-ordinate with the policy of the government and encourage academia to co-operate with industry. The establishment of the Commission for the Promotion of Photochemistry is aimed directly at co-ordinating academia with industry and business, so that research and development may be tuned to the need of industry and thus accelerate the transfer of technology. How can the Promotion Commission and the existing leadership units in charge of technology co-ordinate and co-operate with one another to avoid duplication and overlapping of work? I wish all of you would address this topic and engage in a lively discussion.'

(2)   Chin (Director): 'Mr Ts'ai just mentioned *technology transfer*. That hits the nail right on the head. *Frankly speaking*, a *gap* still exists between our academic and research institutes and the industry. How to *bridge* this *gap*? In my unit, an important criterion for the evaluation of applied science research projects is whether the project is *relevant* to our *immediate problems*. The trouble is, there are too many authorities in charge, and everyone is a *prima donna*, making it very difficult to accomplish anything. If, from the very beginning, the goals of the new Commission for the Promotion of Photochemistry are clearly identified as industrial education, personnel training, and *development-type research*, then it would be easier for it to serve the function of *technology transfer*.'[3]

(3)   Yen (Professor): 'Director Chin, if you had not mentioned your applied science research projects, I would have kept silent. Now that you have mentioned them, however, I'd like to say something. Director Chin mentioned that the criterion for the evaluation of applied science research projects should be their immediate usefulness. This seems a bit too short-sighted. How can one anticipate a positive result from any scientific research even before it is carried out? If we are reluctant to put money and effort in basic research, science will never take root in our soil. If the Commission for the Promotion of Photochemistry can help reduce Director Chin's burden, I for one am all for it; therefore basic research ought to have the support of the Promotion Commission. I'd like to reiterate the old adage: Without basic research, there won't be any applied science.'

(4)   Pao (Research Associate): 'It is a honour to be present at the meeting here today with my seniors. The Dean of my Research Institute has always had the highest esteem for the far-sightedness of Commission Member Ts'ai. Before I came here, the Dean repeatedly instructed me that our Institute would do

---

[3] The italic portions of Director Chin's remarks are in English in the original.

everything within its power to help the Promotion Commission with its job. Although our Institute cannot boast a long history, we are equally enthusiastic about basic research and application development. Moreover, the preparatory work, which I have been put in charge of, for convening an International Conference on Photochemistry in Taipei, is well under way. Commission Member Ts'ai, Director Chin, and Director Chang have all given it their enthusiastic support. On behalf of the Dean of our Institute, allow me to express our deepest gratitude.'

Answer:

(1) Commission Member Ts'ai: 'Since to establish the Commission for the Promotion of Photochemistry is a decision already made by the authorities concerned, nobody should hinder it.'

No one has mentioned who should be the Commission Chairman, probably because it is not yet time. I'd better find an occasion to have a man-to-man talk with the venerable Ts'ai, to remind him that Fan Shu-t'ung is out of the question.

(2) Director Chin: 'I am opposed to the establishment of the Commission for the Promotion of Photochemistry. If it has to be set up, I hope the territories are clearly marked.'

His budget has remained the same for three years, so his position is no longer firm. All the 'corporate bodies' that fly around today are drastic measures taken by the authorities concerned. His opposition eventually will be futile. This man is fusty. It's alright to have some contact with him for concerted efforts, but I must be careful not to be infected with his germs.

(3) Professor Yen: 'I am ready to fight against Chin "What's-His-Name" to the end. Whatever Chin is opposed to, I endorse.'

Old Yen is an outstanding scholar, and he is honestly opposed to Chin. Yet when a stubborn scholar loses sight of the whole picture he will only make things worse. Considering the research of Fan 'What's-His-Name', Old Yen might be willing to have him come and take charge of the Commission for the Promotion of Photochemistry. Although Old Yen has neither position nor authority, he wields considerable influence. If I should fail, pedants like him must bear the responsibility.

(4) Pao Shih-chien: 'I may be young, but I am industrious. I hope you'll give me guidance and help.'

This young man, full of sap, spares no effort showing off. Unfortunately he has joined the wrong camp and followed the wrong leader. I'll try somehow to win him over, though. If he is grateful and reciprocates, then I can use this young man.

Problem 12.   Explain the term 'Politics'.

Answer:

(1)   Politics is the extension of war. When you are unable to use an over-whelming force or naked power, you resort to political means.

(2)   Politics is the purest human relationship. There exists between man and man only one basic relationship—that between master and slave. If you are the master, I am your slave; if you are the governor, I am the governed; if you are king, I am the rebel.

(3)   Political behaviour is a purely rational form of conduct. The art of politics is the highest of all arts because political behaviour is completely rational. All irrational elements are data for policy-making, not the subject of policy-making. Political rationale is a crystalline, pure rationale, untainted by the slightest impurity.

Problem 13.   What is the probability of your successfully preventing Fan Shu-t'ung from heading the Promotion Commission?

Answer: 80 per cent.

First, I will pay a visit to the venerable Ts'ai, to show my support for the establishment of the Promotion Commission. Once it is clear that I'm not in the slightest degree selfish, Ts'ai will be reassured that I will never play tricks on him. When Fan 'What's-His-Name' returned two years ago, he embar-rassed the venerable Ts'ai in public on one occasion. I will just make casual reference to that. If the venerable Ts'ai starts to bad-mouth Fan, then I can be 10 per cent sure of my plan.

When the venerable Ts'ai fumes about Fan, I'll echo immediately, to reinforce the sense of solidarity in the face of a common enemy, and to clearly remind him never to make use of this man. If Ts'ai is thoughtful and silent and says nothing, then I can be 20 per cent sure.

I will then pay a visit to Director Chin. Chin has been bitten before, and he is, unfortunately, rather timid. I should stress the fact that Fan is inordinately proud but very capable. Smart man that he is, Chin can't help get my meaning. If he mentions some other candidates, it means he is planning for the worst, and I can be 30 per cent sure.

I will tell Director Chin that Sung Fu-sheng will come back and take part in the International Conference, and that he might wish to ask Sung to give a lecture in his unit. If Chin appears interested in this, then I can be 40 per cent sure of my plan.

Pao Shih-chien is going all out for this International Conference, most likely to bring in foreigners whose influence he can use to puff himself up. I'll have a chat with him in my office, and point out that a youngster must avoid unwanted publicity. Since foreigners do not understand our situation, they can only decorate the scene; it would be better to give the limelight to true Chinese experts like Sung Fu-sheng and thereby pre-empt criticism. Since I have contributed money to the Conference, Pao Shih-chien will listen to me, and then I can be 50 per cent sure of my plan.

Old Yen is the most difficult to manipulate. I've got to persuade the old man with reason, but appeal to his compassion as well. Sung Fu-sheng is his former classmate, who else should he give a hand to? For the long-range development of science, co-ordination among all members concerned is essential. If Old Yen lends his support, I can be 60 per cent sure of my plan.

Once the groundwork is laid, the other 20 per cent depends on Sung Fu-sheng's on-the-spot performance after his return. If he acquits himself appropriately, sees all those people he should see, says all he should say, and keeps his mouth shut about anything he shouldn't say, then I can be 80 per cent sure of my plan.

(Thirteen years ago I was betrayed by Fan 'What's-His-Name' my resentment remains to this day when I recall the past heartaches lead me to a profound understanding though gone astray I'll find the right path now that I realize my mistake like an old fire-horse I can still answer the alarm a man of stout heart stays brave to the end of his days the great Lien P'o has aged considerably but he's still alive and kicking wait and see if I am not more skilful than ever before an ignoramus no longer I am ready for you anytime)

Key to the Problems

11. (1) 'I am chairing this session as ordered.'

    (2) 'I have no alternative but to come.'

    (3) 'I am an upright man of integrity.'

    (4) 'I am a young prodigy.'

12. Politics attempts to manage the affairs of many people.

13. The probability of success is zero.

F. Do . . .

Problem 14. Shih-hsien is coming over for a vacation. Where are you going to put him up? Is he staying with Shih-chia? Or staying with you?

Answer: He stays with me of course. Shih-chia is too wild; he does nothing but fool around with those would-be stars of the TV company. If Shih-hsien stays with him, he is likely to be misled. Easy-going, Shih-hsien is nevertheless highly principled. He has Mei-fan's strong character; in looks he takes after me. Now all of a sudden he's 22! When I left Mei-fan he was only 9, and Shih-chia 17; we agreed to take care of one each. It snowed heavily the day we left and Shih-hsien quietly put on overcoat and boots himself and followed the car all the way to the end of the lane. I asked him to go back, but he kept standing in the snow. He didn't cry, however; it was Shih-chia in the car who did—

calling to his brother and crying. We see each other once every year or two, and each time he seems to have grown bigger than the last. Mei-fan does know how to raise a child; after all, it's better for a child to stay with his mother. In comparison, Man-ch'ien seems feckless in her treatment of Shih-ch'uan, who has been spoiled rotten. She can't stand being criticized; the moment you bring the matter up, the tears trickle down. What Li'l Ch'uan might become when he grows up, I can't bear to imagine; maybe I won't live to see the day. Now that all three sons are with me, I should be content. If I can crush Fan 'What's-His-Name', I'll have reason to congratulate myself.

Problem 15.   Explain the term '*kai-t'u kuei-liu*' [replacing natives with outsiders].

Answer:

(1)   When the political struggle among various factions is at white heat and reaches a deadlock, usually an outsider will profit from the situation and step in to take charge.

(2)   Troubles at home inevitably lead to foreign invasions. Only after eunuchs start to jostle for power will the queen's relatives rise to prominence. There were Yang Kuo-chung and Kao Li-shih before there was An Lu-shan.[4] Outsiders are serviceable precisely because they lack local support.

(3)   There are many stages in the struggle between the nativists and the pro-foreigners. I used to be one of the pro-foreigners, a beneficiary of the policy of 'replacing natives with outsiders'. Now I am a member of the pro-foreign group among the nativists. The pro-foreigners can be sub-divided into 'foreign pro-foreigners', who specialize in making international connections, and 'native pro-foreigners', who join hands with nativist forces. Native nativists versus foreign nativists versus native pro-foreigners versus foreign pro-foreigners: in a quadrangular battle, the situation is, of course, always ambiguous and confusing. But, 'replacing natives' does not necessarily mean appointing outsiders; 'replacing outsiders' may mean appointing natives.

(Political behaviour is a purely rational form of conduct. All irrational elements are data for policy-making, but not the subject of policy-making. Herein lies the greatest contribution we who have studied abroad have ever made.)

---

[4] Yang Kuo-chung was brother to the favoured 'Precious Consort' of the T'ang emperor Hsuan-tsung; Kao Li-shih, a powerful eunuch of the court; and An Lu-shan, the leader of an unsuccessful rebellion.

Problem 16. (Multiple Choice)
On the first day of the International Conference, foreign guests discovered differences in their travel subsidy. The three who were given less money make a big issue of it and demand increased subsidy or they will boycott the conference by pulling out. How are you going to deal with it?
(1) Resolutely say no to the request.
(2) Pay the full amount requested.
(3) Negotiate with the foreigners and increase the subsidy according to the circumstances.
(4) Other (write your answer in the blank provided).
Answer: Pay the full amount requested.
Pao Shih-chien may be enthusiastic enough about his job, but he is, after all, lacking in experience. One of the thorniest problems in organizing an international conference is the unequal distribution of travel grants. If there are too many monks for the little gruel to go around, complete equality is out of the question; if some get more and some less, the latter are bound to be dissatisfied. Since I am not the organizer of this Conference, I need not get involved in such matters. But the three foreigners, with the backing of other foreigners, are making a scene. If things get worse, not only will all of us be embarrassed, which may be of no great consequence, but our nation may be shamed, which is a serious matter, indeed. In order to settle the dispute and bring about peace, I will advise Pao Shih-chien to pay the full amount requested. This is rather unfair, of course, given the fact that the foreigners Pao Shih-chien invited are mostly impostors—and they have the nerve to make impossible demands. One of them even goes so far as to request a suite at the Grand Hotel, obviously having forgotten the worth of the uncredited university he represents! Unfortunately fellow-countrymen can't tell genuine foreign scholars from phonies and are therefore simply duped. Because so many foreigners are attending this Conference, Pao Shih-chien gets rather high marks. This man is good at manipulating things. I will keep quiet and let him bathe in his glory just this once.

Both Fan 'What's-His-Name' and Sung Fu-sheng have returned to attend the Conference. Fan has certainly pulled a lot of tricks. No sooner had he got off the plane than he called a press conference. Everywhere he goes, he draws a group of followers. Thanks to Director Chin and me, who secretly lend Sung Fu-sheng our support, the latter barely manages a stand-off with Fan. This is going to be a tough battle and the outcome now hinges on Sung Fu-sheng's luck.

Problem 17. Learning that Shih-hsien has come back and is to live at home with you, Man-ch'ien throws tantrums again. What are you going to do?

Answer: Man-ch'ien is just too narrow-minded. Shih-hsien comes back only once in a long, long while. How can I shut the door on him? Usually I forbear and give in to her, but on this matter I will not budge. Luckily we are not officially married, otherwise I would be forced not to recognize my own sons, wouldn't I? In choosing this particular juncture to make a scene, this woman exposes her ignorance. With Fan 'What's-His-Name' invading, I am in imminent danger, yet Man-ch'ien not only shows no sympathy, but seizes the opportunity to make a scene. Sometimes I wonder why I was bewitched by her in the first place. One must never be soft-hearted; soft-heartedness leads to infinite disasters.

Problem 18.   The International Conference on Photochemistry comes to a successful conclusion, and the venerable Ts'ai throws a banquet for the renowned scholars and experts attending. Chinese and foreigners are mixed, and 23 of them sign foreign names, 28 use chopsticks, and 15 use knives and forks. How many Chinese and how many foreigners were there?
Answer: About half and half. All things considered, it was a satisfactory banquet; even the three foreigners who had clamoured for more money were contented. Sung Fu-sheng's performance was not bad, and his thank-you speech was rather appropriate. Judging from the expression of the venerable Ts'ai, he must have a liking for Sung; this move of mine did not go wrong. Fan 'What's-His-Name' played big-shot again: he called up Pao Shih-chien from the Grand Hotel and demanded a car be arranged exclusively to take his wife shopping. When Pao Shih-chien came for my advice on this, I told him to forget about courtesy and formality, adopt a stern sense of justice, and reject the unreasonable demand of the blackguard. Fan was so furious that he even purposely showed up late for the venerable Ts'ai's banquet. He went too far indeed. Who did he think he was to keep everybody waiting? A Nobel Laureate? Fan's presumptuousness not only incurred the wrath of the venerable Ts'ai and Director Chin, but Professor Yen also became impatient and shouted abuse at him. Now that an Anti-Fan group has shaped up naturally, just a few tricks should serve to direct everybody's fire at Fan in the next organizing meeting of the Commission for the Promotion of Photochemistry.

Problem 19.   Fill in the blanks of the following statement:
As the Commission for the Promotion of Photochemistry is being organized, the most important task is to (a) _____ and (b) _____.
Answer: (a)   find a good location
          (b)   construct a large building
You must have a piece of land before you have people. The most important job in the establishment of any agency is the construction of a building. If I am

to succeed in my plan to prevent Fan 'What's-His-Name' from heading the Promotion Commission, I must give serious thought to the location of this Commission. It is unlikely that Sung Fu-sheng will stay in Taipei on a permanent basis. If I recommend Associate Director Wu to be Executive Secretary of the Commission, then the Commission is practically mine. Since it's all in the family, so to speak, things would run smoothly. It would be better to have the Commission for the Promotion of Photochemistry close to where I now work; it's more convenient that way.

Key to the Problems

14. Let Shih-hsien decide.

15. Dismiss officials who are natives and fill their positions with outsiders.

16. Resolutely say no to the request.

17. Coax her with sweet words.

18. There were 28 Chinese and 18 foreign scholars (cf. 'Chickens-and-hares-in-the-same-cage' type of math problems).

19. (a) recruit capable persons
    (b) begin research now

G. End . . .

Problem 20.   You are attending the third preparatory meeting of the Commission for the Promotion of Photochemistry, and suddenly you find all the other members giving you the cold shoulder. Commission Member Ts'ai looks stiff when he greets you, Professor Yen does not even look you in the eye, Director Chin merely nods slightly, and even Research Associate Pao puts on a false smile. What exactly is the reason?

Answer: I don't understand, I just don't understand. It seemed all of a sudden I was turned into a transparent man and nobody took any notice of me. Returning to my office, I find placed on my desk a newspaper clipping, in which there is circled in red a notice: 'Warning Against My Deserter Wife': *Wang Mei-fan: You have deserted our home without reason. If you fail to return in three months, each of us is free to remarry. Chang Pi-ching.* Finished. Completely finished. I am frozen to the finger-tips. Fancy her doing such a stupid thing. She thought a notice in a minor newspaper wouldn't catch anybody's attention, but in fact there are any number of loafers in Taipei who do nothing *but* read minor newspapers. Finished. Completely finished. 'Man proposes, God disposes.' All my plans were perfectly worked out; how could I have known Man-ch'ien would betray me? I didn't even have a chance to guard against it. There are things that can be done but not talked about. Now that she has caused this trouble, how can I face others? 'Warning Against My Deserter

Wife'. A smart woman, indeed! Finished, completely finished.

Problem 21.   Fill in the blanks in the following statement:
The Commission for the Promotion of Photochemistry is formally established.
Its Chairman is (a) _____, and its Executive Secretary is
(b) _____.
Answer: Less than three days after the scandal, the venerable Ts'ai called me
over for a man-to-man talk, in which he advised me to resign my job. Having
anticipated this, I asked for a teaching position at a university; I have
absolutely no wish to hold on to my chairmanship. From the way he spoke, I
knew it was impossible even to teach in the university; I was horrified to have
been denied even this alternative. I said that I had no other choice but to leave
the country. Ts'ai kept silent, and I knew their minds were made up and there
was no use going any further. As I took leave of him, however, Ts'ai's consoled
me by saying that everybody appreciated my hard work all these years and they
were sincerely grateful, so they would never do anything to embarrass me. I
might rest assured, he said, the man to replace me would not be Fan Shu-t'ung.
That made the scales fall from my eyes. I was digging my own grave when I
paved the way for Sung Fu-sheng! The Man-ch'ien incident could have been
overlooked; after all, 'In the whole Chia Residence only the stone lions are
clean.'⁵ All along they wanted to do me in, and the Man-ch'ien incident gave
them a pretext: how perfect! For whom have I laboured and toiled? I hate that
Sung Fu-sheng: under the mask of an honest face, he harboured ulterior
motives. It was a re-run of the story of 13 years ago, and I was still completely
unaware of it. I lived 13 years for nothing!

Problem 22.   Who is Wang Shih-hsien?
Answer: If his friend had not made the phone call, I would not have known
Mei-fan had changed my son's surname! I shouted into the receiver: 'Wang
Shih-hsien doesn't live here! There's no one here by the name of Wang Shih-
hsien!' Yet by my side Shih-hsien, unperturbed, said: 'It's my phone call, Dad.'
I knew you could change your name when you got US citizenship, but I never
thought Mei-fan would be so utterly ruthless. She wouldn't divorce me, she
wouldn't remarry, yet she would change the surname of my son! This is the
stab from Brutus. Man-ch'ien hurt me, Fan Shu-t'ung revolted against me,
Sung Fu-sheng betrayed me . . . but none of them was so ruthlessly venomous
as Mei-fan with this thrust. Boundless though the universe is, there is no place
for me, for Chang Pi-ching. O Heaven, why do you treat me like this?

---

⁵ The Chia family features prominently in the great Ming novel *Hung-lou meng*.

Key to the Problems
20.   They regard it a disgrace to be in your company.
21.   (a)   Fan Shu-t'ung
      (b)   Pao Shih-chien
22.   Chang Shih-hsien.

H. Go To . . .

Problem 23.   You are in the airport. Shih-hsien is carrying your luggage for you, Man-ch'ien crying like a baby, and Shih-chia holding Li'l Ch'uan by the hand. The airport is crowded, a sea of people, and you finally manage to squeeze through them and approach the gate. Shih-hsien says it's time you went in. The ticket and exit permit tightly in your hand, you look around and find no one else to see you off. Write an essay to express your feeling at this moment.
Answer: Political behaviour is a purely rational form of conduct all irrational elements are data for policy-making and not the subject of policy-making herein lies the greatest contribution we who have studied abroad have made a policy maker must be cool careful decisive I am 56 I am very tired 13 years ago at Oakland University I almost made department chairman at the last moment I was betrayed by Fan Shu-t'ung who joined forces with Indian colleagues and the old Jew 13 years after that my prize was again stolen by Sung Fu-sheng I am not an ideal policy maker I am 56 I am very tired betrayal among human beings is nothing to be marvelled at betrayal is also a kind of policy but what's happened to my belief that political behaviour is a purely rational form of conduct all irrational elements are data for policy-making and not the subject of policy-making Man-ch'ien I don't blame you Mei-fan you did the right thing all the troubles were rooted in my own *karma* I am 56 I am very tired *I was about to ride the wind to heaven but fear that the crystalline palaces I was about to ride the wind to it I was about to ride the wind to it I was about to ride the wind.* . . .

The Scholar of Yanghsien

Chang Hsi-kuo

translated by Tzu-yun Chen

TASSEL WHITE, before she bought the erotic bottle gourd from the scholar of Yanghsien, was a normal and contented housewife. Normal, for she was always gloomy. Contented, for Gusty Lin, her husband, owned 973 robots.

When Tassel White promised to marry Gusty Lin, she never dreamed that he would become as prosperous as he was today. Her parents had passed away long ago. Her father, who had been a biblio-maniac, left her a strange name, a robot who only knew how to play chess, and a houseful of old books. The books were sold in batches as antiques; only the chess-playing robot was left without any taker and became her only dowry. Tassel White was born a beauty. Her shining black hair grew so long that it almost reached her knees. Her hands were long and slender; and when they touched the responsive keys of a piano, the most wonderful music was produced. Many a man had been enchanted by her music. Unhappily, because of her name, they took her for a woman of a certain profession, and would never get serious about her. The only person who seriously courted her was Gusty Lin. He was then in a worse financial situation than she was. He did not own a single robot. In the daytime he was a delivery man and when day was done he went to night school. It was only because of his situation that Lin condescended to take her as a wife, for who could possibly want a woman with such a strange name?

The day after the wedding Gusty Lin began to display his talents. Stroking her long hair, he remarked, 'Tassel, beginning today, you need not go to the restaurant to play the piano. We are turning over a new leaf.'

'Gusty,' said Tassel White, greatly moved. 'I was willing to marry you, for I knew you were up-and-coming. I will work a few more years to support you while you finish your night school. Is that a deal?'

'That's unnecessary!' Gusty Lin replied firmly. 'I definitely will not let you support me. You have a robot. Why not let him develop his potential?'

'Are you talking about Mount Chün?' Tassel White could not help laughing. 'Mount Chün knows nothing but playing chess. What can we possibly ask him to do?'

'There are many things he can do. If you have no objection, I will try to enlighten him.'

Having got the consent of Tassel White, Gusty Lin summoned his wife's sole dowry and said to the robot: 'Mount Chün, starting from today, you are no longer to fool around, you have to do something constructive.'

'Nonsense!' The robot whose name was Mount Chün was outraged: 'When my old master was alive, he had never asked me to do any heavy manual work. A robot may be killed but not insulted. If you force me to do anything, I will certainly commit suicide right before your eyes.'

With that the robot tried to dash his head against the wall, but before he could make it Gusty Lin caught him by the waist. Taking advantage of the situation, Gusty Lin retrieved a memory-control board from Mount Chün's belly and replaced it with one that he had prepared in advance. The robot, having undergone this repair work, lost all his pugnacity, and did whatever Gusty Lin wanted him to do quite submissively.

'Mount Chün,' Gusty Lin was all smiles as he said, 'it is time to start working.'

The belly of the robot began to produce strange sounds and before long he opened his mouth and a microcomputer was spewed forth. Tassel White watched all this with wide eyes and her mouth agape. This was the first time that she had ever seen the robot perform a useful task.

From that time on, conditions for Gusty Lin and Tassel White became quite comfortable. Having used his little trick to subdue Mount Chün and convert him to orthodoxy, Gusty Lin then began to direct him to produce many things. This chess-playing robot was actually a very capable machine tool of the A-77 class. Before long he had assembled one robot model B-5 for Gusty Lin. Then another. By the time Mount Chün had assembled his two-hundredth robot, the Lins had become the wealthiest family in the community.

But Gusty Lin did not become complacent. He was very ambitious and went on to enlarge his robot forces and expand his enterprise. He took to writing and published many monographs on the administration of robots, such as *The Robot and You, Gusty Lin's Tips on Money-making*. Every one of his books became a best-seller. By this time he was a nationally-known entrepreneur, a much-revered decision-maker. The Heaven Television Station interviewed him regularly, the weekly news magazine, *Earth*, had a special issue on him; Gusty Lin became the busiest person appearing in heaven and on earth.

Behind every successful man there is always a lonely woman. The busier Gusty Lin became, the gloomier Tassel White grew. There was, of course, no need for her to work in the restaurant. Apart from combing her hair and playing the piano, she had little else to do. Life was as plain and tasteless as a cup of boiled water. The man who was supposed to be her mate for life was so occupied that he hardly had any time to be with her. Even though Gusty Lin became rich on her dowry and therefore theoretically should be satisfied, what did she get out of it?

One night, it was very late and Gusty Lin had still not come back. Tassel

White sat by the window and watched pair after pair of mandarin-duck rocket-ships rushing by by the skyscraper. Her tears flowed. Had she known it would be like this, she would have let Mount Chün go on playing chess. Thinking of this, she felt compelled to throw her tea cup at the robot spitefully.

'Watch out!' cried the robot, and with the soft rubber sucker of his mechanical arm he caught the tea cup nimbly, 'it is against the law to maltreat a robot.'

Having brushed back her long hair with one hand, Tassel White raised her oval face, and with tears sparkling in her bright eyes, she asked bitterly, 'Mount Chün, what shall I do?'

'Find something meaningful to do. For example, join the Cockroach Protection Association. Do you know that there are only 325,642 cockroaches left in the whole world? If there were no cockroaches, can you imagine what the world would be like? You should go around the world and bring this news to its populace.'

Nonsense, thought Tassel White. She hated cockroaches more than anything. Just to think of them gave her goose-flesh. But the robot went on: 'He is busy. You have to be busier than he so he will notice you. We have only one earth, and you have only one husband.'

The last sentence struck a responsive chord in Tassel White's heart. The very next day she became a member of the Cockroach Protection Association and went about crying and chanting for the salvation of this much-despised insect. When Gusty Lin was interviewed by the *Earth* magazine for the millionth time, Tassel White also appeared on the screen of the Heaven Television Station and talked articulately.

'To be sure, the cockroach is not very lovable, nevertheless, it is the most ancient and most enduring living thing on earth. If the cockroach cannot survive, does man have any hope?'

'You were marvellous!' the robot remarked when Tassel White returned home. 'Of course, the script was well written. Your husband must be jealous. He wants me to ghost-write again for the sequel to *How to Administer the Robots*, but I haven't started it yet.'

'I still feel that it is a bit nonsensical,' said Tassel White. Staring at the beauty in the mirror who had her make-up partially removed, she felt she had a thousand charms. 'None of the members of the Cockroach Protection Association is very good looking. In fact, they all have cockroach-like heads and mouse-like eyes. Perhaps I should join in a lion or a camel protection association or something like that.'

'The last lion died the day before yesterday, and in the whole world there are only 11 camels left. The only way to live busily and meaningfully is to protect the cockroach. Remember, the busier you are, the more your husband loves you.'

Tassel White did not know whether her husband loved her the more for that, but obviously other men took great interest in her. The Cockroach Protection Association had very few female members in the first place, and attractive females like Tassel White were nowhere to be found. Many male members courted her desperately, but none found favour in her eye. The most persistent suitor was Peace Chen, the owner of a pharmaceutical laboratory and 974 robots. Taking into consideration the fact that he had one more robot than Gusty Lin, Tassel White repelled his advances with civility, but she was only civil to him. That's all. Had she not met Mr Fan, a reporter for Heaven Television, Tassel White would have been as faithful as a modern Penelope.

Tassel White was in fact a good conservative woman. The reporter, a man dark of brow and large of eye, on the pretext of arranging a programme about cockroach protection, made advances to her with dexterity, but she always had the presence of mind to deflect him before anything improper could take place. But having seen so many shots of ugly creeping creatures, one would naturally seek romance as an escape mechanism. One night when Mr Fan took her home, he seized a favourable opportunity and kissed her. Though the kiss was the lightest of its kind, it made butterflies flutter in her stomach. She had to make a clean breast of it to the robot, for he was her only confidant.

'At long last I have a lover. Mount Chün, do you think Gusty will be jealous?'

The robot did not raise his head. He was practising calligraphy single-mindedly (for after being altered by Gusty Lin, he no longer played chess), and crooned the following words: 'Lake Stonefish, like Lake Tung-t'ing, when the summer tide rises, Mount Chün is green. Every part of the name my old master gave me is an allusion. Look, "*When the summer tide rises, Mount Chün is green*", how beautiful that line is!'

'How about my name?'

The robot did not answer. Instead he said: 'A lover is the image of youth in one's mind. A lover is a scarlet mole on one's breast, the bright moonlight before one's bed. When the image disappears from sight, but appears again in the inner eye—that is a true lover.'

Tassel White thought it over and found Mr Fan ambiguous. She wondered whether he was really in love with her. How about Peace Chen? He was far from qualified as a lover. She became disconsolate. Why did she bother to join the Cockroach Protection Association in the first place? She regretted having been a busybody. The robot seemed to read her mind and remarked: 'In ancient China there was a city called Peking. In its suburb there was a temple called

Tan-che. In that temple there was a huge iron pot, which could cook porridge for several hundred monks. It is said that the fire which cooked the porridge burned day and night. On the stove by the pot there was a statue of the Sad Buddha, who looked on the flames with sadness. No one knew what the Sad Buddha was sad about. Was he sad about being tortured by the scorching flames, or was he sad that the fire might eventually die out? Well, the Sad Buddha might be sad about both. If the Buddha could be so contradictory, how much more so is man?'

'Enough,' Tassel White retorted with displeasure. 'You souless machine, what do you know about sadness? Good—'

Before she could finish the exclamation with 'Gracious', everything went black in front of her eyes. At first she thought it was a black-out, then she suspected that the robot was playing a joke on her and was about to scold him when suddenly everything turned bright again. Looking carefully about, she found herself in a luxuriously decorated living-room, and a fat man stood right before her. He was all smiles and held a bottle gourd tightly in one hand.

'Mr Chen, you . . . Why am I here?'

Peace Chen bowed and said: 'Welcome, welcome! Tassel, your condescending to come to my humble place makes me very happy.'

'Don't . . .' Tassel White dodged a kiss from Peace Chen skillfully. 'Peace Chen, tell me the truth, how did you manage to abduct me here? If you don't, I'll be angry.'

'All done with this.' Peace Chen waved the bottle gourd in his hand triumphantly. 'This erotic bottle gourd is great. Tassel, I long for you so, take pity on me and grant me one tender night.'

When Tassel White managed to get away and returned home it was midnight, and, imagine, Gusty Lin was not home yet. Remorseful and miserable, she summoned the robot.

'Mount Chün, what kind of a magic weapon is the erotic bottle gourd? Can you make one?'

'No,' the robot was telling the truth. 'I know a little about the theory of the Higgs fields, but I am definitely no expert.'

'Higgs fields? What are Higgs fields?'

'This has to be told from the very beginning. When the universe was just born, less than 10^{-34} of a second old, it was as tiny as a sesame seed. In the chaotic universe of this tiny sesame seed all the forces were unified. When the universe began to expand, the unified forces went their separate ways and became gravitational force, electromagnetic force, weak interaction force and strong interaction force. When the universe grew as large as an egg, all the force fields had appeared. Later the universe kept swelling and finally became as expanded as it is today. Despite the vastness of the universe, its miniature was fashioned in the first second.

In addition to the gravitational force, the electromagnetic force, the weak interaction force, and the strong interaction force, there are also the Higgs fields. This could be called a partial mutation taking place in the embryo stage of the universe. Later the fields spread to every corner with the expansion of the universe. Since the Higgs fields are a mutation, the general laws of physics do not apply to them. The erotic bottle gourd is a device which controls the Higgs fields. . . .'

Having got this far the robot stopped, for he noticed that Tassel had fallen sound asleep on the sofa, her profuse long hair in disarray and a tear drop glistening on her cheek.

'How pitiable! If my old master were alive, he would certainly be heartbroken at such a sight.' With that the robot tenderly carried Tassel White to her bedroom, and stationed himself outside to keep watch. Robots do not need sleep. He could of course have turned off all power, but he did not; he went on meditating. The books of his late master had been sold by Tassel White, but he remembered all their contents. Man can never avoid the tragedy of birth, age, sickness and death; he is either tortured by love or enslaved by desire. The robot stood in the dark and meditated with compassion, and he searched for a solution in the vast collection of data stored in his memory. If someone happened to see the robot at this moment, he would very likely have been surprised to find that his steel face appeared to be sad.

Gusty Lin returned just before dawn and at once saw the robot standing in the dark; he scolded him vehemently: 'Mount Chün, have you been idle again? Why aren't you working! I told you to build 10 more C-3000 models yesterday. Have you finished them?'

The robot hung his head and said nothing. After a little while he began: 'Mr Lin, last night my mistress . . .'

'Mr Lin again!' Gusty Lin snapped in a rage. 'How many times do I have to tell you I'm your master? Understand? Don't think I can't get along without you. I tell you, if you're this disrespectful again, I'll send you to the Buffalo-pen Labour Correction Camp for Robots and let you taste being in the ditches on a hill side!'

The robot did not dare to argue. He watched Gusty Lin go into the bedroom and before long heard the sound of a great fight. At noon on the following day, after Gusty Lin had gone to his office, Tassel White summoned the robot. Squinting one black and blue eye, she said to the robot: 'Mount Chün, I want an erotic bottle gourd.'

'Mistress,' the robot said with a sigh, 'you'd be better off without it.'

'No! I want an erotic bottle gourd.'

Hard put, the robot said: 'The erotic bottle gourd—I don't know how to build one. If you want to buy one, I know where you can.'

'Who can I buy one from?' Tassel White was so surprised she forgot the pain in her face. 'Do you really mean there is someone who sells these erotic bottle gourds?'

'I don't know his real name. All I know is everybody calls him the scholar of Yanghsien. If you really want an erotic bottle gourd, I will take you to find the man. However, if my late master were alive, he would certainly not approve . . .'

'I don't care! I want an erotic bottle gourd.'

In the afternoon of that very day Tassel White forced the robot to take her to find the scholar of Yanghsien. Having walked in narrow, winding alleys for a long time, they finally came to a tiny herbal medicine store. Holding a feather fan and wearing a silken cap, the scholar of Yanghsien sat erect inside. When he saw them, he said: 'Another customer for the bottle gourd. Here you are.'

The robot picked up the bottle gourd, scrutinized it from right to left, and said: 'Isn't it a transducer of the Higgs fields?'

'There's a knowledgeable robot,' the scholar of Yanghsien chortled approvingly. 'Knowledgeable people nowadays are few and far between. In someone with an iron head and a silicon brain this is even more commendable.'

Tassel White could not discover anything special about the bottle gourd and asked: 'How do you use an erotic bottle gourd?'

'There are many uses. Moses crossing the Red Sea and Kung-ming using the east wind both depended on this small bottle gourd of mine.' The scholar of Yanghsien went on: 'The merits of the bottle gourd can never be fully enumerated. I know what you have in mind. Just recite 'Chu Lu Ju Mu' once and call his name three times; you will then be able to abduct him. As to its other uses, you've no need to learn them.'

Tassel White committed the spell to memory. The robot remarked, 'This bottle gourd has a language recognition device, and that is not difficult to make, but the way to abduct people is to shrink a person to manageable size and suck him up into the Higgs fields inside the gourd. By reversing the same procedure, you can return him to the original size. This is indeed a very ingenious method. Besides the erotic bottle gourd, do you have other secret weapons for sale?'

'Yes indeed, once I dealt in mirrors called the erotic mirrors.' The scholar of Yanghsien went on: 'Unfortunately most people did not like looking at their reflections in a mirror. The Chia family tried it once, but after that the market for such mirrors was so slow I stopped making them. Erotic bottle gourds, on the other hand, enjoy a bull market. They are exported to every corner of the world and have earned considerable foreign exchange for the country. As a matter of fact, the mirror is illusory and the bottle gourd is real; the majority of people shun the illusory and cling to the real. They don't know that in the art of erotica, true is false and real is illusory.'

After this the scholar of Yanghsien mumbled an incantation, changed himself into a wisp of black smoke and disappeared into a bottle gourd hung on the wall. The robot admired it for a while and then said to Tassel White: 'This Higgs fields transducer is extraordinary, but erotic bottle gourds, as well as erotic mirrors are for the disenchanted. However, ignorant people take the erotic for the romantic, and that is a serious mistake.'

Tassel White did not take in a single word. She clutched the bottle gourd tightly all the way home and once home lost no time reciting: '*Chu Lu Ju Mu*, Liu-yuan Fan, Liu-yuan Fan, Liu-yuan Fan!'

The robot by her side heard and was greatly dismayed. He sighed resignedly: 'This is indeed a predestined illicit affair. If my late master could know this in the other world, he would certainly regret having begot her in the first place.'

From then on, every day after Gusty had gone out, Tassel White would summon Liu-yuan Fan. Occasionally Tassel White would be abducted by Peace Chen. Happily Peace Chen's wife was not a peaceable sort and kept a close watch over him. Since she was not abducted very often, Tassel White took it in her stride.

Gusty spent less and less time at home. Aside from pushing the robot to increase production, he neglected household affairs completely. Since she had Liu-yuan, Tassel White became indifferent to Gusty Lin. The robot, however, when he saw what was intolerable to see, criticized both of them with a few choice words. The robot was out of patience; he would snap at Gusty's instructions, and was less obedient to Tassel White than he used to be. When Tassel White was obliged to find fault with him, the robot would invariably reply: 'I wish I were a water-melon. The water-melon distributes its flesh to accumulate merit, and at least people help it spread its seeds, but me? I've built many robots for you, yet your husband forces me to do more. I wish I were a water-melon.'

'But all the robots in my family are your descendants, Mount Chün! Aren't you satisfied?'

The robot turned on the channel for Heaven Television in a bad mood. The last whale was rushing up to the beach to commit suicide, and the last bee was dying from exhaustion on the petal of a rose. The robot wailed: 'Since fin and feather are extinct, being a water-melon would do no good.'

Tassel White was speechless. She had not taken part in the activities of the Cockroach Protection Association for a long time and wondered whether there were any cockroaches left in the world. Possibly no cockroach had survived, but so long as Liu-yuan was in love with her, the world remained the same to her. She picked up her erotic bottle gourd and recited the spell in earnest: '*Chu Lu Ju Mu*, Liu-yuan Fan, Liu-yuan Fan, Liu-yuan Fan!

But Liu-yuan Fan did not appear immediately as he used to. Tassel White noticed that the robot was watching her with a tragic air. She stared absent-mindedly for a while and said: 'Mount Chün—'

Before the robot could respond, Tassel White was falling again into the void. She could see nothing, and shouted in the darkness: 'Liu-yuan! Liu-yuan!'

She was answered by another voice: 'Tassel! Tassel!'

'Mr Chen, why are you here?' Tassel White was startled. 'I didn't summon you!'

'On the contrary,' the voice of Peace Chen said. 'I invited you with the erotic bottle gourd, but why did you put me into the gourd?'

Tassel White did not know how to answer him. By then the inside of the gourd had become brighter and she saw Liu-yuan Fan standing at a distance and Peace Chen standing absent-mindedly on the other side. Two girls who were strangers to her were also there, as was Gusty Lin! She was befuddled. It seemed to her that the top of the gourd where the light filtered in was rising higher and higher, but no, it was her body that was dwindling. Not only herself, but also the five others, were dwindling rapidly, and their distance from her was lengthening. Tassel White shouted in anguish: 'Liu-yuan!' But Liu-yuan Fan shouted to another girl: 'Hsiung-hsiung!' Hsiung-hsiung disregarded Liu-yuan Fan and cried to Gusty Lin: 'Gusty!' Gusty ran in the direction of the second girl, yelling, 'Hsiao-feng!' Hsiao-feng howled desperately: 'Peace!' But Peace Chen was calling in a shrill voice: 'Tassel!'

Suddenly it dawned on Tassel White. All six of them, independently, had summoned each other with the erotic bottle gourd at the same time. The gourd sucked them into the Higgs fields, but because there was nobody outside the gourd, no one could revert to normal and each and every one of them was growing smaller all the time. Tassel White was desperate with fear, shame and rage: 'Oh, I see, all of you have lovers, and all of you cheated on me!'

She tried to do something in her rage, but it was too late. The six persons in the Higgs fields were changed into six tiny specks of dust rushing forward to the ten-to-the-minus-thirty-fourth power of a second before the beginning of the universe.

Rustic Quandary

Shu Kuo-chih

translated by Hsien-hao Liao

A MAN was moving up onto the yellow, gravely mound. Sand and pebbles fell on his worn out shoes. His dry, cracked hands held onto a protruding stone as he moved a few steps further up and reached the level top of the mound. A puff of wind blew the sand off his shoes. Once on top, he found the mound stretching and winding off into infinity: he was, in fact, on a winding dike. The man narrowed his eyes, perhaps to ward off sandy winds and the rays of the sun, and stood there looking into the distance.

At the foot of the dike was an endless stretch of green field, quite unlike the side of the dike he had come from. There it was, a vast expanse of dry, yellow earth. A cloud shadow drifted over the fields, making them look a darker green. Several distant farm houses formed crimson patches. Closer by were some variegated dots in motion: farmers working in the fields. The wind blew and sucked in directions so changeable it was hard to predict. Sometimes the sand on the arid side of the dike blew over; thus it was difficult to keep the lushness of this side.

In addition to the dike, there were also several rows of lush trees planted earlier to fend off sands blown from other directions. The wind never carried moisture. Over the years, it rarely rained on the dry yellow earth beyond the dike. On this side, further into the green fields, it rained once in a while around the village. But the land around the village was not large enough to support all the inhabitants, so they had to increase production by expanding toward the dike. There was just no other way. Those trees planted on the green side, for instance: some had died after a few years; the few left standing looked odd and isolated. They had been expected to grow into leafy trees, but now they had only their skeletons left. Unable to fend off sandy winds, they now turned into peculiar decorations. The purpose of cultivating the land, of course, is to feed the farmer. Therefore, for scores or even hundreds of years, the villagers had tried to expand the arable area. They worked hard at it and with determination. They tried to get rid of as many stones in the soil and to preserve as much moisture as they could. On the moist, fertile soil they grew rice. The gravely areas were put to melons. The sparse trees that could hardly serve as a wind-break could, nevertheless, shelter a man from the parching sun and refresh him.

A water-buffalo drew a plow, followed by a farmer. The share split the soil open and turned it to one side. The farmer, guiding the plow, constantly darted his glance to the right, watched the man on the dike, looking curious and unsettled. He followed the buffalo to the boundary of a small lot and then directed it to turn around and plough in the opposite direction. While the soil was being split open, his glance was directed again toward the stranger. To do this now, he had to look toward his left. In neighbouring fields, there were other farmers or farmer's wives who also noticed someone standing on the dike. They too looked sporadically in the direction of the dike as they attended to their work. In fact, they looked at the stranger and just as often at their neighbours at work . Everyone was aware there was something strange going on, and felt suspicious. But no one talked to anyone close by. In fact, 'close by' meant some 20 to 30 feet away; you had to shout in order to communicate. Usually the words they exchanged were: 'Oh, here you are', 'Hey', 'Time to eat', 'Let's go'. Or they would sing response folk songs; not necessarily begun by Tom for Dick or Harry or by Mr A in response to Mr B. As for conversation, there was practically none. For though somebody was standing on the dike, nobody knew what it signified and so could think of nothing to say to their neighbours. Should they ask who the stranger was? Weren't they all equally uninformed? In this village, everyone knew everyone else's friends and relatives. Now the mystified look on the villagers' faces suggested that they were certainly going to have a hard time trying to comprehend the situation. They rarely had unusual encounters. Now that they were in the presence of such an unfamiliar phenomenon, it was only natural that they should be uneasy and have to spend some time thinking it over to get it exactly right.

Putting down his hoe, one stout middle-aged man crossed his elbows in front of his chest and frowned, looking as if he were thinking about something, while he fixed his eyes on the man on the dike. Seeing a number of others had stopped working, one old man took out his pipe and tucked it into his mouth. He puffed and casually glanced toward the dike. He could see there was a man standing there, but couldn't see clearly who it was except that the man was someone he didn't know. Only after quite a few people had looked several times at that man did one woman venture a glance at him—though a furtive one. She could at least tell he was tall and was standing upright; he didn't seem to be inclined toward rough or vulgar behaviour. The sight as well as the conclusion drawn seemed a luxurious reward to her, and she again bent down to pluck out weeds and collect vegetables. This she did hastily. Shortly afterwards, as if feeling herself entitled to more reward, she again looked toward the man on the dike. She simply couldn't see his face clearly. She would have seen much more clearly had she been where the pipe-smoking old man was. A child helping his father to plant vegetable seeds accidentally dropped the basket he was carrying and hurried to collect the scattered seeds. The father saw what had happened. He looked toward the dike and then back at the child but didn't scold him. Seeing his father looking toward the dike, the child did the same. He saw a man up there, standing. The father didn't seem to want to continue with the work. Although the child had recovered the seeds and put them in the basket, the father appeared not to notice. Deciding to ignore the whole thing, the child bent down, gathered some wet dirt and made it into a ball. But, when he raised his head, he was looking toward the dike and wondering why the man was still standing there. The child's mother worked in another plot, her hair tied with a dappled cloth which floated with her as she moved about. When she looked around, she was mostly looking at her son and sometimes at the stranger. The few times she did look at her husband, it was because she was watching her son and once or twice her eye caught his. One young man raised a muscular arm to wipe the sweat from his forehead while leaning on the vertical hoe. Having looked at the man, he felt a mixture of strangeness and familiarity: strange because the man on the dike was a stranger, never seen before: familiar because the man on the dike reminded him of an experience a year before while fixing a leak in the roof of his house. Standing on high and looking down, all the villagers seemed to have shrunken in size. But for the moment, the stranger stood motionless; no salient features could be perceived. He was neither a child nor an old man. In that respect the young man felt they had something in common. But that this man's hands had done the same work and his feet had trod the same road as he, was doubtful. It was hardly likely that such was the case—this conclusion increased his curiosity. One old man with a red, dry and apparently festered eye socket, also squinted toward the dike. If his eyesight was as bad as it appeared, what he saw could have been a withered tree instead of a person. If, at this moment, someone had told him there was a man standing on the dike, the old man would have been in a quandary, having to decide whether to believe his own eyes or someone else's words. Such possibilities threatened the old man's perceptions; the sight became much less certain than the hoe he was holding.

The villagers had nearly all seen the stranger, but they couldn't tell whether or not he had looked back at them. It was probably because the sunlight came from the direction of the dike; looking into the glare, only a blurred face could be seen. It could also be that where the stranger stood was so far off, that no one could read subtle emotional changes on his face. It was like the statue of the bodhisattva enshrined in the little village temple; you never remembered clearly what it looked like and never really comprehended its facial expression. Therefore, in every town and village, no generation of bodhisattva sculptors had ever understood the thoughts and feelings of real bodhisattvas. Perhaps this was why they gave up all efforts to know thoughts and feelings and simply decided to carve a wooden figure without facial expression. As a result, all bodhisattva images looked alike; they had eyes and noses but not hearts. In fact, the sculptors didn't put their minds to it at all. Although they could be very deft artisans, they were nevertheless ordinary people who had to open their eyes to see and their mouths to eat and they did things in a matter-of-fact way. Since the gods on high couldn't be seen, how could they treat them with the kind of feelings they did their wives, children or friends?

The man on the dike didn't seem to have moved at all. The villagers, on the other hand, had moved around quite a bit. They didn't stop working as they had before: the old man resumed cultivating work, having smoked for a while. The child again was following his father, carrying the basket. Most villagers were there to work their fields; they spent most of their time addressing the earth, looking up toward the stranger only intermittently. The sun was moving further and further west. A little bug crawled over a leaf—one farmer saw it and began staring at it, but the stare didn't seem aggressive; it was a look without any implicit criticism. A moment ago, he had probably been thinking about the various possibilities of the stranger. Seeing the small bug, he forgot about the stranger. In a while, his mind would doubtless move on to something else beyond the scope of both topics. However, what he was thinking nobody could say, any more than the farmer could say what the bug was doing. If there were holes on the vegetable after the bug had crawled on it, he would have been able to guess that it was eating the leaf it crawled on, but standing upright, he was too far away to observe the bug adequately. He couldn't tell whether it was in fact, eating the leaf. If he had bent over and looked at it from a distance of only two or three inches, he would have known better what the bug was doing. He could have seen the bug was casting excrement, or he could have seen clearly the pattern on the bug's wing-case. Even so, he could not have predicted what the bug's next step would be. For nothing could reveal what the bug was thinking. Even seeing the bug's excreta would not necessarily mean it created the holes on the leaf. Of course, you could suppose that which came out of the bug had been ingested by it. The fact that you saw it defecating one minute didn't mean it had or hadn't been eating the minute before. Certainly, if the bug had not surfaced on the leaf, no one would have been able to see it there. Sometimes, given an ordinary stone, clean, smooth and with nothing on it, some people will imagine that by moving it they will discover hordes of ants underneath. A bit like some people's tendency to believe there are veins of gold, copper, silver or iron underground.

Although the villagers couldn't see the man clearly, they nevertheless were curious about what there might be behind him. The dike, however, was too high for them to see beyond him. If he had been carrying a bag or something, you could presume he had travelled some way to get here. The present fact, however, was that the man was casually dressed, standing there all by himself, and not carrying anything with him. When villager A saw villager B carrying a fishing rod, he would ask, 'Are you going fishing?' Villager B would probably answer, 'Well, yes.' Or 'Just come back.' This kind of interaction was more familiar to the villagers, and made them feel more reassured. Therefore, someone holding a fan was thought to be dispelling the heat; someone clutching a wine bottle was going to get drunk. Their guesses were usually not too wide of the mark. The villagers, however, had never seen anybody just standing on the dike; nevertheless, not every one wondered who he was. Those who liked to guess were guessing, those who didn't, weren't. Those whose minds were filled up with other thoughts would have had to clear some mental space if they had wanted to devote a thought to the stranger.

One farmer who had been bent to his work for some time raised his head to find that the stranger had sat down. The farmer wasn't certain he was the first one to have made the discovery so he looked at others around him, but they were all bent down, working hard. Once in a while, one of the other farmers would look up and be somewhat surprised by what he saw, but more often they remained undisturbed and bent down again to their work. After seeing all this, the first farmer was even less sure whether he had been the first to have noticed that the stranger had sat down, but then, what did it matter if he were the first? The fact that he had been surprised by his discovery would seem less significant if he had not been the first discoverer. Had someone else discovered it and had then gone on to inform him of it, would he have felt any surprise? And if he had been the first but had not informed others of his discovery before they made it themselves, the others could have thought themselves to be first and they could have been surprised—had they been the kind of people easily surprised. Besides, being the first to have discovered the situation, he certainly deserved some kind of special attention, but since it hadn't attracted any, he felt an inexplicable sense of disappointment. He remembered one spring when a village youth had found a strange flower and reported it to the elders in the village. Everyone had gone to look and all had been amazed. While praising it, they had not forgotten to smell the flower; they either nodded in appreciation or stuck up their thumbs as a gesture of praise. Fingering his beard and appreciating the flower, one elder had suddenly thought to ask: 'Who found this?' The crowd pointed out the young man. The elder had looked at the youth and tapped him on the shoulder; he said nothing, but praise of the youth 'having contributed to the welfare of the district and well entertained fellow villagers' had been fully expressed in his very silence.

Many villagers had noticed by this time that the man sat there motionlessly. They looked at one another as if they'd found something curious, but nobody seemed to want to discuss what they'd found. In fact, it was quite easy for anyone to discover what the others had; he had only to raise his head. There was no need to inform anyone. During a life there were quite a few times when saying nothing was preferable. Therefore, it didn't matter that for a while nobody said anything. Many times when A said something to B, B might not listen carefully—or, even if he did, B might not understand. One of the mothers working in the fields wouldn't expect her child to understand what she'd told him. While still a babe-in-arms, she had nattered away to him about what she felt and had never cared whether or not he had understood and couldn't have done anything about it if he had. Ordinarily, nobody was bothered by the fact they couldn't communicate with the deaf by speech; if facial expressions would do, they used them. Right now everyone was using facial expressions: you looked at him, I looked at him and you looked at me and I at you. After enough looking, a conclusion was reached: the stranger had sat down on the dike. This was what you got from looking at one another, and that was all that mattered.

The man on the dike was simply sitting there with his legs crossed. 'Why was he sitting with his legs crossed?' wondered the villagers. One villager, known as Fifth Wang, was in the habit of working at the crack of dawn; either making rice porridge, turning the gristmill, or simply cleaning house. When he was not doing anything, he would sometimes sit in a chair. Sitting in a chair of course can be considered doing something or doing nothing. After years of living on their own, the villagers achieved a kind of rich and solid training. They saw and heard things; they learned new skills, uttered new words. They planted in spring and harvested in autumn. They worked during the day and rested by night. Born into the world between heaven and earth, like all other animals, they could make fitting response to the myriad of changes and illusions of the universe in a manner fitting their way of life. When there was a storm, they protected themselves; when there was an earthquake, they fled from it. Beyond this, they prayed, they offered sacrifices, they shook their heads, waved their hands; performed all kinds of rituals, devised from spells and symbols, and chanted sounds. In the worst case they broke their arms, or bit their lips. They could do all these things—or maybe not.

Villagers over 40 had seen the village ransacked by bandits and could still remember things that had happened. The bandits stormed into the village, their legs clamped around their horses bellies, waving their leather whips. The dust they stirred up formed a vast curtain; behind it men screamed and horse-hooves thundered, but now as the older ones looked back, the sounds were no longer as clear as they had been. The heavy breathing of the men on horse back, the clenching of teeth, the sweating, none of these reappeared with any sound. Even the speed at which those men ran toward the villagers had slowed down in memory—they kept running nearer but never reached you. Perhaps it had all happened too long ago and the impression of it had faded. As if rain was now falling in a scene where there had originally been no trace of rain: and there was no dust floating, only muddy earth everywhere. Or it was like viewing a scene on the bottom of a basin filled with water. The picture was veiled with ripples, and every time the water was disturbed, the scene changed. First it was a horse trampling the breasts of a naked woman, leaving the imprint of its hooves. Then you looked down again, and saw a simple man with wide and distraught eyes running by in panic but stopping, unable to move, before a whiskered bandit with spear in hand. The bandit bursts into laughter and then stops, his expression turning evil and fierce. He thrusts his spear and the man stumbles flung to the ground; the tip of the spear is smeared with blood.

Those old men who had gone through the raid could remember only so much; the younger ones, born after the troubles, could only learn about it from the elders. Often the old men had so few teeth left they couldn't speak clearly; so the young men could hardly understand them. Some able to talk more clearly often added details they had made up and created their own sagas. Still others supplied only a few details and let the young make up their own story by cutting and adding. Others again had hidden in root cellars during bandit attack and hadn't personally seen anything of the battle, but years later they were actually able to tell coherent stories about the incident. Although they hadn't witnessed what had happened, they had heard garbled noises and had later seen dead bodies scattered all over when they climbed back to daylight. They suffered no lack of material for story-making. Among the dead, who had killed whom and had in turn been killed by whom else; whether A had killed B and then gone on to kill C, or had been in turn killed by C, couldn't be verified. It was only natural, then, for those hidden in the cellars not to know exactly what had happened. Even if the dead should revive, they couldn't have said with certainty who had killed whom because it had all happened in such a mêlée. It was like two villagers in a fistfight being finally pulled apart; neither would know how much he had hit the other or how much he had been hit by the other, they wouldn't even know exactly where they hurt.

When too many people tell the same story, the audience is hard put to decide on one version, and since it had happened a long time ago, it couldn't be summoned back for eye or ear. Had a village youth claimed to have seen a wolf while tending the sheep on the hillside, the villagers could look into it by going there in a group and seeing for themselves. Even so, those who had difficulty walking and couldn't go along would say, 'What's to see? Just be a little more alert for it. Going that far . . . really!' There was also a type easily disturbed by the mention of anything whatsoever, and were inclined to make a mountain out of a sesame seed. Their attitude would be similar to the farmer. The elders who believed the shepherd, however, would immediately respond, 'Little Three wouldn't lie to us. Anyway, he is not an old man, how should he have lost his sight?' Many's the lad with clear eyes but little knowledge who had raised clouds of suspicion. Once someone had taken a very fat cat for a tiger, and this actually happened.

The stranger hadn't done anything; he still sat off in the distance like a stone, so the thoughts of the villagers were still free to soar. As always the sight of the dike stopped or diverted the train of thought. There were always priorities and different people conceived their priorities differently. A would marry a woman to help him with household work; B to have a child to support him in his old age. A pair of big hands disentangled themselves from the fields, possibly having worked there long enough. The hands rubbed each other and a few cakes of dirt fell from them. This movement was what farmers did when they were ready to call it a day. Our man, however, didn't seem to be standing up. He scratched the back of his neck a few times while looking in the direction of the dike. When his gaze withdrew, he looked at the other farmers in passing and again buckled down to work.

Farmers never finished work in the fields. No man-made rules about what time you went to work or what time you got off, how much you planted or how much you harvested. Sometimes when your family didn't bring lunch to the field, you could go on working as if you didn't expect a break. The sun was still up so you might as well go on working—why not? The stooped old man worked slowly—one up, one down, but bit by bit the work got done, didn't it? He showed no signs of quitting, but perhaps that clouded mind could only conceive of one hoe-stroke after another and would continue cultivating until somebody ordered him to stop? You could think of it this way; but there was another way, and that made the situation different: The old man was absorbed in his work; nobody gave him any orders. A young man, Second Liu, also working the field, had wanted to advise his aged father working near him not to look toward the dike, but didn't know how to begin. Second Liu realized that everyone had been looking though none looked too frequently. Or they did it surreptitiously: either while wiping off sweat or when raising a hoe. Unlike the others, however, his father just stared at the dike. A bout of work and then a stare, then more work. As though looking was part of work. Second Liu was upset by this, but didn't know how to speak his mind; he suspected that one or two of the farmers knew how he felt. Even if Second Liu told his father it was not decent to stare at the dike in such an obvious manner, he might not listen. Years ago, the old man's oldest son had once suggested that he leave this arid village for some other place where he could spend the rest of his life peacefully. This was one example of vigorous young villagers breaking away to seek a better living and returning to relate the prosperity of other places. The elders were fascinated by the stories and would argue the pros and cons with each other. Some thought it would be worth while to take a trip to those places, but that it might be better if they could travel as a group. However, organizing such a project wasn't easy and couldn't be done in a short while. Older and feebler folk were afraid that something might happen during the trip, and they decided not to go. Nevertheless, precisely because they felt their lives were coming to an end, they felt a craving for the trip. If they went, at the very least they'd have seen for themselves the glories of the outside world. Having feasted their eyes on such scenes they could close them without regret. Most older villagers had decided not to leave for other places. Much as they would like to, the few things they had heard about the outside world were not enough to help them make up their minds. However hard the young people who had seen the world tried to persuade them, they wouldn't change.

It was all very well to talk about leaving the village to see the world, but doing it was a different thing. There were many things which were nice to talk about, but couldn't really be done if only because the time wasn't right. It was like running into a sudden rain: it was always better to wait under the eaves till the rain stopped; you could always resume what you were doing after it stopped raining. Then you could fetch that stick under the tree over there. Then you could go home, wash your face and eat, and once you were home someone might visit and chat a bit. One thing after another, there were endless things to do. When you had finally finished everything that needed doing, and your hair was properly combed, a whole life had been used up. Without leaving home at all, you could leave home; leaving, you could still stay home. Things unexperienced leave no traces on the tablets of the mind: an old man who never set foot out of his door in his life would not know what time in the morning the main gate opened and what time in the evening it closed in a city 500 miles away, but bitten by a swamp snake when young, the sight of a rope will make his heart skip a beat for years.

Those young men who hoped to make it big began to miss their families soon after they left the village. They would figure how far away they were from home each time they passed through a town. When they boarded a ship, they would always look back at the way by which they had come, though all they could see was the flow of a vast river. These fellow villagers stopped or ate at a hotel and felt lonely and out of place as they watched other travellers. Nevertheless, they carried on anyway—later thoughts didn't overwhelm their earlier ones. To be sure, they had hard times, but if you were born in times of war, you couldn't moan and sigh that your luck was worse than your ancestors' who lived in times of peace and prosperity.

Among those young men who had settled away from home, some hadn't found a decent job and had taken the risk of committing crimes, and had no place in the world to take refuge. The best they could do was return home in secret at the Festival of the Dead and shed tears as they offered sacrifices at their ancestral tombs. They could settle in no place on land or sea but had to go wherever the wind blew. To the old people living peacefully all their lives in the village the rites and sacrifices were so familiar they didn't have to give them a second thought, but if a kid lost one of his parents, in the midst of his grief he wouldn't know what to do at the funeral service. Fortunately, you did get the hang of it after doing it a couple of times. There was a locust tree about a mile away from the village on the dike. Behind the tree was a shallow fish pond. Kids often frolicked around there all day until dark. If you just remembered the tree and the pond behind it, you could always go back there. Grown-ups often feared their memory would fail them, and when they ran into somebody they knew but couldn't remember his name, they felt they had committed a great social fault.

Today the villagers had inscribed in their memory the stranger on the dike, but they couldn't do anything else about him, so they continued with their work.

As they went on with their cultivation, 'bu-u-u' came the unmistakable sound of a fart; everyone recognized it as such. All they had to do was wait for the smell and it would be confirmed. There was no other way. As soon as the fart was let off one after another stopped to look toward the dike. The man on the dike was too far away to hear or smell the fart, of course, so he sat completely unperturbed. Although the 'b-u-u' sounded like a fart, it *could* turn out not to be one. The villagers often heard a 'bu-u' sound while sitting in their courtyard cooling off and enjoying the moon, and thought it was a fart; only to discover it to be the scraping sound made by moving their stools about. When the droppings of an insect were found on a leaf, that was substantive and an idea capable of being grasped, but to claim an insect farted would be baseless because there would be no visible evidence for it. Of course, sometimes a child or two would say to their father, 'This morning I heard a bird talking to me.' Not all people are equally endowed; most of us should be reticent about such things. 'Being reticent' means not expressing any opinion whatsoever; expressing no opinion resembled the man on the dike. The man on the dike hadn't farted; had he done so, and the smell reached the villagers, they would at least have been able to guess that there might be something wrong with his digestive system, but as it was, the villagers were completely mystified. One farmer happened to see the expression in the stranger's eyes while dumping pebbles he had dug up near the dike. The stranger wasn't looking at him, but judging from the way he looked, he was looking neither at other villagers nor the horizon. For, in either of those cases, the farmer would be able to tell right away. The way the stranger looked would neither help him focus on things close by or things far away. It wouldn't allow him to see; one simply couldn't see things with that gaze. Then, wasn't it like closing eyes or being blind? Of course, a slight difference there was: the blind could never see, but closing your eyes was sometimes to avoid strong light, sometimes for the sake of preserving energy, and sometimes the result of being asleep.

The farmer walked by where he had dug up the pebbles and took up his original position. People near him all darted glances at him and at one another, their eyes filled with concern. The farmer could offer no new information. Everyone was his own governor working in the fields and no one would say anything about another's way of doing his work. All the villagers had silently shifted their positions a bit without knowing it, and were now working even harder because of that. They worked as though weeds grew so fast that they couldn't stop for a second. Shifting positions didn't seem to involve time, since they all felt a very short time had passed, but when again someone raised his head and looked toward the dike, it had gotten darker: more startling, the man on the dike was gone. It was probably an effect of darkness, but a few farmers were astonished and transported by this discovery. It was getting darker and darker. Ordinarily it took quite a time for dusk to fall, but now it was as if dusk had wings and arrived in the blink of an eye. Some farmers, probably those slower or older ones, but who knows, were quite comfortable with the way things were going; sunrise and sunset always came at right and proper times. Quite right; for some people it was just natural to feel hungry at precisely noon time; there were more people who always used the outhouse at dawn. A couple of the children seemed very different from others: having watched the circus of the day, these would become magicians during their sleep at night and would perform magic whose effects could reach the farthest end of the world. At this moment, all the farmers stood and faced the dike, but there was nothing except the sand blowing over it. The villagers looked as though they stood at attention for sunset. Tomorrow when the villagers came to the fields, they would look at the dike again, but it was not certain that the man would be there. If he were not, then yesterday's viewing of the dike would be like drifting clouds which passed without leaving a trace, but this would concern them only after the night had passed. For now, sunset had painted the sky orange and the monster-shaped clouds in the west were about to swallow the sun. The villagers were quite clear: this was not the proper time for working in the fields, and shouldering their hoes to return home was as natural as the world canopied by the sky and supported by the earth.

Notes on the Authors

CHANG Hsi-kuo was educated in Taiwan before he went to the United States and earned his doctorate in electrical engineering from the University of California at Berkeley. Now a professor at the Illinois Institute of Technology, he is a prolific writer especially well-known for his promotion of science fiction.

CH'EN Ying-chen is the pen-name of CH'EN Yung-shan. He also writes under the pseudonym of Hsu Nan-ts'un. A native of Taiwan, Ch'en graduated from Tamkang University with a B.A. in English, and was a middle-school teacher for some years. He attended the Writers' Workshop at the University of Iowa in 1983.

HUANG Fan is the pen-name of Huang Hsiao-chung, a native of Taipei. A graduate from Chung-yuan University, he did not get his first novella published until 1979, when he was 30. Since then, he has many books to his credit and has many times been the winner of major literary prizes in Taiwan.

LIAO Hui-ying, born in Taichung, graduated from National Taiwan University with a B.A. in Chinese. First-place winner of the 1982 *China Times* Literary Prize in fiction, she is best known for 'The Rapeseed', represented here, which has been made into an enormously successful film.

LIU Ta-jen, a native of Kiangsi, was brought up in Taiwan. After graduating from the Department of Philosophy at National Taiwan University, he studied for short stints at the University of Hawaii and the University of California, Berkeley, before involving himself in political movements concerning China. He now works at the United Nations.

LU Fei-yi graduated from National Taiwan University with a degree in library science. Winner of *China Times* and *United Daily News* literary prizes, he writes television and movie scripts in addition to short stories.

Pao-chen is the pen-name of CHIANG Pao-chen. A scientist by training (he holds advanced degrees from UC-Berkeley and Swedish University of Agricultural Sciences, and is now teaching at National Chung Hsing University), he has won many literary prizes.

P'ing-lu is the pen-name of LU P'ing. She graduated from National Taiwan University with a B.S. in psychology before moving on to the United States, where she earned a master's in statistics. Winner of many literary prizes, she has published short stories, novellas, and essays.

SHU Kuo-chih graduated from the Department of Film of the World College of Journalism in Taipei. 'Rustic Quandary', his first short story to be published, won him a *China Times* literary prize in the category of prose for the year 1980. He is noted for his experimental prose style.

SU Wei-chen is a graduate from the Department of Film and Drama, College of Political Warfare. After the publication of her first novel in 1979, she has subsequently won many literary prizes and has many books to her credit.